INTENTIONAL WAR MAGE

INTENTIONAL WAR MAGE

TOMAS J. McINTEE

Podium

Podium

INTENTIONAL WAR MAGE

CHAPTER ONE

In Which I Learn of Business and City Life

The open fields and pastures we had traveled through had been pretty but startlingly empty; they would soon fill with lambs and calves brought out from their wintering places. Dab, on the other hand, was ugly and far from empty.

I am told the population of Khoryvsk is more than ten times that of Dab. On the rail journey we passed through Khoryvsk, but we had not stopped there, so I hadn't been afforded an opportunity to see a bigger city. If one counted the whole cluster of nearby towns that had sprouted up next to it as one metropolis, what I was faced with was easily a hundred times the size of a regular village and larger than any town I had ever been to before. The density of people living within its walls was impressive. When the guardsmen told me that there were probably rooms enough to spare at inns and common houses to quarter my entire force without displacing anyone, I was dubious; but after I had walked the streets and taken in the scale of Dab, I believed that claim in full.

My doubts about the resources of the townsfolk met with doubts from the town guards about my purposes and the wisdom of permitting my heavily armed force entry into their city. We were an unwelcome reminder that war was never very far away. Our choice of cover as a mercenary company was a good one; we were not the only, nor even the first, mercenary company to arrive in town that season.

We set up headquarters in a pair of vacant warehouses, obtained at a reasonable rate through a local factor who had done business with some of the Rimehammers' kin. The arrangement was a little complicated. We looked around at what was available and told the factor which ones seemed suitable; he then purchased the warehouses and leased them to us for use as barracks. This was substantially cheaper than leasing directly from the current owners, especially after considering the issues of credit and profit-sharing arrangements.

I should explain that Captain Felix Rimehammer took the opportunity of working out lodging arrangements via a connection of his to simultaneously renegotiate his contract with me; we ended up with a relatively complex three-way arrangement between myself, the local factor, and the Rimehammer family as represented by Felix. He pointed out—rightly—that we might need to take on additional jobs as a cover in the course of our mission, and had several interesting, if complicated, proposals as far as financing and profit-sharing went.

After that unexpectedly long meeting concluded and the warehouses were essentially ours to occupy, I told the men and women of the battalion that they were welcome to arrange more comfortable lodging for themselves if they wished; that they were at liberty for a while, but not to misbehave in such a manner as to bring trouble upon us; and, finally, if they wanted to terminate or re-negotiate their contracts, now would be a particularly convenient time to do so. I delegated contract negotiations to Captain Felix, the problem of making the barracks habitable to the older captain, discipline to the younger captain (reminding her briefly of my anti-dueling policy), disbursement of payroll to Vitold, and took Katya and Yuri out around town.

As I mentioned, we were not the only, nor the first, mercenary company to set up shop in Silesia; others could smell which way the winds of war were blowing. Sigismund II had taken ill during the winter, neither of his granddaughters were likely to inherit, and in the borderlands Lithuania loomed dangerously close. The city council was presently considering a resolution to ban the open carriage of arms, uncomfortable with the number of well-armed strangers in town.

The city folk compared us to vultures in whispered comments as we passed—a fine example of the pot calling the kettle black, I felt, with the impressive local population of carrion birds attracted by the slaughter operation. I could see crows perched on nearly every building in the city.

Even with the wind blowing most of the stench away from the slaughter yard to the south, the city was dirty and smelled bad. I have since been told that aside from the contributions of the slaughter yard itself in the butchery quarter, Dab is unexceptional among cities in this regard, but at the time, I was unpleasantly surprised. However noisome the urban environment, there was something I thought I could find in Dab. From what I had heard, a person could find nearly anything for sale in a big city, and Dab seemed huge to me. I had something fairly expensive in mind; or, at least, usually expensive as a finished product. Two somethings, in fact.

I had made a promise to myself to buy Katya something nice, something that would make up for my having given Lieutenant Gavreau a pair of enchanted pistols and perhaps lift her out of the slough of depression she had become mired in. Initially, she had been elated at her unexpected survival and occupied with the immediate intense pain, but that rush had worn off, along with the physical pain, and her awareness of what it meant to deal with missing both a leg and arm had expanded, leading to pain of a less physical variety.

As crippling as the loss of two limbs is, this is the modern era, and great scientific and medical strides have been made since the days when the best you could expect was a simple peg or hook; these days, there are fully functional mechanical limbs, with joints that bend, with hands capable of grasping and manipulating. I once met an officer with an artificial hand, in fact. In a great city like Dab, perhaps I could find such devices available for sale. They might be expensive (perhaps beyond my means, one reason I had not told Katya of my intentions), but I owed Katya my life several times over, and had a lingering sense of guilt over the way that she had lost her limbs and nearly her life in a chain of events that started out with the two of us having an angry argument.

Something which costs an arm and leg is fairly expensive, and buying them back is almost as dear, but I was hoping for a good deal on limbs; if I could afford the price of an arm and a leg, I would buy both, and failing that, try to at least buy one of them.

In the common geography of cities, altitude is status. The elites position themselves on a hilltop; the dregs deal with poorly drained swampland, with correspondingly thicker and more pungent air. It was in the wealthier section of town where I hoped to find a doctor or mechanic who might have mechanical limbs on hand. I learned some lessons that day as I attempted to explore the better quarter of town.

First, scruffy foreign mercenaries are generally unwelcome in good neighborhoods. This was made clear to me several times and in several ways. Second, mechanical limbs must be custom fitted to the recipient, accounting for their size, the amount of natural limb they have remaining, et cetera; and thus are generally not kept in stock, even by doctors and mechanics in great towns the size of Dab. It's the sort of item typically custom-built and fitted to the user.

After having learned those two lessons, I was holding onto Yuri's collar with one hand—while wiping my face clean of mud with the other, courtesy of a carriage driven by someone who had swerved through a muddy puddle to underline the first lesson—when I heard a voice greeting Katya in thickly accented Romanian.

"Please! My apologies for my countryman's poor manners." The voice had a nervous edge to it, but anticipatory rather than fearful. I would expect fearful were Katya waving her pistol about. "May I introduce myself?"

When I opened my eyes, blinking reflexively—I had perhaps not gotten all the mud off my face quite yet—I could make out a young man, perhaps in his late teenage years or early twenties. Though he might have been older than I was, he seemed young to me, between the nervous way he was staring down at Katya's chest and the lack of hard wear on his face. He had better, I thought to myself, apologize for his own poor manners next; and then I took note that he wore an amethyst pin.

Katya was wearing her amethyst pendant, a very distinctive item she had picked up so long ago off of a dead rebel. When considering his possession of a similar piece of jewelry, it seemed more likely to me that he had recognized the necklace rather than ogled at her breasts. (That is not to say that I think poorly of Katya's feminine anatomical features; but her bosom is of the smaller and less eye-catching variety under ordinary circumstances, and months of short military rations had left her chest nearly as flat as a man's.)

As I processed this, Katya scowled suspiciously. The language of the Wallachians was not a language she associated with trustworthy individuals; and some inner patriotic instinct was aroused, something that told her that this was not a man who toasted to the good health of the deathless Golden Emperor. He had managed to get through his name, title, and lineage when I spoke up.

"I see you have recognized us, but please, let us not draw attention," I said quietly in Gothic, slipping my arm around Katya's waist possessively (in the event that he had been staring at more than her necklace), and speaking with what I hoped would sound like a light Romanian accent (in order to further any delusions he might have had as to our origins).

"We are glad to be here in Dab, but you never know who might be listening. Perhaps there is somewhere else we could become more closely acquainted, somewhere less public?" If I couldn't buy Katya a replacement leg, perhaps I could make progress on the mission General Spitignov had assigned to me. The noble's choice of jewelry, his recognition of Katya's, and his attempt at trying to welcome us in what he thought to be our native tongue suggested to me that he had some connection to Wallachia. He could be one of those who financed rebellion within Wallachia; and if he wasn't, he likely had friends who did.

"But of course! Please, call upon me this evening at my manor house." He paused, and frowned, looking at my mud-spattered clothes. "Though . . ." He seemed unwilling to finish his sentence, then made a decision, waving at a manservant. "Frederick, I believe I can make it back unattended. Would you see to . . ." He frowned again. "I am afraid I do not know your names."

"Colonel Marcus Corvus," I said, as I shuffled through my memory.

Katya's false identity, which we had prepared paperwork for at the beginning of this venture, made her out to be a native of Moravia. This would not pass convincingly in Dab company, and I strained to remember a suitable Romanian surname. "And this is Leontina Odobescu," I added, choosing the first surname that popped into mind.

Later, I would recall that the name belonged to Radu Odobescu, the man who had chosen to try to kill me rather than sign a contract, a man whose throat Katya had slit to make sure of his demise.

"Delighted!" The young nobleman seemed to actually be delighted, rather than just pronouncing the completion of the formal ritual of introduction, which made me regret that I hadn't paid the slightest bit of attention to his name when he'd introduced himself. "Yes, Frederick, do see to it that Lady Odobescu and the colonel get an appropriate consideration from a good tailor, on my account."

I mentioned that scruffy foreign mercenaries are generally unwelcome in the better parts of towns. This should be understood to include upper-class tailor's shops, but it is worth noting that the proprietor's attitude underwent a remarkable change when he was dealing with scruffy foreign mercenaries in the company of a liveried footman. There were, then, two new lessons for me to learn.

First, it is possible for clothing to fit neatly and snugly yet comfortably. I had never worn clothing fitted to me before; growing up, my clothing had been bought large with the expectation that I would grow bigger soon enough, or it was more often handed down from older family members. Since joining the army, my attire had been issued by impartial authorities who saw no need to tailor things to fit, and my more recent mercenary gear had been scrounged from disparate sources. Second, you can examine every naked inch of a woman's body without really knowing what she looks like wearing a dress. It made her look younger, somehow.

The tailor even managed to come up with a peg leg of sorts for Katya to rest her stump on and stand with. It was a far cry from a fully functional artificial leg, lacking even as much as a knee joint; he built it in haste from a walking stick and a shorter peg leg he'd found in his back room.

CHAPTER TWO

In Which I Pay for a Pony

Katya, I think, had not realized that nobles were supposed to eat slowly and delicately, as if one was bored rather than hungry; but she did have the ready excuse of being short an arm for her clumsiness. After she hastily misjudged an olive during a salad course and sent it flying across the table, I begged the matron's forgiveness and asked if I might be permitted to assist Katya in dining, breach of normal decorum though that might be, on account of her not having adjusted to the lack of an arm.

This request broke the ice of the matron's cold disregard for me; she had judged me to be a rogue and a scoundrel the moment I had been introduced, but she found it difficult to keep exhibiting a poor opinion of me. If she had reacted coldly or angrily at that point, she would have looked particularly mean-spirited, and I suspect she either didn't want to think of herself as mean-spirited, or was reminded of someone she was fond of. Whatever the case, she went from contemptuous to neutral at the drop of Katya's salad fork.

The matron, who spoke a clean and clear dialect of Gothic, which suggested she had moved a considerable distance when she married, proceeded to warm up to me further (though less suddenly) over several excellent courses, most of which were completely unfamiliar to me. I politely praised each one in vague terms; not so warm as the praise that would be considered good manners among normal folks upon encountering something that clearly had been labored over extensively, as I sensed that would be out of place, but enough to keep the conversation mostly on the meal and culinary tangents.

Dessert came and went, and after the servants cleared away the dishes, I could hear the butler count the silverware under his breath—his attempt at a low whisper perfectly audible to me from two rooms away. Like his mistress, he had judged me to be a rogue and a scoundrel the moment I had walked into the foyer of the mansion. Unlike his mistress, though, he remained constant in his attitude.

We settled into the sitting room for casual conversation after dinner, a cozy room with comfortable furniture and an old painting of a sailing ship. Writ in small letters at the ship's stern was *Gertrude*, the matron's name. The conversation quickly turned away from food, weather, and other inconsequentialities to more substantial matters; the butler pointedly commented that "Corvus" was a very unusual surname.

"Of course! It's a pseudonym," I said, with a wink (directed to the matron, using the eye the butler couldn't see from his vantage point) and a grin (directed to the whole room). "Wouldn't want imperial interests to concern themselves with my real identity! Why, there could be unfortunate repercussions for, well, I shouldn't talk about that."

Every word I had said was perfectly true, and yet each contributed to a deceptive whole. I tried to include as much truth as possible, not to assuage my conscience, which continued to twinge regardless, but rather in order to be as convincing and consistent as possible. The easiest way to lie is to tell the truth, just not quite the whole of it. There are so many different things that could be left unspoken that nobody ever guesses the most important missing part, such as teaching a fox how door latches work or being a soldier in the service of the Golden Empire. In the latter case, I wasn't entirely sure if I was still a soldier in the service of the Golden Empire; I'd done my best to evade orders, but here I was, trying to find out more about its enemies.

"Besides, it is catchy," added the young nobleman who was responsible for our presence at the manor. "You have to get your name around to advertise your services, and a catchy name helps with that."

I wasn't quite sure what he was talking about. I could blame my grasp of the local dialect, which was loose, but to tell the truth, I was quite unfamiliar with the idea of *advertising* entirely. In an ordinary-sized village, everybody knows everybody else, and some people know enough about some of the folks in nearby towns to trust them to make deals. The idea of spreading your name around so that people would recognize it and prefer your service, or your goods, over someone completely unfamiliar . . . Well, it made sense once I heard it put that way, but it took me a little while to work out what he was talking about.

"To be honest, I'm not really looking to pick up any new business for a couple of weeks," I said. "I think the men would mutiny outright if I pushed them into a pitched battle tomorrow. That said, I do always have to be on the lookout for the next job, and I suppose I should be looking toward the long run like that. Call it a happy coincidence, then, I didn't even pick the name for myself. Wouldn't have chosen a raven either. They're clever birds, but completely unprincipled. Always waiting around to clean up someone else's mess, or getting in a fuss over shiny things like coins . . ." I shook my head.

The young man lit up with laughter. "So perfect for a mercenary, then! How did you get that name?"

I paused, trying to recall the circumstances, and then what parts of those circumstances fit with my cover story. "I think one of our prisoners came up with it, but it caught on like wildfire with my soldiers. Next thing I knew, I was Colonel Raven, and that was that; it wasn't as if I could afford to work under my real name anyway. It's better than being boring old Colonel Marcus."

"I told you we should have killed her," Katya said. She knew exactly who I was talking about.

"Was this how you lost your arm?" The young man seemed eager for a story from Katya.

The matron winced a little when Katya didn't immediately answer. Katya had not said very much over the course of dinner; her Gothic was far from fluent, and the difficulty she had eating unaided left her visibly embarrassed.

"No, it wasn't," I said, answering for Katya. "This was back when Leontina here had all her lovely limbs." I patted "Leontina" on the shoulder, and shifted topics from the past to the present. "You know, we were trying to shop around for some mechanical prosthetics when we ran into your son," I told the matron. "No luck, alas. I fear we're too far from the sea, and I've heard that's the place to go if you want a well-made prosthetic. Something to do with the sea trade, I've been told. Perhaps you know better than I how dangerous the ocean really is to the limbs of sailors—I can't say I've spent much time on seafaring ships."

The matron clucked her tongue and aided me in shifting the topic to a discussion of the benefits and detriments of coastal life. The young man who'd brought me there would have rather listened to stories about gore and glory in service to the resistance, I suspect, but with both his mother and I cooperating to push the conversation away from the subject, he hadn't a chance.

There's something surreal about the way names work. I've always just been plain old Mikolai Stepanovich; that is to say, Mikolai, Stepan's boy. When you're living in a reasonably sized town, you don't really need any more than that, not unless you're trying to prove something about how proud your lineage is. And who does that, aside from nobles and those trying to make themselves look more respectable by emulating the nobles? I'd never laid proper claim to a surname. The general titled me as "Yagin" for reasons that remain unclear to me, the druid dubbed me "Raven," and there was yet a third false surname sitting somewhere on mercenary paperwork we'd put together a long while ago.

If I had a legitimate claim to a real surname, it wasn't one I knew about or cared about. Given that, I think I should be forgiven for having made the mistake of putting the particular surname "Odobescu" on Katya, which made things a great deal more exciting than they needed to be. The whole point of using a Romanian name had been to try to settle any suspicions about our origins, which would in turn help deflect attention away from said origins. If all the answers are simple and boring, inquiry soon comes to a halt. Unfortunately, the name "Odobescu" was associated with a well-known noble family, which had the effect of drawing more attention to us.

The young noble who'd met us on the street didn't think we were independent mercenaries who had recently worked for the rebels, but instead thought we were a group of rebels working as mercenaries to build up funds and strength. The distinction between these two is subtle, but important to nobles, much like the status implied by the name "Odobescu." Thus, the invitation to dinner and the unusual yet inevitable follow-on consequences.

The morning after our first dinner in the nobles' quarter, a sour-faced, familiar fellow, who I knew to be employed as a butler, arrived with a long wooden box and a letter. He handed them to me with a sneer and a roll of his eyes and left without further explanation. I'm not sure why he chose to undertake that errand personally; he surely could have delegated the errand to one of his underlings. The box and letter were addressed to "Miss

Odobescu," and the latter explained that the former contained an old mechanical arm that once belonged to the sender's uncle, who no longer had use for it, and gave directions to a local mechanic who could adjust the arm and would be quite respectful if we dropped the appropriate name.

After a minute puzzling over the signature, I decided that the letter and box had come from the matron. Katya was quite excited about what the letter said, until she opened the box.

"Oh," she said, and her face fell.

Being that I was holding the box while she lifted the lid, I could easily see the reason for her disappointment. The young nobleman was a slight fellow, and his mother of perfectly ordinary dimensions for a woman her age, but his granduncle must have been cast from a different mold. The arm was as long as mine—in spite of being fitted for a man who still had about half his upper arm left. That is to say, the prosthetic, going from mid-bicep to fingertip, was as long as my whole arm, shoulder to fingertip. It was also quite bulky; while Katya was herself not exceptionally small as women go, she was still shorter than most men and quite slender, and all the more so after the rigors of our journey.

"It's more of a size to be a replacement leg for you," I said. (She didn't laugh at the joke, simply nodded as I held it next to her remaining leg, agreeing with my assessment sincerely.) "We'll manage to get some kind of work out of it, Katya. Besides, there's a good word for the local arm-and-leg-smith here. I'm sure we can bring him around to getting you something a little less conspicuous and a little more"—I searched for an appropriate word—"like you. Beautiful."

I kissed her, as it seemed an appropriate moment; and then there was a throat-clearing noise behind me from someone who thought it wasn't an appropriate moment for me to be locking lips with my favorite subordinate officer.

Captain Rimehammer wanted my attention. Well, he insisted that it was my company and men that needed my attention, but he really just wanted to give me a short stack of reports, get my signature on several new documents, and have a discussion with me about what ought to be company policy regarding soldiers who ended up in the town jail after getting up to mischief.

It turned out this last item was entirely non-hypothetical in nature. The level of mischief soldiers are likely to get up to upon getting leave turns out to be directly proportionate to how long it has been since their last leave and inversely proportionate to their available spending money. While our financial situation as a company was not too bad on paper—thanks to the local factor and our three-way deal—what Vitold had paid out last night was well short of the total sum of back pay owed. Hence, mischief.

To this day, whenever someone mentions "brothel," "pony," and "greasepaint" in the same sentence, it brings to mind the exasperations I had to deal with through the rest of that morning and some of the afternoon. Since I could hardly send Katya hobbling off by herself to deal with the mechanic, we did not make it to the mechanic's shop until late afternoon, and I had markedly less confidence in my ability to pay said mechanic to apply his expertise in prosthetic limbs on Katya's behalf. Mechanical limbs are, as a general rule, quite expensive.

Granted, I had a line of credit in the company's name, the letters of credit taken from the ogres, and some of the jewelry looted from the dead king's tomb (which I thought of as being as much Katya's as mine—she had saved my life there, and it was she who had shot the king to pieces), but it took every penny in my pockets to pay for damages, missing livestock, and the bail money. The company's cash reserves had already been doled out as pay to the troops in hopes that putting spending money in their pockets would generate some goodwill.

Hopefully, the letter of recommendation would be enough for the limb mechanic to work on credit.

CHAPTER THREE

In Which I Am Not a Witness to Murder

N o, no relation whatsoever," insisted the man who looked like a slightly grayer and balding older brother of the young nobleman.

"I'm just an old mechanic who's done a fair piece of work with them—we're good friends, nothing more. I worked with her husband, used to manage the accounts during his longer voyages, as I get seriously sea-sick when not on solid ground. Even the riverboats up to the coast are too much for me. That was before they inherited the estate from her uncle, of course. Now the estate staff handle all the books, and I only visit the manor on social occasions."

I peered more closely.

The mechanic's nose was a great beak similar to the young nobleman's, large with a distinctive downward bend, almost hooked. The matron, known to be the mother of the latter and unrelated to the former, had a nose that was pert—small and straight but for a slight upturn at the end. Both the mechanic and the young noble had earlobes that attached to the head all the way down their length. The matron's earlobes, by contrast, hung free. Both of the men had the same lively green eyes, while the matron's were a clear, calm blue.

In addition to the little facial details, both the mechanic and the young nobleman were a bare inch taller than Katya and quite similar in bulk, built compactly but solidly. Both men had long, bony fingers, with unusually short pinky fingers, while the matron's fingers were uniformly stubby, short and slightly plump.

From observing how they walked, I could guess that both men numbered among the population whose second toes were longer than their big toes. By contrast, the matron's gait suggested the more common pattern of a shorter second toe. While I had not seen the bare feet of any of the three at any point, I would cheerfully bet a solid silver Romanian denarius against a copper imperial kopek that there was a common difference in foot structure based on the obvious difference in gaits.

"My apologies for the mistake," I said, remembering belatedly that not all familial relationships are acknowledged ones and that this topic becomes particularly sensitive with noble families. "I am, you understand, not from around here, and you all look a little alike to my eyes. I'm just lucky I erred with someone who wouldn't take offense from it. Imagine if I had mistaken the lord of the manor for being your kin, instead of the other way around!"

"Hard to do," he said. After checking to make sure we were talking about the same family, he informed me that the lord of the manor had been blond, with unforgettably piercing blue eyes. The lord had also been a head taller than him, with a bulk that had made the artificial arm look proportionate. He had been all around quite a bit more impressive looking than the mechanic.

"Speaking of smaller and larger folks," I said, deciding that I needed to get down to business and avoid discussing the matron's evident infidelities. "I have a fairly small woman here, missing two limbs, and a very large arm offered to her as a gift. I'm sure no offense was intended, just as I meant no offense with my guess that you were yourself of noble heritage, but it is a little awkward. Especially, as you see, my lovely little lady just doesn't have as much arm left as the great lord did."

I carefully pulled Katya's shirt aside to expose what was left of her shoulder. She had a sour look on her face at that point; I wasn't entirely sure why, as it was clearly necessary to show the man what we had to work with in terms of attaching an artificial limb.

"Leaving aside the problem of size, she simply doesn't have a stump left that can fit into the bracing socket here," I said.

"I see! Yes, a most unusual problem. I've never dealt with a case quite that bad before. I wonder . . ." The mechanic frowned, then felt around the site of the amputation. Katya gave him a dirty look, then turned the dirty look to me, to my exasperation.

"Hold still, I'm going to need to take some measurements."

After taking measurements around her shoulder (what was left of it) and her chest, he paused, then lifted Katya's skirt up to check on her other missing limb. As I prevented Katya from striking him (the usual reflex of a lady in polite company having her skirt unexpectedly pulled up by a stranger), he (unaware of the danger) clucked his tongue.

"That's what you're using for a peg? It's a wonder you can even stand! That, I can fix today."

He ducked off into another room, muttering under his breath. I quietly whispered to Katya that while it might seem he was taking indecent liberties with her sense of modesty, he really did need good measurements to do a proper job, and that it really was a better idea to refrain from killing the man who seemed our best hope for getting her some nice replacement limbs. She frowned and then nodded reluctantly to me.

The balding man returned with a toolbox. "I have a brilliant idea. I'll have to build the attachment for the arm from scratch completely, and the old lord's arm is heavy enough to make that even more difficult. Bracing, you understand? However, while you probably would have never thought of it, this old monster is practically the right size to make a replacement leg for the lady."

He looked at us. It seemed a natural enough idea; I'd made the comparison earlier. We nodded, and he seemed disappointed at our lack of surprise. In a very short time, he had removed the thumb, switched the joint attachment, and by the strategic addition of bracing, transformed the hand into a passable foot.

"Hop up on this table, and we'll see about getting it fitted and adjusted," he said.

Katya perched herself on the table and gingerly pulled up her skirt to reveal her stump. The fitting process took a little while, and I busied myself poking around his workshop. He had quite a collection of tools, and also (as I drifted to the section that resembled a sitting room—the man clearly lived in his shop) quite a collection of history books and knickknacks.

I was halfway through a treatise exploring possible methods of automating sail-handling when I heard the characteristic clatter of a workman putting away his tools after he is confident the job has been completed.

"And there we are!" The mechanic announced this in a grandiose manner, as if he were a servant preceding a high-ranked noble into a tavern of an unfamiliar town who wished to make sure his master was accorded an appropriate number of awed looks from the peasantry upon his entrance.

I turned to look and saw a thin-lipped Katya narrowly avoid falling over.

"It'll take a bit of practice to get used to it," the mechanic told her. "I'm sure you'll be back up to full speed in no time."

She took another determined step, and I hastened to offer my arm. She continued lurching forward, practically dragging me out of the workshop.

"Wait!" When Katya didn't stop, the mechanic put down his toolbox and hurried after us, consternation visible on his face. "There is the small matter of payment!"

Katya continued forward. Too excited with being able to walk under her own power, I supposed.

"It is no problem," I said over my shoulder, trying to sound like a noble who didn't care about money and wasn't to be bothered about it. "I'm sure your rates are fair."

"I suppose I'll send you the bill, then, Colonel Raven," he called out, as we turned down the street. He looked confused.

Once well out of earshot, I whispered to Katya. "What's gotten into you?"

"He kept squeezing my butt," she said. "Not to measure it. Because I did not do anything about it."

I stopped, angry, and turned to head back to the shop.

"Wait, Mikolai. Is it not better to 'refrain from killing' the man who is making me a new arm?" There was an angry edge to her voice. "Or at least wait until after he finishes it? I have already paid the price of 'indecent liberties.' I may as well get a new arm out of it."

I couldn't argue with that logic. "I'm sorry," I said.

The merchant tapped his fingers on the counter. "I can even see the tool marks. With the work being this crude, it's probably got all the gold content of my grandmother's brass candlesticks. You simply don't work in precious metal with a piece of this mass, not without spending a lot more on craftsmanship."

"I told you, it's old." I hefted it, testing the mass. It was clearly too heavy to be brass. "They didn't have as sophisticated metalworking techniques back then. Look, feel the weight of it. Solid silver or lead wouldn't weigh this much. It's not perfectly pure gold, of course, but it's more than half gold by weight."

"And I suppose you want even more for it, on account of it being an artifact of great antiquity!" The merchant hefted the necklace and frowned.

"It does have an honest sort of weight to it," he admitted. "I could have an alchemist assay it and see if there's any gold in here. I can't promise more than metal value, though."

"Sure. We'll leave it with you. You do that," I said, handing him a card on which I'd scribbled the address of our headquarters. "Send a message here. Tell them to ask for the colonel. That's me. The sooner, the better."

It was like a light went off inside the man's head. His eyes lit up, and he cracked a wide smile; even his nose seemed to brighten, and he adjusted his posture subtly.

"Ah. I see. Colonel Marcus Corvus! My deepest apologies, I hope no offense was taken." He tucked the card into a pocket, beaming a bright smile in my direction.

"The one and only," I said, with a flourish and a bow that I hoped seemed like the correct response to his sudden transformation in manner. "I'm sure you're a very busy man; we'll be on our way now and out of yours." I strolled out of the shop and Katya followed, not saying anything.

She hadn't said anything at all to me that day. The last couple of days had been full of tension between me and Katya. Following the eventful fitting of her new leg, we had a lengthy discussion on the topic of who had permission to grab her derriere and exactly what should happen to someone who did so without permission.

After having accidentally ordered her to let a local mechanic do so while fitting her for a new leg, my own derriere-grabbing privileges proved to be endangered, in spite of my fervent apologies and my insistence that I had every intention of helping maintain the exclusivity of that privilege. We had never really talked about that before. Looking back on it now, I think my efforts to conceal my jealousy had worked against me.

When we walked out of the merchant's shop, I heard a familiar voice around the corner, echoing out of the alleyway.

"So, what else can you tell me about Colonel Marcus Raven?" It took me a minute to place the voice. It was the mercenary with the fancy sword cannon, the one working for Captain Winslow. A clinking noise spoke of the exchange of two—no, three—coins. French deniers, minted relatively recently by the crisp sound of their anti-shaving ridges; I would have found that sound unfamiliar before my arrival in Dab, but the border town saw all kinds of currency clinking about.

"Well, guvnor, there was this pony, see," said a voice that sounded worn, old, and a little drunk.

It was early in the day for drinking by ordinary standards, but then, the speaker was evidently familiar with the seedier parts of town and was able to relate the story of the pony at great length (in a form somewhat more embroidered than any of the versions I had yet heard, but these things have a way of growing in the telling), so early morning drinking was probably not unusual for him.

I stood in front of the shopfront, uncertain as to whether I should stay and listen, or make a quick exit from the scene to avoid a direct encounter with the Loegrian mercenary. If he was asking questions about me, that wasn't a good sign. In fact, that he was here instead of patrolling the deep woods with his captain was a bad sign in and of itself. I shook my head to clear it. Then again, he was a mercenary, and I was purportedly a mercenary. He could be looking to sign on to my company, or looking on behalf of his current employer to offer me a job.

Still, it didn't feel quite right, and I didn't want to walk into a situation where I'd need to explain the less respectable antics of my soldiers during their first night out on the town again. I walked in the other direction. This was away from the warehouse serving as our headquarters; so, in case my movements were being watched, I stopped at a bakery and bought some pastries—which cost me the remaining contents of my pockets—to provide an explanation for my detour. Haggling with the baker took a while, and when I came out, I saw Katya bent over, a young boy whispering in her ear. I froze and busied myself counting the pastries, pretending not to have noticed. She stood up.

"Do not worry," she said, tousling the boy's hair. "I trust Marcus. If he wanted to do something bad to me, it would have happened before. The person who sent you is wrong."

She handed him a local copper pfennig, and shooed him on his way.

"What did he tell you?" I asked very quietly.

"Not here," she said, her voice tight with tension.

When we arrived back at headquarters, she tearfully told me that the boy had been looking for Leontina Odobescu. He had brought Katya the message that she was in grave danger because I was secretly in service to the Golden Empire. She added that her pistol would have been too loud, and that she didn't think she could drag the boy into an alley to cut his throat without being noticed, so she had simply told the boy he was wrong about everything, hoping he would believe her. However, she was fairly sure she could pick him out of a crowd from a rooftop with a pistol, though she cautioned me that it might take a little while, and she wasn't sure who else he might tell in the meantime.

A chill ran down my spine as I thought of Katya setting up on a roof somewhere and shooting at children. I told her to stop crying, that she had exercised good judgement in playing it cool, and that since the boy had probably been told that by whoever had sent him to find her, the boy himself wasn't really our chief worry in any case. She didn't have to go shooting people from the rooftops, and I thought I had a good idea who might be the source of the rumor.

CHAPTER FOUR

In Which I Question a Good Fit

The hinged piece reminded me of a breastplate, but it was too short, only covering the upper half of Katya's torso; and, for that matter, it was not tempered in the manner of armor, but rather, forged from the quality of steel used for structural members, not armor plates. Any good mechanic learns to tell the difference quite quickly by touch; the qualities of structural strength and of resistance to penetration call for somewhat different metallurgical techniques, and they feel as different to the bare skin as a chair made from maple and one made from oak when you sit down in them.

It's really quite obvious, but since most people don't regularly work with good steel, they don't really have the opportunity to accustom themselves to the difference. By contrast, something like the difference in the feeling between oak and maple chairs is something that many people will have the chance to familiarize themselves with; I should think that only someone living in an area without both types of trees, or someone opposed to sitting down entirely, would manage to avoid becoming familiar with the characteristic differences in hardness between the softer maples and harder oaks.

Rather than having the function of armor, the purpose of this breastplate-like object was to serve as a padded brace for an artificial shoulder to attach to. Short of bolting the artificial arm directly to Katya's clavicle and scapula, I couldn't think of a more elegant solution in terms of minimizing the bulk of the device, and with the artificial arm being stronger and heavier, trying to attach it directly to Katya's skeleton would have been not only messy, but a risky piece of structural engineering— bone is simply not as strong as steel.

The miniaturized form-fitting cuirass braced the artificial shoulder against the entirety of Katya's upper torso. The mechanical arm and hand themselves were a little more worn-looking. The mechanic had freshly polished them to make a good impression, of course, but they had obviously been something he already had on hand, with minor adjustments made to fit them to each other and to the newly constructed mechanical shoulder.

Even with only the shoulder and the brace for it being of entirely new construction, the turnaround had been very quick—barely more than a week. It was likely that the mechanic had several talented apprentices to shop much of the work out to, but even so, it really was quite a remarkable piece of work. All this was running through my mind as I checked the fit on Katya. It fit very well. Of course, the mechanic had been very thorough with his measurements, to the point of undue familiarity. I felt a surge of jealous anger as I thought about the older man's hands on Katya, touching and feeling. I opened the brace, taking it back off Katya and setting it on a workbench.

"Mine," I growled under my breath, running my hands up and down her bare torso.

"Here? Now?" She blushed, gesturing at the door.

"Yes," I said.

I shoved one workbench against the door to ensure our privacy and cleared off a second one with a sweep of my arm. She bit her lip and nodded, and I set to the task of laying a fresh claim to every inch of her body.

A slightly too-short while later, we were interrupted by a loud crashing noise, and I was reminded in a very unpleasant manner that the door was hinged on the other side, and thus opened out into the hallway, not into the workshop. This meant that my barricade was completely ineffective at preventing the door from opening, though it did present an obstacle to graceful entry into the room.

As I was processing this startling reminder, Vitold picked himself up off the floor amid fragments of wood and machine parts (a mixture of the too-fragile crate he had been carrying, its contents, and the contents of the workbench he had just tripped over) and a stream of curses. Another soldier stared goggle-eyed from the hallway, holding an intact (and presumably full) crate. After Vitold had run out of angry curses, he added two non-profane words, in a tone of incredulity.

"Here? Now?"

It was my turn to blush.

"Sorry," I said.

A wrench bounced off the wall near Vitold (a demonstration of Katya's displeasure), and he ducked back into the hallway, closing the door behind him. Several more apologies and promises later, I left Katya to work on getting used to controlling her new arm on her own and went off with the intention of supervising some drills or dealing with some paperwork. I found myself having a discussion with Vitold.

"Mikolai, she's bad for you."

Vitold's arms were crossed, and he had an unusually serious expression on his face. A mix of negative emotions had congealed and set into a firm and dire expression, by which indication I thought he was changing the subject from Katya's effects on me to the state of our company.

"We can't keep going on like this; it's just not going to work out."

"Why? Why not?"

I closed the door so as to ensure a little bit more privacy and lowered my voice, since I did not want to feed any rumors. "Look, we've just gotten enough cash and credit to pay everyone, and if the troops are awash with rumors about the colonel and his lovely captain, well, we are for all practical intents and purposes a mercenary company. No regulations to deal with from up above, and if I'm hauled back in front of an imperial military court, charges of inappropriate fraternization would be the least of my worries."

"That's not the point," Vitold said. "Well, it sort of is," he added, "but I was talking about Katya."

"What about Katya?"

"She's a patriot as well as a monster. As long as she's hanging around your neck like a stone, you're never more than two steps away from getting shot in the head, and never more than three steps from getting hauled in front of a tribunal. How long can you keep pretending we haven't deserted? Katya has to be the only person in the whole company who thinks we're still following orders from Tanais. If someone from one of the ministries came sniffing around tomorrow, she'd tell them everything she knew about us at the drop of a hat, and cheerfully. She could also blow our original identities to the locals or foreign spies. I don't think our charter could pass close inspection by a lawyer."

"I trust Katya," I told him.

"That's a big mistake," Vitold said.

I gave him a measured look.

"She's a monster as well as a patriot. She doesn't love you, she loves what her twisted little mind thinks you can do for the Golden Empire. She's a remorseless killer. She doesn't think like us, she's hardly even human. She doesn't hesitate. I think she likes killing people, Mikolai; she's a sniper for a reason. We need to get rid of her before she decides to get rid of us. And if it's the . . ." He hesitated, and made some suggestive gestures awkwardly. "Hire a courtesan or something. You've got the cash, and they won't kill you if you sneeze at the wrong time."

At my shocked look, he cleared his throat and continued.

"Or just sell off all the hardware and get yourself a wife here. We could make a pretty nice new life here for ourselves in Silesia with that kind of stake, Mikolai. Just not with that red-headed, bullet-spitting monster glued to your side."

I looked at Katya's slumbering form. In sleep, she looked so peaceful; she breathed peacefully and evenly, a warm snuggly weight not quite heavy enough to impede my own breathing. She looked small, fragile, vulnerable; and innocent of the accusations Vitold had levied against her. Vitold's words kept coming back to me, echoing in my mind's ear. I had never known Vitold to be so passionate in declaring someone evil. He would talk about people being crazy, mad, pig-headed, stupid, or stubborn on a regular basis (he did love to complain); but I couldn't remember him being so scathing, even when he had been talking about our infamous general, a man with far more blood on his hands. Her own hands were far from clean, but . . .

Hand, singular, rather. I clasped it in mine, gently, careful not to wake her. Was this the hand of a monster and a patriot? It was true that she killed ruthlessly, and without hesitating, but her quick and accurate shooting had saved my life. In the service of our country, though. But she loved me, simply and purely, did she not? I could still remember her urgent and earnest whisper: "You are a good man and I like you." I could also remember how much Katya had struggled with trying to pretend to be something, or someone, that she wasn't; if she couldn't lie smoothly to nobles at a party, how could she lie to me?

Do monsters love? What is a monster?

When I was young, a woodsman from the next village over was mauled by a bear. To him, the bear was a horrifying monster, one that nearly tore his arm off before chasing him up a tree, tormenting him for hours through a long, sleepless night for no reason but to delight in his suffering. When I spoke with the bear, I was told that a horrifying monster with an ax had dropped a tree on her cub. She loved her cub, she told me, and its death had simply infuriated her. The woodsman, of course, had been working hard all summer long to raise enough money that he might be able to make a bid for the hand of his beloved. What he had was barely enough to buy him a good funeral when his wounds went septic.

I can't blame either the woodsman or the bear for calling the other a monster. Bears don't really understand the idea of a careless accident, and the woodsman didn't know (and never lived long enough to learn) the reason he was being tormented so. And there is something monstrous about killing the animal equivalent of a small child; something monstrous, too, about mauling a man and spending hours tormenting him as he clings, terrified and helpless, to a branch above.

What Katya was willing to do in the service of her country had no boundaries that I had yet found. Her job was murder—murder of our own officers, if necessary, or of civilians. I could remember her crying recently because she hadn't been able to conveniently slit a young boy's throat when she suspected he knew a state secret (to wit, my imperial affiliation, and a fabricated belief that she and the boy shared that I was up to some sort of sophisticated skullduggery on behalf of the less overt side of state service). If failing to commit an atrocity made her cry, what wouldn't she do in the name of the Empire? Even if she did love me, well and truly, would that be enough if she realized I wasn't following any orders at all?

I shivered in spite of the warmth of the blankets, and of the woman snuggled up on top of me beneath those blankets. She stirred, pulling her hand out of mine to tug the blankets higher, and mumbled something into my chest before settling back down. Her only dilemma might be whether or not to cry herself to sleep after she slit my throat. Maybe she would spend the rest of the night quietly mourning me, snuggled up against my corpse until it grew cold, I thought to myself, a sick feeling growing in my stomach as I pictured a far more sinister version of the scene at hand.

Vitold was right that I could not expect—not reasonably, anyway— that she would continue to believe in the delusion that we had not, for all intents and purposes, willfully deserted. I had a letter, sitting amongst my personal effects, calling for my arrest—or summary execution—as a confirmed enemy spy. (Why hadn't I simply gotten rid of it? Well, it had largely escaped my mind, to be frank.) Sooner or later, the truth would come out, and it would mean my life—unless Katya died first. It would be easy enough for me to kill her first while she was helpless and asleep in my arms, as she was now. Physically easy, anyway. But I could not bring myself to cause her death; not by my own hand, not by sending her out on a suicide mission. What might be easy for my arms was far too hard for my heart.

And as loyal as she was, she would not leave my side on her own; and whatever task I ordered her to, I could expect her to return. Even if I ordered her to go back to the imperial capital in Tanais, I should expect her to return (though in that case with a team from the capital with orders to ensure my capture or execution). If I simply absconded, or went away for a mission of my own, she would come looking for me when I didn't return, to rescue me as she had done time and time again. Sitting there in the dark, holding warm and winsome red-headed death in my hands, I couldn't think of any good options. I didn't want to die, and I didn't want Katya to die. I didn't want our time together to end either, but that seemed a better choice than the death of one or both of us.

As that thought crossed my mind, the distinctive sound of a large piece of steam-powered machinery deliberately crashing through a wall sent me tumbling out of bed and onto the floor.

CHAPTER FIVE

In Which I Roll Out of Bed

I reacted to the sound of machinery crashing through the wall by bolting upright and startling awake, though I am not quite sure in which order those two things happened. In either case, I was only briefly upright before Katya yanked me into a tumble off the bed and onto the floor. This was no mean feat for someone half my size with half the number of working limbs, but Katya was willing to fling herself to the floor and yank me on top of herself regardless of incidental bruising.

I rolled off of Katya as she groaned, but stayed low to the ground. Had the bed been a lovely piece of wooden furniture like the one in the manor, I would have rolled underneath it, but my bed in the warehouse was really just a pile of straw padded with blankets. Gunshots rang out, and a mech took down my bedroom door with a heavy smash of its arm, following up on its entry with what I could only assume was a grenade to the center of my bed, sending a cloud of straw and cloth spinning up in the air in a dull explosion.

The mech cast its head back and forth, peering as if it couldn't see perfectly well through the floating chaff, its boiler growling loudly. The starlight that leaked through the cracks in the wall glittered off the floating bits of straw most distractingly, true, but they were hardly a solid barrier to vision.

It seems difficult to grant a mech ordinary human visual acuity. I had heard that some wizards can learn to see through the eyes of their mechs on occasion, but I had thought I hadn't yet learned the real trick of it. On the occasions where I had perceived myself to be looking through the eyes of the jury-rigged steam suits, they seemed to have abysmally bad vision.

Past a very short range, things would get very blurry—imagine looking out on a forested hill, and seeing simply textured green in the distance—not merely being unable to make out the veins of leaves and patterns of bark on the distant trees lining the horizon, but not even being able to distinguish individual leaves, entire trees reduced to little more detail than a smudge of green paint.

However, I have never seen through the eyes of a proper, professionally constructed mech, and it is possible that they have better vision than the jury-rigged machines I had been working with. In that case, the elemental spirit providing the motivating guidance may simply have not been clever enough to process the confusing scene in front of it and compare it with the orders it had been given by its master.

I whispered to Katya that she should ready herself to grab a gun. I would distract the mech, I told her. Then I counted down from three, leaping up onto the bed waving my arms. As I did so, the mech reeled under the weight of a canine projectile, impacting it at a truly remarkable velocity for a dog only given the space of a small room to accelerate in. Someone behind the mech cursed loudly and ordered the mech to "hurry up and kill them," the phrase being notably ambiguous and in French.

Katya groaned weakly as she lay there, her moan blending eerily closely with the groan of bending metal as Yuri tried to tear the faceplate off the presumptively French mech with his teeth. He dropped the hot piece of metal with a yowl, and the mech thrashed around noisily, trying to connect with its attacker in the darkness as Yuri dashed around the room. The mech seemed to think the ambiguous order included, among the selection of possible targets, the dog that had just attacked it, and was prioritizing what it saw as the most dangerous target out of the three in the room.

Unfortunately, the mech seemed to have chosen wisely. Yuri was the only being that seemed likely to threaten it. I was unarmed, and Katya seemed dazed and confused. Looking around the room for a weapon, I spotted Katya's rifle, but hesitated. Picking up her beloved rifle felt like sacrilege of a sort; she was very particular about the treatment of her rifle, and I had never fired it before.

After overcoming my initial hesitation and picking up her rifle, I started looking around for ammunition. Where did Katya keep the ammunition for her rifle? For that matter, how did one load it? I remembered a mallet was involved somehow, as the rifling made it impossible to simply drop the bullet in. It wasn't quite the same as the arquebuses Vitold and I had briefly trained on, and now was no time to be fumbling around figuring out how to properly load an unfamiliar weapon. I tossed the rifle away with a flash of guilt for mishandling Katya's precious weapon and grabbed a pistol—not as potent a weapon, but at least one I was familiar with.

As soon as I fired, the mech, identifying a more dangerous target than the dog, turned toward the sound. The tube mounted on its shoulder oriented toward a point above my right shoulder and fired, narrowly missing me. Between the loud report and the painful blast of the grenade's explosion, striking me everywhere from the top of my head to the backs of my ankles, I thought I had been hit, but as I had not yet died, I loaded and fired again, aiming at its boiler.

Steam whistled out as it clattered toward me like an angry teapot. I lashed out with the now-empty pistol, and a line of magical force followed, looping around the mech's midsection in the shape of a noose and crushing it. Either I had grown to be much stronger in the ways of casting spells, or this mech was more lightly built than the ones I had encountered before.

Thus reminded that I was in some fashion a wizard, I closed my eyes and reached out mentally to my familiar jury-rigged mechs, awakening their elemental spirits and commanding them to go forth and fight. Had there been anyone alive inside them, instead of just machinery, they would have cooked in the bath of steam that bled out through the valves during the sudden jump-starts of the boilers; a surge of elemental power consuming a quarter-load of charcoal in seconds is not what those valves had been designed to contain.

A growl and a bark reminded me that the mech had a controller of some sort nearby—now in rapid retreat from Yuri's wrath, fortunately—and that my other faithful bodyguard, the human one, had yet to reach her feet. (Foot, I suppose, but you catch my meaning.) I bent down to check on her. Lying on the floor next to the bed, she had been spared most of the shrapnel from the grenades fired by the mech, but she seemed dazed, her pupils mismatched in size and not focusing on me as they ordinarily would have. I pushed some blankets (such as they were—smoking and shredded from the effects of the grenade) off the bed and on top of her, to keep her warm and out of sight between the bed and the wrecked mech.

Then I jogged off toward the sound of Yuri's barking, pistol in one hand and an ammunition pouch in the other, the night air cool against my skin. A warehouse, or rather a pair of adjacent warehouses converted into an impromptu military compound, is not a very large place, when it comes down to it. In less than a minute, I was looking up and down the street, trying to catch sight of enemies. I called back Yuri, then returned to the warehouse. There was some shouting going on, a lot of confusion, and as the officers began to put order to the chaos, light from lanterns filled our barracks.

"Sir! Compound two reports all clear, sir!" Lieutenant Rimehammer was among the living. He looked concerned. "Sir, are you alright?"

"I'm fine," I told him. "Just a little winded."

I looked down at myself, just in case, and remembered two things. First, with the warm spring nights (and warm redheaded bed-companion) I had been sleeping without any sort of night clothes on. Second, I had experienced a near miss from a grenade. The shrapnel had opened up shallow wounds across my entire exposed side, including several cuts in my scalp that were bleeding profusely.

"I suppose I should get cleaned up," I said in as neutral a tone as possible, "and perhaps put on some clothing. I was not expecting an attack."

I would soon find out that there were very few casualties from the nighttime attack; it had been an assassination attempt aimed at me, not an attempt to destroy the company by ambush. Two soldiers on watch duty had been shot and left for dead (one of them was indeed deceased, the other might yet live); there were several injuries, most of them minor, from identification errors in the dark; and one man had broken his leg when he left his bunk a little too quickly in response to the call to action. Katya's bump on the head and my dose of shrapnel were among the more serious injuries to treat. I pointed the former out when the Swedish lieutenant emphasized the latter. As a compromise, we went to my room together, where I found Katya with her pupils dilated to uneven sizes, a combination of relief and confusion on her face, and otherwise much the same as when I had last seen her.

"There you are! You are not just little bloody scorch marks! What has happened?" She seemed distraught.

I explained, briefly, that we had been attacked and were now putting together the pieces of what had happened.

"There are little bloody scorch marks," she told me, pointing down at the dirt floor. "I thought you were just little bloody scorch marks." She paused, staring downward.

I handed her some clothing and told her to put it on, and then tried to follow suit when I remembered that my entire backside, from head to foot, had been caught in the blast. Trying to pull a jacket on over the combination of cuts, burns, and shrapnel that one receives from a proximate grenade blast is quite painful, and now that I had reminded myself of that injury by aggravating it, I was having difficulty breathing evenly.

"Sir, you really should come to the infirmary." The lieutenant sounded concerned. Yuri was also concerned, and licking my leg, as dogs are wont to do to themselves or their wounded companions (usually other dogs, but dogs tend to think of humans as no less worthy than dogs).

"The little bloody scorch marks are bloodier now," remarked Katya, gesturing at the floor as fresh blood dripped down. She giggled, waving the long coat I'd passed to her in the air for emphasis. "And you are not just little bloody scorch marks!" She dropped the coat and touched me with her fingertips carefully, as if making sure I was corporeal and not some ghost-Mikolai come to haunt her. She gripped me a little more firmly, and the lieutenant looked away, embarrassed.

I imagined staggering, bloody and still naked, into the infirmary. The dirt floor seemed to be a little less steady than usual, and so in light of that, I added the spectacle of my falling over from pain and weakness to that mental image. It went from undignified to downright embarrassing.

"I think it will be better if we have clean bandages and such brought here," I said, deciding that the less said among the men about me charging off naked to battle, the better, and laid myself face-down on top of the shredded pile of cloth and straw that had previously been a bed.

"Yes, sir." The lieutenant bustled off, muttering something under his breath about gods and idiots.

"Little bloody scorch marks." Katya paused, then changed the subject. "He is licking you, Mikolai. Why is he licking you? Does that mean he wants to eat you? You're not just little bloody scorch marks."

"It's what dogs do to try to clean an open wound," I told her. "They don't have hands to hold a cloth with, so they lick things to clean them off."

"Does it work?" she asked.

"Well enough for them, I suppose," I said. Since there was only one dog in the room, the second thing that started licking me must have been Katya. I was still trying to figure out what to say to that when the licking suddenly stopped.

"Ow." A pause. "I got one of those little sharp pieces in my tongue."

"You have hands, Katya," I said. "You don't need to lick things to clean them off."

"You are not just little bloody scorch marks," she replied. "What has happened?"

Hadn't I already explained that to her? "We were attacked," I began.

"Where are they?" she asked, interrupting me. She paused. "There are little bloody scorch marks on the floor." A brief giggle escaped her, and then she shifted back to a concerned tone. "Mikolai, you are bleeding." She gingerly touched me with her fingers.

"Yes, Katya, I'm bleeding. Now go put on the coat." I pointed in the general direction I remembered her having dropped the coat. I heard a rustling of cloth, then the door opening, and forced myself to raise my head. The lieutenant was back with clean bandages, vodka, and an alcoholic surgeon. The surgeon pulled each individual piece of shrapnel out with a pair of tweezers. Fortunately, he was of the opinion that vodka should be applied both topically and orally to the patient in generous measure, and I passed out partway through the painful process.

From the diary of Helen Maude Victoria Winslow

March 14th

A monstrous abomination attacked this morning. That is to say, a monster was sighted east and a little south of our camp, heading south by southwest, and Jacob, having taken this heading as being for our camp while on watch in the pre-dawn gray, opened fire. (Alan checked over the tracks later. He thinks it wasn't coming any closer than a hundred paces; it was making a path as straight as an arrow.) The blighted, eyeless horror, whatever it was, went down quick enough once the mechs were up in action, but when Caleb cut apart the body trying to find something worth taking as a trophy, we found a handful of metal artifacts—belt buckle, coins, buttons, boot clasps, and a locket—that strongly suggest the rider we sent was eaten without delivering his message.

I dearly hope that was a pure and foul coincidence. If it is someone trying to prevent word of Colonel Raven's battalion from reaching the margrave . . .

I have made the command decision that we ride back to the margrave's castle posthaste to report our findings, all of them. I have a bad feeling about this whole business. Maybe it's just Caleb's paranoia rubbing off on me—he thinks, of all things, that their latrine ditches were too well dug for them to be real mercenaries—but I think there's something more to it all. And whether or not Colonel Raven is right about Koschei and his minions being too busy holding Wallachia to make mischief for Leon, we're better off keeping close by with our patrols.

March 15th

I have always disliked special agents of the crown a little. Every one I have met has little respect for rank or property, whether military or social. I've worked very hard on my etiquette and my properly Parisian court French.

I am hardly one to shoot peasants for sport, as a cousin's friend claimed he'd seen done at a country resort once. That said, I very much want to shoot one particular Silesian peasant. Let him go running, get a little head start, and then BANG, shoot him. Maybe first shoot him in the arm, to make him think he might get away, then a leg next, to see him quail in fear and crawl sobbing for cover, then BLAM, shot to the head. SPLAT.

And now that I want to, I won't, because the man is supposedly a special agent in the Lion's service, and that might even be the truth. It turns out that Colonel Marcus Raven is called "General Mikolai" by his bedmate when the two of them are talking over a pillow, and that they have some greater mission they're urgently trying to carry out. The agent has written notes on that and a thousand more things, a journal full of his notes investigating Marcus Raven! I took them away from him over Jacob and Alan's objections and read through them by lamplight late last night. He just didn't want to let me know until he felt like he was a safe distance from Colonel Raven. And then the little coward demanded I give over a horse to him, because he wasn't going back to within a day's ride of Colonel Raven.

I refused, of course, saying I couldn't possibly let military property into the hands of a civilian specialist without supervision, and then Jacob nobly gave over his own horse, which of course is his own personal property rather than a military horse, and the agent was off like that.

He's made me look a fool. Christ, forgive me, but I want to kill him. Painfully. Even if he has done us a service . . .

Addendum: And even though his notes are painstakingly detailed. At times, luridly fascinating, for which I feel a little guilty. When he had a chance to set up undetected with a good pen and surface, his notes will describe every word, every sound, every act, no matter if a normal person would have stopped transcribing out of a sense of personal decency and modesty. I am embarrassed enough by what I read that I cannot bear to share it aloud with the others and have refused to share the journal, lest I have to hear too many coarse jokes.

I should only admire his thoroughness and dedication, to keep recording even then. But I still detest him with all my heart . . .

March 17th

After a hard day and a half of riding, we have come to the end of the trail. We came across signs of battle first—dried blood, uprooted trees, fragments of metal, cloth, and bone, freshly turned mounds of earth; but whatever they fought in these dark woods did not stop them, for the trail continued and led to a camp. As we inspected this camp for clues, Jacob came up to me to announce proudly he had worked out the mathematics of it, and that based on how long we had taken to reach their camp, we might catch them by the night after the following night.

Alan was skeptical about that, and we soon all became downright pessimistic. Roughly a mile from where they set camp, their trail ends. It does not stop with a halt, so much as simply fades into unbroken brush, the medley of deep ruts, hoofprints, broken vegetation, and mech prints fading to a scattered handful. The last fifteen yards show only a single set of hoofprints and wheels, growing lighter with each step. Alan has taken his pessimism being proven particularly hard. He is right now sitting on the ground, staring at a hoofprint. I think he wants to cry, but refuses to do so while the rest of us are watching.

We have sent men out in a search pattern to find anything.

Addendum: They have found no signs, and it is getting dark. We will set up camp here. I am looking back over the spy's notes to see if I can shed any light on the matter. Christ preserve us from whatever evil that lurks in these woods. I feel a chill in my bones.

CHAPTER SIX

In Which I Dance Carefully

"Miss Winslow? Would you be so kind as to honor me with a dance?" Out of uniform and made up for a high society dance, the Loegrian captain looked significantly different, but a thick layer of face paint—changing her complexion from weathered brown to the pallor expected of those who diligently stay in manor houses throughout the daylight hours—a very tight corset that narrowed her waist, and a pile of petticoats, which rendered the lower half of her body completely indistinct, were not enough to render her unrecognizable.

Her eyes were the same, certainly, and I could see certain other small details were the same. The little bumps in people's skulls, the thickness and texture of their hair—she had dyed hers to a dark auburn, but it remained fine and wavy—even the way the skin swirls on people's hands are all distinct. Though, as she was wearing gloves, that was little help, as I could not catch a glimpse of such swirls. Not that I had memorized her appearance perfectly, but I remembered it well enough to distinguish her from the local upper crust.

"I'm afraid you have me mistaken for someone else, sir." She demurely fanned herself.

"Delighted to make your acquaintance, then, miss," I said, bowing and kissing her hand and, while she was slightly off balance, tugging her to take a first step out onto the dance floor with me.

She had the choice between either making a scene or following my lead, and chose the latter. In the distance, I heard a wineglass shatter, then the pieces tinkle to the floor. The Loegrian captain looked over my shoulder toward the noise with some alarm. A musician paused in surprise, a brief hiccup in the music that drew the attention of the room to Katya, the source of the interruption.

"Your companion, good sir, she seems to have suffered an accident," she simpered, leaning close. "Perhaps you should go see to her?"

"How observant of you to note that we are acquainted," I murmured back, "especially given that we arrived separately, and I haven't spoken with her yet."

"Well, she looks jealous," the captain murmured into my ear as I spun her around, pulling her wrist firmly behind her waist as I steered her around in a flourish. "I could only assume."

Katya was, I was delighted to see, gesturing at her wine-splattered mechanical arm apologetically. I could only guess that she had remembered to play off any mishaps as being due to the newness of her prosthetics. She shot me a brief but intense glare when she saw me looking her way, and I looked away. She seemed to have recovered from the knock on her head, but she was still not a particularly subtle person. I probably should have told her to stay behind, but her false identity as Leontina Odobescu meant that she had been explicitly invited. By going separately, we were each able to bring an escort, doubling our presence at the party. Katya had come with Lieutenant Quentin Gavreau (who was better able to guide her through the minefields of noble etiquette than I) and I had arrived with the infantry captain (who would help keep an eye on Quentin, lest he end up in some sort of foolish mischief like his attempted duel with Lieutenant Kransky).

After we had come up with that plan, Quentin had spent the entire afternoon teaching Katya what she needed to know. I sat in on the discussions, first just to be sure he wasn't trying to charm her away from me, and then because I was learning things about high society that I would never have learned while stumbling around on my own.

"You're quite fond of making assumptions," I told the Loegrian officer dressed as a demure young civilian as she stepped on my foot—perhaps accidentally, perhaps not. "I believe the cost of your assumptions has become entirely too high. And you could at least have considered wearing something other than the boots from your dress uniform. You'll mark up the floor." I dipped her sharply, taking the breath out of her as she attempted to formulate her next response. After I brought her back to vertical, we danced through several measures in silence as she considered my words and closed her mouth.

"Very well. I am Captain Helen Maude Victoria Winslow, and you are General Mikolai something-or-other, and the two of us are dancing at a reception to which neither of us was invited," she said.

I wondered how she had managed to learn my name. "Not entirely accurate, but now I know you've dug far enough to have a very dangerously poor idea of what I'm up to." Technically a true statement in its own right. I wasn't a real general, I had no idea what I was up to, and she seemed to know enough to be dangerous to me. "Which explains the inept assault," I added.

"What assault?" she said, her face the very picture of innocence.

I swung her around, dipped her again, and brought her back up with her arm pinned behind her back. "You really shouldn't lie about the obvious things. It helps me learn what you look like while lying. Just a tip; I'm not offering to take you under my wing. My operation is entirely too delicate to have a clumsy oaf like yourself stomping around in it." I tapped her boot with my foot—not putting my weight down, but giving a gentle reminder that I, too, could step on toes if I chose to.

She looked like she was going to say something in response, but then another couple slammed into us. They were engrossed in one another to the exclusion of paying attention to the rest of the dance floor—as, for that matter, we had been. Presumably, the other couple had more pleasant reasons for being distracted. The collision effectively interrupted the entire dance; for the four of us, because we were picking ourselves up off the floor, and for everyone else, because the collision drew their attention and disapproval as the musicians stopped. I helped Helen to her feet and bowed.

"Thank you for the dance, miss," I said at a volume I usually reserved for giving orders to my fellow soldiers. Lowering my voice to a level I hoped would not be noticed, I continued, "Your intentions are lovely, but I am afraid that my toes are a little too sore to dance with you again tonight, as delightful as you are. Perhaps another night."

I bowed again, as deeply as I felt I could without risking my balance. A few giggles from nearby women demonstrated that with the music stopped, I hadn't spoken quietly enough to avoid being overheard. I ignored the giggles, pretending that the comment had been private between myself and the young woman I had just danced with. I had learned enough about the cut-throat dynamics of high-class social affairs to understand that the pretense of privacy was an important shield for both of us.

After exchanging a lengthy series of flowery apologies with the couple who had bumped into myself and Captain Winslow, I wound up back on my way to the dance floor in the arms of a charming young lady with hair the color of well-aged—but not moldy—cheese, which is to say blonde but not bright enough to stand out. Her friends had shoved her at me, and there had been, of course, nothing left but to catch her, keep her from falling over, and then politely ask her to dance at that point. It would have been rude not to.

As I spun around the floor with her, I concentrated simply on dancing well. The point of the previous dance had been an exercise in psychological warfare—to frighten, intimidate, confuse, and interrogate Captain Winslow. Ultimately, my intention had been to try to put the brakes on any plans she might have for the evening, and to find out if she had anything else planned in the wake of the failed attempt to murder me in my sleep. This dance, however, had no such purpose; it was simply a hazard of the evening that might reveal me to be someone or something other than what I pretended to be—a mysterious but potentially highborn mercenary.

There were no major missteps this time—no collisions, no trod-upon toes, nothing of the sort—and I thought I was out of danger when the musicians finished the piece. I bowed to my partner, and she curtsied and thanked me for the dance.

There are three things I should state now, though I did not figure them out until later. First, most of the young men in the room had, by that point, collected around Quentin Gavreau to hear stories from a heroic warrior who had fought against the evil soldiers of the distant Golden Empire in faraway Wallachia. Some of them may even have been true.

Second, the main form of acceptable entertainment for young women of the noble variety at parties like the one I found myself at is either dancing with or speaking with unmarried men of the noble variety.

Third, the blonde who had been practically shoved into me was enmeshed in a plot that caught me unaware. Her friends—I am using the term "friend" loosely—had shoved her at me in the hopes that I would create an embarrassing spectacle, as I had with the Loegrian captain. I hadn't. Instead, I had shown the blonde a good time on the dance floor. Granted, some commented that I had held her "scandalously close" and was "daringly energetic," phrases which I found very odd to apply to my dancing. Among normal folks, rather than nobility, those phrases would respectively suggest I had slipped a hand somewhere more intimate than the outside of her corset and was working up a sweat.

Doing so promoted me swiftly up the ranks of potential dance partners, something that there was a decidedly short supply of—most of the other men present were bald, gray, or both. I ended up back on the dance floor with another young lady shortly. Then a third; and then the young lady who'd been shoved at me earlier reclaimed me for the next dance. This continued until my feet and arms were sore.

For some reason, I hadn't expected my arms to be sore, but it made sense after the fact. Women are, as a general rule, considerably heavier than sacks of vegetables, even if they usually do most of the work of holding themselves up, and my arms have been sore from spending less than half as long loading sacks of vegetables onto a wagon to bring to market in the village. By the end of the night, I thought I understood the reason for the giggled whispers about my being "daringly energetic." A man who had planned on dancing that many times would likely have chosen a more sedate pace.

When I finally escaped from the dance floor, I found that etiquette required I make a series of polite and pleasant statements to the young blonde lady and her friends that they were perfectly good company and I was simply exhausted. By the time I finished extricating myself from the unexpected social situation, I could not see Katya anywhere, and the infantry captain seemed to be very preoccupied with the exercise of dragging Lieutenant Gavreau away from the party. The infantry captain had deployed a clever ruse of feigning excessive drunkenness. (At least, I hoped it was a clever ruse. She made a very convincing belligerent drunk.)

I didn't want to call attention to the fact that my original escort for the evening was departing, or to Katya in particular, so I felt like I had no ready excuse for leaving early. In retrospect, I should have left and gone looking for Katya at that point. Any old line about simply being entirely exhausted and requiring rest would have worked just fine, but I was nervous and had little experience with high society and the manners of the rich.

Consider how sometimes the obvious and correct course of action eludes you: The word sits on the tip of your tongue but won't launch itself out of your mouth. That was how I felt when I was searching for a good reason to brush off the young ladies I had been dancing with. It is true that the young ladies were charming, friendly, and attractive, but in spite of what certain individuals have suggested, that had nothing to do with my lingering late into the night.

Unlike people who work for a living, nobles aren't obligated to get up early in the morning, or even in the morning at all. The noblewomen talked for some time—until the dance floor completely emptied, the musicians packed up their instruments, and the older matrons started dozing off. At this point, they began to talk about leaving. The blonde who had been initially shoved at me clung to my arm, pleading dizziness from what she referred to as an "exhausting night with so much twirling and spinning about," citing the fact that I had danced with her several times that night as justification for why I was obligated to make sure she didn't lose her balance and fall over somewhere.

As I look back on the events of that night, I am not sure whether my escorting her down to her carriage and waking the dozing footman on the front bench saved her life or heedlessly endangered it. I didn't feel like asking the person who could have answered that question with authority; neither answer would have been a particularly comfortable one to work through, and I decided to avoid the subject entirely.

At the time, though, I merely felt flattered and more than a little awkward as the young woman first told the footman that her aunt was sleeping on a couch in one of the host's rooms and was surely ill-disposed to be disturbed, then tried to persuade me to keep her company on the carriage ride back on the grounds that it was near midnight and she would soon fall asleep. The footman looked relieved when I declined.

Midnight. Had I really spent that long talking? I looked up to the stars to confirm the lateness of the hour. Dab, a bustling town, had less clear air than most places I had been; the smoke from many people doing many things for a long time means the air itself remains hazy, an extra foul note on top of the other smells associated with a large city full of people. As I brought my gaze down from the stars, I spotted Katya. Her face was blackened with grease paint, she was no longer wearing a fancy dress, and she was covered in . . . Was that a net with roofing shingles tied to it? It was. It broke up her outline against the night sky.

She also had her rifle with her. Had she gone back to our base of operations and then come back? I looked more closely and saw that on the backside of the sloped roof, facing the other way, was a weedy-looking fellow I recognized as another sharpshooter. I waited for a carriage with several more nobles to pass out of earshot before I called to her.

"Katya? Come down, please. It's time to go home," I said.

She froze for a moment, then sighed deeply, turning toward the weedy-looking man. "This makes things hard," she told him quietly, then extracted herself from the net, handed down her rifle, and then climbed down, dangling from the roof's gutter for a moment before dropping to the ground, landing with a muffled clanking noise. (It is hard to land quietly when half of your limbs are made of metal.) She signaled to the weedy-looking fellow, then took her rifle back from me.

I held out my arm for her, but she just started walking toward the warehouse district. I hastened to follow. We were halfway back before she broke the silence.

"You had a very good time dancing." Katya's flat tone sounded accusatory.

"She's a nice girl," I said defensively, thinking immediately of the blonde girl I had escorted out of the party. "It's not her fault her family owns a foundry, and they mostly make bells anyway. It wouldn't have been polite for me to turn her down, and then her friends started in . . ." It occurred to me that Katya might have been jealous of the young woman with aged-cheese-colored hair. I had danced with her several times that night; and I had been smiling, making eye contact, and being otherwise quite friendly. The young woman had taken that as interest in her; I could hardly blame Katya if she made the same judgement.

"You danced with her, too?" The extra emphasis on the pronoun reminded me I had danced with more than one woman and had not seen Katya in the crowd any time after I finished dancing with the Loegrian captain.

"Yes. Several times. It was a long party. I had to be polite. You left early?" I asked.

"I did not want to stay after seeing you dance with that first woman. There are better things for me to do than break glasses at parties and listen to old people say mean things. I left the ballroom then and left the party not very much later. There was talking in the library to hear. Do not tell me you were just being polite when you danced with her. You were almost rude when you dragged her onto the dance floor." Her voice was measured, even, and very tightly controlled. "You danced with her like you were bringing her to bed."

"That was Captain Winslow," I told her.

She stopped in her tracks and blinked several times. Several incoherent noises escaped from her lips—the start of one word, then the start of another word. She sat down right there in the dusty street, eyes unfocused and staring in the distance as she tried and failed to find words. I knelt in the street and gently took her by the shoulders.

"That was Captain Winslow," I repeated. "The Loegrian woman."

"That did not look like . . ." Katya paused, then her eyes focused on me. "You are sure?"

"Yes. Dressed differently and wearing a great deal of make-up, but I am quite certain that was the same woman we met in the woods." Maybe Katya hadn't gotten a clear look at her. "She was wearing the same boots, too."

Her eyes widened, and she looked at me with a strange expression in her eyes. She opened and closed her mouth several more times without actually saying anything.

"I was trying to intimidate or confuse her off our tracks. I'm not sure if it worked or not. She certainly seemed affected," I said.

"I should go back and tell Pavel," she said, looking back over her shoulder the way we had come. "One of the men might have seen where she went."

It suddenly dawned on me what Katya had been doing on the roof. The distant pops of hunting rifles I had heard during our walk took on a more ominous flavor. Most people did not favor the middle of the night for hunting, and I could not imagine that the hunting was very good anywhere within several miles of the city. I was simultaneously horrified and impressed.

Horrified, because I realized that sudden death was stalking the streets, and I felt a little uncomfortable with the idea that the people I had been dancing with, drinking with, and speaking with were lying dead in the street, executed by Katya's orders. I could imagine very vividly a spill of hair the color of well-aged cheese across the cobblestones in the middle of a bloodstain, a young woman's life cut short because her friends had pushed her to dance with a mysterious stranger.

Impressed, because it was a display of initiative and competence that I had not been expecting. I had never really thought of Katya as exercising real control over the troops that were under her command. Her immediate subordinate, Lieutenant Quentin Gavreau, was in charge of her entire nominal command and had been under orders to answer to all four captains' demands. With Katya's capture and injury, he had been the one to lead them on the battlefield.

"She'll have taken precaution against being attacked, especially after her man came after us with a mech. Not a good idea for Pavel and the others to go in half-cocked." Holding her shoulders, both the metal one and the flesh one, I drew her close, looking straight into her eyes. I whispered as fiercely as I could. "I'm tired. I want to go to bed. And I want that bed to have you in it. Not some silly Gothic noble, not some homicidal Loegrian soldier, you."

I slid my hands all the way down her back and then squeezed gently. Katya broke eye contact, looking down. Some of the tension left her as she leaned into me.

"It's you that I love," I said. "One woman is enough for me; I'm not like Ilya was."

She stiffened, and I realized I had made a mistake by bringing up her dead lover.

CHAPTER SEVEN

In Which I Do Not Hear Bells Ring

I slept poorly that night. It was chilly and lonely, and I could feel the beginning of a headache coming on before the first time I fell asleep. My dreams did not help; the most pleasant of them was one where I and several young noblewomen stripped ourselves of our clothing and then were interrupted by an attacking mech that, for some reason, looked like Misha, one of the other steam knights from the squad I had been assigned to so long ago. He, Gregor, and Ilya all featured in my dreams that night; I had plenty of time that night to reflect on my dead comrades.

That dream, at least, had a pleasant prelude; the next one began with shoveling headless bodies into a mass grave and ended when I woke up Yuri with the noises I was making. It was neither my first nor last time having that particular dream. I will never forget that little Wallachian village.

I don't know whether or not Katya also slept poorly that night.

Vitold was irritatingly cheerful when he brought my breakfast in the morning. I was in a foul mood. My feet ached (from dancing), my arms ached (also from dancing), my head ached (from drinking surprisingly strong punch), and my heart ached (because of the rift that had opened last night between Katya and myself). Tea (with sugar and cream, since we were in the midst of prosperous civilization), eggs and toast (with butter), and even sausage (which Yuri eyed hungrily). I thanked Vitold automatically and ate methodically as he filled me in on how the morning had gone. I had slept in a little bit. Unsurprising, given the circumstances, though a poor example.

The rampage of Katya's men in the night had not gone unnoticed. It had, miraculously, not been blamed on us. Yet. However, it was stirring a panic among the noble folk of Dab, and they were worried. Worried enough that some of them had already contacted us, seeking to hire protection beyond what the town guards could offer. The other mercenary companies in town were probably entertaining similar offers. I was surprised by how quickly news and rumors had spread—I had thought that in a very large town like Dab, with so many people that most do not know each other's names, it would take a while before word of the shootings spread widely.

Dab may have been too large for most to be able to hear urgent news from a single town crier, calling loudly from the center of town, but it had newsboys and two or three weekly publications. The targeted assassinations of more than a dozen prosperous members of society in the streets of the city presented a significantly profitable opportunity for someone who owned a printing press and was willing to set type by lantern and rush out a news-sheet. And, in a great city like Dab, there could be two or three such people, competing with each other to be the first to spread the news.

There was, in fact, a nobleman already waiting for me as I ate breakfast. After Vitold told me that, I wolfed down the rest of breakfast quickly and hastily changed back into the fancier jacket I had been wearing the previous night. I was, I reminded myself, supposed to be the commanding officer of a presently unemployed mercenary battalion, and as such, having noblemen beating down my door looking to hire me was something I should be happy about. Yes, we had arrived in the town in disarray and in need of some time to recuperate, but I should be starting to sound quite eager to get to work.

The noble rose to his feet when I entered the room. He was tall, with sandy hair, the sort of ambiguous shade that is either the light blond of a young man or somewhere in the range of light brown to dark blond and starting to gray with age. After noting the wrinkles around the corners of his eyes and reminding myself that nobles tend to be a bit less worn by their years, I decided it was probably the latter.

"Sorry for the delay, your lordship," I told the noble. "I am apparently in great demand this morning."

He smiled for a moment at the word *lordship* and then his face smoothed back over. Evidently, I had used the wrong form of address, but he hadn't

been offended by it. "Colonel Raven. I'm glad to make your acquaintance."
He shook my hand. "I need your help."

"So I was told by my officer, but I'm afraid he didn't provide any detail
beyond that." I sat, gesturing for him to sit back down. "I should warn
you, though, we're a front-line combat unit with serious firepower, most
of which we aren't allowed to use in town. If it's bodyguards you want,
we might not be the best choice."

"I don't need more bodyguards." He paused. "Well, I do need more
bodyguards, too, I suppose, but as you say, your company is rather large
for such a job. What I'm worried about is a full-scale assault on my facili-
ties." He hesitated, then lowered his voice, speaking softly. "Can I trust
you to keep quiet?"

I nodded.

He kept his voice very low. "Six of the victims of last night's shootings
were either investors or customers of mine. I recently signed a contract
for a major purchase which required some additional external up-front
investment in order for me to fulfill it in a timely fashion. I've reviewed
what the news-sheet says about where and when they were shot, and if
the people who did that are willing to expose several teams of sharpshooters like that, they can hire themselves a small army to assault my facili-
ties. I wasn't sure who I could trust, but then someone reminded me you
were at the festivities last night, giving you a clear alibi; and I was able to
find people able to vouch for your loyalties in general terms."

"Surely, if the backers are dead, the project is as well," I pointed out,
matching his whisper. "Are you sure you can afford to hire us on a hunch?"

"They weren't the only persons involved, and their estates will be bound
to fulfill their obligations regardless. I may even be able to get some of
the others to shell out a little extra to cover my expenses, but I'll be hanged
before I let myself get intimidated out of an honest contract." With that
fiercely whispered declaration, his voice returned to a normal volume. "My
complex isn't here in Dab. It's a short trip by rail, but not far enough for
me to fool myself that it isn't in danger. I have a load of ores scheduled to
leave here tomorrow morning, and I can arrange for some extra cars to
be added to the tail of that train easily enough."

"Well, if you're sure enough to hire us, and the rates are agreeable, I'll
be happy to take the job," I said. I wish I could say my decision was part
of a deeper plan, but his proposal simply sounded like an opportunity
that a real mercenary colonel should be eager to jump on, and I didn't see

any good reason to turn down the offer of employment—especially given that I knew the risk of my company being attacked by its own sharpshooters was quite low.

The last train I had ridden on had taken me from mechanic to steam knight officer. This train took me from a man posing as a mercenary to a real mercenary. Whatever can be said about the legitimacy of how we ended up in that situation, the truth of the matter is that we were being paid for our services as soldiers on a contractual basis, and that made me a mercenary as surely as any of the sellswords we had impressed into our company. This train ride was much shorter, but the transition was no less unsettling because I had the time to reflect on the transition consciously.

The captain of the heavy armor and Yuri were my two companions at the table in the first-class cabin our status as senior officers commanded. The infantry captain felt the need to supervise "certain lieutenants," the Swedish captain was dealing with paperwork in the corner, and Katya was avoiding me. As far as my two companions went, Yuri, as I mentioned before, is not a very talkative dog, which I think is due to the fact that he was raised by a very temperamental man, and the older man had mastered the art of taking naps. I am given to understand this is a skill that good soldiers usually learn. I could not have arranged for hours of uninterrupted contemplation intentionally, but by sheer luck I had it.

I was not sure which bothered me more: my transition to a genuine mercenary, or the fact that I had secured the job because my own subordinates had gone on a murderous rampage. Being hired in anticipation of an attack by my own army seemed somehow dishonest. I had never considered the possibility, and I cannot imagine that Katya did when she ordered the sniper attacks either.

If I had my way, I would not have become a soldier at all, but no son of the Golden Empire has the choice to avoid military service. I only "volunteered" when and where I did because the alternatives tended to involve getting shot, arrested, or both, and even then I might have risked it if that little old grandmother hadn't convinced me I could manage to avoid the worst of the army if I volunteered.

This had seemed like a smart choice until I made the mistake of wearing the wrong dress uniform one day and found myself mistaken by a madman for an experienced steam knight. I hadn't wanted to kill or die in the service of my country; now I was promising to kill or die for a fistful of coin. I was a little disturbed, and then more disturbed by the fact that I was only a little bit disturbed. Shouldn't I be horrified?

Vitold's comments came back to me. If I simply sold off the mechs and walked away from this, I could set myself up easily enough in a new life. Some homicidal maniacs might want to kill me even if I did so (the general himself; Katya, who, though near and dear to me, certainly had enough blood on her own hands to qualify; also perhaps Captain Winslow and the mysterious "I.V.T." from Colonel Romanov's letter), but it could hardly be riskier than continuing to fight on a professional basis.

Doing so, though, felt like a betrayal of the men and women who had placed their trust in me. I could perhaps take a couple of people with me; Vitold, for example. But what of the rest? What if the Gothic manufacturer's fears were founded, and he was attacked? What about the Rimehammers, who through a local had made a financial investment—albeit a risky one—in me? What about Katya? What about the old veteran captain dozing quietly in front of me?

What about the mission I had claimed for my own? According to everything I had been taught in the army, Wallachia was a small, poor country with no real prospect of standing on its own, and the most the rebels could accomplish would be to advance the designs of the Golden Empire's imperial rivals. If they became independent, they would soon enough be a vassal of the Magyars or the Turks, or a puppet of Leon I or Sigismund II. Their old prince, known as the Dragon, had been powerful enough to carve out his own realm if he had survived; but his magic had died with him.

Perhaps they could weaken the Golden Empire enough for the sultan or the Lithuanians to smell an opportunity. I would dislike seeing the horrors of war visited on my home village or, more realistically, on the other villages not unlike it in the border regions of the Empire. I may not have had Katya's fanatical fervor in service of the state, and I may not have wanted to join the army, but I did have some love for my homeland and the people living in it. By this logic, I nearly convinced myself that my declared mission of disrupting the stream of foreign money and weapons funneled into Wallachia was a contribution to the greater good.

In the end, I decided that I would continue on as if everything had been part of some great plan from the start. With, I hoped, as few massacres and murders as possible staining my hands with blood. This hope brought my mind back to Katya. I did not want to see the events of the night after the party repeated; I also did not want her to stay angry at me. My love for her felt uncomfortable.

I wasn't sure which sensation felt worse—the guilt I felt for the unseen deaths of several innocent members of local high society or the empty feeling of Katya not being with me. Intellectually, I knew the former seemed like it should be more important, but I still loved her, even if I felt horrified by the blood on her hands. If she'd stayed glued tightly to my side, she wouldn't have been able to surprise me with large numbers of civilian deaths. I had to have her back, I decided. Not only for the sake of our happiness together, but for the sake of anyone else who might be in the line of fire the next time she thought she had a mission involving murder.

Having constructed a justification for why my relationship with her was for the greater good, I stood up and went from car to car to search for Katya. She might be the death of me, but until then, I would keep her close. If she killed me, perhaps I deserved it. I reached the end of the train without finding Katya. Staring out the back end of the train held my attention for a little while.

It may have been early summer, but it was not unpleasant at all, and less stuffy than the cabin. Inevitably, though, my mind turned back to Katya. I went back over the events of the night. Katya had departed the room during my first dance, what she had seen upsetting her enough that she didn't want to watch. Then she had done something else at the party; she hadn't left immediately, simply gone elsewhere for a little while. Perhaps upstairs to the library, though I did not peg her for a literary type; I knew there had been a number of local worthies gathered there, including the fathers of at least two of the young women I had danced with that night.

Then she had sent a message to Quentin through one of our host's servants—she was feeling indisposed and he shouldn't wait up on her account. She had taken one of the horses from her carriage and ridden with good speed back to our barracks, rounded up several sniper teams, and posted them in key locations in the city with a list of targets.

She hadn't wanted to talk to me more than the minimum necessary yesterday or this morning, and I hadn't pressed her on it. My hands were full, organizing our deployment. Did we want to leave some of our own behind to look after our base of operations, or hire someone to look after them in our absence? Did we want to bring all of our mechs? Was it a good idea to sell off some of our matériel before leaving? We ended up bringing almost everything. The artillery, the mechs, the horses. They all came with us, and we sold most of what we didn't feel like bringing.

We left behind an empty-looking office with a lieutenant, a single lonely cannon, a stray acolyte, and a handful of men to look after the place. I also left Fyodor a fast horse and told him that he might need to use it if the notables of the city figured out who was really behind the sniper attacks the other night.

Katya, I remembered, had been in charge of the horses, and had seen them aboard the train. I had seen her get on the train. That I hadn't seen her inside any of the cars suggested several possibilities. First, she had left the train while it was in motion. Second, she had managed to pass me without my noticing. Third, she had hidden herself amidst the cargo. I gazed back along the tracks, thinking. Katya had disappeared on me before.

At the manor house, she had gone out through the window and up to the roof. In the deep forest, she had left unhappy with me; I had found her up a tree, where she had climbed to escape trolls who had already injured her severely. And after the party in Dab, she had gone up to the rooftops to shoot people. There was a pattern there. When Katya was in distress, she went up to escape from it. People usually don't look up, something Katya was well aware of as an experienced sniper.

I climbed up onto the roof of the caboose, Yuri watching anxiously below, and looked toward the front of the train. She was perched on the roof of a car near the front of the train, rifle across her lap. I thought about climbing quickly back down and giving her privacy to think in, but thought better of it. She had not come to me to close the rift between us; I needed to go to her or I would lose her for good. The train ride was almost over in any event, so she'd already had plenty of privacy in which to reflect and come to her own conclusions.

I carefully crawled my way toward her against the strong headwind of our forward travel, Yuri's anxious and increasingly distant whines reminding me what a bad idea it was to run around on the top of a moving train. The roaring wind made conversation impossible, so I didn't try; I just sat down next to her. She tensed, looking over at me. I waved at her—a sort of silly gesture when you're sitting next to someone—and then looked out at the Gothic countryside.

Several moments passed, and then she leaned against me a little, relaxing. I put my arm around her, and we watched together as our destination came into sight, the train slowing. Once it had come to a stop, it was quiet enough to hear, and she spoke.

"I asked the others about Ilya. The ones who knew him." Her voice was flat.

"Do you want to talk about him more?" I asked, equally quietly.

She paused, considering, and came to a decision. "I do not want to talk about him right now," she said. "I . . . loved him then. I really did. He is dead now."

"Are you angry at me?" I said.

"No. Yes." She sighed. "I am a little bit angry at you. They looked pretty. The one you were dancing with first, and the one you were with when you left." Katya gestured at chest level. "And I cannot dance with you the way they did." She tapped her artificial leg.

"I'm sorry," I said. "You'll get used to the new leg, someday, and I promise you that when that time comes, I'll try my hardest to show you a better time on the dance floor than I showed any of them. Just so long as you don't shoot me first," I added, trying to get her to laugh. Laughter dispels anger, or so my mother told me once.

She tensed and turned toward me. "Mikolai." She cupped my chin in her hand, turning me to face her directly and looked straight into my eyes. She wasn't laughing at all. "I promise I will not shoot you. I will not shoot you if I want to. I will not shoot you if I am ordered to." She paused. "Unless I miss someone else and hit you by mistake," she amended. "I like you very much." A hesitation, then, as quietly as I had ever heard her voice get, words I hadn't heard from her before: "I love you."

A Letter addressed to Yaroslava Ivanova, District of the Lower Tanais, Rome-Upon-Tanais, Upper Quarter, Palace of the Seventeenth Heir-son, Eastern Wing

Dearest Cousin Yarka,

I write with good news and bad. The bad news, as I have heard it from the mouth of Major-General Spitignov, is that your eldest brother is deceased. The good news is that I have been assigned as the general's new assistant, or perhaps I should say minder, which is in some minds effectively a promotion to acting brigadier. I hope your grandfather (my granduncle) may find in the news some cause to reconsider the matter I broached with him back in April.

Though I am sending this by special post, and it should thus not be grubbed over by the army censors, I will be circumspect and give you only the details which should not matter if the wrong eyes fall upon this page. Hopefully it is not opened so often as to let out the scents of the flowers I have pressed within these pages; there is an excellent greenhouse in the Istros District Military Headquarters, primarily for the growth of reagent and medicinal plants, and I was permitted to sample it.

As you know, the Wallachian prince was said to have been swept away in a storm, leaving the Ceres to make port at Tanais as a ghost ship. However, we now believe it is possible—say this not in polite company, I tell you this in confidence—that he was never on the ship in the first place. His father was a most puissant wizard, known as Vlad the Dragon.

The young prince, also named Vlad in an unimaginative decision of a similar sort to what your father made (rest his soul) in naming your brother (unfortunate), was supposedly kept suppressed at the sultan's court. But if the sultan won him over from an early age, who is to say that he was not trained in the sultan's court? That he is not loyal to the sultan?

A man matching his description was sighted several times heading north and west along the Tauridan coast—lands held jealously but not loyally by the sultan, we have reliable sources there. That Yalita was put to fire is perhaps some sort of ruse by the sultan, who has sent this prince from Taurida across the western part of the Axine Sea to raise rebellion.

Yours truly, if you will have me—
—Igor Vladimir Tsarevich

P.S. The general is not so fearless after all. Mention of Vlad the Dragon when I briefed him had him startle in his seat and begin to breathe in and out very quickly, until he was reassured that the Dragon was long ago dead by the hand of his successor Vladislav, known as the Dragonslayer. I had thought the man fearless, but he has perhaps gotten old before his time. Hopefully, the Dragon's son is less fearsome.

The oddest thing is that he has requested "another" apprentice, saying he was quite pleased with the first one. I am quite confident he was not assigned an apprentice, and I've already been through the very short list of gifted officers assigned to his last command (from Major Pavlov on down to Banneret Teushpa) without finding a match. Ivan did not leave behind any documentation of an apprentice—did he write anything to you about this man? I am puzzled, and I do not like mysteries.

CHAPTER EIGHT

In Which I Cause Friction

At the depot, several dozen tons of coal, ore, and mercenaries traded places with half a dozen cast bronze bells, a gear the size of a small mech, and a large number of sealed crates marked with abbreviations and numbers that meant nothing to me. Then we headed down to a compound just over a mile from the depot, accompanied by relieved-looking oxen pulling empty wagons. This was a slightly inconvenient distance, but not a long one. It was sort of a modern village, a collection of a dozen boxy buildings set beside a fast-moving stream, surrounded by a low wall to discourage wildlife from wandering in. My first priority, I decided, was raising the height of the wall in case of more serious trouble than wandering wildlife.

It was, I learned, an exceptionally clever arrangement, made possible only by an exchange of favors between the actual owner of the land (the margrave) and the industrialist. The industrialist, in spite of his wealth, was a lesser variety of noble, one not high enough to merit being called "your lordship" or dispense high justice in his own name, but could act as the higher noble's proxy by appointment.

Specifically, he referred to himself as a baron, which Gavreau explained to me as being a sort of French title comparable to the local title of *freiherr*. I pointed out that the industrialist in question looked like he'd grown up on the wrong side of the Gothic Empire's border with Lithuania rather than west of the Istros; at that point, Gavreau assumed a mournful look, saying the industrialist was likely a "jumped-up merchant with blood more gold than blue."

I don't think I will ever quite understand nobles.

The shrewdness of the baron in locating his factory in the middle of the countryside and purchasing the right to act as a lord over the lands in the area requires some explanation. It would have been initially less expensive for the baron to have set up his factory in Dab, or one of the other towns clustered together in the area, but there were a lot of costs associated with being in a city in the long run. This included taxes, criminal activity, competitors stealing his trade secrets, and increased net expenditures related to his labor force.

This had to be explained to me at length before I believed it. It turned out he wasn't paying his workers less than they would earn in the city. Instead, he was paying them slightly more than the going wage, a measure necessary to convince skilled workers to move to a more isolated location. At least on paper; in practice, much of it ended up back in his pockets. Beyond charging roughly a third of their base pay rate for food and lodging—a rate that he claimed was a heavy discount—he also sold them various goods and services.

The workers could pay to take a train to Dab when they had days off, shop in Dab, and return; or they could buy things directly from the industrialist's own general store. His general store carried everything from candy to drinks to books to clothing; the prices were a little higher than in town, but not so high as to outweigh the cost of a train ticket for anything less than a major shopping expedition. There was a public house for drinking, separate from the mess hall. Drinks were rationed out carefully by the bartender, as the baron did not want his workers to drink to excess (any who did so more than once were likely to be fired), but even so, the gross take from alcohol sales alone was roughly one-fifth of his workers' payroll.

He had an apothecary, a church, and even a small school, which mostly operated at night. His more ambitious workers could take basic lessons for free and could pay to be tutored privately. A quarter of the fee went back to the baron, a quarter to the sole full-time teacher in the baron's employ, and half went to whoever was actually teaching the lesson (sometimes, but not always, the teacher, who preferred quarter-pay for doing nothing). The baron's accountant regularly taught mathematics and finance, and visiting aristocratic youngsters commonly made arrangements to earn a little extra pocket money on the side by teaching. It wasn't just a scheme to get money back out of the hands of workers; it helped the baron identify workers who were ambitious and capable, who were then good prospects for promotion (and likely to leave to try to find better work elsewhere otherwise, once they had more of an education). It also helped cast the baron in a more positive light.

All in all, about four-fifths of what he paid his permanent employees didn't leave the compound before getting spent in one way or another. I know this because I got his accountant very drunk one evening. Most of the time, close to a fifth of his workers were in debt to him. On top of managing to get back most of his workers' salaries, the control he exercised over his workers' lives by isolating them from the outside world meant less absenteeism, fewer trained workers being recruited away by competitors, and less theft. Exactly how the baron had come up with this arrangement in the first place, I don't know, but he seemed to be making money hand over fist with his foundry.

I describe the setting of the baron's compound carefully because, as it turns out, when you have constructed a carefully planned community that amounts to a modern industrial village where everybody works for you like one large well-oiled machine, suddenly introducing a large number of strangers at once who don't have a thing to do with smelting, casting, and machining metal is a little disruptive.

To start with, there was the matter of housing. We were not only a mercenary company, but a large one, one large enough and with enough heavy equipment that I could afford to use the word *battalion* without getting laughed at very much. We had filled up two warehouses in Dab. Even with a reduced quantity of livestock, we required a significant amount of space, which required shuffling about furniture, people, and materials in order to make room. Those people and things that were displaced would become uncomfortably crowded, and this would in turn lead to dissatisfaction with our presence.

After some discussion with the baron's castellan and a consultation regarding the precise terms of our contract, we ended up occupying the smallest and oldest of the workers' dormitories (bunking two to a room, mostly), and most of the guest quarters in the baron's mansion. The latter were far more luxurious than the former, so they became officers' housing. I was a little uneasy at the idea of sleeping in a separate building from most of my men—emergencies could arise at any time of night—but being an officer is almost like being a noble. If I wanted to maintain an air of social prestige, I could not simply tuck myself, Katya, and Yuri away in a small room with a single bed.

Since it wouldn't do for one of my junior officers to have something grander than I, that meant I ended up in the baron's third-best bedroom. The canopied bed was the size of a small hut in a poorer village, and unbelievably soft, softer than any mattress I had ever slept on. My first morning waking from the bed was memorable.

"You may go. I will ring if I need anything." The voice that woke me was unfamiliar and muffled-sounding, as was the sensation of feeling like I was buried in silk. It was a woman's voice, but not Katya's. I could smell a rich breakfast laid out—tea, eggs, toast, griddle cakes, and sausages. The firm weight on my stomach was a woman's head, and the warm soft weight sprawled over part of my leg was, logically, the arm and shoulder of the same woman.

Another moment, and I woke up enough to be confident that while the muffled voice had not been Katya's, Katya was indeed the woman using my stomach for a pillow and half-sprawled over my leg, an unusual position that suggested I was sleeping in something far less cramped than her tent or the makeshift straw mattress at headquarters. I opened my eyes, seeing the surrounding canopy blocking most of the light of morning, and finally woke up enough to remember where I was and why. The sheer size of the bed still amazed me. Yuri had lain down in the corner of it and wasn't even near to touching me or Katya, as sprawled out as we were among—and mostly underneath, especially in Katya's case—a variety of pillows and blankets.

So, who was the woman outside the bed? The voice sounded familiar, I was sure I had heard it before. A small delicate hand, one not much used in manual labor, grabbed hold of a section of canopy and pulled it aside. A familiar face peered in—it was the young lady with hair roughly the color of well-aged cheese, with whom I had danced several times at the party several nights ago.

She looked down at me—or, particularly, as much of me as was visible underneath the covers, which was mostly the upper part of my torso— and blushed fetchingly, presumably because I wasn't wearing anything.

"Ah, I see you are awake, Mr. Raven." She spoke softly. She reached out and tentatively touched my shoulder. "I thought I might break my fast with you this morning."

Katya got up rather quickly at this point in the conversation, her head coming out of concealing blankets and pillows, revealing herself and most of the portions of my body that had been previously covered. If looks could kill, she would have added a young Gothic noblewoman to her body count right then and there. The unfriendly sound she made woke up Yuri, the dog thumping to the floor with a dull thud and a scrabble of surprised claws.

The young noblewoman's mouth gaped open in surprise. "I'll just, um." She let the curtain drop closed. "There's breakfast over there. Ring the bell when you're done for the servants to clear it," she added, rushing through the words, embarrassment lending haste to her articulation.

Katya glared back at the closed canopy. The sound of a door closing and receding footsteps announced the young woman's hasty departure from the room. "Mine," Katya declared quietly in the general direction of the doorway, gripping me possessively with her hand as she sat on my leg. Yuri flicked an ear and circled twice before lying down in the corner of the room, letting out a soft exasperated whuffling noise.

"Yes, yours," I said, smiling and running a hand through her hair.

Katya decided to spend a certain amount of time securing her claim to me before we ate breakfast. I am not sure if she wanted more to reassure me or herself that her declaration of possession was true or if she wanted, somehow, to prove something to the now-absent blonde noblewoman who had woken us up.

By the time we got to breakfast, the eggs were cold and the tea lukewarm, but we had built up enough of an appetite to make up for that. There was no meat on the breakfast tray, though I had been certain I had smelled sausages. An empty plate with a tracery of canine saliva and a slightly guilty look on Yuri's face suggested that my nose hadn't been playing tricks on me.

My thoughts returned to the woman who had woken us up. What was she doing here? I went through what I knew about her, which was not very much. She was an attractive and healthy young noblewoman, with very soft hands. She was more curvaceous than Katya, though in truth not much thicker around the waist—and likely not at all once Katya recovered the weight she had lost on short rations. She was shorter and less muscular than Katya, but this is not measured against a woman in the ranks of society. If anything, the opposite is true.

What about the people around her? Her friends were unkind enough to her to shove her at a man they hoped would embarrass her on the dance floor. I thought about that for a minute and felt quite sorry for her.

Finally, I remembered that the young noblewoman's father owned a foundry that cast bronze bells. She had spent a little time talking about bells. I remembered seeing bells loaded onto the train when we disembarked, considered the probability that there were two bell-casting foundries in the neighborhood, and reached the appropriate conclusion: The young noblewoman was most likely either the baron's daughter or the daughter of the higher noble who owned the land underneath the baron's compound. The second possibility seemed less likely in the light of the cruelty of her supposed friends, but I could not eliminate it.

So. My employer's daughter—or possibly the daughter of the higher noble on whose good graces his business operations relied upon—had come into my bedchambers with breakfast, dismissed the servants, and then gone to wake me up. Katya had snarled at her, distressing her and sending her fleeing from the room, and I had lain there blinking sleep out of my eyes as this happened in front of me.

This would need to be handled delicately. "I think we should befriend her," I told Katya.

Katya bristled. "She is already too friendly to you. I do not like her."

I explained that the young lady's father was someone whose goodwill resulted, directly or indirectly, in us getting paid and pointed out that she could cause us a great deal of trouble if she was upset.

Katya suggested permanently removing her capability to make mischief.

I returned that this was likely to cause immediate trouble for us and that it would really not be very nice.

Katya scowled.

I told Katya that I didn't care if she wasn't endowed with the more generous physical assets that the young noblewoman possessed.

Katya looked upset. Our conversation spiraled downward from there. A lesson I should pass on: If your lover is concerned with a potential rival who has certain attributes generally considered more attractive, I recommend you refrain from commenting on them. Most especially, do not give your lover a specific list of such attributes, and do not supply any estimated measurements.

CHAPTER NINE

In Which I Read Tea Leaves

As a general rule, soldiers serve three commanders: their superior in the military chain of command, their cause (country, coin, sense of self-preservation, religion, et cetera), and—last but not least—boredom. Boredom, unfortunately, has an assortment of lieutenants to delegate to, e.g., "mischief," "alcoholism," "gambling," and "inappropriate behavior involving livestock." I am not sure whether my soldiers were boastful, or if the story about the pony had preceded us by other means, but I overheard one of the baron's machinists retelling the story to one of the baron's clerks.

For the most part, I felt I was contending with General Boredom for my soldiers' attention. Besides being senior to me in both rank and experience, General Boredom has a particular knack for commanding soldiers during assignments of this sort. Guarding an industrial compound located a deliberately inconvenient distance from any town is not a terribly exciting activity.

I could, and did, set soldiers to the task of surveying the local geography, and some handful to the task of watching the walls, but there was not a lot to do that did not feel like makework. For that matter, the whole job had that feeling to me in particular, since I knew that our employers' worries had been generated by Katya. There was one large labor-intensive project I wanted to undertake to keep them busy: building up the walls. Unfortunately, the baron's castellan dug his heels in and insisted that I must clear detailed plans with not only him but the baron's architect and a representative of the margrave, whose permission was evidently required before constructing any fortifications higher than a man's shoulder.

The older captain took charge of drawing up the detailed plans because he had far more experience than the rest of us with such things. Quentin Gavreau was kept quite busy with the project of making very good maps and, as the maps developed, responding to the older captain's demands. Captain Rimehammer was involved with protracted discussions with the baron's own logistical personnel (suppliers, cooks, inventory clerks, and accountants) and generally documenting everything that was going on. Katya was busy trying very hard to stay in character for her role as Leontina Odobescu while glued possessively to my side.

For those of you counting officers, that accounted for three out of four of the captains of Colonel Raven's battalion, as Quentin was only a lieutenant. The remaining fourth captain, once a proud captain of the infantry on the fast track for rapid promotion, and now the captain of the infantry division of Colonel Raven's battalion (officially "the Raven's Claws" or "4th Company, Raven Battalion" on the paperwork) had set up a watch schedule and then gotten thoroughly drunk, which state she returned to as frequently as she could arrange it.

I did not remember her having been a very heavy drinker before, but she was now drinking heavily enough to be in competition with our surgeons, whose profession gave them easy access to liquor for medicinal purposes. When she had to be bodily carried out of the pub a second time, I decided this was a problem.

I assigned the job of keeping an eye on her (and, not incidentally, carrying her back to her guest room in the baron's mansion if it became necessary yet again) to a reliable corporal, by which I mean the physically largest of her subordinates. The man looked like he could be one quarter ogre by heritage. I figured that his imposing bulk, in addition to giving him the muscles to make hauling a non-cooperative adult woman up the stairs easier, would render him resistant to getting drunk himself, and discourage any unwanted trouble from the baron's workers. (The Loegrian captain's own massive bodyguard may have influenced my thoughts on the matter.)

Second, I sat her down for a private talk—truly private. I sent Katya off to go pay her respects to the baron's daughter, asking that she try to mend fences, and sent Yuri off with Katya, giving him strict instructions not to bite any noblewomen, even if they bit him first. Being drunk may not be a crime, but excessive drinking is still unwise for an officer, and

I had some stern words to give to her. They would be hard enough for her to swallow without anyone else listening in on them. I asked her to set a better example, told her I was assigning her an aide to help her avoid future embarrassments, and asked her if she knew what her men had gotten up to the previous night.

When she told me that she didn't know (having woken up with a very thick head and not much recall), I may have clucked my tongue, shaken my head, and sighed, much as my mother had done when I (or one of my siblings) misbehaved, waiting for her to guess her way toward scolding herself. I realize now that my mother had been quite clever; we were much more likely to believe we had misbehaved if we had to prosecute and judge ourselves than if she had simply piled accusations on us and left us to defend ourselves from them.

She soon realized that if she was drinking heavily every night, she would find herself in the position of having to punish her soldiers for their mischief after the fact and make amends to offended civilians (in this case, the baron's workers), while if she was in charge of her own faculties most of the time, she could preempt at least some of the mischief that would otherwise occur. The captain berated herself quite effectively on the topic and stayed apologetic even after I told her no serious mischief had come to my attention the other night, aside from having to carry one of my officers out of the compound's pub.

After the conversation had ended, I realized the supply colonel, that old alcoholic I had demoted to the position of lieutenant, was no longer with us. I hadn't noticed his departure. Consulting Captain Rimehammer's records, which I was suddenly thankful for, showed that he hadn't signed any of the new paperwork. I couldn't even remember if he had still been with us when we marched into Dab in the first place. He had been a disagreeable souse, but he had also been—in terms of genuine official rank—the highest-ranking surviving officer. I felt a little twinge of conscience realizing that I didn't know where he was now. Then the guilt was replaced by alarm as I imagined how much influence a colonel might have back in Tanais and how much trouble he could cause for us if he found his way home on his own.

After the baron arrived, approval to construct fortifications went through quickly. Lord Erasmus von Vasco (informally "Asman" if we were in private conversation) also told me that it would be better that the margrave never heard a thing about my battalion's presence; there was "no reason to worry the fellow unnecessarily" by contacting one of his representatives. In their relationship, penance was cheaper than indulgence.

Later that afternoon, I got one of the heavier mechs fired up to help with improving the fortifications. There was a surprising lack of complaint from the soldiers about being put to work, something which I attributed to the fact that I was getting my own boots muddy right along with them. Who can complain about pointless work when your commanding officer is working alongside you? If anything, the elemental spirit caged in the mech seemed more sullen about the task than my living soldiers.

Sullen and rebellious, I thought to myself, staring at its gemstone eyes after the fourth time it knocked over one of the wooden frames. I concentrated, moving one of my hands slowly and carefully. "Delicately," I muttered under my breath. The mech's fist mirrored my own deliberate motions, clutching and unclutching delicately to pick up individual pieces of lumber without crushing them.

I knew that I somehow commanded the allegiance of the elemental spirits caged within the mechs I had built from my former comrades' steam suits, but communicating with the spirit originally bound by some unknown Ruthenian military mage years before and a thousand miles away was a considerably more conscious affair. Fighting certainly is complicated, but it wasn't a thing I liked to think about a lot. Instead, I thought about what was going on with everything else, and my mechs simply acted the way I needed them to.

Digging was simpler, in principle, but this mech seemed unfamiliar with the task. I could make it do the work precisely and correctly only if I concentrated on each step, giving it verbal orders and demonstrative gestures. Mechanically, the mech was capable of doing the work; but if I let my concentration slip, mud went everywhere.

The elemental cages built by the thaumaturges of the Golden Empire were less sophisticated than the ones the Wallachian rebels had gotten their hands on. The heavy mech was more robustly engineered than my slapdash efforts, including mechanically devised reflexes that could be tripped by a crude control. In combat, or covering broken ground, those reflexes might have been helpful, but in the construction of earthworks, a rapidly triggered punch or actuated swing of an arm is frequently less than helpful.

The elemental spirit seemed to want to knock down the wall we were building up, not make it higher, and I had to concentrate quite closely to get it to dig an even trench line. It was like trying to use a knight's destrier for farm labor instead of a peasant's mule. The destrier may be larger, stronger, and faster, but mules are smarter than most horses, and warhorses have had most of the common sense trained out of them. The worst part, of course, is that their owners frequently take exception to this misuse.

This is true of knights and their horses, and I could not help but consider it was likely also true of the Imperial Army and mechs belonging to them.

The next day at our morning meeting, Vitold told me that some complaining happened in the places where I hadn't been, but that complainers were swiftly silenced by their own comrades in arms rather than the officers. He also told me that the supply section had been swamped with requests for gun oil, cleaning cloths, and ammunition that night.

Apparently, many of the soldiers were convinced that if I was getting my own boots muddy working to improve the fortification, it meant that I had, by some supernatural means, determined that we were going to be attacked soon. The barracks were alive with activity, and discipline was tightening up of its own accord.

Superstitious beliefs, in other words, were accomplishing what common sense and experienced officers hadn't. The only drawback was that with the soldiers discussing my alleged skill at divination, the baron's daughter, some of her friends, the maidservants, and once even the baron himself started asking me to read tea leaves for them.

I was happier digging than reading tea leaves, even with the frustrations that came with exploring the curious link between mage and spirit that allowed a war mage to personally command a powerful army of armored steam-powered machines. Being spattered with mud by a clumsy mech while trying to make it dig in the dirt seemed somehow a more dignified occupation than handling a barrage of questions around a drawing room table, especially since the tea leaves didn't provide direct answers.

Tea leaves don't spell out simple answers like "yes" or "no." They form patterns with simple symbolic meanings, like "bear," "livestock," "dismemberment," "old woman," "waxing half-moon," et cetera, the arrangements of which the tea leaf reader then compiles together into some sort of syntactically sensible sentence like "my aunt's livestock will be ravaged by a bear at the next half-moon." Which really is a matter of sheer guess-work, even if it wasn't simply peasant superstition that assigned one shape of clump of leaves to "bear" and another similar one to "livestock."

Frustratingly, if you get the prediction right in such a case, your aunt is likely to get mad at you when a bear does happen to kill one of her pigs the next month, as if making the prediction caused the event to happen. If I had been wrong, she probably would have gotten mad at me for predicting misfortune that failed to materialize. Practicing fortune-telling of any kind often gets you blamed for whatever happens next regardless.

Sometimes, what the tea leaves say hasn't the slightest possible relationship with the questions being asked. "Wolf looking over three full moons, rabbit sleeps" can't really answer a question like "Will my true love be a tall handsome man?" or "Can you tell me if next year will have a good wheat crop?"

I suppose I could have lied and just said "yes" to both shouted questions, or asked one of the quieter girls to repeat their questions to see if I could connect it to one of the other questions, but I felt guilty enough going through the superstitious claptrap. Mud, on the other hand, just made my boots wet and squishy and sometimes spattered the rest of me a bit. Boots are far more easily cleaned off than dignity or self-respect.

CHAPTER TEN

In Which I Am Bushed

I was bone tired after yet another long day working on the fortifications—a day in which I had successfully avoided engaging in anything resembling reading tea leaves. Unfortunately, I had overestimated my growing rapport with a certain elemental spirit and wound up getting hit dead-on by a giant shovel full of dirt. Then the weather turned cold, and I'd wished I was reading tea leaves in the warmth and comfort of the baron's parlor instead.

While I was busy feeling sorry for myself, a vise-like grip clamped onto my shoulder, digging in painfully.

"It is time for dinner," Katya told me. She was becoming more comfortable with her mechanical arm and beginning to think of it more as if it were part of her own body rather than a tool she was using. I think she would have been wearing it to bed if she slept alone, metal plate and all.

"I take it we are invited up to the baron's table again?" While the baron and his daughter were both in the compound, formal dining was a frequent, if not completely regular, occurrence.

She nodded assent. "He asked what was taking you so long, so I came down."

I frowned, then directed the mech to see itself to the stables and hastened to the baron's mansion, stopping briefly at our chambers to quickly change with Katya's help. Either Katya or one of the servants had already laid out something resembling attire suitable for a high officer or minor nobleman. The servants were taking away the remains of the soup course when I finally arrived in the dining hall, arm-in-arm with Katya and out of breath.

Katya sat next to the baron's daughter, who dimpled at me briefly. I sat next to the baron's accountant, who afforded me a very cool glance before staring into his cup. The baron was talking about the price of copper. Somehow, this was related to the health and welfare of sheep this season; I listened with a polite minimum of attention and comprehension as the servants brought out finely slivered bits of something drizzled with a bright yellow sauce.

After several tries, I determined that attempting to spear the slivers with the fork that had been provided by a servant was a losing strategy, but they could be scooped with the tines if you were careful and didn't mind eating slowly. I was, I discovered after my first few bites, quite hungry, and I cleared my plate with a speed that bordered on indecorous. (I'm not quite sure which side of that border I was on, but I did at least manage to refrain from using anything except the fork for the course.)

The wait for the next course was long, and while I had been concentrating on clearing my plate, the subject had somehow moved from the relationship between wool and copper to the effect of the growing season on next season's fashion, and in particular on the recent trends in matrimonial gowns. Katya later informed me that the intermediate topics had been textiles and dyes, with a new alchemically synthesized dye called cerulean being all the rage in France. It was in limited supply outside of Paris and Corsica, making the price hideous.

By this turn of topic I inferred that either the baron's daughter or one of her friends had managed to wrest control of the conversation from the baron. What I didn't know was that the baron himself had brought up the topic. This was the baron's way of trying to subtly remind his daughter that she should start thinking about marriage and in turn helping her father make some advantageous connections while doing so.

Katya restricted herself to terse comments, nervous about her ability to pretend to be Leontina Odobescu when the subject turned to something noblewomen were supposed to know a great deal about. Even if she had been one to follow fashion trends before volunteering for the Imperial Army, she'd been posted in Muzga before being transferred south to join General Spitignov's task force. Muzga was a tiny backwater town near the Lithuanian border, far from Emperor Koschei's court in what the Golden Emperor insisted on referring to as Rome-upon-Tanais and impossibly remote from Emperor Leon I's winter palace in Corsica.

I restricted myself to listening with interest until the next course arrived. I do not quite remember what it was, but it was solid, delicious, accompanied by rolls . . . and most importantly, the maidservant who brought out the course on a rolling cart placed one of her baskets of rolls right next to where I was sitting, with a wink and a grin that let me know the proximal placement was deliberate.

I concentrated hard on not eating too indecorously, but I was applying myself methodically enough to the task of eating that my concentration was on table etiquette rather than following the conversation.

"Well, what of that, Marcus?" The baron mentioning my name brought my attention sharply back to the conversation.

I chewed and swallowed a mouthful of fresh-baked buttered roll, as soft and fluffy as a cloud and utterly delicious. "My apologies, your excellency, I was slightly distracted." I tapped my ear. "What was it that you said?"

"I said, I thought you said we weren't going to see much rain this season, but I hear thunder," said the baron, a little loudly but not seeming to be offended. A muffled snicker from somewhere down the table suggested someone else thought I was supposed to feel mortified for paying insufficient attention to the conversation and too much to the food. Quentin's lessons on noble dining etiquette hadn't focused sufficiently on pretending to ignore the truly delightful efforts of cooks and bakers that went onto the baron's table in favor of boring conversations.

I cocked my head. A distant rumble caught my ears (thunder, indeed), and then a closer, sharper clap of noise (not thunder). The hairs on the back of my neck raised. That was a gun being fired. From the pitch, timbre, and volume, it had to be a relatively small gun, fired somewhere nearby.

"Sounded close," remarked the baron's accountant, staring out at a leaded window, the small diamond panes affording a blurry view of the sky. "Though I suppose we'd know better if we'd seen a flash to count from," he added, as if to show off his command of natural philosophy.

I looked around the table. Could they really not tell the difference? "Excuse me, your excellency, but I really should go see who is shooting and why." I stood up, and stepped around my chair. "It may be nothing to be concerned about, but I would rather make sure." I reached out, reconnecting with my recent digging partner and jump-starting its engine, just in case. Coal is cheaper than blood, I reasoned, and it was better to burn coal foolishly than lose blood carelessly.

The baron looked puzzled for a moment, and then gave a worried nod the next. "I hope your concern is mislaid," he said. His expression was carefully neutral.

The accountant, meanwhile, gave me a funny look, as if he thought I was crazy, then shrugged, trading looks with the baron.

The balcony or the stairs? The former would afford me a quicker and better view, but if there was something wrong, the latter would let me get on the scene more quickly. I headed down the stairs as quickly as was safe in the dress boots I was wearing. Dress boots being like cavalry boots, only with worse traction, this was slower than I would have liked, and I nearly fell down the last flight of stairs in spite of my frustratingly slow descent.

Leaving the mansion, I noticed a light rain was falling.

When I arrived I could hear shouting. I stepped quickly, several tons of bipedal war machine following in my wake, the noise of its imperial-built boiler doing its level best to drown out the noise from ahead. Once I worked my way up the new fortifications, I could see the source of the noises.

A scruffy-looking man, with a hat that looked both expensive and badly worn, was gesturing with a pistol. He was on the wrong side of a ditch, on the other side of the earthen rampart, atop a horse that was eyeing said ditch dubiously, and the man was shouting to make himself heard to the sentries who had challenged him and were demanding his name and his business.

"We have more guns than you factory slaves," he was saying. "Just bring out the baron's money and we'll be on our way without trouble. We know he has at least two full chests of coin. Force us to come climbing over and you'll regret it."

He had about two dozen friends. Between them, they did have a considerable number of guns backed up by a wide assortment of other weapons; most had an arquebus and at least one pistol. One particularly vicious-looking fellow had eight pistols, which were hanging on three separate belts along with pouches for ammunition. I wondered how long it took him to put them all on before setting off on the trail—or did he just sleep with them already on? It was an impressive collection, even if none of the pistols looked to be of impressive size or quality individually.

The sentries shouted back a number of derisive comments. One particularly creative fellow—originally from Khoryvsk, if I remember correctly—decided to first insult the scruffy fellow's father and then his mother's husband, using terms I do not care to repeat.

The scruffy-looking fellow waved his pistol menacingly in the sentry's direction. "I'll blow your brains out if you don't go running to fetch me the money! This is your last warning!" The fact that he hadn't reloaded his pistol yet robbed the statement of some of its immediate menace, as did the arrival of soldiers by ones and twos on my side of the wall. He was not aware of the latter, but surely was aware of the former; everyone knows that a pistol with a single barrel has but a single shot to fire.

The sentries, I realized, were now looking over at me. I nodded and jerked my thumb back toward the building serving as our barracks, and one of them jogged off to roust those who weren't already awake or investigating the noise.

"This facility is under the protection of Colonel Raven's battalion," I shouted at the scruffy-looking man. "Go off on your way and we won't have to kill you."

The scruffy-looking man pointed his empty weapon in my direction and clicked the trigger (doing nothing), then turned back toward his comrades as if he expected them to carry out his threat for him. Seeing as I was not wearing my armor, or even armed, I ducked back down out of the potential line of fire, concentrating instead on the machine behind me, guiding it in what I hoped would be a graceful vault over the wall, consciously directing it to grab the scruffy-looking man.

The part of this maneuver where the mech grabbed onto the top of the palisade with both hands and pulled went just as I envisioned; however, instead of the mech going up and over, that section of the wooden palisade tore loose in one piece and collapsed outward, creating a wooden bridge over the surrounding ditch. The mech continued forward, the logs bending alarmingly under its weight as it staggered across.

Gunfire crackled, and then thunder from above. The rain began to pour in earnest.

"Take prisoners if you can!" I shouted. "I can't question the dead!" It occurred to me that it would be very good to learn more about why these men were here. They sounded like simple bandits, but they also seemed confident in their knowledge of the target. Who had directed them here? Had they robbed this compound before? The workers were usually paid in paper scrip and only cashed out when they went to town, so why were the bandits so sure that the baron kept an ample supply of cash here?

My thoughts were interrupted by the scream of a horse flying over-head. Its rider was nowhere to be seen. I ducked low and winced when it landed in a tangle of broken limbs behind me. I got up and assessed the situation: the bandits were scattering away from the heavy mech, and my men were starting to pursue them.

"Alive!" I yelled, jogging forward.

A soldier with a smoking arquebus looked back at me and cringed sheepishly. Then he gingerly stepped over the corpse at his feet and relayed my orders forward.

"Aim low for the legs!" he shouted. "The colonel wants prisoners!"

Hoofbeats from behind and to my left suggested that some of our own mounted troops were entering the fray—or chase, I should say, as the bandits were transitioning from a fighting retreat to a panicked rout. They had not expected serious resistance, and a charging mech backed up by a rapidly increasing number of experienced war-hardened soldiers qualified as serious resistance.

I continued jogging toward the heavy mech, hoping to keep near enough to it to have some control over the developing situation and the berserk machine. It was not long of a jog before I had counted more than a dozen more bandits down. Some were wounded; some dead. One, I noted, appeared to have bled to death as a result of an injury to the major artery in the leg. None, however, wore the distinctive hat of the bandit leader.

Then there was a distinctive report of a rifle, some shouting, then hoof-beats. One of the mounted scouts was carrying a distinctive-looking hat with a hole in it; the other carried the scruffy owner of the hat, who looked rather the worse for wear. He had a sucking chest wound. Sucking chest wounds do not flatter the looks of anyone, and the deathly pallor of his face suggested he might not have much longer to live.

After I got back to the mansion, Katya apologized profusely for missing the bandit leader twice. The wind and rain had made it difficult to aim, she said.

CHAPTER ELEVEN

In Which I Learn Two Truths and One Lie

picked Katya up and hugged her until she stopped apologizing. Then I told her she had done well enough, and she smiled. Then I told the baron's butler I would not be returning to dinner, as I needed to attend to the aftermath of the attempted raid. The bandits had been routed quickly, I told him, but there was much to be done. Then I suited action to words and hastened back out into the rain. Yuri followed, unbothered by the rain, eager to play, and impatient from having missed my earlier stroll around the compound; Katya, less interested in getting wet, did not, announcing that she really needed to take apart, dry, and clean her rifle thoroughly.

I was cold, wet, hungry, and bone tired—even more than when I had finished the day's work on assembling the fortifications. I got progressively colder, wetter, and hungrier rounding up the men in the rain, making a good count of the dead and injured, and taking care of everything else that needed to be done. I made sure that the bandit leader got the attention of the more sober of our two surgeons to further the chances he might be in a condition to answer my questions at some point; organized double-strength shifts of sentries for the rest of the night; and finally got the night shift manager of the factory calmed down. Convincing his foremen that we neither required nor wanted their help was another task entirely.

The whole time, the rain continued to fall and the air continued to get colder. When I staggered back up to the mansion, I was too tired to go looking for food. I peeled off my wet clothes and handed them to an anxious-looking servant, who gave me a towel in exchange. I applied the towel to my still-wet self, then more or less controlled my collapse into bed, burrowing under the covers and next to Katya, who was warm, if somewhat startled by the chill touch of my skin.

She scolded me in some fashion; I cannot recall the words, for my consciousness was already in rapid retreat. She seemed in a better mood when she woke me the next day, perched on top of me with a surprisingly shy smile. After a certain period of time, I discovered that she had brought (or arranged to be brought) breakfast, although it had grown cold after she had finished waking me up. I was hungry enough that even cold scrambled eggs tasted good.

The bandit leader's life had not lasted the night. The rain, on the other hand, had; though it was falling more lightly than it had during the night. The handful of bandits who had been captured and survived could provide little of the information I had so wished to gather from their leader; they were local to the area, in the broadest sense of the word *local*, which is to say that they were from elsewhere in Silesia or Moravia. However, none of them claimed to have been with the group for more than a few months.

None of the bandits had previously visited the compound either, but that was a nearly meaningless piece of information, considering the brevity of their membership. For neither the first nor the last time, I spent a brief moment wishing that Katya was less thoroughly deadly. I could hardly fault her for being skilled, particularly as I owed my life to her exemplary skill, but sometimes I felt like the man in the fable of the diligent work mech, standing in the middle of the plowed field that used to be his neighbor's barn.

It was my responsibility to be careful of what I said to her so long as she remained my loyal and dedicated officer, bodyguard, and lover. Blood on her hands would stain mine, at least until such time as she stopped obeying me—at which time my blood would surely stain her hands, as I could not imagine killing her. I wondered if the emperor or his ministers had entertained similar thoughts about my former commander.

In spite of his dubious morality, sanity, and severe case of halitosis, Ognyan was deeply loyal and obedient to the crown. At least I had the excuse of love on my side—or was that truly unique? Perhaps someone in Tanais loved Ognyan in such a way, and felt the same deep reluctance to do away with someone who had murdered and would murder yet again.

Not that the bandit leader's death qualified as murder, really—a bandit who has just attempted to rob you is usually considered fair game—but I was reminded of the numerous less justifiable deaths on her hands, such as the partygoers in Dab. I tore myself away from that line of thinking. I had ridden this train of thought before, and it led directly to Vitold's complaints about Katya and the inevitable doom of our love affair; unfortunately, I loved her too much to do any of the sensible things Vitold had suggested.

Focusing on the positives that might ease my burdened conscience, I told myself that I no longer had any cause to worry that I was taking unfair advantage of the atmosphere of terror created in large part by Katya in Dab. Whatever had inspired the baron to hire me to protect his compound, the money had been wisely spent, and I could not possibly classify stopping the bandits as anything but a good deed.

Considering that possibility led me to several others, as well as the realization that the bandit leader was not the only one who could help me divine answers to my question.

I asked the baron if the compound had been raided before, or if any of the bandits we had gathered, living or dead, had ever worked for him or visited the compound under more ordinary circumstances.

To the first question he responded in a definitive negative; to the second, he replied that he wasn't sure, and that I should ask his accountant.

His accountant told me that he recognized the bandit leader (and several other dead men) as having come by to extort money several times, beginning two years ago, the last time being a little more than half a year ago. This was a surprise to me, since the baron had told me that the compound hadn't been attacked before. I returned to the baron with this new insight.

This had a number of effects, both immediate and long-term. The accountant was dismissed from his post and then put to work reconciling the books with the promise of final punishment later. Putting these actions in a different order might have made more sense, because the accountant ended up disappearing into the forest after burning the account books. He may or may not have filled his pockets from the compound's treasury on the way out.

Captain Felix Rimehammer ended up working overtime *pro bono* in order to ensure that our pay was successfully accounted for. After that accounting was complete, the baron found an urgent need to travel in order to obtain either a loan or advance payment on the cannons he had been contracted to manufacture; we did not see him for several months. His daughter and her friends, however, continued to come and go.

We didn't see any local bandits for the rest of our time working for the baron. Presumably, survivors had circulated word that the baron's foundry was well defended from attack by bandits. However, it had only limited defenses against the curiosity of investors or customers.

"Check," I said, pushing the mech across the board.

"That was a mistake," Vitold said, interposing his knight between my mech and his emperor.

"Really?" I said. I captured his knight with the mech. "Check again."

"Yes, really," he said, frowning at the board. "Would you go get us some refills? My throat feels awfully dry."

When I returned with full mugs, my mech had been captured by Vitold's mage, which was also putting my own emperor in check. "Ah, I see," I said, politely not mentioning the inexplicable way in which Vitold's mage had jumped straight over his pawns. "Well, no point in continuing, I think you have this one. Think the men are ready for inspection yet?"

Vitold shook his head. "You don't see Miss High-and-Mighty around, do you? If the men were ready, she would probably be around here by now." He was referring to the infantry captain. Vitold, at this point, would not address her by name, only as "Captain" or "ma'am" to her face and "Miss High-and-Mighty" when she wasn't around to protest.

"Fair point," I said. I peered around the pub carefully. If she was here, I should have noticed the ogre-like corporal I'd put in charge of shepherding my infantry captain. I hadn't heard of any incidents of serious drunkenness on her part after assigning her a minder, but she was still inclined to spend most of her off-hours in the pub drinking—just not as much. After a second close look, I was satisfied that she hadn't managed to slip her minder and go to the pub without him.

I had mixed feelings about telling my men to have their gear in parade condition for tomorrow. When I had been a mechanic in a garrison, I had loathed inspections and being paraded out for senior officers and officials to look over, and here I was now ordering the same thing. Now, I was the senior officer and I had nothing to do at the moment but wait for my subordinates to finish supervising all the cleaning and polishing.

I understood the idea of parade condition better, though; the baron wanted everything in the compound to look very nice when the customer arrived to inspect the first batch of cannons he'd manufactured for them. I, in turn, wanted the baron to feel like he could afford our continued presence; and so I wanted the baron to impress his customers enough to shower money in his direction. Some would then spill over onto us. (And perhaps, I added to myself, whoever wanted the baron to build them cannons would also be hiring mercenaries in the none-too-distant future.)

Remembering how irritating it was to have officers wandering about the barracks offering "helpful" suggestions, I thought that it would be better if I made myself scarce until the troops were ready for inspection. It made me feel lazy, though.

"Black or white?" Vitold's voice interrupted my musing. He'd finished setting the board back up.

I looked at his two outstretched fists and tapped the left one.

He took his left hand away and opened his right hand, revealing a black stone. "Black, then. I won't have to trade seats." Vitold sipped the beer and pushed forward an ivory pawn, signaling the start of a fresh match. "So, then, who do you think the younger Rimehammer's eye is on? He's been getting that sort of distant look. One of the baron's people, maybe?"

I shrugged, dismissing the question. It was hard enough to concentrate on the game. There were so many other things to think about. My mind was on the baron's mysterious business partners, what might impress them, and what that might do for us. I gave limited attention to carrying my part of a conversation with Vitold, who was inclined to gossip about . . . well, everybody else in the officer corps, with the notable exception of Katya. He'd already made his opinion on the subject of her perfectly clear and offered plenty of advice; and I, in turn, clearly hadn't taken any of that advice.

"So. The baron's daughter," Vitold paused, moving his knight, but keeping his finger on the piece. "You have to fill me in."

"What about her?" I asked, guardedly. I looked at the board, and reached out to move my mage.

"Wait, no." Vitold slipped his knight back and then into a different position, using the knight to pantomime a lewd act with his mage. "I think I'll go here instead. You ever think about doing that with her?"

"That seems unwise," I said in as neutral a tone of voice as possible, frowning at the offending pieces, "for several reasons."

"Cute, isn't she?" Vitold put his knight back on the board, completing his original move, then redoubled his offensive by bringing his other knight forward.

"I haven't moved yet," I pointed out. "Give me a minute; it's not your turn yet."

"Well?" Vitold pulled his knight back into place. "Isn't she?"

"I won't argue the point," I said, castling cautiously. "She is well-formed. And yes, before you say anything, yes, she comes attached to a fair sum of money, isn't crazy, and isn't likely to shoot me in the head."

"Now, now," Vitold said. "Why would anyone ever want to shoot you in the head, Colonel Marcus? Surely you aren't bedding down with a psychotic murderess of some kind." He pushed forward an exposed pawn, transparently baiting me.

I refused to take the bait, steadily moving my left mech into position. I lowered my voice and leaned forward. "Look, in all honesty, I'll admit that describes what I've been doing, but . . ." I sighed deeply, my imagination vivid enough to evoke her familiar scent mingled with the perfume she had started wearing since our stop in Dab. Behind me, I could hear rapidly receding footsteps and a small choked sob.

I froze. The perfume had not been my imagination. I turned sharply. A strand of hair in a familiar shade of red lay on the floor behind me, faintly reflecting the sunlight. "Kat—" I started to say, then corrected myself, remembering I was in a very public place. "Leontina!" I called out after the footsteps.

"I didn't say anything about her!" Vitold said, waving his hands. "That was all you!"

I shot him a dark look and chased off outside, in the direction the footsteps had gone, around the pub and to the back wall. "Leontina? Leontina!" I looked around, examining the impressions of boots in the mud. The toes pointed back toward the pub, the heels on the side nearer to the wall. Had I gone the wrong way? The sound had been perfectly clear, and clearly Katya, down to the faint mechanical sounds of her prosthetics.

I followed the footsteps back into the pub, noting several trails leading in, but while I saw several of Katya's boot prints pointing in toward the pub by the entrance, I saw none leading out. I placed my foot next to one of the prints, looking down and sinking it into the mud. Yes, those were definitely Katya's footprints. I could even still smell her, the faint whiff of perfume stirred up but not completely dispersed by my rapid passage and not yet quite washed out of the air by the light drizzle.

Vitold was putting my left mech back on the board. "You knocked over some of the pieces," he told me, by way of explanation.

I glanced down at the board. I must have been very distracted indeed, for the board looked quite unfamiliar. "Looks like I was losing anyway," I said. "We'll play again some other time."

The troops were ready for my inspection near sunset—or perhaps I should say I was ready to inspect them near sunset. This was fortunate, because the baron's business partners arrived early, having taken a train on their own schedule rather than waiting to hitch a ride with the regular supply shipment scheduled for tomorrow. I had wanted to inspect my troops in their gear the night before the baron's business partners arrived, so we would feel well in order.

As it was, when the baron's customers arrived shortly after I had finished reviewing the troops myself, my battalion took this as a sign that I had somehow divined their early arrival by uncanny means. This was the latest in a long line of episodes "proving" my supernatural ability to predict the future. Even my decision to keep the men busy building and manning fortifications was taken as a sign of my skill at divining the future—who else had expected bandits to attack?

I'm not entirely sure what the baron himself made of it. He gave me the strangest look as he adjusted his hat, peering at the oncoming carriage. I had told him that sometime around late afternoon I would be busy reviewing the troops to make sure they were looking their best for tomorrow, so it was not as if he was unaware of my plans or the real reasons for them, but the coincidence of it seemed to strain his sensibilities.

If anything, he knew that I hadn't had enough foresight to accurately guess how long it would take the infantry to polish their kit or the mechanics to touch up the paint on the mechs. Afternoon had passed into early evening with my attention mainly on the mysterious disappearance of Katya, searching the compound high and low to find where she had gone. Watching their commanding officer climb up the rooftops and around smokestacks may have presented a distraction to my soldiers, thereby delaying their preparations.

Standing at a military parade rest seemed unfamiliar and unnatural. When was the last time I had stood "on parade?" I struggled to remember. It seemed like a lifetime ago. Had we ever been paraded in Wallachia for senior officers? His task force had spent most of its time in the field, and other senior officers had preferred not to spend any more time speaking with the general than they had to. I came to the conclusion that the last time must have been before the fateful train ride that had taken me away from that garrison the previous year.

Of the half dozen people who climbed down from the carriage, I recognized three as having been at the party, their appearance familiar to me. The fourth was unfamiliar in most regards. He was an older man and well-dressed. Among his extensive collection of jewelry, one of his necklaces bore a familiar-looking amethyst pendant. I had often seen its twin hanging around Katya's neck.

CHAPTER TWELVE

In Which I Expose Someone

I was still processing the significance of this when the fifth passenger, a thin girl with a very serious expression, stepped into view. Her eyes locked on mine, widening with surprise and recognition; she nearly tripped due to the shock of seeing me here.

For over a week, I had been held prisoner by partisans in Wallachia. The girl had brought me food, water, and promises to murder me, which she never could quite bring herself to fulfill. Her hatred was understandable because I had been part of the unit that had massacred her village, killing her parents, grandmother, brother, and sister at the orders of the infamous war mage General Ognyan Spitignov. I had also buried her alive in a mass grave.

In my defense, I had made sure to bury her with a shovel in her hand, an act of gruesome mercy without which she probably would not have survived. In a state of shock, coping with a vivid flashback, I didn't even see the sixth person to step out of the carriage. I know it must have happened because there were six of them standing in front of me when the baron's voice brought me back to the present day.

"And this is Colonel Marcus Raven, who is handling the security for our little project. Marcus?" The baron cleared his throat loudly.

I saluted smartly, or at least saluted in a manner that I hoped came across smartly. "Pleased to meet you, good sirs; I am at your service," I said, guessing vaguely at an appropriate form of collective address. Judging by Quentin Gavreau's eye-roll, I had chosen poorly. "I believe some of you may have made the acquaintance of Lieutenant Quentin Gavreau, my special liaison officer, who will be seeing to any special requests or concerns you may have," I added.

Quentin recovered nicely from the surprise of being given the new title of "special liaison officer" and moved into action automatically, years of ingrained training in the social arts of the nobility taking over. I could not cope with this. My efforts were entirely concentrated on retaining my composure and not betraying the fact that I had recognized the fifth occupant of the carriage.

For her part, she didn't say anything either, nor was she introduced by name. She was simply mentioned as being the ward of one of the men; that introduction complete with the obligatory comment about being pleased to meet the baron, she faded back into obscurity. Standing behind the men, she stared at me quietly.

"And where is Ms. Odobescu?" The question, posed entirely too casually by the unfamiliar man with the amethyst pendant, caught my ear.

Quentin caught my eye. I shook my head in what I hoped was a subtle enough fashion not to be noticed. The girl was staring right at me. "I'm afraid she's feeling indisposed at the moment," Quentin said.

I muttered something about double-checking security arrangements and fled the scene with as much combined decorum and speed as I could muster. I could feel that girl's eyes burning a hole in the back of my head the entire way.

As the saying goes, whether you're trying to cheat death or trying to cheat the taxman, you are liable to end up both penniless and dead in the end. I say this to justify why I apparently had no sense of self-preservation left, and thus decided to give death a free pawn and put myself in check in the same move. That is to say, after fleeing the girl and the uncomfortable memories she brought up, I climbed on top of the roof of the main factory compound and up the side of its tallest smokestack.

I had already been on the roof but had given climbing all the way up the smokestack a pass before because the maintenance ladder bolted to its side looked rickety. I had met the factory's chimney sweeps, the men who used those ladders regularly. They were all quite small—short bandy-legged men comfortable with tight spaces and lacking any sensible fear of heights. The state of the maintenance ladders didn't bother them, but I feared I might weigh as much as any two of them put together.

This was, of course, not the only danger. I recalled that a Katya in distress, or a Katya waiting for a good shot, was often found in a high position. She was likely up a tree, on a rooftop, or something of that sort. I do not know if it was her training as a sniper or some deeper-seeded habit involving her childhood, but I had found Katya hidden high up too often for it to be a coincidence. If she was anywhere nearby, it was probably somewhere high, with a view of her surroundings.

With her deep affection for firearms, she likely was cuddling her favorite rifle, though I had not seen whether or not she was carrying it when she fled from me. I had just called her an insane psychotic woman likely to shoot me in the head. This left me with one thought in mind as I carefully ascended the ladder:

She might be inclined to prove me right.

I half hoped to find her at the top of the smokestack, in spite of the unlikeliness of it as a hiding spot, but she wasn't there. I walked carefully around the top of the smokestack, avoiding stepping on the grate that was intended to dissuade birds from flying in during down periods; I wasn't sure if it would take the load of my weight. I circled the top of the smokestack four times, each time casting my gaze a bit farther before pausing to consider. The main factory building roof; the main production centers; the outer buildings; and then the fortifications we had built.

I stopped as I looked at the wall, peering at the spot where Katya's tracks dented the ground. I could still make them out, as I knew where to look for them. They started at the wall itself and went directly to the door of the pub.

On the other side of the wall, where I hadn't looked before, I could make out a set of footprints leading away. It was difficult to tell if they were Katya's prints, softened as they were by light rain and several hours; perhaps if I had been closer, I would have been able to tell for sure, but at a hundred fifty yards through the deep shadows of a setting sun, I was doing well to spot the shallow depressions in the mud, make out which end of the prints was a little narrower, and note the direction in which the broken and bent foliage pointed.

The tracks led through the cleared fire zone and out into the woods. It was the work of a minute to spot the glint of a spyglass, two-thirds of the way up one of the taller trees. A few seconds more, and I had made out Katya with her rifle, outline broken up by sticks and leaves, face daubed with stripes of something dark.

"I'm sorry, Katya," I said quietly in her general direction and then climbed back down.

On the ground, I found one of the baron's servants waiting for me, impatient for me to get cleaned up and join the baron and his business partners for dinner. He seemed particularly distressed that "Leontina Odobescu" would not be joining the baron for dinner—to the point of demanding an explanation on the pain of the baron's wrath.

"She's not even in the compound," I told him. "That's about as thoroughly indisposed as you can be. I would rather not account for anything more specific than that—matters are dangerous enough as they stand."

I wasn't lying. There was, after all, a very dangerous (and not very happy) sharpshooter out there, perched in an elevated position with a good view of the compound. Granted, she hadn't shot anybody yet, but as Vitold was fond of telling me, she had a lot of practice shooting people and very little practice feeling guilty about it. I could not help but agree with Vitold that she was likely to shoot me eventually, once her sense of patriotic duty told her to do so.

That sense of duty had been on my side so far. Her belief that I was a loyal and capable imperial officer was strong, but that faith was founded on fragile delusions. Love shields delusion, as a wise old woman once told me. If I had lost Katya's affection, those delusions could shatter at the slightest blow. Any careful reflection on Katya's part would hammer those delusions repeatedly, with the particular combination of delicacy and volatility that one might associate with an attempt to use a steam-powered shovel to mix unfamiliar and experimental ingredients in an alchemical laboratory.

All of this reasoning expressed itself as a psychosomatic itch between my shoulder blades that only faded once the door was closed behind me and returned each time I passed a window. As I dressed (or, more accurately, was stuffed into what the baron's servants thought was appropriate attire for the occasion) I could not help but note that my room had a view of the forest rather than the compound, meaning that it was on the same side of the baron's mansion as Katya's tree. It is fair to say I felt very exposed during that process.

"The Colonel Marcus Corvus, of the Raven's battalion, *amicus* the family Rimehammer of Sweden." The butler's pronouncement was halfway between a drone and a bellow—dispassionate and monotone, but somehow also loud and pretentious. I had fobbed his attempts at prying lineage and additional titles off on Felix; the Swedish captain apparently decided that the most important extra title he could slap on was a statement that I was a "friend" (business partner, really) of his extended family. The stentorian introduction left me unable to avoid notice.

"Please be seated," the butler said, only slightly less loudly. "The second soup course will be arriving shortly." He gave me a look as if he was worried I would do something highly inappropriate, only lifting his gaze off his nose once I had taken my seat between the baron's daughter and one of her visiting friends.

This put me directly across from the man with the amethyst pendant. Sitting next to him was a girl. *That* girl, the one who brought recurring nightmares to mind. We avoided eye contact with one another as I sat down. I stared intently at my wineglass instead and thought about getting very drunk to numb the mounting feelings of guilt, horror, and fear.

Thinking about getting very drunk didn't do very much in and of itself, but staring intently at the wineglass caught the attention of the butler, who took it as a signal of sorts and made a gesture to one of the servants. I did not see the servant fill the wine; my vision was instead filled with flashes of unpleasant memories. The massacre; the aftermath; my time as a prisoner in the hands of Wallachian militants. When the memories faded, I saw a full glass of wine in front of me, which I drained promptly.

I no longer knew what the first soup course had been, but the second soup course was a very thin, lightly peppered broth with some sort of translucent slivers of green, slivers of water chestnuts, and bits of mushroom. I wasn't quite sure what the slivers of green were. This was served in a wide saucer that was shallow enough that it was difficult to spoon out the soup.

As a servant leaned over my shoulder to top up my wineglass for the third time, I thought to myself that I had drunk tea that seemed more substantial. If a meal consists of many courses, making them individually small and light made a certain amount of sense. In some ways, this was similar to dancing at a noble party. Nobles danced with little vigor because they could afford to have parties that lasted a long time and didn't want to tire in the first hour.

The baron cleared his throat noisily. I looked up.

"Colonel, I asked what you thought of wider versus narrower caliber of shot for the same weight of gun," he said. "As a professional military man, you must have an opinion on the topic."

"My apologies, I was considering the soup," I said. "It's quite interesting." I shrugged and sipped my wine. "Well, my experience is that you use what you have," I said, then paused to take another long draw from my glass, choosing my words ahead of time carefully to dance around the inconvenient fact that what I had in terms of cannons mostly consisted of guns issued to General Spitignov by the Imperial Army, subsequently winnowed by transportation accidents and battle damage down from a regimental-scale battery to a company-scale battery and then amplified by the Swedish walking-guns.

The baron nodded patiently.

"The battalion's gun battery is a little . . . ah . . . mix and match. It makes sorting ammunition fairly tricky. Since I wasn't expecting to need to reduce any fortifications to rubble, I left my chief artillery officer back in Dab. I'm sure he would have a lot to say about such matters," I said, buying myself a few more precious seconds in which to think. "Weight for weight, a longer and narrower gun can shoot a smaller ball faster, and this is easier to aim with less need to correct for windage. Wider cannons can more easily handle an exploding shell, however. A larger shot from a shorter barrel, such as a mortar, experiences a lesser shock from firing, and can hold more powder."

I reached into my pocket, intending to take out materials with which to draw diagrams illustrating the nature of the difference, and then realized that all of my pockets were empty, courtesy of my hasty change into dinner-appropriate attire. I frowned.

A light hand patted me on the thigh consolingly underneath the tablecloth. I leaned back in my chair, schooling my expression. The baron's daughter and her friend exchanged looks past me, and then both giggled.

The baron steered the conversation in another direction with more determination than grace, moving the subject to the recent war between the sultan and Emperor Koschei. One servant reached around me to retrieve the soup saucer; another topped up my wine glass.

The third soup course arrived. This time I recognized the vegetable component: leeks. Leeks sliced crosswise and then boiled until nearly transparent and nearly (but not quite) flavorless. The shallowness of the saucers used was no longer much of an irritation; while the previous soup had reminded me more of a peppery tea, this one was barely substantial enough to register as more than tepid water, a sort of spacer better used as an excuse to avoid talking.

The wine, of course, served a similar purpose while being considerably more flavorful and, unlike the soup, was constantly being resupplied by servants. I wondered if the first soup course had been something more hearty, or at least more interesting, but didn't know how to politely broach the topic without reminding everyone present of my failure to arrive punctually.

Then, as my thoughts turned to the topic of missing food and hunger, my eye caught on the amethyst pendant of the man sitting across from me. The pendant he wore was a match for Katya's, and I wondered what Katya was eating. If she was eating anything. The thought of her sitting up in that tree, cold and hungry . . . I blinked, looking into the bottom of an empty wineglass, one hasty emotional gulp having drained it completely.

The man across the table from me leaned forward, a curious look on his face, but said nothing.

"I'm sorry," I told him, quietly. I didn't want to draw attention. "I was thinking of . . ." I paused, deciding to better avoid the subject of Katya, my eyes involuntarily flickering back to the man's amethyst pendant. "I was thinking of an absent friend." Out of the corner of my eye, I could see a servant leaning over my shoulder to refill my empty glass.

"Ah. Yes, the war has left many of us with absent friends." He raised his glass. "To absent friends," he said in an uncharacteristically quiet toast.

CHAPTER THIRTEEN

In Which I Have Difficulty with Numbers

Somewhere between four and six courses later, I felt unsteady in my seat, and had some difficulty focusing on the empty space that previously had contained a plate. How much wine had I drunk? I eyed my glass and hefted it carefully, feeling the weight of it and estimating the volume of its contents. It was, not unexpectedly, full to the brim.

I had drained it only once, but the servants had attentively refilled it whenever the level dipped more than two fingers' width from the top, something that had happened more than once in each course. Two to three fingerwidths, multiplied by more than once per course, multiplied by somewhere between four and six . . . add in that glass I had drained in one gulp . . . The arithmetic wasn't quite coming together for me, but I suspected that it added up to an excessive quantity. I gave up on my attempted calculations when a servant tapped me on the shoulder.

His hand reached toward my half-empty glass, pausing politely. "Perhaps Sir Colonel would like to change to a sherry? It will go well with Sir Colonel's cheesecake."

I blinked. There was, in fact, a slice of cheesecake in front of me. When had the dessert course begun? I nodded to the servant and glanced around the table quickly. The baron, quite careful with his food, was almost halfway through his slice; the man across the table from me had only a few bites left, but was too busy talking to attend to the remaining share of the slice. To my left, the baron's daughter had artfully arranged the remaining third of her slice and was considering it idly; while to my right, her friend was pursuing a geometric series of bites of declining size, taking a cautious third of the remaining piece onto her fork at a time.

The girl—the oh-so-familiar girl I had spent most of dinner trying to avoid looking at—was staring at me over an empty plate. I looked back down. Well, at least I didn't need to worry about finishing my dessert too quickly, I thought, and paused. There were two forks left. I looked furtively to the left to identify the fork used by the baron's daughter. She caught my eyes and smiled.

"Colonel Raven here can read fortunes," she said to the girl across the table. "Have you ever had your fortune read?"

The girl shook her head silently and then toyed with her fork, looking down at her empty plate. Then I remembered I wasn't supposed to be looking at her. Why wasn't I supposed to be looking at her? Something about the fact that I knew her. Where did I know her from?

A hand squeezed my knee.

My fork clattered out of my hand onto my plate, and I blinked. I looked down. A small crumb from the crust of the cheesecake and a few streaks of sauce told me that at some point I had eaten my dessert.

The baron was saying something about the smoking room. The man sitting across from me caught my eye for a moment, trying to signal something.

I made some polite excuses and waved him off, and then made some more polite excuses to the effect that I would be delighted to converse at greater length tomorrow, but it had been a long day for me. Intense concentration was required to pull my chair out and get up without knocking anything over. This was a bad sign, and after pushing my chair back in after myself, I paused, spending a moment trying to recall how much wine I had drunk. I closed my eyes for a moment, then opened them.

I was, I noted, in the hallway, and my shins hurt. I put my hand on the wall and looked down. There was, I noted, a low table there. I reassessed my position. I was not in the hallway, but had walked straight from the hallway into a sitting room. Fortunately, nobody was sitting in it at the moment. I sighed in relief, closing my eyes.

Someone considerably shorter than I was, with soft hands, was helping me stay upright in the hallway outside of my bedroom. They were more or less underneath my left arm, so I opened the door with my right and then tripped over Yuri, who I suddenly realized had been sleeping in the hallway outside of the door to my bedroom.

Yuri yelped, wanting to know why I had kicked him.

I sat up on the carpet and tried to explain that I hadn't noticed him there and was very sorry and didn't mean it. I heard a giggle behind me, started to turn, but then the carpet lunged up at me, backed up by a stone floor underneath it. The giggle turned into a gasp right before everything went white for a moment.

The next thing I remembered was lying on top of the covers of my bed, with someone pulling my boots off. I put my hand to my forehead, and it came away with a smear of blood attached. Then I fell asleep and stayed that way until the next morning.

I was undressed and under the covers. Yuri was poking his head in through the curtains around the bed with a vaguely concerned expression. The light peeking through the edges of the curtains seemed very bright, and my head was sore in two different ways: I was wearing a bandage over a scrape that had scabbed over, and I also had a hangover. I put my arm up against my face to block the painful light and succeeded in pulling the bandage loose.

The resulting hiss of pain alarmed Yuri, who offered to lick my face until I felt better.

"I'm fine, Yuri, or at least I will be once I get my wits together and get some breakfast," I said by way of demurral. I opened the canopy of the bed with more determination than comfort. After my eyes adjusted to the light, I spotted a tray with cold tea, cold eggs, cold scones, and a carafe of juice. An empty plate with several streaks of dried saliva glinted in the light, suggesting that if I had woken up earlier, I might have seen some sausage there.

I didn't bother to dress, but walked over to the tray and, braving the painfully bright sunlight, sat in front of the open window, trusting in the curative powers of breakfast and fresh air to solve my hangover problem.

When I made my way outside with Quentin in order to check on Katya, the tree was empty. Katya had slept the night there, woken there, and made a meal out of a hardtack biscuit in the morning. I could see that by the obvious enough signs—some small crumbs, a bit wider than a hair, which had neither been gathered up by insects nor dampened by morning dew.

She had climbed out onto a surprising number of branches, from the marks she left behind on them. Her metal limbs left behind very distinctive scratches. Perhaps she had wanted to make sure she had the best view from moment to moment based on what was going on in the manor; perhaps she was simply restless.

Yet . . . somehow, I could not find any sign that she had come back down to the ground in the morning; no bent foliage, no divots in the dirt, no marks on the ground for thirty feet around the tree. The only signs in the dirt beneath the tree were the ones that Yuri and I had left behind and the faded tracks she had left the day before.

It was another mystery, and one that I disliked. Her backward vault out of the compound had left puzzling enough traces, but that could be ultimately explained. Here, the only signs on the ground were a day and a half too old. Had she learned to fly? I climbed up the tree and nailed a note to a likely looking branch, telling her that I loved her very much, was very sorry, and to please forgive me and come back. I thought about signing it "Your Dear Mikolai," but then I thought better of it—incriminating evidence—and signed it with just my initial.

When I climbed down, Quentin asked me why I had chosen that tree to climb. Apparently, he couldn't recognize the clear signs that Katya had been there. Perhaps he was getting a bit near-sighted? I pointed out some of them, motioning him nearer to take a closer look.

"If you say so, sir." Quentin had a blank look on his face and then pointed at an undamaged section of bark. "So these scrapes, here?"

I spent a moment reconsidering the wisdom of putting an unobservant Parisian noble in what was effectively direct command of our scouting forces, but in truth, he had done well so far.

"No, here. See the parallel lines in the bark, about three times the width of a hair? That has to be from her mechanical arm." I said.

"That's alright, sir, I should be fine." Quentin fidgeted, and looked back toward the compound, reminding me that I had pulled him off of noble-wrangling duty for this.

"Have the scouts ride out through the woods. Long sweeps, three-man groups, concentrating in this direction out from the compound. She might have doubled back, and she's probably not too far. Tell them that if they run into her . . ." I paused. What could they do? "Have them tell her that . . ." I groped around for words. "Tell her I need her."

"Sir, I'll get right on that," Quentin said and hurried off.

It wasn't until I was directing the set-up of a firing range outside the compound that I realized I hadn't told Quentin to come back and handle the visiting nobles. The man with the amethyst pendant kept hanging around while I was setting up targets for the baron's cannons, peppering me with questions about Leontina Odobescu's health and other topics I didn't want to discuss with him at all.

I was sure Quentin could have kept the man distracted; moreover, Quentin, as a mere lieutenant, could claim ignorance a lot more convincingly. Granted, Quentin was not particularly familiar with artillery pieces, but our expert in that was—as far as I knew—still cooling his heels in Dab. I should have someone fetch him. If this visit by the baron's investors and customers extended for long enough, his expertise would be highly welcome.

I sent a message to the older captain, explaining to a messenger that I wanted Fyodor swiftly fetched from Dab. The older captain could take his place supervising our warehouse in Dab or delegate the task to another lieutenant, whichever he thought suitable.

Delegation is an important leadership skill, one which I was then still learning. Quentin knew how to handle nobles far better than I; and I could see signs of Katya more easily than he could. I had let my frustration with chasing futilely after signs of Katya push me into a highly inefficient distribution of tasks, I thought to myself. Then the man asked about "Leontina" again.

"Well, it wouldn't do to spread this too widely," I said, letting slip a partial truth. "I'll tell you this: Leontina is in charge of our reconnaissance element, and her being indisposed has more to do with being absent than with ill health. I wouldn't want to worry the baron, but there are bandits about in this area and it is therefore prudent to send out long patrols." All technically true statements. "Doubtless she is very disappointed to miss you."

That last line was something of a lie, as far as I was concerned, though I supposed it had the potential to become true in a more literal sense if she had an opportunity to shoot at him. He had some kind of connection to the Wallachians, and I felt increasingly certain that the cannons were destined for purposes Katya might consider inappropriate.

"But enough about Leontina. My employer would be very disappointed if I didn't tell you more about these cannons. They are cast bronze, cast in much the same way he casts bells. It's not just a choice of convenience! While there is a premium price attached to working in bronze over iron, there are some advantages to doing it this way." I wracked my brain, trying to remember what they were. "First, bronze cannons don't rust, of course. Now, I know you might not be putting these on a sea-going vessel, but weathering can be a concern anywhere."

"I see," the man said politely, fingering his pendant. "Is there anything else?"

There was something else, but I couldn't remember exactly how the baron had put it to me. Something about how many cannons would burst unpredictably, even after being proofed. I put it out of mind, deciding it wasn't a good time to talk about poorly made cannons bursting. The baron's men had set up the first one on a set of wooden blocks and were loading it with a charge.

"You might want to cover your ears," I said, and shortly thereafter did so myself.

When the smoke cleared, the cannon had come off the blocks but was still intact.

"Was that supposed to hit the target?" The man rubbed his ears. "Damnably loud, this close."

"Ah. Well, sir, that was a proofing charge. It was just meant to make sure the construction was sound. Usually that is at least a double charge. As you can see, it holds up well against the blast." I looked over at the target I'd set up, back at the blocks that had not held the cannon in place, and concluded the baron's men did not have prior experience with cannons.

"I see. So next, you will have them fire at the target?" The man crossed his arms.

"Ah, no," I said, searching for an excuse that didn't single out the baron's men as incompetent. "Today is just a day for doing proofing, and they'll need to go over the phoenix stone with a jeweler's glass to check for cracks or any loosening in the setting. Besides, we'll want to finish setting up the targets."

I walked briskly over to the baron's men to inform them of the change in plans. I hoped to delay the demonstration until Fyodor arrived. At the time, it seemed like a reasonable plan; the unfortunate consequences came as a surprise.

A Letter addressed to Yaroslava Ivanova, District of the Lower
Tanais, Rome-Upon-Tanais, Upper Quarter, Palace of the
Seventeenth Heir-son, Eastern Wing

Sweet Cousin Yarka,

It pains me to say that with the rail line having been destroyed by inimical forces just short of Tyras—if you sent me any letters, they must have been mislaid along with the last batch of our supplies. This letter will be the last to arrive by special post—I must return to Aegyssus posthaste—as the last train to attempt to reach Tyras is now a pool of cooled slag and ash covering nearly a desyatina of land. It is a state secret that the rail line has been cut, but I cannot see how it will be restored in less than several months.

The disaster occurred in the dark of night and left no survivors, so it is anyone's guess if it is some unknown catastrophic form of sabotage of the firebox engine or an attack by some great mage or elemental spirit. Given your access to the libraries of Tanais and your well-rounded education, I invite you to speculate at your leisure, for we are all confounded. I do not know which possibility is more concerning—if a firebox engine of the size used in a locomotive is capable of such thorough destruction, it will rewrite the rules of modern warfare. If a mage can call forth such volume and intensity of elemental fire in a sudden strike, then the greatest new mage of our generation works for our enemies.

I have not had any news from your grandfather, which saddens me, but please do tell him that I have the trust and affection of our most whimsical general, for I delivered him not one, but two apprentices—both of low birth for their talents, in case his whimsy proved fatal—and he has taken to trying to teach them.

This exercise has proven fruitful in gaining a description of his previous apprentice, which has resolved one mystery and created several more. This was a person that your dear departed brother brought to my attention. I am now reconciling his correspondence with the descriptions of the general, and am now greatly concerned that we may encounter this apprentice on one side or another of the borders of Wallachia.

With deepest affection—
—Igor Vladimir Tsarevich

CHAPTER FOURTEEN

In Which I Am Taught Officers' Ways

It is difficult for me to accurately represent what happened in Dab during this period, as my knowledge of the events in question is indirect. My account is therefore necessarily vague and may contain some inaccuracies. I am given to understand that Lieutenant Fyodor Kransky, lieutenant of artillery, well-born Ruthenian, and the trusted officer left in charge of our base of operations in Dab, did not supervise his men very closely.

I do know that he had a solid bed constructed with a goose-down mattress and purchased some surprisingly expensive bed linens. I also know that he spent a considerable amount of money in Dab. In particular, my summons found him with substantial unpaid debts at a dressmaker's shop and a less substantial unpaid debt at a bakery that had inexplicably extended him a line of credit.

The old captain (by which I mean the captain of the heavy armor company) was not particularly happy to deal with this. Within the context of the company accounts, this was small change, but the debts measured quite substantially against a lieutenant's salary. He also described the lieutenant's quarters as "fancy, like a room from a house of ill repute." While speaking with the enlisted men under Fyodor's command later, I discovered that the lieutenant had been keeping late hours, squiring the acolyte about town and spending a great deal of time with her; she then began to look rather round in the belly. At that point, there was a marked change in the tenor of their relationship.

When the recall order arrived, along with the old captain, it was evening, and Fyodor had a considerable amount of packing to do. He and the acolyte had an argument of some kind, and Fyodor slept on a bench in the front office. In the morning, there were two things conspicuously absent from our base of operations: blonde women and fast horses.

There had been one of each: the "fair maiden" that Fyodor had been willing to duel Lieutenant Gavreau for, and a good, fast roan stallion that I had left with Fyodor. That had been Banneret Teushpa's favorite horse, left behind only because I had asked that the fastest horse in the company be left with the lieutenant. At least, Banneret Teushpa claimed it was the fastest; granted, the man also claimed magical talent, which I had yet to see any evidence of, so I didn't entirely trust that finding.

According to the old captain, the young lieutenant had appeared both surprised and distressed at this particular turn of events, but was not willing to talk much about it past establishing that he didn't know where she would have gone and that her absence distressed him considerably.

This led to a chewing-out and a dressing-down, in that order. (Evidently, older officers start to differentiate between the two. I can't explain what the difference is myself, but the old captain was insistent that he had done both separately.) The phrases "dereliction of duty," "desertion," and "eaten by crows" apparently figured prominently in the latter, while the former involved talking about the role of testicles in cognition.

What I received on the train from Dab the next day was a very depressed artillerist. Lieutenant Kransky's uniform was rumpled, his eyes were bloodshot, and his vocabulary consisted mostly of monosyllables and honorifics, most notably "yes," "no," "sir," and "ma'am." The first night he came back he got monumentally drunk, and his captain had to be called in to peel him off of the table.

She revoked his pub privileges entirely, and spent the better part of the next morning trying to "tear a strip off of his hide" with her tongue. When I asked her if this was different from a dressing-down or a chewing-out, she said it was. She added, I think in jest, that she hadn't used her teeth and had left his clothes intact, and then asked if I needed a private demonstration of being dressed down and chewed out.

I wasn't sure what the punchline of the second joke was, so I didn't laugh. I began to suspect that officers' school involves classes on the finer distinctions between different types of verbal discipline.

Later, I learned from Vitold that this experience had given her a little more sympathy for my handling of her excessive drunkenness, and that I had been a "soft touch" with her. She also complained to Vitold that if

I could enchant the acolyte with lust for Fyodor, surely I could enchant Fyodor to make him forget her. Or maybe enchant him with slothful impotence, so he wouldn't care about his bed being empty. Witches could do that, right? So surely I could.

Apparently, the infantry captain had spent a long while talking with one of the cooks, trying to figure out what ingredients I might have used to brew a love potion. Where that woman gets her ideas about me, I don't know. Evidently, she also had some personal complaints about me that Vitold didn't want to pass on, saying it was best if I just remained ignorant of the details. He told me I should take her complaints as compliments, adding that her frustrations were her own fault.

Around lunchtime after Fyodor's arrival, I had the baron's cannons and my artillery team locked in a room, with Fyodor ordered to perform a detailed examination of the cannons for the baron's business partners. He would, of course, report to me first. Then I had second thoughts about leaving him by himself in charge of a team of men and a variety of explosive devices in his present state, so I told his captain to go in and keep an eye on him. (I found her talking to Vitold. She stopped mid-sentence when I walked into the room, but was quick to follow my orders.)

Next on my list was checking in with Quentin on his progress in finding Katya. Quentin had yet to uncover any signs of Katya. He suggested that if the baron had the appropriate permissions on the land, perhaps we could go on a hunt. It would give us an opportunity to go out riding through the countryside looking for signs of Katya without seeming like we were trying to avoid the nobles.

I decided that Fyodor probably needed a day or two to shake off his mood, so I agreed. "Go ask the baron and see what he thinks of it," I said. "I don't know how the hunting is around here, but tell him I think I can get a much better demonstration of his products if we get his business partners out from underfoot for a while."

Quentin nodded. "The quality of game in the area doesn't matter too much. We can stretch out a hunt for longer if game is scarce, in fact. Not that you and I will actually be hunting; it's just the excuse of the matter."

The baron approved of the idea of holding a hunt to entertain his guests, and spent two days preparing for it. Lieutenant Gavreau and Banneret Teushpa, more familiar with the ways of nobles, quietly snuck off on their own. I, unfortunately, found myself partnered with the baron's daughter and some of her friends, by which I mean she followed and caught up with me when I was watering my horse at a stream. Her attention was so focused on me that she didn't even notice Banneret Teushpa when he came riding back to check on me.

There was nothing to be done at that point but to ride deeper into the woods with her and her friends, as if our meeting had been coincidental. Her friends came and went by ones and twos, and when the last one took off at a gallop after a reddish-colored bird, shouting "fox," we found ourselves alone together in the woods for a few short minutes.

Then a loud crash reached my ears, and the scream that followed wasn't human. I did recognize it, though; it was a horse ridden by one of the baron's daughter's friends. The horse's description of its rider's probable ancestry was, if unimaginative, likely accurate, from what I remembered of the party in Dab.

"Stupid mean human with stupid mean damn and stupid mean damn of damn and stupid mean damn of damn of damn" may seem harsh, given that I had not met the young lady's great-grandmother, but her mother, aunt, and grandmother had been among those using phrases like "scandalously close" to refer to my dancing at the party.

The friend in question had shoved the baron's daughter at me in the hopes that I would cause her as much embarrassment as I had caused the Loegrian captain on the dance floor. All things considered, that move seemed both stupid and mean. And yet . . . the baron's daughter still thought of her as a friend, enough to be delighted at the prospect of putting her up for an extended visit, which had run two weeks so far.

The baron's daughter had even seemed to admire her supposed friend's horsemanship, which was athletically inspired . . . if, as the present situation demonstrated, less than entirely sensible.

She had spurred her horse into a headlong gallop through thick underbrush in the middle of a light rain because she mistook a reddish-colored bird for a fox . . . and then, from the thumping noises I had heard after the horse's first scream, she had also managed to put her horse right into a rabbit warren, ignoring all the signs in front of her. I rode forward slowly toward the rabbit warren, telling my horse to step carefully and try not to step on any of the burrows.

"Oh, no, Carmen! Are you alright?" The baron's daughter was following close behind me. "What hurts?"

Carmen—the baron's daughter's friend—was more or less uninjured, having landed upside-down in a bush. Her legs wiggled in the air, crossing each other.

"I'm alright," she said, as the horse tentatively tapped the ground with its leg, and screamed again. Gunshots in the distance suggested that someone else thought they had sighted something worth chasing after, and Yuri went running off in the direction of the shots. (Yuri was having a grand time. The horse's leg wasn't any of his concern, and neither were the young ladies.)

I dismounted and rushed toward the horse. Carmen could wait. I told the horse to hold still and to lie down—something a horse really doesn't want to do, generally. After helping the horse lie down, I began examining the leg. Most of the sounds involved with the crashing noise had been that of snapping woods, but there had been one that sounded like bone breaking, and it was easy enough to tell that the horse's leg had broken. In addition to the main break, several other bones seemed to be cracked as well. The horse screamed again as I prodded a particularly tender spot.

I told it that I was trying to help and to hold still and not scream quite so loudly, please. I took a deep breath, not really wanting to tell the horse that his leg was broken. Horses with broken legs almost never recover. Many of them know it's a death sentence. It's possible, theoretically, for them to recover, if you can get them to hold still for long enough, but even if you splint up their leg, tell them over and over again that it's really important that they keep that leg still and try not to stand on it, make a little rolling support cart for them to lean on with a sling in it to hold their leg off the ground . . . Well, at some point while you're off feeding chickens or pulling up turnips or something else that leaves them unsupervised, they'll either forget or get frustrated and try to walk again, and re-break their leg before it's healed.

I gently put the gelding's leg down and moved over to his head, patting him on the nose. "Hey, big guy," I said to him, looking him straight in the eye. He was one of the larger geldings from the baron's stable and had been very proud of that fact during our previous conversations. "I've got some bad news for you, big guy."

A gunshot sounded behind me, and the gelding jerked and started screaming again, blood pouring from his neck. While I was blinking and rubbing my slightly singed ear and the horse was screaming something uncomplimentary about the "mean stupid human," Carmen hurriedly reloaded her hunting rifle.

I stood there surprised for a moment and then opened my mouth as if to speak. Carmen chose that moment to line her gun up next to the horse's eye and shot again. The gelding stopped moving, and I closed my mouth. Well, at least he was out of his misery now, I thought to myself, though I really would have preferred to explain things to him before offering him a mercy killing.

"Oh, thank the saints that awful screaming is over," Carmen said. "It just sounded so horrible! Mr. Corvus, please, would you get my other saddlebag out from underneath that thing? And try not to get any of that stuff on it." She waved her hunting rifle sideways with one hand in the general direction of the blood and brains pooling out on the ground, fluttering her other hand for emphasis.

While I attended to that, the baron's daughter dismounted from her mare.

"Carmen, you can ride my horse for the rest of the hunt. I'll ride pillion with the colonel on his horse." The baron's daughter emphasized the word *colonel* as she dismounted from her mare.

"Oh, no, it was my mistake for picking that clumsy horse in the first place. I should have known he'd trip on me if I pushed him to a gallop. Don't put yourself out on my account; I'll ride pillion behind Colonel Corvus." Carmen was the picture of demure innocence as she took a turn emphasizing my military title. For the record, the big gelding had been a surprisingly agile fellow for his size.

"I insist! As your hostess, it's my responsibility to keep you in mounts. Besides, you're the better rider by far. It's a wonder that I wasn't the one to take a fall on this outing. It's safest if I ride with the colonel." The baron's daughter crossed her arms resolutely, trying to look down at Carmen. Since Carmen was about half a hand taller, this was a futile exercise.

"Ladies, the two of you put together have to weigh close to what I do, it makes more sense to put the two of you together on one horse while I ride the other," I said, mounting my horse and hastily setting him into motion. "Now mount up and follow me without any more galloping after foxes, real or imagined. We've gotten ourselves separated from the rest of the hunting party."

I could hear gunshots in the distance.

CHAPTER FIFTEEN

In Which I Am Hounded

I followed Yuri's trail. He had heard the other hunters just as well as I had. My hope was that with any luck, his eager and noisy bounding would scare off any wildlife that might distract the young ladies I was with. The last thing I needed was for either of them to see something that might make a good hunting trophy. They had already traded one imagined fox for a dead horse, which was not a fair trade.

The aforementioned ladies were seated double on one horse. They were distracted with a fiercely whispered argument of some kind, which I didn't care to follow. It involved lots of vague references I didn't want to try to untangle and a certain amount of gesturing and jabbing at one another. A confused snort came from the mare they were riding, and I called back to the mare to just hurry up and follow after me.

Another gunshot in the distance, a single loud sharp report. A flock of starlings took flight, heading away from the noise. A few crows flew the other way, cawing optimistically about carrion to each other. Something wasn't quite right, I thought to myself, and then turned my course, pushing my horse into a trot as I made a hasty detour. Something large was approaching, crashing its way through the underbrush with more haste than stealth.

The mare followed obediently in spite of Carmen, who was shouting something along the lines of "Stop, you stupid beast, stop!"

A wild hog burst into view not far behind the mare, and Carmen hastily grabbed at her rifle as it passed by. The boar had made it another forty yards or so before Carmen managed to get her gun untangled, at which point she fired at one of the branches off the left side of a willow tree. The boar careened off the right side of the trunk, leaving the tree swaying as it turned right and continued onward.

"Ow! That was right in my ear!" The baron's daughter wasn't happy. "Are you trying to deafen me?"

"Stick your fingers in your ears, then; I'm shooting again," Carmen said, grabbing the baron's daughter's unused rifle from the side of the saddle. She aimed to the left, squinting off into the distance, and then fired again.

"This way, ladies," I said, pointing back in the direction the hog had come from. "The rest of the hunters should be somewhere back that way."

"But the boar went that way!" The baron's daughter seemed a little confused as she pulled the mare around. She was pointing in the direction Carmen had shot, which was about twenty degrees off from the direction the boar had fled.

"The hog came from that way, and it was running away. He left a fairly obvious trail, so the other hunters should be following along it soon," I said, directing my horse forward and telling him to be ready to stand aside if men with guns came riding the other way. "Boars are dangerous, and it would be irresponsible of me to encourage you to chase after one. Especially if it's wounded."

My horse stepped forward into a nervous trot, commenting that he didn't want to get shot like the gelding. He had a point; it wouldn't do to get mistaken for a boar among the shifting shadows of the trees and accidentally shot.

"Stop," I said, holding up a hand. "New plan. We step to the side of this trail of flattened vegetation and wait for the hunters to come for us, not making any particularly sudden motions." I dismounted, and looked behind me at the disorderly pile of clothing in front of the now-riderless mare. I squinted.

The pile of clothes wiggled, resolving itself into two very irritated young noblewomen. The mare flicked her ear, telling me that she was good and had stopped immediately when I told her to stop, even though it was hard to stop that quickly, and asked if she could have a carrot now.

Carmen's language, although not particularly harsh by the standards of the local workers, veered into creative and highly insulting territory as she yelled at the baron's daughter for getting them both dismounted. The baron's daughter was protesting her innocence.

"I didn't do anything! She just threw me off when he told her to stop." The baron's daughter looked up at me, frowning. "She's not supposed to listen to you like that! Not when I'm her rider!"

The two of them seemed to be having trouble standing up. I walked over to assist, starting with the baron's daughter, pulling her up by main force. A ripping noise accompanied my effort, and one of her petticoats came most of the way off, attached to one of Carmen's spurs. Having her foot suddenly lifted up flipped over Carmen, who shrieked indignantly.

"Sorry, miss," I said, and set down the baron's daughter feet first on the ground. She persisted in clinging to one of my arms, so I found myself required to help Carmen one-handed. She, after a quick look at the baron's daughter, clung every bit as fiercely to that other arm even after gaining her footing.

"Your mare is stupid, and so are you," Carmen said, talking to the baron's daughter past the front of my chest. "I'm riding with him from here out, like I suggested before. I should never have gotten on that stupid horse with you."

"Colonel Raven, I'm just no good at riding; you have to let me ride with you," the baron's daughter said to me, hugging my arm and pleading with wide open eyes that reminded me of a puppy begging for table scraps. When I didn't immediately respond, she looked over at her friend. "Carmen, you're an excellent rider, I'm sure you can handle Socksy if I'm not in the way."

I looked over at the mare. She looked back at me with sympathy in her equine eyes. Then she winked, sympathy replaced by amusement as she whickered out several inappropriate comments. I closed my eyes out of sheer embarrassment. The two young noblewomen continued to argue, tugging on my arms for emphasis; fortunately, neither one seemed to understand the mare's comments.

Then I heard the baying of hounds and the snapping of branches. I tried to get out of the way, but there was no graceful way to jump out from between two noblewomen both yanking on my arms without risking hurting one of them. The pack of hunting hounds nearly bowled us over. Moments after the pack finished pushing by, Yuri showed up, panting heavily. He decided that since the ladies were both jumping on me, he may as well join them in doing so rather than try to catch up with the hunting dogs.

A fully grown war hound can weigh more than a full-grown noblewoman. Add in the weight of two noblewomen trying to pull me in two different directions, and I was in trouble.

"Off, all of you," I said, shaking vigorously.

A horse trotted up, riderless. Pulpy chunks of blood, bone, and brains were splattered across its mane.

It wasn't long afterward that I found myself needing to explain the riderless horse in order to defend myself.

"A flawed theory," I said. "There are three difficulties with it. First, it's wrong—I haven't shot anyone today. Yet. Second, you can see for yourself that my own hunting rifle hasn't been fired at all today. Have a look at it yourself. It may be a bit muddy, but the inside of the barrel is as clean as it was this morning. I even still have my full allotment of ammunition. Third, even if I had another weapon stashed somewhere, these ladies haven't let me out of their sight for long enough to retrieve it, wait in ambush, fire, and then stash said weapon . . . wherever it is supposed to be now. Fourth, even if I were trying to set up an ambush, I couldn't have possibly anticipated the way in which the lot of you went haring off to the northwest after we got separated."

Having exceeded my number of originally promised reasons, I paused uncertainly, my thoughts disorganized and turning inward. To clarify the reader's thoughts, the riderless horse had been followed promptly by several additional horses. Those additional horses were carrying several riders and a half-headless corpse wrapped in a blanket. I was addressing the suspicious riders.

"I've fired my gun," Carmen announced helpfully, bringing my attention back to the present. "Several times!" she added.

"Yes, you shot your horse twice, and then you shot over that way." I said, pointing at the poor inoffensive willow tree she had shot at in her hog-fueled confusion. I turned back to the hunting party. "Seeing as you've arrived from the opposite direction, I think that makes Carmen an unlikely suspect as well. But she does inadvertently raise a valid point: Could it have been a stray bullet fired carelessly by someone in the distance, shooting at game? If it is fired at an upward angle, a bullet can travel surprisingly far before coming to ground."

This proposition was greeted by skepticism. Unfairly, I thought; it was a simple and elegant explanation. Given the short notice any assassin would have had of a hunt and the disorganized execution of the hunt, an assassin would have had to have either already been among the hunting party, or possessed of extraordinarily good fortune, which made their initial leap to the conclusion of an assassin among the hunting party superficially reasonable.

On the other hand, I didn't think they had considered motives. The hunting party consisted of the baron's family, several of his employees and retainers (including, technically, myself and Quentin) and the baron's business partners. I struggled to think of why the baron would want to murder one of his business partners, or why they might want to murder one another.

Careless and inaccurate shooting, on the other hand, seemed common noble practice if Carmen's actions were any indication. The hunt having been a very impromptu affair organized on short notice, a hostile assassin would have had little opportunity to set an ambush. Moreover, the hunting party had deviated so wildly from our initial intended course that an assassin sent out separately to rendezvous with us would have been left waiting in vain.

In retrospect, I had a very naive perspective on issues of business. I was, by that point, still mostly unschooled in the ways of finance and business, at least in the ways that merchants, bandits, and criminals practice such things. My assumption that business partners' interests necessarily align was grossly ignorant.

Eventually, the baron arrived with the remainder of the hunting party, which appeared to be short a horse. The girl—that girl, the all-too-familiar one to whom I had once given a shovel, and who had once been my prison guard—was riding double with the baron's brand new and nervous-looking accountant. The front of her cloak was spattered with blood, but not brains or bits of bone, unlike the riderless horse that had run by earlier, and the back of her cloak was ripped and stained with mud. There was, I noted, a neat round hole in one of her sleeves. These clues pointed in a very ominous direction.

Several accusations and a short screaming match later—half of which was carried out next to my ear, though, fortunately, not directly into it—I felt obligated to revise my estimation on the accidental nature of the gunshot. Two accidental gunshots are doubly improbable, but two deliberate shots are nearly as likely as one deliberate shot.

Moreover, no additional motive was required to go from shooting a nobleman with connections to Wallachia to shooting the horse of the ward of said nobleman with connections to Wallachia. However unlikely it might have been for a gunman in service to one of their enemies to have somehow run across them and recognized them in the woods, it seemed the likeliest explanation.

I told everybody to stop shouting. I may have shouted in the process of doing so. Having gotten their attention, I explained that everyone should get back on their horses and start riding back toward the compound with haste. I may have picked up and placed several persons on said horses with a lack of proper decorum, and then started giving orders directly to the horses.

This had mixed results; horses may generally be very obedient creatures, but they are also not possessed of great intellect or understanding, and some riders will give them very clear and firm directions of their own. Carmen, for example, was very skilled in the basic techniques of riding, even if she was dangerously lacking in prudence. This posed a small problem, which I decided to solve expediently rather than diplomatically.

We reached the compound tired but in good order, with Carmen lying over my saddlebow sideways as I brought up the rear. Interestingly enough, she was quiet, in contrast to the volume of the piercing shriek she had made when I had placed her there.

As the compound came into sight, I heard a crash of thunder.

CHAPTER SIXTEEN

In Which I Fire My Mouth Off

There is something relaxing about rain. It can make life a great deal more complicated for you if you rely on the ground being firm, powder being dry, your clothes warm, and your iron rust-free, but the plants generally like as much of it as they can get. The feel of rain is relaxing, and the sound of rain upon a well-made roof is a sort of music. Faced with the prospect of standing around in a light rain and the threat of a coming storm, the hunting party hurried inside the baron's manor quickly, and with almost no argument.

After I dismounted and helped Carmen to her feet, I told her to go straight to whatever room she was staying in and straight to bed. She obeyed on wobbly legs and with wide eyes and a tightly sealed mouth. I didn't think I'd ever seen her simply do what anyone asked of her in such an obedient manner, and was confounded by the sudden change in personality. I had barely laid one hand on her, and not at all violently. She was not that heavy, and her hunting outfit had included a sort of sturdy over-corset thing that made for a convenient handle, making the use of a second hand unnecessary in removing her from her saddle and placing her across mine.

It was as if the startled squeak she had emitted in that instant had been an exhalation of her entire store of willful rebellion, a physical exhausting of a psychic quantity. I will not pretend to understand noblewomen.

In the foyer, I spared a moment to watch her on her way upstairs before proceeding to the dining room. The baron, Lieutenant Gavreau, the baron's surviving business partners, and company had collected there, at the end of a trail of mud-spattered coats, jackets, and boots. Servants had already begun to erase the trail as best as they could, but that was not done so quickly that it prevented me from tracking it to its end. I squeezed past a horrified maid coming to grips with the realization of why the "mud" on the cloak she was gingerly folding was sticky and red and found the discussion in progress.

The baron's daughter was present, sitting next to her father. She showed no interest in leaving his side to go upstairs and join Carmen; she clung to the baron's arm in reassurance. I am not sure if she was intending to reassure him or herself that way, but it probably worked both ways. They were not, as a general rule, given to displaying filial affection in any but the most formal ways; though, as far as I knew, the two of them did hold deep love for one another as father and daughter.

Lieutenant Gavreau was trying to similarly reassure, or perhaps console, a certain Wallachian girl, who was having none of it. She showed little sign of distress to start with. Her face was like a mask carved on a glacier—cold, rigid, and with a measure of implacable purpose behind it. She had faced far worse horrors in the past, I recalled, than a near-miss from a bullet. Being buried alive in a pile of corpses, for one. Experience had hardened her.

Quentin Gavreau was having trouble recognizing that his reassurances were neither necessary nor welcome. When I noticed the girl fingering the handle of her knife, I sent the lieutenant to provide a detailed briefing to my captains, something I ought to have done at the start of the meeting; better late than never.

Of course, while experience hardens some, it shatters others. I gathered that the white-haired man rocking back and forth had been a soldier once; now that the heat of the moment had passed, he was reliving past horrors.

At several points, I wished that Katya had been with me, not just for the emotional reassurance of having a loved one cling to my arm but for her expertise. She would have insights into the techniques of assassination and of the ballistics of rifle shots—useful knowledge to have on hand. My nerves had grown harder by then, and my main source of distress was not the no-longer-immediate threat of an assassin in the forest, but the anger and suspicion from the baron and his business partners.

After the third time Yuri growled at someone on my behalf, I sent him upstairs and told him to go keep an eye on Carmen. The mood around the room didn't improve. The baron's butler anxiously arranged for finger food; a while later, we retired to a drawing room. The baron used this as an excuse to send his daughter to bed; the Wallachian girl followed her upstairs without attracting comment, even though the baron's daughter's room was quite far separated from the guests' quarters used by the baron's business partners.

If you are not in the habit of drinking tea and liquor in close succession, I will offer four pieces of advice. The first is that tea has stimulant effects while alcohol has a disinhibiting effect; this combines, in some cases, to produce a sort of manic mood. The second is that, manic moods aside, most people still only have two hands with which to juggle a teacup and a glass, which means that one ought to set them down carefully before trying to light incense or sketch out an idea. The third is that angry persons in manic moods are prone to starting fights. The fourth is that for exceptional liquor of sufficient strength, it is flammable enough that striking a matchstick across your teeth before swallowing your drink is ill-advised.

These four pieces of advice being offered from experience—in addition to being explicable through sound medical and alchemical theory—will suffice to explain why I was so close-mouthed the next day, in addition to the purple decorations on the faces of two of the baron's business partners and the baron's grimly worded declaration that his surviving business partners would sit through a demonstration of his cannons, or otherwise prove themselves guilty of complicity in the attacks and thereby earn themselves a role as a target in said demonstration.

The baron did not repeat that statement in the morning, nor the mangled Latin phrase he'd muttered after I'd learned my fourth lesson of the night—something about vines being useful divining implements. I was too busy comparing the pain in my mouth to the pain of ignorance to sort out what an ablative declension might mean for a leafy plant and revelations of divine truth. I think it was traditional, in olden days, to read entrails for omens; but if he was referring to that practice, I have no idea how the baron might have mixed up vines and entrails. Nor did he need to; while some were sullen and others hungover, his visitors were all ready and waiting before my artillery lieutenant.

When Fyodor Kransky finally arrived to put his teams of artillerists in order, he was wearing somewhat unseasonable earmuffs and moving stiffly and deliberately, shading his eyes with his hat protectively. Optimistically, I chalked this up to a case of nerves and a desire for caution while working with a large number of artillery pieces at close range. More pessimistically, those practices could also have been explained by the aftereffects of having drunk a large quantity of alcohol the previous night.

A proofing charge, as it is called, is used to test a cannon. The uninformed reader might presume that this is a lesser charge than a full combat load, perhaps a series of such put in at once. Instead, it is a significant overcharge, the aim being to cause the cannon to fail catastrophically during testing, if at all possible. Note that with this greater charge comes a correspondingly greater recoil, which can be particularly impressive if the ground is slick and muddy. Rather than trying to build better bracing contraptions, Fyodor had mechs backstop the cannons with superior mass and strength.

The Wallachian girl excused herself with some haste as soon as the demonstration began.

As a demonstration of the baron's products, it was largely a success. The cannons themselves did not burst. As a demonstration of the capabilities of Colonel Raven's battalion, it was an embarrassment. As a method of providing a distraction to the baron's business partners, it was a qualified success; but the rifts of suspicion were too deep to paper over.

To accuse one another of treachery and murder tends to create deep breaches; for when someone accuses someone else, it is only natural to air one's private grievances, suspicions, and dislikes to justify that accusation. I think that the search for evidence in favor of the accusations caused more harm to those relationships than the accusations themselves.

On the point of how the demonstration reflected upon Colonel Raven's battalion, well, I will summarize matters by saying that one of the baron's business partners, a noble with shipping interests, commented under his breath that if this was how well Colonel Raven could plan a simple demonstration, I could be excused from any accusations of skullduggery by virtue of sheer incompetence.

This put a fire in my belly, as the saying goes. I had a discussion with the captain of the infantry, who filled me in on some of the details—and added some lurid speculations—about Kransky and the acolyte. In the interests of keeping him out of mischief, the captain suggested putting him in charge of a search party to locate Katya, noting that it would keep him busy and out of the way. She had a list for the search team already drawn up; I told her she could go ahead and make it happen.

Regrettably, I did not look closely at the list, even after she told me it mostly contained troops who hadn't served under Kransky, either recently or back during the days that she and Kransky had been regular imperial soldiers rather than deserters posing as mercenaries.

Soon enough, it was time for one more interminable formal dinner. Most of the baron's business partners left mid-afternoon, escaping before it began; the dining hall felt cavernous. With the sudden shift in the number of guests, the portion sizes shifted from artfully small to pleasantly ordinary. I enjoyed the food perhaps more than any other formal dinner I had yet attended. In the wake of the sudden changes in plan, the baron's servants accidentally gave me medicated wine, which I returned to them—I guessed that one of the older men among the baron's business partners had difficulty sleeping, so they had prepared a bottle of medicated wine for him before discovering he wasn't staying for dinner and replaced it among their supply without taking care to mark it as adulterated.

The scent was painfully obvious to me, but the servants seemed unable to tell the difference when I quite pointedly confronted them, waved it under their noses, and suggested they taste it. I would not have been so rude, except this was the fourth time I was handed a medicated glass of wine. After that, the baron apologized for their ineptness and directed them to bring a fresh set of bottles out of the cellar for "the Colonel's discerning palate."

The baron, it seemed, thought that if I possessed a discerning nose, I ought to give my opinion of some of the various vintages he had available. He had the servant pour himself the first glass of each bottle, pronounced it good and unadulterated, and then asked my opinion. After being directed to pay close attention, I began to realize in how many subtle ways various wines differ. Even wines from the same place but of different ages had marked differences, once I knew to look for them.

As we were discussing some of the finer points of those differences, I watched with curiosity as the line of nine empty wine bottles blurred into eighteen, each bottle next to an identical mate, and then the floor jumped up to give my head a solid knock. After a brief grappling match with that particular hardwood assailant, I closed my eyes to get my bearings and

then woke up with a headache that was being made no better by the sunlight streaming through the window.

I was, I noted, abed, the curtains of the canopy bed left wide open
instead of closed against the encroaching sunlight. Oddly, Yuri was not
in the room, and my boots had been placed neatly as a pair by the side of
my bed, my clothes folded on the bedside table. Carmen, smelling faintly
of the medicated wine that the baron's servants had been so sloppy with
the other night, was snoring next to me. The second unusual scent that I
identified (other than the medication from the medicated wine) was less
explicable: Sheep's blood, mostly dried, spotted the sheets.

There was a perfunctory knock on the door, and the click of the handle opening.

CHAPTER SEVENTEEN

In Which I Am Out of Orders

The man who entered was familiar—he was one of the baron's business partners. I had dined with him the previous night. For reasons unknown to me, he had an onion in one of his pockets, freshly sliced in half.

"Oh, no," he said in an even tone. "What do I see here? Is this the daughter of my dear second cousin? Let me see." He tugged on the sheet.

I tugged back, preferring not to be exposed suddenly.

"Ah, I see blood! You have robbed her of her virtue!" He tugged at the sheet harder. "I said, let me see!"

I was impressed with his persistence as well as his ability to see the lower sheet spotted with sheep's blood in spite of the fact that the upper sheet still had not been tugged free of my grasp. I reassured him that however she had come to be in the same bed with me, it was merely sheep's blood daubed on the sheets, and therefore her virtue ought to be intact.

He reached into his pocket, rubbing the onion with his fingers, and then rubbed his eyes. Tears welled in his eyes as he wailed. "Carmen is ruined! She will never be able to find a good marriage now! What man will take what you have stolen, you thief?" He paused, choking back a sob that was very short and sharp, the corners of his mouth twitching upward momentarily. "You . . . um . . . thief of virtue?"

Carmen stirred, then rolled onto her back and resumed snoring.

"I swear to you, her maidenhead is untouched!" I sat up and immediately remembered how many bottles of wine I had seen the previous night. Sudden motion was regrettable in an intense fashion. "I clearly remember passing out. I must have been carried to my bed. I have no idea how she ended up here."

When I said "untouched," the man bit his tongue, lips pursing as he choked back a short, sharp snort of a sob. After I had finished speaking, he took a deep breath before energetically shouting. "I do not care that you claim you do not remember anything! It is enough that you are here with her in the same bed! You are responsible for what you have done!"

"I have done nothing to her!" I shouted back, instantly regretting my decision. "Nor would I want to," I added at a less-painful volume, rubbing my aching temples. "She's unkind to her friends and doesn't take good care with horses."

At this, the man seemed genuinely insulted. "She has a fine seat, taught by my wife. You couldn't wish for a woman better schooled in a side-saddle!" He paused. "Now, where was I?"

"Responsible for what you have done," I said. "Except I didn't do the deed."

He nodded, taking a deep breath. "You are responsible for what you have done! And you must marry her at once!"

"Except I haven't done anything," I said. "I don't think anyone did the deed you're suggesting. I'm telling you it's sheep's blood spotting that sheet, and Carmen is just as much of a maiden as she was when she arrived in this bed. However that happened." Feeling disadvantaged in the argument by my lack of trousers, I stood and began putting them on.

"Aha!" he said, yanking back the sheet. "I see blood! You have robbed her of her virtue!"

"You said that before," I said. "And as I said before, that is clearly sheep's blood. Taste it if you like."

"Of course not! That would be disgusting." He shook his head, then paused, his eyes lifting upward as he counted on his onion-stained fingers for a moment. "Where was I?"

"You said I had to marry her at once," I supplied helpfully. "And I said no."

He advanced his count by another finger, then rubbed his eye, a tear welling up. "What? And now you demand a dowry for despoiling the daughter of a lord? Sir, you will not only dishonor me, but beggar me in the process."

I tossed on my tunic. "I didn't say a thing about dowries," I said. My head hurt and I was beginning to get angry. "I haven't laid a finger on your kinswoman. Yet." A cold wind swirled around the room. "Now collect her and be on your way. Save your anger for whoever gave her too much medication."

The man stared up at me, mouth opening and closing. "But . . . don't you want her? She's quite comely. And her lineage is impeccable. You would be marrying up into landed nobility. I've seen your table manners; you're country gentry by birth at best."

I stared down at him for an angry moment. Then, with my right hand, I took hold of Carmen's ankles, pulling her off the bed and upward in one swift motion. While she was considerably heavier than a sack of vegetables, I was angry and had been doing a great deal of ditch-digging recently. Her hair trailed on the floor as she swung like a pendulum toward her kinsman, who staggered backward as he caught her around the waist. She yelped, waving her arms, her eyes flicking open in surprise and confusion.

"Take her," I said, letting go of Carmen's ankles; the nobleman wobbled, struggling with the awkward burden. "Take her and go."

As the nobleman staggered out of the room, I could hear a confused Carmen put a sleepy voice to some of the questions I wished I had answers to. How had Carmen ended up in my room? Had she walked there on her own, or had she been carried? Her drugged stupor suggested the latter. There weren't so many people who could have put Carmen in my bed, but I couldn't think of a single good reason why anyone would do that. My head was pounding, my emotions were inflamed, and I lacked answers. After I had taken care of morning necessities and drunk several cups of tea to ease my headache, it occurred to me that my reaction had been hasty and perhaps unwise.

Marrying Carmen would have brought wealth and prestige. What reason did I have for turning her down? That she was reckless with horses and played petty, childish games with other young noblewomen? Surely, such vices were the sorts that the young grow out of as they grow older. And whatever claim Katya may have had on my heart, we weren't married, nor even engaged; in fact, she had refused to take my apologies and fled. I might not have stolen Carmen's maidenhead, but rationally, the marriage seemed beneficial in very pragmatic ways. There are worse reasons to marry than money and social status, or at least that's what my mother had told me; for my part, I had seen that few married without attending to the issues of money and social status.

Try as I might, I couldn't argue myself into wanting to marry Carmen. If someone had told a sixteen-year-old me that I would turn down an offer of marriage to a beautiful noblewoman from a wealthy and well-connected family, I would have laughed in their face. Awkward, gangly, young Mikolai would have walked through fire just to get the blacksmith's daughter to dance with him. She had giggled and said that the smoky smell reminded her of her father, which I took badly. Looking back on it now, that was likely meant as a compliment, given how daughters usually feel about their fathers, but at the time I only thought of the fact that the man had a face that looked like a horse had sat on it while it was being molded.

The manner in which I had issued my rejection of the proposal was also unwise, I decided. A blunt rejection that turned Carmen's exit into a spectacle visible to whatever servants were walking the halls had been undiplomatic. I should have left Carmen in the bed and exited the scene myself, directing the nobleman's attention to his drugged cousin, deferring and delaying the heated discussion until after she had woken up and provided her account of what had (and, more importantly, had not) happened.

Next time I found myself waking in bed with a drugged noblewoman and bloodstains on the sheets, I told myself, I would try to resolve the situation more amicably. Then I heard a scratch at the door.

Yuri's arrival was welcome, though when I asked him where he had been, he hunched his head, curling his tail between his legs. He had, he admitted, been distracted from guarding my room by the application of sausages. After two of the baron's servants had carried me into bed, ignoring his growled questions, one of them had returned with a sausage, taunting him from outside the door.

There was, of course, nothing to be done but chase after the sausage at that point, catching up to the manservant and said sausage near the kitchen. In the kitchen, there had been bread, and several playful children, and the cook's dog, and it was fun. Recounting this, Yuri's tail wagged cheerfully.

"But why didn't you come back?" I asked.

His tail curled back down between his legs, and he said once he had finished, I hadn't let him in when he scratched at the door. The hallway was very uncomfortable for sleeping in, so he had gone looking and found a door that was cracked open. The room had been just visited by the same people he smelled on my door—Carmen, her older cousin, and a couple of the baron's servants—but the bed was empty and comfortable, and nobody had shooed him out until morning when Carmen staggered in, smelling like onions.

She had sat on his tail, Yuri added, which was not comfortable. His tail curled between his legs as he added that Carmen had a loud and piercing voice when she was angry.

I reassured Yuri, telling him that I was not angry with him, and asked him to sniff about the room. After searching the room, he informed me that Carmen had been in the bed, and so was sheep's blood. The sheep's blood smelled nice, but was dry enough that it was hard to lick up. It was nice to hear what I already knew confirmed, but I had hoped for more— some insight, some clue that would make sense of a terrifically confusing episode.

Someone had decided that it was to their advantage to make it appear as though I had deflowered Carmen. Who? How? And why?

My headache was beginning to subside, but I was out of tea and hadn't any breakfast at hand. I decided that the most prudent course of events was to make my way to the kitchen and finish taking care of my hangover before trying to discuss the situation with the baron. The problem with this plan was that the baron had drunk far less wine than I had and suffered from less of a hangover. Thus, while I was still recovering my equilibrium, the baron was acting and reacting. I was halfway through a plate of eggs and toast when a footman arrived.

"Colonel Marcus Raven, sir, the baron wants you in his study," he said.

"Just a minute," I said, holding up a finger.

"Immediately, sir. The baron is most insistent, and most annoyed." The footman crossed his arms.

I sighed, stuffing one last forkful in my mouth before standing up.

The baron's study was occupied by the baron, his new accountant, his daughter, Carmen, and Carmen's second cousin once removed. I took a seat and sent Yuri off to the stables.

The baron cleared his throat. "My business partner informs me that you have insulted his family honor, that he proposed a remedy, and you have refused his proposal. Is that true?"

"I refused his proposal because this has all been a terrible misunder-standing," I said, trying to rush my words out.

The baron shook his head. "I am afraid it is paramount that I maintain good relations with Carmen's family. You leave me no choice but to dismiss you from my service."

CHAPTER EIGHTEEN

In Which I Am Bankrupted Only In Honor

Ask your servants how Carmen really ended up in my bed," I said. Diplomatically, I refrained from accusing the baron of having ordered Carmen placed in my bed, even though I thought it was a real possibility. "Ask them where the blood on the sheets really came from." I would have continued, but I was interrupted.

"What?" The baron's daughter's exclamation was accompanied by a spray of tea. "You . . . and you . . . after I told . . . and . . . How dare you!" Her face was red with fury, and she pulled back her arm as if to fling her teacup.

I ducked and dodged to the side, reflexes honed on the battlefield serving me well. There was a dull thud of ceramic cracking against flesh, then a tinkling crash as the teacup impacted the floor and shattered into dozens of pieces.

"Ow," said Carmen. She sounded as if she were not quite fully sensible yet, the drug still leaving her woozy.

I looked up just in time to see a small thin red line on Carmen's forehead disappear under an alarming quantity of blood. Scalp wounds, even minor scalp wounds, tend to bleed profusely.

"I'm sorry," Carmen continued, holding up a hand to her forehead, "but I just don't remember anything from last—ah!" Seeing the blood on her fingers had startled her.

The baron's daughter let out a wordless, angry noise. It was almost a roar but for the treble range of it, as if a lion the size of a mouse had a thorn jabbed into its paw.

"My little treasure, please calm down," the baron said to his daughter.

The baron's daughter stormed off. "I hate you," she shouted over her shoulder. As she didn't turn around all the way to look at us, I wasn't quite sure which one of us the statement was directed at—myself, Carmen, or the baron . . . I doubted she was saying it to the baron's new accountant; she barely knew him. (Editor's Note Regarding Linguistics: While Mikolai's account arrived already translated, it is worth noting that in Gothic, the formal and informal second-person pronouns are distinct [as are singular and plural forms of the informal second-person pronoun]. As it is unthinkable that the baron's daughter would use the formal second-person pronoun to address her father, Mikolai's uncertainty implies that Mikolai and the baron's daughter had a close familiar relationship where she addressed him informally.)

Carmen, in the meantime, was shrieking bloody murder, wiping her forehead to keep blood from dripping into her eyes and waving her bloody hands around. In the distance, I could hear Yuri barking in the stables, trying to let me know that he heard the screams of an injured human. (He was not aware that I was already on the scene of the incident.)

The accountant looked to be on the edge of fainting when a pair of alarmed servants arrived. The baron directed the servants to stop Carmen's bleeding and take her elsewhere to have her injury treated while he continued a private conversation with me. The accountant stayed, color slowly coming back to his face as I laid out my case to the baron.

"I passed out cold. When I woke up, I could smell that Carmen had been drugged," I said bluntly. "Both of us were likely carried to bed by your servants. It's not likely that she made it into my bed on her own. Your business partner isn't strong enough to carry Carmen comfortably, much less myself, and the only other scents that my dog noticed were those of your servants."

The baron shifted uncomfortably. "I did have you carried to your room, but whatever you imagine you smelled . . ."

"It was the same medication I smelled on the wine I refused," I said.

"None of the rest of us smelled this alleged medication." The baron shook his head. "Not to mention, any such smell would have faded overnight on Carmen. It's preposterous for you to claim she was drugged and carried unless you did it yourself."

I folded my arms. "I couldn't have done anything of the sort."

"Couldn't you?" The baron shrugged. "I saw you lift her onto your horse with one hand the other day. Drunk, you might have needed both hands to carry her, and you could have ensorcelled her into a deeper sleep. It's an easy spell, according to the margrave—one of the first ones his sons learned."

"I don't know any spells," I said, then paused, thinking of the lines of magical force I had used to battle mechs. "Well, one, perhaps." I thought back to the incantations I had read out from the Wallachian wizard's diary when I was binding spirits into elemental cages. "Maybe even more than one, but I haven't formally studied as a wizard, and I've never learned a sleep spell."

The baron looked at me with a strange expression on his face. "Fine," he said. "Suppose someone else stole Carmen's virtue . . ."

"I'm telling you, the blood wasn't hers," I said, digging in like an offended mule during the muddy season. "It was sheep's blood. I could recognize the smell; I grew up on a farm. Her virtue is as intact as it was before she was placed in my bed."

"Nobody can tell a few blots of dried sheep's blood from a maiden's," the baron said. "Stop being ridiculous, Colonel Corvus."

I glared back.

The baron sighed. "Suppose you're innocent, and someone else had their way with Carmen, and then dumped her in your bed. And suppose that somehow, you convinced my business partner of your innocence, that some unknown actor was to blame instead of you. Who do you think Carmen's family would blame, if not you?"

Pausing, I considered the question carefully. "You? You're the host. It would be easy for you to have me set up."

"If Carmen's family blames me for their daughter's loss of honor, I am finished," the baron said. "This whole enterprise will have to be folded up, and you'd be out of a job anyway because I couldn't pay you. Look, Marcus, I believe that you think you're innocent."

My head bobbed down and up in a curt nod.

"But even if the drink didn't rob you of memory—even if you really are innocent—you have to admit that the most practical course is for you to take the blame here," the baron said. "Can it really be so bad, marrying Carmen?"

While I wasn't sure, I wasn't ready to say so. But a thought came to mind. "I don't know why someone wants to force me into marrying Carmen, but if they had my best interests in mind, they could have secured my cooperation in that endeavor by talking to me about it. The fact that I was set up suggests otherwise."

The baron winced. "I didn't . . . I understand your logic now, Marcus. But you leave me no choice at all. At least I won't have to ask you to extend credit on the next payment."

The accountant looked away when I glanced in his direction. I turned back to the baron and put as much resolve into my voice as I could muster. "We've upheld our end of the contract. If you release the battalion through no fault on our part, your obligation to us doesn't simply evaporate."

"I'm sure the margrave will rule it your fault for tupping his wife's favorite grand-niece," the accountant said.

I uncrossed my arms, stood, and then pointed at the baron. "I fully expect you to abide by the terms of the contract. If we are not protecting you, we do not need room and board, but you will provide the promised pay or regret the breach of your promise."

The morning light dimmed as a flock of dark birds flew by the window, but my attention remained focused on the baron as I stood there. A damp spot appeared in the middle of the accountant's trousers.

"I will go now. If you do not have cash on hand," I said, glancing at the accountant, "you may discuss alternate arrangements for satisfying your obligations with Captain Felix Rimehammer. We can take payment in barter if necessary."

The older of the two Swedish brothers would also be better able to guess if a letter of credit issued by the baron would be accepted at face value anywhere or not.

When I found him, I discovered Felix was very annoyed with me. I could tell that he didn't believe my protestations of innocence, and he seemed skeptical that I had been offered Carmen's hand in marriage at all, much less decided to turn it down. I told him that while I understood he didn't have a good reason to believe my innocence, I trusted him as a representative of his family—and therefore of a stakeholder in the incorporated mercenary company in question—to negotiate an equitable and legally sound early conclusion to our contract with the baron.

If we were turned out with neither pay nor a decent reputation, the battalion would be bankrupt very soon, I added. Our abrupt dismissal from the baron's service would be widely remarked upon locally, and Carmen's relatives would be ready to whisper in the ears of any prospective employer.

Felix begrudgingly admitted I had a point.

Rather than trying to argue the point further, I changed topics, warning Felix that the baron was apparently short enough on ready cash that he had been planning on asking us to extend him credit on his next payment. He might need to get creative with what we accepted as payment; it was up to him to figure out how to ensure that the battalion had the resources to last the coming winter.

After he left to find the baron's accountant, I began looking for my other officers to help with the unenviable task of preparing for our departure from the compound—and, if necessary, to prepare for any further treachery on the part of Silesian nobility. The elderly captain of the armor company had been officer of the night watch and was sound asleep; I decided not to disturb him for the moment.

The captain of the infantry was nowhere to be found, and her erstwhile keeper, the ogre-like soldier, was off with Lieutenant Kransky's search party. With Captain Rimehammer busy with negotiations and Katya missing entirely, I was down to junior officers, and not all that many of them either. Fyodor was (as previously mentioned) off leading a search party through the woods, Quentin was hungover and keeping out of sight inside the manor, and Ragnar (the younger Rimehammer) had been sent off on an urgent errand of some kind by the elder Rimehammer.

I would much rather have walked into the woods and not dealt with anyone else for a while, but there simply wasn't anyone else to whom I could delegate the other necessary tasks of command. Watches needed to be set; soldiers needed to be accounted for; equipment needed to be inventoried and prepared for travel; and I did not trust the baron to simply acquiesce to my demand for payment.

While I had not been a mercenary for long, I knew from reading history that bloody treachery was sometimes offered as an alternative to pay, and I had cause to worry.

INTERLUDE

From the diary of Quentin Gavreau

In the morning, I shall have my first duel. It is over a woman—she is very comely, receptive to my advances, but Fyodor is also pressing his suit. We shall settle matters. My mother might question my decision, as concerned as she is with proper breeding, but while the lady in question has offered no pedigree, she has strong magical talents. In Paris, that is as good as a title, and I have never met a weather-mage before.

It is a frustrating day. I did not die, clearly, but I did not win either. Colonel M has forbidden dueling and seems to find the custom offensive. He has, however, granted me the most marvelous pair of pistols in exchange for my letting Fyodor have the weather-mage. They are nearly antique, and of the usual single-shot variety in contrast to my honeycomb pistol, but they are enchanted.

The baron's daughter, Amelia, has her eye set on Colonel M. As for myself, she has misremembered my pedigree three different ways. I have tried to build a friendship with the baron, but it has not been easy.

Glad I took the guns over the girl—the slattern abandoned poor Fyodor in Dab. And they say she is pregnant! No sensibility from either of them, clearly.

Rumor has it that Colonel M is a bit of a brute. Took Amelia's friend, picked her up, and tossed her across the front of his saddle like she was a shot fox. One-handed, if that's not an exaggeration from the rumor mill. I was not there—was searching farther afield, and then returned to the compound.

Colonel M made a spectacle of himself at dinner, so I made myself scarce as soon as practical, as did a few others. ~~Ended up sharing a bottle of wine in the stairwell with Amelia's friend C. Charming girl, though I don't remember the latter half of the conversation.~~ *Woke up on the floor of my room with a blanket and pillow and a sore neck.*

There is some sort of great scandal that has the servants abuzz this morning involving the girl Carmen, one of Amelia's friends. She seemed a comely sort, though I can't say I have come to know her well.

Addendum: The baron has sequestered Amelia and her friend. Evidently, we have been dismissed in disgrace, and I am filled with shame. I want to know why, but I also hope that the reason remains a buried secret, so that it will not reflect on myself or the Gavreau name.

CHAPTER NINETEEN

In Which I Am Salty

In western Lithuania, just on the other side of the dark forest, there is a city called Krukov—literally, the city of crows. Knowing crows as I do, I have no intention of visiting, but in the earth near Krukov, there is buried salt that can be mined like rock out of the earth. Most salt is boiled down from brine; so large is the deposit of earthen salt there that Krukov salt is cut in great blocks. Farther west, it can fetch a good price, as it is thought to be of better quality.

The baron had a full ton of it sitting in one of his storehouses. According to Felix, salt regularly fetched ten times the price of wheat, bushel for bushel; and he had gotten the lot for a credited value of a thousand silver pfennigs. It was one of the most stable trade goods that could be salvaged out of the baron's account; Felix and the baron's accountant haggled over everything from spices to cloth to heavily decorated small bronze cannons belonging to an order canceled in the ruckus.

It was not clear to me that we needed more guns; but Felix seemed to think that they would help in cashing in the letter of credit that the baron had drawn up for the heavily negotiated remainder of the balance of payment. They bore his mark, and we needed every bit of credibility we could afford if we wanted to try to cash in the letter with someone who knew of the baron.

I was overseeing the loading of the blocks of salt into a wagon when Fyodor's search party returned. The first to ride into camp was Banneret Teushpa. He was perched on his favorite horse—a horse I thought had run away with a young weather-witch sitting on top of it.

"Well met, Banneret. Your horse came back?" I asked.

Banneret Teushpa's face fell into what I could only describe as a pout. He sighed as he made a broad gesture with his hand. The two soldiers next to me gasped with surprise, apparently startled by the gesture, dropping the block of salt they were carrying between them as they looked over at the banneret. I lunged to try to catch the block, but the sides were smooth and my hands were damp with sweat. The block squelched into the mud.

"Yes, sir," the banneret said. "Brought a woman along, as well. Fyodor's missus. He'll be along soon, sir. He's riding slow on account of her condition."

I sighed as I bent over the block, trying to help lift it back up. "Any word of Katya?"

"We found a couple spots where we think she camped. Left signs in case she came back to them. She's out there somewhere." The Cimmerian shrugged. "She knows where we are. Just be patient, sir. I'm sure she'll get over her mood, even if it takes a week or two. It's not as if we're going anywhere anytime soon."

I grunted, then stepped back as the original pair of block-bearers took possession of the mud-spattered salt block. "About that," I said. "There's been a change of plans."

By the time I had finished explaining the situation, Fyodor and the others were riding up, the acolyte riding astride in front of Fyodor on the placid draft horse that the artillery lieutenant had selected as his mount for the expedition. I found myself obligated to repeat myself. After an awkward silence, Fyodor refrained from asking me questions about Carmen and instead gave his version of the report on the campsites that likely had been made by Katya, adding that he'd spotted a few foxes out and about.

I had many questions about the acolyte's decision to return to Fyodor, if that had been her intention, but I stayed them out of prudence. The ground was muddy enough, and I didn't want to risk setting off the temper of a pregnant weather-witch while we were loading wagons. If having six older brothers had taught me anything, it was that a pregnant sister-in-law coming from a long ride on a horse would likely not want to spend long chatting before excusing herself to find a privy.

I was sure I would learn more details than I wanted to in due time, if my sisters-in-law were any guide.

Once I was back inside, dry and warm, my first priority was checking on Felix's progress in negotiations. He had settled terms that he felt satisfied with, even though they involved the baron writing up a letter of credit to cover a significant fraction of the payment. However, a new wrinkle had emerged in their discussions.

Though the baron could not possibly employ the Raven's battalion due to the dishonorable conduct of its eponymous Colonel Corvus, he still had some security needs he wanted filled. Could we perhaps detach part of our force to provide continued security under a different banner? And wouldn't that reasonably discount the pay owed, if he wasn't dismissing all of his hired soldiers?

I told the baron that I would allow some of my soldiers to stay behind if they wished to quit the battalion, but that he would need to pay for any equipment owned by the battalion. The details of that arrangement would need to be worked out with Felix. Privately, I told Felix I trusted him to work out the details, but I would send him a messenger as soon as I could with my assessment of which equipment and how many soldiers we could spare. It was obvious that any additional payment Felix got from the baron would be in the form of some additional letter of credit.

Leaving the baron, the baron's accountant, and Felix behind, I went looking for Vitold.

Vitold and Ragnar had already been going through our inventory of heavy machinery, assessing equipment on the basis of size, weight, condition, usefulness, and potential value. They had many questions for me about exactly what we needed to bring with us on our trip. The most difficult part of traveling with a mercenary battalion is accounting for heavy cargo and the provision of fuel.

Would we bring our self-propelled charcoal kiln? It had been immensely useful in getting us through the sparsely populated border region between Avaria and Lithuania. It would be immensely useful if we tried to go back the way we came. If we were staying within the Gothic Empire, it might be less useful, as fuel was rarely in short supply.

The answer to this question—and many others—depended on where we were going next, and I simply did not know. A few thoughts had crossed my mind, but nothing detailed. I sat down with Vitold and Ragnar for a wide-ranging discussion of our possible next steps. The decision would ultimately be mine, but I wanted to make a good decision, and that meant exposing my reasoning to criticism as I explored the possibilities.

We had rented a warehouse in Dab; however, Carmen's relatives were numerous among the local nobility. Even if those relatives didn't exert themselves on behalf of Carmen's honor, the simple fact of our sudden dismissal from the baron's service would raise many questions among potential local employers.

There was one potential local employer who was both desperate for troops and high enough in status that he might hire us anyway and quash the critics: the margrave himself. The accountant had said Carmen was the margrave's wife's favorite niece, but the margrave had the responsibility for the security of the whole border region and might be inclined toward pragmatism.

If we were to transform the baron's extended credit into cash, we needed to cash them in with someone who could realistically expect to extract eventual payment from the baron. The margrave, perhaps, but if not the margrave, then it would likely have to be someone well connected within the Gothic Empire. We talked about what we knew of the geography of the empire and the kingdoms within it.

Midway through this conversation, Yuri arrived and began to persistently lick my knees and shins, slobbering all over my trouser legs. When I reached down to turn his head away, he redirected his attention to my hands. Evidently, enough Krukov salt had dried on me to make me irresistible. I scolded Yuri for his poor manners and resolved to take a bath to wash off the dried mud and salt.

After a hot bath and some time alone to think, I had a plan of action and a set of priorities. The only patron worth considering locally was the margrave, and that seemed too risky. Not only was Carmen reportedly his wife's favorite niece, but he employed Captain Helen Winslow. I did not trust the Loegrian mercenaries; indeed, I suspected that Helen or one of her officers had tried to have me killed one night in Dab.

My grasp of the geography of the Gothic Empire was hazy, but I knew one time and place where the wealthy and powerful of the Gothic Empire could be found assembled in great numbers: Sigismund II's winter court in Oenipons. It was a great distance away, but there was a rail line that headed south from Dab to the Istros, meeting the great river of Europe at a city named Vindobona, not far from the western edge of Avaria.

From there, we could travel up or at least alongside the Istros to the Oen, which was navigable to the imperial capital. Logistically, the main difficulty would be our heaviest equipment. We decided not to leave the self-propelled charcoal kiln behind—with a little modification it was a perfectly serviceable self-propelled wagon. At worst, with the engine disengaged, it was a pile of useful spare parts bolted together on top of a wagon.

The purpose-built imperial mechs—that is, the mechs built in the Golden Empire—were extraordinarily difficult to stop on the battlefield, but they were also slow, heavy, and awkward. We would leave them behind, selling them to the baron or breaking them up and taking the most valuable parts with us.

The elemental spirits directing their motions were not nearly as seamlessly obedient to my orders as the ones animating the steam suits I had transformed into light mechs. Nor did I want to give up the other steam suits, though I would let the steam knights muster out if they wanted to. The heart of the Gothic Empire might be a trip too far for many of my soldiers; and the fewer soldiers I brought with me, the easier the trip would be.

My captain of armor—the old man—was the seniormost volunteer to stay. Having designed the baron's new fortifications, he was the best suited to command their defense, and he was concerned with leaving the baron in the lurch. This would leave Captain Rimehammer in direct command of the main heavy armor company in combat, as well as outside of it; but both Rimehammer cousins had fully earned my trust in the blood of the battlefield, and the Rimehammer family was financially invested in the success of Colonel Raven's battalion.

I tried to push the infantry captain into staying with him, as I was concerned about her reliability. I talked about her history of drinking too much; emphasized that we would be going farther and farther from the emperor whom she had sworn an officer's oath to initially; and then went as far as to say that loyalty to Colonel Corvus in Oenipons might make one a traitor in the eyes of others. Subtlety, I will admit, is not my strength.

She took this talk in with a series of shamefaced nods, not meeting my eyes. I thought that would be the end of it, but the next morning she showed up with a dozen fresh volunteers taken from among the baron's employees—each and every one of them eager for adventure with Colonel Marcus Corvus, slayer of bandits and seducer of noble Silesian women. The infantry captain met my eyes with defiance, her rumpled clothes and the faint scent of beer testifying to a long, sleepless night.

The baron's second letter of credit, the one that would pay for the Ruthenian heavy mechs and the other equipment left behind, came with a caveat— it could not be collected on until two years had passed. When I asked if this made it less valuable, Felix shrugged and told me yes—but it wasn't as if we wanted to drag the equipment with us, was it?

As we assembled in front of the compound before our final departure, I saw a flash of hair the color of aged cheese out of the corner of my eye, but when I turned around, there were only a few pairs of boots visible underneath a wagon. Someone with hair the same color as the baron's daughter, I thought to myself; and then, thinking of women, thought about Katya.

"We are going to Oenipons," I said quietly, facing in the direction of the woods, wishing that Katya could hear my words. "South to the Istros, and then up the Oen tributary. Please forgive me. I . . . I still think I love you."

CHAPTER TWENTY

In Which I Presume Innocence

Final arrangements were made in Dab. We cleared out the pair of warehouses we'd converted into barracks and rented out from a local factor, selling some supplies and buying others, mostly based on what Felix thought was advisable. We even bought some more Krukov salt. To keep relations sound with the local factor (he'd done business with the Rimehammer family before), we had some of the men doing carpentry, trying to ensure the buildings were in better shape than when we'd first rented them out.

Though he did not say directly, my impression was that the factor intended to subdivide the barracks further into tenements. Dab was a great big bustling and rapidly growing city, or so it seemed to me at the time; I had caught only a brief nighttime glance of the much greater city of Khoryvsk, and I had not yet laid eyes on Vindobona.

If Katya had been with me, I am sure she would have wanted to send a letter home from Dab. Personally, while I missed home, I did not want any high-ranking officers or ministers to take notice of my continued existence. General Ognyan Spitignov might yet believe I was doing his bidding; no sane official of the Golden Empire could possibly believe likewise. Not when I planned to go west up the Istros, not east through Avaria and back to the Golden Empire through its newest province—Wallachia.

After I collected a few letters to be sent home, including one from the aging captain, who had stayed behind to join the baron's service permanently, I asked Felix where I could find a messenger willing to take them east. Felix bluntly told me to hang onto the letters until we reached Vindobona. Post would travel far faster and more reliably going downstream on the Istros than by land across Lithuania and the hinter-lands of the Golden Empire.

As the train pulled into its station, I felt as though something was wrong with it. Something was off, unfamiliar; it took me a while to realize it was the fact that the locomotive wasn't presently burning any coal. Intellectually, I'd known that fireboxes alone could provide power; but on the trains of the Golden Empire, fireboxes were treated as strictly aux-iliary, supplemental power that helped save a little fuel here and there or allowed a stranded locomotive to creep back to the station after running out of fuel—surely leaving its cargo cars behind in the process.

This locomotive was a triple-firebox model with an auxiliary coal engine, the coal burners being brought online for express high-speed trips, unusually heavy loads, or steep mountain grades. Any arcane engine was worth a fortune, even the simplest fireboxes. Lightning flux engines, hydraulic circulator engines, and wind engines were in another league; the lightning flux engine that powered my own rebuilt steam suit was at least as expensive as an elemental cage.

This, in turn, meant that the chief engineer of the train was himself a wizard; he gave me an uneasy look as he dismounted his steel horse to direct us to the cars we were supposed to load onto. When our eyes met, I gave the friendliest smile I could. He was likely a thaumaturge, even if he wasn't the same one who had built the fireboxes in the first place. Remembering what Katya had said about the Loegrian captain, I wondered if the gun at his side was loaded with a metal cartridge; I could not see any spare ammunition, and the barrel was fully tucked into a thick leather holster.

It might not even be loaded at all; I didn't know how often he might have to worry about bandits attacking a train, or if he was expected to risk himself in the defense of the train and its cargo as part of his duties.

Though I'd been hoping to take a closer look at the engine, the engi-neer and his assistants directed us to a string of flatcars and boxcars near the very end of the train. An extra caboose was attached in front of our cars; upon reflection, that seemed a sign of distrust that went deeper than the engineer's nervousness at sensing my magic. They were clearly pre-pared to cut us loose. I decided to load the self-propelled charcoal kiln in our first flatcar along with my armor.

Wordlessly, the mechs I'd built, along with their living steam knight brethren, began boarding the next two flatcars. This wasn't part of our original plan, or my freshly revised one, and while it seemed ill-advised, I limited my criticism to pointing out that they ought to secure their steam suits well if they were to ride a flatcar instead of a boxcar.

There were almost as many human steam knights standing behind me as there had been in the Wallachian wintertime, in spite of the fact that half a dozen steam knights had died since then. Only two suits had proven beyond repair, taken apart for spare parts, but there always seemed to be another man willing to step up and take whatever secret vows bound them together. This fact reminded me of something that puzzled me about the steam knights.

We'd sold two functional heavy mechs for credit to the baron—all that he was willing to pay for, even with a delayed letter of credit. I'd taken a third apart for practice, releasing the elemental spirit from its cage and binding a new one to prove to myself that I really knew how. Then, I rebuilt it as a smaller machine, using parts from the two destroyed suits to build another mech that looked little different from the steam suits of the knights around it.

With a Ruthenian elemental cage at its heart, it had fewer and cruder controls for its motion than the more sophisticated cages we'd found in Wallachia, but I had learned more about how mechs worked and did a better job at connecting control rods and joints together. It was still a little clumsier than its predecessors overall. Strangely—according to Vitold; I did not ask them directly—the human steam knights called it Peter. That had been the name of a steam knight crushed under the foot of a three-headed dragon. For my part, I struggled to believe Vitold's claim; surely they understood that it was a mech rather than a man, a steam suit animated by an elemental spirit with no flesh.

But Vitold insisted, and I felt I could trust him on this. He seemed as confounded as I was by the spontaneous generation of a solemn sacred brotherhood of steam knights who addressed mechs as if they were dead brethren. We had been lying to cover for the absence of our comrades when we claimed that my first three steam mechs were devout men who didn't talk because they had taken vows of silence. At first, we had thought the other steam knights had taken up the joke; yet now they seemed deadly earnest in their spirituality.

Because the brethren had decided to tie themselves down on flatcars instead of going into the shelter of a boxcar (human and mech alike), we ended up leaving behind some wagons that would not fit through the doors of the boxcars. Hopefully, we would have no trouble picking up replacements in Vindobona, I thought to myself, and then realized that if we were simply loading everything onto a riverboat after arriving in Vindobona, we probably wouldn't need replacement wagons until we reached Oenipons.

Other than leaving behind wagons, the process of loading the train went smoothly. People, guns, machines, horses, mules, et cetera, all were crammed into boxcars or strapped down to flatcars with minimal incident. I kept waiting to hear the roar of a hostile mech's engine, angry shouting in Loegrian or French or Magyar, the crack of a redhead's rifle fired from a rooftop, or something, but there was nothing of the sort.

The last to board was the better of our two surgeons, fussing over the proper stowage of his tools and possessions. As the man was also a physician—a very unusual background for a surgeon—he'd come to be quite well liked as surgeons go. He'd been the one to amputate the ragged part of Katya's leg. He spoke Venetian like a native; remembering that, I decided I wanted to ask him questions about the imperial capital, reasoning that on the map, Oenipons and Venice had looked much closer together than Oenipons and Dab. Maybe he'd been there.

The less said about the worse of our two surgeons, the better; I was glad he'd decided to stay as a barber in Dab. We'd need a replacement before we went into battle, though. One surgeon could be easily overwhelmed, injured, or might be inconveniently incapacitated by his own anesthetic liquor.

Given my recent experiences with Gothic nobility, I was not in a trusting mood myself. With the loading finished, I perched on the charcoal kiln, where I could keep an eye on the connection between our cars and the rest of the train. If they cut us loose at the most obvious junction, I would have warning, and possibly be in a position to prevent it.

A plume of thick black smoke announced that the auxiliary coal boiler was being put into service to get the laden train into motion. I watched as Dab receded into the distance, and thought about what I was leaving behind. Somewhere in the forests surrounding Dab, there was a redheaded woman with a piece of my heart. I hadn't been able to talk to her or apologize to her.

There was also an old man, whose loyal and lengthy service to the Golden Empire had just definitively come to an end. I didn't know what terms the baron had negotiated with those who decided to stay, but I imagined it involved an oath of fealty that amounted to forswearing the one the captain had sworn to Emperor Koschei all those years before.

There was a baron, a Gothic noble who had handed me two letters of credit, one post-dated. He would have to settle matters with Carmen's extended family, who seemed to believe I had ravaged her and stolen her virtue. That the alleged incident had happened under his roof left him with a share of the responsibility, and I doubted that it would stay secret, even if Carmen and her relatives wanted to keep it under wraps rather than pressing for recompense openly. Carmen waking up in my bed also seemed to have destroyed her friendship with the baron's daughter.

When Vitold came to offer me a kopek for my thoughts—one of the few he'd kept with him since our time in Ruthenia together, before our trip west began—that was the subject I had in mind.

"Once upon a time," I told him, "I danced with a stranger, a young woman with hair the color of aged cheese. From there, I failed to keep her father's clients and business partners alive and then ruined his relationship with one of his few remaining business partners." I sighed. "I know I've done worse," I added, remembering a whole village rendered into screams and blood. That day still haunted my nightmares. "But . . . I still feel bad about it."

Vitold snorted. "He paid for protection, and we delivered. With the troops we've left behind, we're still delivering even after he fired us. Remember the bandits? They would have had the run of the place if we hadn't been there to stop them. Not our fault his old accountant robbed him blind. Not our fault that he tried to stab us in the back. You, in particular, though with a knife that winsome, I wouldn't blame you if you'd just let him do it."

I sighed. "You think he was behind it," I said.

Vitold nodded. "You're not practiced in underhanded thinking," Vitold said. "He probably had his own drunken way with her and then needed to find someone to blame."

I shook my head. "I told you, it was sheep's blood. Nobody stole her virtue that night. And the baron hadn't been in my room, not that Yuri could smell. Just the servants and the cousin. And they seemed to want to keep the incident quiet. The only reason it was all over the compound is that I made such a fuss of it. I should have left the room myself instead of tossing out Carmen."

"Suit yourself," Vitold said. "Maybe nothing happened to her that night, but the baron is the one the servants take orders from. I'd bet you if I thought we could ever settle it."

I held up the kopek and chuckled. "I think you have," I said. "I'll just hold onto my winnings until you can fully prove the baron's guilt. Not that I believe in his innocence."

Vitold laughed. "You old cheat," he said. "With Carmen drugged, the only people who would know the baron set you up are him, his servants, and maybe that daughter of his. Not that we'll see any of them again."

I pocketed the kopek with a wink.

INTERLUDE

Two Letters

From a Mother to a Son

Dear Son,

I hope this letter finds you well, and that it finds you at all. We have received a letter from Pesht, from a woman I will only name as Damoiselle E—— in case this letter falls into unfriendly hands. Dlle E—— informs us that you fell in battle, but that she did not see you die. She inquires if we might be able to supply funds toward your recovery, funding perhaps a rescue attempt or ransom.

Septima is most distraught and thinks you must have died heroically fighting the hordes of the Golden Empire, for she thinks you the bravest man in the land. We are all concerned over the lack of any news directly from you or your captors, if the report should be correct. Your stepfather thought perhaps you found Pesht too distracting, and for the first time I find myself hoping you have been dissipating yourself through carousing with Magyars and gotten distracted from pursuit of your rightful inheritance.

Your stepfather says he hopes you made a clever escape and are hiding in Wallachia. The news is that half of Rumelia is aflame, Prince Vlad is back from the dead (one of the sons of the Dragon—do you remember what I taught you?), and the sultan is threatening to wage war against Koschei. The man carrying this letter has been paid for his trouble, with a promise of more if he brings back a reply from you. You are to include a drawing of Septima's favorite flower and a line from your stepfather's favorite book, so that we know you have written it.

Your stepfather and I may be able to come up with a ransom if one is required, but I would prefer to focus on getting him to pay for Septima's tutoring—the thaumaturge I hired says she has memorized half of a book of the basic practice cantrips letter for letter, and if—no, when—she gets her magic in, she will be more able than some of his grown students. If you have died a hero, I will be proud of you, but also sad.

Remember all that I told you about the princes—if you are there in Wallachia, you may have to make a choice. Just be careful that they have not promised your inheritance to another. Also, whatever Dlle E——— may have told you, there is no shame attached if you swear to a liege who then bows to the Golden Empire, not as long as that means you gain your title and lands.

Mme. Flavia Gavreau

P.S. Have heard the Undying Emperor is sending one of his princes to Wallachia, out of the fourth empress's line—my maternal grandfather's sister Maria was sent south to Rumelia and had a childless marriage with a man named Bogdan. The fourth empress's nephew's seventh son, who also died without issue, was a man named Bogdan who married a woman of uncertain lineage named Maria, picked up somewhere as a prize of war. Depending on the course of politics, this could be a useful connection to draw if you find yourself discussing lineages in the Golden Empire—just avoid any unnecessary precision about dates and places.

To a Different Mother from a Different Son

Dear Mother,

I am writing to tell you that, by the time you receive this letter, you may have become a grandmother. You said to never count chicks before they hatch, but I do not know if I will live to see this egg hatch or eaten by a fox. Matters seem uncertain. My deployment has taken me off the map, and I dare not say where I have been or where I am going now.

I will describe the potential mother. Zaleska has fair hair the color of wheat in harvest. She is tall as women go, though not so tall as most men. Her eyes are the gray of a thundercloud, dark but colorless. She will probably wear a gray cloak, which no rain can soak through. Due to the circumstances of her raising, I do not know if she was well-born, and she has no family to rely upon; however, she is magically adept, and you know how few of the Kransky line have any magic in my generation. I myself can barely read the wind; Zaleska can call up a gale strong enough to blow over trees.

Should you meet her without me, with her bearing a child who looks of the right age to be born a few months after I wrote this letter, please welcome her and accept that the child is mine. If she has no child, welcome her anyway, and hopefully I will come home after. Support her even if I have died and am not just delayed or separated, perhaps see if she might marry Vyacheslav if you have not found a wife for him yet. He has enough magic to start a fire, which makes it all the more likely she would bear him mage children.

I wish I could say more, but I do not know who else may read this letter. Your boy has fought dragons and phantoms and rebels and bear-men and won. I will come home when I can, and write again if I have a chick to count. But, for now, I write to warn you that there is an egg.

Fyodor Kransky

CHAPTER TWENTY-ONE

In Which I Stand Vigil

Once the auxiliary coal burner was turned off and we left the plume of black smoke behind, the sun set and the stars came out. It was the night of the new moon. From my vantage point, perched on top of my steam suit, which was strapped on top of the self-propelled charcoal kiln, which was in turn strapped on top of a flatcar, I could see the starlit terrain all around us. Once bright Venus dipped below the horizon, it was a nearly shadowless night, the only real shadows being those cast by the lights men brought with them.

The lantern light dimly seeping out through the shutters of the caboose windows in front of me lasted only two hours past sunset. With the crew in the car in front of me sound asleep, I might have relaxed and slept as well—but we were gaining a little elevation, and I found the view of the starlit lands beautiful. They were so lush and green in the gleaming diffuse light of the stars . . . it looked like a painting by a talented but lazy artist, who had decided to leave off painting in shadows. To the left, I could see what I could only assume were the westernmost reaches of the great Sarmatian range.

That is not to say it was silent. The still, starlit lands around us were contrasted with the raucous noise of railroad travel. On the flatcar behind me, the steam knights sang for a little while, their voices contending with the noise of the train. The wind rushing by felt as fast as a galloping horse, a dull but inconstant roaring that tore snatches of music away here and there. Villages dotted the land, and larger towns hugged the railway.

Those towns flickered to half-wakefulness as we came through, the noise of the train significant enough to draw attention. We stopped in three of them, the train off-loading passengers and cargo as I watched anxiously, but the crew in the caboose in front of my flatcar remained asleep, their lanterns dimmed and hooded. To them, the stops were routine, not worth waking for. Each departure was signaled with a new plume of coal-black smoke rising into the sky. Then the tension in my gut eased as the tension rose on the linkage between my car and the next, the locomotive pulling us once again into motion.

I was thoroughly tired by the time the gray pre-dawn light began washing the stars from the sky and the rosy light of dawn began to peek over the distant Sarmatians to the east; but still, I did not sleep. The shadows of the mountains crept up the foothills as we moved south, and when the blue ribbon of the Istros came into view, it was lit by bright morning light. With that came my first view of Vindobona, nestled beneath the foothills of the Alps.

It made Dab look like a backwater village. The only comparison I had was Khoryvsk, but while Khoryvsk spans the Slavutich, growing from settlements perched on both banks, Vindobona began life as a Roman fortress with the Istros guarding its northern frontier. The city's ancient stone walls, while not in any way short, barely concealed most of the buildings within, a profuse crowding of tall buildings. One particularly tall cathedral spire stood out near the center.

Surrounding the old walls of the city was a desolated, jagged span of new fortifications under construction, barren earth and jumbled stone surrounded by open firing lines. A canal pulled water from the Istros into a defensive moat. I took the decision to construct a new moat and bastions as firm evidence that Emperor Sigismund II placed little trust in the security of the old fortifications. (Later, I learned that decision had been the responsibility of the local margrave, even though the imperial capital was not so far away.)

About a dozen bastions were in various stages of construction at points between the old wall and the new moat, each one a pointed protrusion jutting out from the city. At one, men and mechs were digging out a foundation; at another, a trio of thaumaturges were going through the laborious process of laying enchantments in silver wire stretched across level stones. One bastion looked finished, with no workers rushing to it; a priest and his attendants were walking away from it in the wake of a crowd of well-dressed city folk while a handful of men in armor stood on top of the bastion wall near the point, engaged in conversation.

The rail line ended short of the river, the rail yard surrounded by a cluster of wooden buildings. We had arrived, and nowhere along the way had we been attacked or betrayed. Had my vigilance been necessary? I didn't know. What I did know was that I needed sleep; once I was confident my officers had matters in hand with organizing the unloading, I wrapped myself in a blanket and climbed into a wagon to take a nap.

As sleep took me, so did dreams. First, I dreamed of home, of blue skies over golden fields. Then there was a dog, cheerfully bounding along. Not Yuri; not one of the dogs that had sadly watched as I'd left the family farm for the last time; it was a long-legged hunting hound with sharp green eyes. The dog saw me and began to run at me, barking with excitement, yet didn't come closer. Instead, the dog receded into the distance, shrinking to an elongated rust-colored spot.

I looked down. My shoes were made of iron, and the ground was zooming behind them smoothly. A trio of small orange birds with long sparkling tails were tugging me along by the hem of my tunic, which was embroidered with tiny runes. The runes were gripping the birds, I realized, reading them and trying to commit them to memory. I reached into my pocket, pulling out a golden ducat.

"Where are you going?" asked a woman in heavily accented Magyar. Her face was covered with a mask that looked like a doll's carved face, with perfect pink dots on her cheeks. Her dress was made of silver coins, stitched to each other with strings through holes punched in their centers. Each coin had her face, except the face was gone.

"I'm just trying to get paid," I said. "I have a letter of credit that can't be called in this year."

She laughed, braying like a donkey. A delicate golden circlet fell from her head, chiming as it hit the ground. "You're funny," she said in a Dalmatian dialect, her accent betraying that this was not her native language either.

I looked down to see where the circlet had come to rest and saw that the ground was gone. A river swirled beneath my feet, and I was swept under. Through the distorted surface of the water, I saw the dog leaping over the river, rust-red fur lightening to a brighter orange on her belly. Down I went, and then up along the smooth pebbled bottom of the river as it flowed upward to the top of a snow-capped mountain. I washed out of the river at its source, a hot spring on the top of the mountain.

I slowly stood to my feet, hot water dripping into the snow and melting it around me. Beneath was emerald green grass, ripe for pasturing. I stared, fascinated. Then an old lady clucked her tongue at me.

"Kolya, I need you to chop wood," she said. "You're late. And where are the eggs?"

"I have a rock," I said, pulling a rough hunk of quartz from my pocket. It dropped into the river. "Oops."

"Clever boy," she said, "but I don't need a special egg. I'm just making breakfast. Go to the chicken coop."

I groaned, picking up a wood-splitting axe and starting the long walk downhill toward a miniature wooden barn. The barn slowly skittered away from me on hundreds of tiny legs, its faded pink pearwood boards creaking nervously as it accelerated.

"Oh, come on," I said in an exasperated tone. I broke into a jog, then a run. The miniature barn jumped off a cliff, and I followed, leaping with my axe held high. I landed on its roof, which lifted itself by one end, opening under my feet. I balanced cautiously on the lip. Inside, there were seven pregnant women.

The distant voice of the old woman echoed in my ears. "Eggs!" That's right. I was supposed to chop wood for her and bring her eggs. But I had to chop firewood.

"Excuse me," I asked. "Are you firewood?"

The women shook their heads mutely.

"You must be eggs, then," I said, and then in the distance I saw the dog, its rust-colored fur distinct as it swam up the river. "Well, I guess if I'm in a hurry, I could chop some pearwood," I said, looking at the walls of the miniature barn.

The lid wobbled, and I lost my balance, pitching forward into the women. I landed on them with a cacophony of squeaks. Then the lid closed on me, and everything went black.

I sat up with a start. The sun was low on the horizon, hanging over the high mountains of the west. The Istros gleamed with reflected sunlight.

"Sir?" There was a soldier standing nearby. He shifted uneasily, wanting to tell me what to do without sounding like he was giving me an order.

"Sir, Captain Rimehammer arranged a house for the officers tonight. If you'll . . . I mean . . . I could show you the way, sir, if you would like."

"That will be fine," I said, stretching and covering a yawn. Perhaps I should have stayed awake to help arrange matters. Had the local authorities refused to let an unfamiliar band of heavily armed mercenaries inside the city walls? Perhaps. Perhaps it was just cheaper here in the little unwalled village perched up the hill on the other side of the river.

We passed several larger houses before reaching the officers' house, which was built on the side of the hill. The owner, a thin man with a long nose and a very flat hat, came out to greet me, ushering me in with polite deference. Stairs led down from the door, and past the tall entry hall, I could see a balcony lined with half a dozen doors. It was a surprisingly compact inn, and with the way it was built into the hill, it was probably easy to keep warm in the winter.

I was in time for dinner, or perhaps our host took my arrival as his cue to bring out food. Each of my officers wanted to talk to me about one or another decision they'd made in the absence of any instructions. The artillery lieutenant had led the inventory of our supplies, making sure that nothing had fallen off the train along the way. The infantry captain got the new recruits out of the way for basic close-quarters training. One cavalry officer had headed to the city docks to find a boatman willing to take mail downriver; the other rode through the city to "gather intelligence," a process that apparently involved visiting coffeehouses and bars and having a good time.

The older Rimehammer cousin wanted to talk to me about our itinerary. He wanted to spend a day or two trying to convert some of the baron's goods into cash before heading upriver. He'd gotten some offers in the little town that clustered around the end of the rail line, but he wanted to see if he could get a better price in Vindobona proper inside the wall.

For my part, I wanted a chance to see the city, so I agreed without a second thought.

CHAPTER TWENTY-TWO

In Which I Bury a Lie

Vindobona. Eastern gateway of the Gothic Empire. Bastion against the Magyars to the east, the Turks if they should overtake Avaria, and the Golden Empire if it should ever begin to reach the breadth of the Undying Emperor's desires. Once the northern gateway of the original Roman Empire—original, as Sigismund II was one of the emperors claiming to hold the imperial scepter of Rome (or, as the sultan called it, Rum), and the Gothic Empire was sometimes called Roman.

Vindobona. One of the great cities of the Empire, arguably the greatest city of the Istros, which was without question the greatest river west of the mighty Kama. Not so great as Rome was, but a city of culture, learning, and intellect. It even had a university, one of the largest in Europe. Moreso than Oenipons, the capital city, the greatest mages and musicians of the Empire were said to gather in Vindobona. They would cluster and chatter in its cafés, bars, and—or so Lieutenant Quentin Gavreau told me—a few special clubs of ill repute.

As an adopted French nobleman who had voyaged much of the navigable length of the Istros on his way to a theoretical inheritance in Wallachia, Quentin had been through Vindobona before. He'd also been educated on it ahead of time, with his mother emphasizing the availability of Turkish-style coffee and the importance of avoiding any place where many women wore yellow squares on their shoulders. This was, he informed me with sparkling eyes, the mark required by local town authorities of a working woman.

Why he might have a particular interest in which women worked puzzled me—didn't all women work, at least those who weren't nobles? We were both embarrassed that he was required to explain what he meant. He told me a working woman was a woman working professionally as a woman. That is, paid to be a woman in the special ways that a woman is not like a man. He clarified further that he was not referring to a wet nurse, but a profession requiring a bit more exposure, and that he was not referring to a painter's model, at which point I realized what he meant and Vitold spent what seemed like an hour laughing on his side.

My oldest available friend, Vitold—whom I had promoted to lieutenant of mechanics—had grown up in a bakery in Lviv, near the western edge of the Golden Empire, and he was keen to taste the city's breads, pastries, and (since Quentin had mentioned it) delectable yellow-square-wearing women. He thought perhaps such a visit would do me well, as I had been looking morose lately and could hardly expect another naked noblewoman to mysteriously materialize in my bed for my entertainment.

Not that I had taken advantage of Carmen. I had passed out cold from an excess of wine when someone—perhaps our erstwhile employer—deposited the drugged noblewoman in my bed, and did not wake up until an older male cousin of Carmen's barged into the room. No, I did not miss Carmen, nor did I wish for a repeat of that incident. I missed Katya, the redheaded sharpshooter who had saved my life more than once.

I'd loved her—I still did. She'd loved me—I hoped she still did, but she'd been angry enough with me the last time I'd seen that she ran off into the woods of Silesia . . . and we were hundreds of miles from there. Maybe I did need to find a woman wearing a yellow square on her shoulder to put Katya out of mind, but one of my older brothers once told me that a visit to a prostitute to cure a broken heart was more likely to leave a man in need of having another part of him cured afterward than to address the broken heart.

What I wanted to see was the university. I had not known I was a mage when I began my journey, and I knew that wizardry was a high-learned art of great sophistication. Perhaps I could learn more about my gifts and how to better use them; I might even be able to find someone to tutor me, a teacher willing to travel with us for a little while and pass on his knowledge. I felt as if I was fumbling around in the dark.

There were two problems with my desire to see Vindobona. The first was that almost all of my officers wanted to go to Vindobona, but we could not march a small army of soldiers through the city gates. The local authorities were concerned with the security of their city. The second was the crows.

When we had traveled by train, we had gone faster than a crow could fly and gone farther than any crow wanted to fly. But crows are inveterate gossips, and they are able to describe men to each other quite well. Whether it was because of the battles I had fought, the distance I had traveled, or the fact that we carried a raven banner, the corvid grapevine had apparently been filled with stories of me. One or two birds had seen me napping at the train station, and then flown off to tell a couple of friends that I looked like the man in the stories, who had in turn, each flown off to tell a couple more birds. By morning the little town across the river and up the hill from Vindobona was full of very curious crows.

They were all eager to get a look at this man they'd heard so much about and were crowding around and cawing out questions without the slightest sense of shame. Worse, many of them were poor listeners and not particularly creative thinkers, so many of them were cawing out the same questions, with more informed crows giving out the same answers. I found it annoying.

My officers found it unnerving and recommended that I stay behind and supervise the troops. Obtaining entrance through the city gates might be complicated if they walked up accompanied by an unusually large murder of crows; indeed, it could be more alarming than trying to bring our artillery into the city. While I had only negotiated my way into one walled city before, I could see how being followed by a conspicuous corvid crowd might make things complicated.

That is not to say that the crows didn't complicate matters even as I stayed out of the city.

"Alright, men, present arms!" The infantry captain's command voice pierced through the cawing loud and clear.

"Yes, ma'am!" they chanted back, voices mostly lower in pitch. Mostly.

I walked along the line slowly, looking over each recruit from head to toe, trying to commit their faces to memory. Today, the captain had felt ready to trust them with unloaded arquebuses. Yesterday, they'd been drilling with fork rests. I paused, gently pulling a hand off of a firing lever here, a finger out from underneath a phoenix stone there. Some of the recruits had never held an arquebus before, and it showed.

The recruit at the end of the line had hair the color of aged cheese—a young beardless recruit in ill-fitting clothes and oversized boots, struggling to grip the arquebus and fork at the same time in too-small hands.

I frowned and then walked back to the infantry captain.

"What is the baron's daughter's maid doing here?" I asked under my breath, gesturing at the row of trainees. The maid had a close resemblance to the baron's daughter, including hair the same shade.

"What do you mean, sir?" The infantry captain looked at me with a cool expression.

I pointed at the end of the line. The baron's daughter's maid's face flushed pink, and she gripped something attached to a necklace under her ill-fitting men's clothing.

"Georg?" The infantry's captain's voice quavered uncertainly. She looked at the baron's daughter's maid with a puzzled expression. "Georg is a man, sir," she whispered.

"Uh, what is the problem?" the baron's daughter's maid said, shuffling a few steps back in oversized boots. She looked uneasily over her shoulder. The crows had grown quiet and were staring at her with interest.

I frowned. "Georg, come walk with me," I said, loudly enough that she didn't have to pretend she hadn't heard the whispered exchange between myself and the captain. With any luck, the other new recruits hadn't been paying attention.

The baron's daughter's maid gulped nervously. For convenience, I will refer to her as Georg; I never learned her real name. It was not the custom of Gothic nobles to address servants by name if they could help it, or I might have learned it earlier. Georg stepped forward; I took her arquebus, handing it to the captain, and then walked uphill. She followed.

"Did you desert your mistress?" I asked, once we had put some distance behind us and the crows had returned to their raucous conversations.

"My mistress? What do you mean?" Georg was breathing heavily, a consequence of having to keep up with my stride with her short legs and ill-fitting boots.

Consciously, I slowed. "The baron's daughter. I know you as her servant."

Georg made an empty pinching gesture in front of her chin as if she had a beard to stroke. "And if I did work for her, what is it to you if I've left her service?"

"Trouble, if she misses you," I said, stopping and turning to face her. "Or if the baron thinks you needed his permission to leave his service. And that's if you've truly left the baron's service."

Georg leaned heavily on her fork rest, breathing heavily as she caught her breath.

"You strike me as the loyal type," I said. I was lying; it was a wild guess, and I was hoping she would react.

She did. "I work for her, not him," she said. "Milady asked me to join you and send word back about where you went."

"To spy on me," I said.

"That . . . She doesn't mean you ill, sir, I swear. Just wanted to know where you ended up next." She looked at me so earnestly that I couldn't help but believe her. "And I've always wanted to see the world, sir."

"You do realize that you've signed up for a rather dangerous occupation?" I looked at the maid in her ill-fitting clothing and oversized boots. "Well, if the captain decides you pass muster, you can stay with us, but I wouldn't be in this vocation if I had the choice of an easy life."

"Really, sir?" she said. She looked puzzled. "But . . . didn't you turn down . . ." She clamped her mouth shut. "Sorry sir; forgive me for my insolence."

"Forgiven. I can accept insolence in private," I said. Then I pointed down. "Get boots that fit better, or find yourself extra socks. Soldiers spend a lot of time marching from place to place. If anyone asks, I was talking to you about proper kit and fit, and alternatives to the arquebus. You are rather small." I paused. "Do you ride?"

"Not as well as my mistress," she said, deferentially, "but yes. And I have my letters."

"Hm. Useful," I said. "Well, do the best that you can for now. I'll let the captain know you have other skills that might be useful. And remember about the boots."

"I will, sir," she said, giving me her best impression of a military salute of some kind.

I waved her away and she walked down the hill in what would have been an awkward silence, if not for the continued chatter of the crows. It seemed like every crow within seven leagues had come to watch the famous Colonel Marcus Corvus.

"I wish I could visit Vindobona," I said, eyeing the crows with irritation. "I'd trade the whole load of Krukov salt for an hour in the university's library."

CHAPTER TWENTY-THREE

In Which I Ride the River

I decided to send several of the new recruits home after a third day of training. Georg wasn't one of them; I issued her a blunderbuss and made her Felix's assistant (as far as he was concerned) and bodyguard (as far as I was concerned). She had been a good personal servant to the baron's daughter, and being a good personal servant requires attentiveness more than anything else.

The fact that her loyalties lay at least partially with the baron or his daughter didn't bother me. Perhaps she technically was a spy, but I didn't consider the baron a threat. He had no reason to want us dead—not once we had passed on his letters of credit to someone else, at least, and I intended to do so as soon as it was practical. Besides, it was hard for me to take a spy seriously who looked like a child dressed in her father's clothes, much less one who had confessed her status so quickly.

As spies went, she had too many nervous habits that drew attention. She tended to grip a pendant of some kind whenever too many people looked at her, sometimes muttering nonsense phrases in mangled Latin. Superstitious charms someone had taught her, or prayers, perhaps. She wiggled her fingers in front of her chin as if stroking an imaginary beard.

I hadn't thought about my good-luck stone much since I had discovered I had magic of my own. Georg clearly didn't have any magic, so she needed a good-luck charm of her own, I supposed. We'd also picked up a couple more recruits—or at least fellow travelers—in Vindobona, one of whom did have magic. Johann was a student thaumaturge who had run out of tuition money. Or, more precisely, he had run out of tuition money in a different quarter of the city from the university and needed to address his finances before returning to Vindobona. He arrived wearing a large hat that covered much of his face.

I wanted to ask Johann if he could teach me about magic; but at the same time, though I wanted to learn more about magic, I didn't want to display my level of ignorance and reveal that Colonel Marcus Corvus had no formal training in wizardry.

The flat-bottomed boat that took us upstream on the Istros was powered by an elderly firebox driving a paddlewheel, assisted by a coal boiler. If we'd been going downstream, the boat captain told me, he wouldn't have bothered with burning coal, but the arcane engine frequently gave out. A leaky chimney lifted most of the smoke above my line of sight.

I frowned. "We just picked up a thaumaturge," I said. "Perhaps he could look at it."

Captain Felix Rimehammer turned to his new assistant. "Fetch Johann. Tell him to bring his equipment with him."

Georg clicked her heels together and saluted before dashing off. She was wearing better-fitting boots now, though still wearing ill-fitting men's clothing.

"Bright young man," Felix said, watching the blonde woman trot off. "Officer material."

I shrugged. It was good if he thought Johann was officer material, but a moot point since the student had been brought in at the rank of banneret. We could hardly do otherwise; he was well-born and had a proven magical talent, making him every bit the social equal of the Cimmerian who kept pretending to be an illusionist.

Johann wouldn't open up the firebox until it had been turned off and cooled back down, the barge anchored in place. Opening up the firebox revealed a glittering array of orichalcum bands, fused into place on the cast-iron shell. The bottom was plated with a layer of silver, originally polished to a mirror shine and now dusty with soot.

Johann muttered under his breath, light briefly flickering from his fingers. "I see," he said. "You have two problems. The first is that it's dirty. You could get a little more heat if you cleaned it out and polished the base plate. The elemental portal opens flush on the reflection, and the soot can't fall through, it's material."

"Polished it?" The boat captain looked puzzled. "My father never polished it."

"I can see that," Johann said dryly. "I've never seen this much accumulation. Has this boat been running since King Koschei's coronation?"

"No," the boat captain said. "My great-grandfather commissioned this engine especially."

"Well, that's your other problem," Johann said, stepping back from the open firebox. "The enchantment is wearing off, and it's old enough that it's not a standard inscription. I can tell that it starts here, on this band, but the runes are so worn I can't read them. Boosting the enchantment is impossible without knowing the original spells used in the process, which takes it from a journeyman task to a master's work. You need the inlay stripped and re-laid with a new enchantment, and that's a bit beyond me."

Curious to take a look at the firebox, I poked my head inside. Once I wiped the soot away, I could see my reflection clearly as if in a mirror. The inscriptions seemed legible to me; perhaps Johann simply didn't want to risk messing up a difficult task in public, I thought to myself as I followed the orichalcum bands with my eyes, mouthing the words under my breath. They seemed familiar; it was dactylic hexameter, at least, even if I couldn't place where I might have seen something similar.

There was a flash of orange light. Surprised, I flinched, banging my head against cast iron. That hurt. I blinked a few times to bring the boat captain and Johann back into focus. Johann's eyes were wide.

"Well, I cleared out the soot, at least, so maybe we'll make up the time from the stop," I said. "Hopefully, the enchantment won't wear off entirely before we reach the Oen."

Johann and the boat captain closed the firebox back up, tucking it into place on its boiler. I leaned over the back rail, waiting as the boat lurched back into motion and watching as Vindobona slowly disappeared into the distance. The boat captain didn't start the coal burner back up, so the rest of our slow trip upriver was smoke-free; I presumed that he was worried about pinching pennies to afford a replacement firebox once the boat's old firebox gave out.

I understood that sentiment. As a mage with no education in wizardry and a mercenary commander who'd never been trained as an officer, I felt like I was riding on an engine that could give out at any moment.

Then I heard a crow cawing. A piece of paper was fluttering down from the sky. I grabbed it before it could flutter off the back of the boat.

I looked up; more pages were falling, and a murder of crows was loudly demanding that I give them payment in exchange for their bounty.

After some negotiation involving as many brass bits and copper pennies as I could scrounge up, I came up with enough of a payment to satisfy the crows. While I wasn't sure why they had chosen to deliver a collection of papers to me, they seemed to think they were doing my bidding, and I thought that was an attitude worth encouraging.

Especially since the alternative would be annoying them. As I mentioned earlier, crows gossip; they can be vindictive and petty when slighted. Politeness seemed the best course of action, and if it cost me a double handful of pennies, that was a price I could afford to pay.

It was a book about magic—or more specifically, about alchemy and the regulations governing it within the Gothic Empire. The author meandered from techniques for partitioning powder to the legal status of love potions without interruption. What was delivered to us started partway through the second chapter, and ended mid-sentence partway through the ninth chapter. With no table of contents, it wasn't clear if the ninth chapter was the last chapter.

Piecing it together in order occupied most of my attention during the trip up the Istros from Vindobona to Batavis. The firebox never gave out, and I found that if I stared out at the river, my thoughts turned to Katya. From Katya, my thoughts would turn to sadness, and then time would pass dimly until someone had the nerve to disturb the brooding Colonel Corvus.

How the crows had gotten their beaks on the alchemy text, or where they had taken it from, I didn't know. The obvious possibility was that they'd stolen it from somewhere in Vindobona, quite possibly from one of Johann's former classmates or teachers. Johann claimed not to have any familiarity with the book; it was mostly well outside of his specialty. He worked with materials created, purified, and treated by alchemists but had little idea of how the alchemists accomplished such things.

His lack of interest bothered me. Johann was a student; he'd had a chance to learn this material, and he had the education that let him make sense of it, yet he was incurious. Vitold showed more interest in the subject, even though Vitold couldn't read the Latin the book was written in and hadn't an ounce of magical talent.

I quietly decided to start writing out a translation of the texts in Slavonic. It would keep me busy during dull periods of our trip and would help me learn the material better. If nothing else, I could pass the Slavonic version on to Vitold and give my friend the gift of dreaming about alchemy. Also, if the original owner returned demanding his stolen book, I could return it without any loss of knowledge.

CHAPTER TWENTY-FOUR

In Which I Reach a Fork

When the sun set on our first night on the river, we were between towns. The boat captain told us he would rather try to continue through the night rather than tie up in an area that could be infested with bandits, so we set watches and pushed on through the night.

Sometime late in the night we slipped by a sleeping toll castle, much to the boat captain's delight; I don't know exactly where or when, though Ragnar told me that there had been a chain that scraped across the bottom of the boat during his watch. The water had been running high with rain.

During the day, the current ran higher still, and our forward progress slowed to a crawl. Several times during the middle of the day, I looked up from my translation efforts and saw the same man in a dusty blue coat, leading a heavily laden donkey as he walked along the towpath parallel to us. Still, we were moving forward, slowly and steadily, other than a short stop to pay a toll at another river fort. With the river running high, most traffic was moving in the other direction, though we saw some anchored barges that might have been waiting to be towed.

The next sunset found us near a town, but the boat captain, with gleaming eyes, suggested we continue through the night, forgoing both the comfort and expense of resting in a town. And if there were bandits awake somewhere along the river, well, there was a well-armed mercenary company aboard his vessel, was there not?

We reached Batavis at night. The firebox had operated steadily and continuously, and we hadn't stopped for any real length of time since Johann's inspection of the antique arcane engine. I had received several distinct excuses for pressing onward and had thought privately of another: Perhaps after Johann's assessment, the boat captain was worried that the next time he cut off the arcane engine, it would never relight again, the elemental portal forever sealed.

It was a pity that Johann hadn't been able to fix it. I had cleaned out the built-up soot, but the services of a master thaumaturge would not come cheaply. Remaking an arcane engine would require considerable power and likely some expensive quantity of orichalcum and other materials. From my brief discussions with Johann, I was coming to understand that even a thaumaturge who was generous with his time could not work cheaply, not if an enchantment was meant to last.

"This is the fastest I've ever taken the leg from Vindobona to Batavis!" The boat captain beamed at me as he pulled the lever to vent steam, the boat slowing as we approached the confluence of three rivers by moonlight. "Thank you, Colonel Crow. Thank you!"

We must have overpaid for our passage, I thought to myself. Cheating our way past one toll might have expanded his profit margin a little bit, but it would hardly pay for a master thaumaturge. "It's been a pleasant journey," I said as the man hugged me. "Peaceful, even. I'm glad we didn't encounter any difficulties."

The boat captain released me from his grip. "Where do you want to land?" he asked. Lantern light from below gleamed off of his broad smile. "If we stick to the middle of the river, we could slip by the bishop's toll house," he added. "That is, if you want to go further up the Istros."

Batavis sits upon the confluence of three rivers, the Oen and the Ohe joining the Istros together from opposite sides like a pair of mischievous children. The main city lies on the spit between the Oen and the Istros; on the other side of the Oen, there is a monastery, and then between the little sister Ohe and the Istros, there is a small toll fort directly on the water, connected by a narrow fortification to a larger fort on the crest of the hill—the seat of the ruling bishop.

In the distance, I could see campfires on the side of the hill near the castle. Distant glimmers of lantern light danced back and forth along wall tops, showing that the lower and upper fortress were both on full alert with double-duty watchmen on high alert. I pointed to my right.

"Hold here before we approach," I said. "I think I want everyone awake and ready before we get any closer. There's a force encamped outside the castle, and I don't want to walk into a battle with half my men asleep."

The boat captain's smile fell from his face, plunging deep into a river of disappointment and shock. He squinted. "I do see fires," he said, "now that you have pointed them out."

Approaching a castle under siege at night is a delicate proposition. After discussing the matter with my officers, I decided that our approach was best left to daylight. We tied the boat up against the bank, making ourselves ready—a process that involved most of the company taking at least another two-hour nap, as I did not want us to exhaust ourselves unnecessarily.

It turned out that the old bishop had recently died, and there was a dispute over succession. The local cathedral chapter had elected a replacement; another replacement had then arrived, claiming appointment on authority delegated by Rome. The first presumptive bishop held the castle; the second presumptive bishop was outside with a small but not insubstantial escort of knights and men-at-arms from his older brother's duchy.

The knights were steam knights of the grand Teutonic style, which is to say that they were not men in humanoid steam suits; they were men in heavy armor with headless eight-legged steam horses to carry them. There was also a mech, distinctively lacking a smokestack and therefore powered by an arcane engine instead of a coal boiler.

With the value attached to the letters of credit issued by the baron and the uncertainty I attached to his willingness to eventually redeem them directly, I had come to the conclusion that our clear priority was exchanging the letters of credit for cash rather than seeking mercenary employment. A well-placed imperial noble might be willing to treat them at close to face value based on superior leverage to compel full payment from the baron. Logically, the best place to find such nobles was the court of Emperor Sigismund II.

However, if an opportunity to earn a better sum fell into our laps before arriving at Oenipons, I would be remiss as a mercenary commander (and therefore less plausible) if I did not at least try to take advantage of it. I also reasoned that it would be imprudent as a military commander in unfamiliar territory to approach the lower fort without being prepared for a hostile reaction.

I write this, therefore, to clarify my reasoning behind approaching the lower fort with my battalion arrayed in such a manner as to display our wares to best advantage. In retrospect, it would have been wiser to send a messenger ahead inquiring as to our prospects for employment rather than approaching directly.

We approached the lower fort arrayed in parade formation. I stood at the front of the boat, my steam knights (and mechs) lined up behind me. As it was essentially a flat barge, the soldiers in the lower fort would be able to see us clearly and note that we were not in a hostile posture. After all, assaulting the riverine wall of the lower fort was not an easy enterprise, and had we been hostile, we would have begun by reducing the wall with our artillery from a distance.

The soldiers in the lower fort reasoned differently. We were an unfamiliar force, heavily armed and approaching them; there were hostile foreign troops besieging the upper fort; therefore, we must be approaching to attack. Our boldness in not firing guns during our approach was perhaps some kind of trick. They opened fire when we were about two hundred yards away from the fort, arquebusiers firing in a ragged, undisciplined volley that lasted a dozen tense heartbeats.

At that range, it was not accurate, but it did not need to be to cause harm; I heard the screams of at least two wounded men.

As I was front and center, I attracted a disproportionate share of aimed attention, and somewhere between ten and twenty bullets bounced off my armor, protective enchantments flaring with turquoise light. I squeezed my eyes shut. I could picture the runes on the inside of my armor, silently mouthing the words they spelled out. The armor would hold; and hopefully, the men on top of the wall would fire straight at the most protected target in their line of sight.

To the aft, a loud hiss announced that the boat's engine was now leaking steam. The soft splash of the boat captain diving off the rear of the boat into the safety of the water was barely audible, but it was impossible not to notice that the boat was completely out of control as it spun sideways in the cross-current of the Ohe merging into the Istros.

Behind me, I could hear the crackle of scattered return fire as the boat careened slowly toward the fort, losing steam pressure and therefore usable power as it went. If I didn't do something, we would crash sideways into the wall of the fort, then slowly drift away in the current as the soldiers in the fort continued firing.

Possibilities flashed across my mind.

"Hold your fire!" I shouted, gripping the forward railing. "Someone grab that tiller and straighten us out!" To the right and left of me, my mechs gripped my arms. Turquoise light flared brightly in my peripheral vision.

Ahead, the first arquebusiers had finished reloading. They began to fire, a steady hail of bullets that could not be considered a volley by any reasonable standard.

"Hold your fire!" I shouted again, my voice distant in my own ears as I hoped that my soldiers wouldn't be the only ones who listened to my plea. Through my armor, I gripped the railing tightly.

For a moment, I thought the soldiers of the bishopric had heard me; their fire began to falter. In the tower overlooking the outer walls of the lower fort, the dark circle of a cannon's muzzle rolled into view. Then it vanished in smoke.

CHAPTER TWENTY-FIVE

In Which I Take the Low Path

I flinched, squeezing my eyes shut. The railing vibrated, and I heard a splash in front of me. Somehow, they had missed. I opened my eyes, my peripheral vision still filled with turquoise flashes. The offending cannon had rolled back with the recoil from its shot but was still visible—and a short bandy-legged man was swabbing the barrel in the first step of preparing to reload it. I felt unaccountably tired, but I knew that they were unlikely to miss twice in a row.

My fingers twitched, tying an invisible knot, and I lashed out with a line of magical force. The cannon resisted the motion for a moment before lurching forward. I pulled harder with my arm and my mind, and it plummeted down, landing in the courtyard of the lower fort with a sound like a giant hammer striking an anvil.

I heard that sound clearly because silence had fallen over the soldiers on top of the wall. For a minute, the only other sound was the dying hiss of the steam engine as the boat slowly crept ahead in the direction of the fort. Then an enemy soldier raised his arquebus vertically, a white cloth tied to the end. The other enemy soldiers were laying down their guns and holding their hands high.

"A surrender!" he shouted, the early morning light illuminating his impromptu white flag from behind. "We surrender! Mercy!"

Some tell a different version of the tale, but it is not true that I broke the Batavis fort without firing a single shot. At least a dozen of my men had returned fire before my order to the contrary. Nor is it true that I took it without any deaths; I had two wounded and one missing, likely dead and fallen overboard, and two of the defenders died, one by return fire and the other slipping off the edge of the wall by accident.

Nevertheless, it is true that the lower fort surrendered to me before I had even reached its walls. It was miraculous that there had been so few injuries; true, the first volley had been offered at a great range, but we had been well within killing range after that. In truth, I think the same fear that had led them to start shooting desperately at a boat full of unfamiliar soldiers had left them with unsteady arms, ready to surrender once they had an excuse to do so.

Having taken the lower fort, we sent one of the surrendered soldiers to the upper fort as a messenger. Of the others, we released any who were willing to give their parole and promise not to promptly take up arms against us again, though we didn't give them back their arquebuses. This proved to be most of them, though some preferred to take a launch across one of the rivers rather than travel up the causeway to the upper fort.

When I wrote my message, I didn't know how to explain that I hadn't intended to take the lower fort, so I did not try. Knowing that the audience was a member of both the nobility and the clergy, I wrote the message in the most flowery Latin I could come up with while saying as little as possible: I had possession of the lower fort and was willing to consider any reasonable terms that the would-be bishop cared to offer.

As far as I was concerned, I was a neutral party in their conflict in spite of having been unjustly attacked. A mercenary ought to be pragmatic about such things. Pragmatically, I also sent one of my own men as a messenger to the force arrayed outside of the upper fort, indicating my willingness to discuss matters with them. In the best case, I might provoke a bidding war.

It seemed better to sell possession of the fort than to sell my services. The fort seemed valuable, and I had been freshly reminded that mercenaries earn coins with their own blood. One missing (likely dead) and two wounded was a distasteful price to pay for having approached a prospective employer too closely, and possession of the lower fort seemed like something that either party would be willing to pay for.

The first replies from both parties were belligerent, so I put Felix and Georg to work making an inventory of the fort's potentially salable contents.

Fyodor, Ragnar, and the infantry captain were put in command of emplacing artillery and planning defenses. The upper fort held the advantage of height on us in any exchange of hostilities, but the range was not terribly far in either direction.

I sat in the tower and stared at a sheet of blank paper for a while, uncertain how to reply. After the candle burned down a full mark, I put the would-be bishops' accusations of banditry to the side and worked on my Slavonic translation of the alchemy text for a while. Alchemy seemed far simpler than figuring out how to deal with nobles.

The breakthrough was when I realized that for someone who had seen my advance on the fort as a bold attack, I was a bandit as long as I wasn't working for either one of them. However, if I was working for the other, then I was a simple mercenary. Inspired, I jotted down my notes and sent for Quentin.

"Here's what I'm thinking of telling them," I told Quentin, waving the paper.

"Your holiness," Quentin started, then paused. "That should be excellence, not holiness," he said, then looked back down at the page. "Various pleasantries—I can rewrite this part for you . . ."

"Yes, please do," I said, "but do go on."

Quentin moved his finger down the page and then cleared his throat. "Perhaps I failed to make it clear that the pretender has, unfortunately, failed to pay me. My services are not cheap, and I will not serve a master beyond his breach of contract, which places me in an awkward position following my arrival," he said. "Really? We're going to just lie to them?"

"It's not false," I said. "He hasn't hired us, but he also hasn't paid us."

"Which one is this letter going to?" Quentin asked.

"Both of them?" I looked at Quentin.

Quentin rubbed his forehead. "Hm," he said. "This is going to be a long night, and I think I want Georg to help with this. He's clever with a good turn of phrase."

Georg absently twirled a lock of her blonde hair that had come loose from under her cap, biting her lip as she held the quill over the page. "I think that will do it for Hellenbodus, but we really have to start over for the other letter," she said. "Sending the exact same message would be a mistake. This version is long, flowery, personal, and we're dropping the hint six different ways."

"Good man," Quentin said, clapping the woman on the back.

I drained the last of the tea in my cup, rubbing my eyes sleepily. "I think I'll take a walk," I said. "Can you two keep working on this without me?"

"Yes," Quentin said. "Georg and I have it handled; you can go get some sleep."

Georg nodded eagerly, unconsciously licking her lips. "Definitely," she said in the deepest voice she could muster, straightening her shoulders out.

I looked between the two of them. "Alright," I said with a shrug. "Just try not to lie outright. I'd feel bad about that. See you in the morning, then." As I walked, I heard Georg's voice.

"The best lies are mostly the truth," she said under her breath.

Looking back, I think she was correct. The best lies are truths told very carefully.

For my part, I did go for a walk before turning in, greeting the soldiers on watch and inspecting the placement of our artillery. I had no intention of second-guessing my lieutenants' choices, as both of them knew more about artillery than I did, but it felt good to familiarize myself with where each gun was placed.

The troops on watch were also happy to see me on the battlements. When I had put myself front and center on the flat deck of the paddle-wheel barge, I had worried that my troops might think I was vain. However, my choice also made me a target. Every bullet that was fired at me was one less bullet fired at the troops behind me, and the soldiers didn't know that I had blinked when the cannon was fired at us. The armor had concealed that, and as far as they were concerned, I had put myself between them and cannonfire without flinching.

One of them called me "Lord Corvus" instead of "Colonel" or "sir." It was so strange that I didn't know what to say back to him. While systems of primogeniture vary slightly, all would at least put the surviving half of my father's older brothers in line ahead of him, and all three of them had children of their own. Even if a title had been bestowed on my father in my absence, I had half a dozen older brothers between me and any paternal inheritance.

Yet "noble" meant "virtuous," not just born to inherit wealth and authority. To that soldier, I was noble enough that I simply had to be a lord. My actual birth status was irrelevant; I had authority, virtue, and perhaps even divine favor, and that meant I deserved the greatest level of respect he could grant with his words.

After walking the battlements and inspecting guns, I checked on the infirmary, where two of my men and three of my erstwhile enemies were dancing with death. Even a small wound could inflame and lead to death, and those five had all been wounded seriously. I spoke with the two of them who were awake. One was a Khazar arquebusier who had spent five years in the service of the Golden Empire; the other was a local, who in his delirium apologized three times for shooting at me, saying that I looked like I was important.

In the morning, we buried three men and sent two messengers. The Khazar was doing better, as was the apologetic local; the rest had not survived the night. During the ad hoc ceremony, the surgeon looked as if he wanted a conversation with me, glancing in my direction often, but then turned and left without saying a word.

Even if nothing the letters said was truly a lie, I felt a twist in my gut as the messengers left. What was I doing trying to bluff myself into some measure of respectability? And what business did I really have taking sides in a local conflict over who was supposed to become the next bishop?

Protecting a factory against bandits and other malefactors seemed much simpler, morally speaking. I hadn't wanted to become a soldier in the first place and hadn't wanted to murder for the cause of the Golden Empire. Offering to murder for the cause of profit seemed no better. I had another handful of deaths on my conscience as a result of a simple, imprudent decision, and now I was offering to add dozens or hundreds more.

Still, it was the path I had chosen—that we had chosen—and stepping off that path had its own risks. With any luck, my intervention in this succession crisis would leave matters no worse than whatever would have happened if I had taken the left fork in the river and gone directly up the Oen without stopping at Batavis.

After seeing off the messengers, I retreated to the tower, returning to my self-assigned task of translating the alchemy text. With the lower fort's walls being directly on the river, the watch team on top of the tower had a much better view, and working on the top floor of the tower meant that I would be one of the first to hear any news they had. It was a good place to wait.

INTERLUDE

The following excerpt is taken from *Ragnar Rimhamar,
Gentleman Adventurer*, with permission of the publisher.

*Vindobona deserves to be known as the City of Books. It is the home of the
greatest mage college in the Gothic Empire, and today its enchanted fortifications are world famous. I myself was able to stand atop the ramparts as they
were being constructed, and listened to one of the city's future master wizards
as he explained to me their plan of defense.*

*It is a great city, one which I have visited many times since, but that was
my first visit, and you never forget your first! My Gothic was passable—it is
not so different of a tongue, and I had picked it up readily—and I needed no
translator to make myself understood. Vitold, that funny little man, had
appointed himself my partner in exploring the city. It was an understandable
choice for him; women tended to overlook the man as short, a little rotund,
and grimy around the fingernails from his mechanical works.*

*On the other hand, I, as a handsome and exotic Swede (as we are thought
of in the lands farther south), would attract enough attention from women
for the both of us. Indeed, so popular I was with the women of Vindobona
that I had to thank Vitold for his service in distracting some of them.*

*The man also had an excellent nose for food; out of the ten best pastries I
have eaten in my life, seven entered my mouth on that trip. Situated where
we were in the middle of the Istros, we paired our pastries with wine from
the west, coffee from the east, and crisp golden lager brewed locally. We spent*

the night in an inn whose sign simply consisted of a golden square, returning in the morning to the Raven's battalion in its camp outside the city.

From there, we went west up the Istros aboard a boat driven only by a firebox; while coal was cheap enough locally, my cousin Felix had wanted to make sure we did not get ourselves separated on the river. Some riverboat captains are little better than bandits themselves, pirates of the inner waters eager to slit the throats of outsiders who won't be missed and take their money, and Felix's trust was far shallower than the waters of the Istros.

In the space of two days, we sped swiftly up the Istros to Batavis, the famed City of Swords. There was a pretender to the local throne who had claimed the title of prince-bishop without proper authority, a usurper.

The light of the setting sun blinded the defenders of the fort as we approached. Once, twice, three times they fired, crisp volleys of a hundred arquebuses each; Mikolai each time raised his hand, and the bullets dropped into the water. The Batavisites jeered, and then stood aside, for their cannons were loaded now; they had ten of them, and they were aimed straight at us.

We held our nerve, and still did not fire back. Those who had beaten trolls and dragons would not be intimidated into flinching by mere men, and we had our orders. The colonel had told us that even if we were fired upon, we should hold our fire until his signal—for if it was truly needed, he would give the order, and our men would rake the walls with deadly fire.

The cannons roared, and Mikolai waved his hand again, the cannonballs returning straight back at those who had fired them. The cannons were knocked off the wall, landing with a cacophony like a collapsing belfry.

"Mercy!" screamed their leader, waving a white flag. "Mercy, oh God, have mercy on us!"

Mikolai gave me a look, and I know that he wanted—needed—my help for what would come next. So, I gripped Mikolai by the shoulder and nodded, touching my hammer to the water. A stairway of ice erupted from the summery waters of the river, and Mikolai walked up the stairs to accept their surrender. I followed behind him, hammer in hand. It was then that I saw, standing on the roof of the tower, a woman with brilliant blonde hair: Giselle, the would-be bishop's daughter.

For one magical moment, her distant eyes locked on mine, and from the awestruck look on her face, I knew that I would not sleep alone that night if she had anything to say about it.

We took the soldiers' surrender (and their arquebuses) from their trembling hands with grace, and then prepared for the next stage of our operation.

The colonel, of course, had devised an intricate plan, the details of which he kept close to his chest in case of spies. The lower fort functioned as a toll castle for the river junction; while it was not the site of the bishop's main treasury, it had its own storehouses containing ample trade goods.

Our own guns were brought up and positioned to cover the causeway connecting the upper fort to a lower fort; the upper fort was within range of those guns in case we wished to start shooting, though the difference in elevation would rob them of some of their force in such a case. However, it was not time to shoot; it was time to wait. We had taken the lower fort without a shot, and a lesson like that does not sink home all at once.

CHAPTER TWENTY-SIX

In Which I Collect Taxes

As the level of the Istros lowered back down to its usual levels, we saw a surge of boat traffic—in fact, we saw it quite close at hand, since the lower fort functioned as a toll castle. Every boat that came down the Istros or Ohe had to stop at the lower fort. The boatmen who worked those rivers were accustomed to obediently stopping without tempting the wrath of the bishop's men, and most of them paid their tolls without asking why foreign mercenaries now stood atop the walls instead of the bishop's men.

At least, that is what I was told. I stayed in the tower, either working on my translation of the alchemy text or watching from a distance. The difference in height between the tower and the walls of the lower fort was substantial; I could see the upper fort and the impatient army camped outside. I could even see the town of Batavis itself, sited on the spit between the Istros and the Oen, which went about its business with little visible concern for either prospective ruler. And I could also see the river traffic, boats lining up obediently to pay tolls at the lower fort.

In addition to the traffic up and down the river, there was a steady trickle of small boats back and forth across the Istros. Goods and people moved toll-free, presumably a mixture of camp followers and enterprising locals with goods to sell to the encamped army. If the town had a militia, and I would be surprised if it didn't, the militia should have the numbers to be able to intervene decisively, but the townsfolk seemed to prefer to avoid taking sides in a dispute between nobles. If they chose wrongly between the two, Sigismund II might send an army to correct the matter, and that would be unpleasant.

Similarly, those aboard the larger boats traveling downriver from further west on the Istros surely noticed that a small army was camped outside the upper fort, but boat captains are generally sensible men who prefer not to inquire about the disputes of high nobles if they can stay out of them. They were just happy that the river wasn't blocked and that—whichever side had hired us—we hadn't increased the tolls.

I assume that some of them shortchanged us because of our ignorance about what the customary tolls actually were, but I didn't greatly care about that. Some of them paid in cash; others paid with a share of their cargo. Captain Rimehammer diligently recorded and valued all of it. After nightfall, he brought the list to me, remarking that it didn't seem bad for a day's work.

I stared at the list for a moment, and then inspiration struck. "Felix, if you don't mind, I'd like to borrow your assistant," I said, gesturing at Georg. "Georg has a way with words, and I think I want to write another message to our neighbors."

"Ah. You want me to send Quentin again, too?" Felix rubbed his chin.

I nodded. "Just so," I told the Swedish captain. "A good commander knows his limits, and those two know a great deal more about the foibles of nobility than I do."

Felix shook his head. "Just take care which insults you sign your name to. Lads that age are full of trouble."

Georg flushed momentarily, her cheeks turning bright red with anger, but she held her tongue.

Realizing that any outburst would have amounted to a spirited defense of Quentin, I paused in thought. I hadn't thought her attached to Quentin, but now I guessed that she must be in order to leap to his defense. Why else would she bristle at a comment singling out young men as troublesome? Internally, I began to question the wisdom of leaving the two of them together alone to work on messages for me; then I explored the consequences. True, fraternization might be improper given the difference in their military ranks, but the maid and Quentin were likely not actually that far apart in social status.

After all, the maid's looks marked her clearly as a relative of the baron's daughter; she even had the hair the same shade (that of aged cheese). Quentin might have actively presumed a right to a title, but that seemed a distant possibility at this point. A marriage between the two of them would not even qualify as a social scandal, and it would be hard for me to say that the Raven's battalion had a consistent tradition of barring fraternization.

Besides, whatever else the two of them might have gotten up to after I'd left them alone to work, they had succeeded in writing letters full of eloquence and subtlety, with all of the appropriate formalities, stating nothing outright while implying everything indirectly. While their first round of messages hadn't gotten the desired results, neither would-be bishop had begun preparations to carry out an attack against the lower fort.

Then Quentin arrived, cutting off my train of thought and clapping Georg heartily on the back by way of greeting, almost bowling over the petite maid. "Good man," he said, looking at Georg. "I hear you've come up with an idea to sell the bishop his own river tolls back to him? Brilliant!"

I wasn't sure why Quentin looked at Georg when his words suggested he was addressing me as the only other man in the room, but I provided the two of them with Captain Rimehammer's list, talking about the value of the tolls and trying to extrapolate what part of the bishop's income likely came from tolls rather than traditional tithes and taxes. Most of the local tithe income probably went directly to the cathedral in Batavis proper and the monastery situated on the opposite side of the three-river confluence.

It was Quentin who informed me that the town of Batavis was home to a substantial number of skilled craftsmen—as far as he was concerned, this city was the fourth-best place to buy swords in the whole world. Between the prized wolf-mark swords—which made the city's thaumaturges famous even among French nobility—and the commerce fueled by its position at the junction of three rivers, the city of Batavis was quite wealthy and had the bishop as its direct liege lord.

At that, Georg assumed a thoughtful look as she made a stroking motion with her fingers in the empty air in front of her chin, nodding. These other sources of income probably weren't being collected during the partial siege either; the most convenient method of delivering them would be by boat to the lower fort. The direct river access of the lower fort meant that a full siege required blocking off the river, and the encamped army was either unwilling or unable to do so.

After being assured that the two of them felt fully able to come up with ideas to use our toll collection activities as a lever to encourage negotiations, I went down the tower to speak with my troops, inspect the battlements, and deliver the finished Slavonic translation of the alchemy text to Vitold. The man might not have any magical talent, but if

I understood correctly from the text, much of alchemy involved letting the natural magics of materials invoke themselves. The author seemed to even think that baking was invoked a type of alchemy, simply one so widely learned as to have lost its mystique.

"You want me to hold this for you, sir?" Vitold frowned. He held the sheaf of papers dubiously.

Hearing the formality in Vitold's speech, I frowned. "I meant it as a present for my friend Vitold, not as a burden for Lieutenant Szpak," I said, an edge of complaint entering my voice. "You seemed to be a lot more interested in it than Johann," I added.

"But . . . I'm not a wizard," Vitold said. "I'm a mechanic. I'd be a baker's boy if I wasn't. No point in me learning alchemy, is there?"

"There is, if you want to learn," I said. "Or rather, even if there isn't, if you have fun reading about alchemy, it's as good as a storybook, isn't it? I penned it out for you in the simplest and easiest-to-read Slavonic I could so that you can read it for yourself, and if you don't want it, you don't have to take it, but . . ." I stopped. I wasn't quite sure what I wanted to say.

"Oh," Vitold said, flipping through the pages. "So, all that time you were shut up by yourself, you were writing this out? And for me?" He counted under his breath, then paused to eyeball the size of the stack of paper in his right hand compared to the stack remaining in his left. "Oh. Thank you, Mikolai." He turned away from me suddenly, rubbing his eyes with the back of his sleeve. "I'll put it somewhere safe for now, my friend," he added.

This time, the two letters sent out in the morning were nearly identical. They thanked His Excellency (granting both presumptive bishops the full honors of their jointly claimed title) for providing an advance deposit ahead of the conclusion of negotiations for my services, but informed them that my honor would require me to eventually return it if we did not come to mutually agreeable terms. A copy of Felix's itemized list of tolls collected was enclosed. The message also included extensive praise for the architecture and interior decor of the lower fort.

I was assured I didn't need to be more direct than that. My first thought had simply been to tell them I would keep the money from the tolls until one of them came to their senses and made me an offer to vacate the castle, but Georg and Quentin convinced me that acting as if I were more interested in honor than money would pique their interest. I should act as if occupying the lower fort indefinitely was beneath my dignity, something that I had been forced to do by circumstances.

For my part, I felt that the main insult upon me had been the soldiers shooting at my troops when we had done nothing wrong. Several men had died because of a foolish misunderstanding. Holding the lower fort ransom in exchange for having been unjustifiably attacked, however, was not as respectable as pretending I had been lured by false promises, been refused my rightful payment, and was too proud and impractical of a noble to directly admit that I'd been tricked into attacking the lower fort.

To me, that seemed less believable than the truth. Feeling pessimistic, I started drawing up plans for leaving the fort under the cover of night. If I didn't have the leverage to force either of them into making a decision, then eventually the dispute between the two would-be bishops would be resolved without me. At that point, there would be one actual bishop with the authority, resources, and inclination to evict a stray mercenary company from the lower fort.

My planning was interrupted when the infantry captain rushed in to tell me that an envoy was arriving from the bishop.

"Which bishop?" I asked. "The one in the upper fort, or the one with the steam horses?"

"Oh. Ah, the one in the upper fort," she said, holding her hat in her hands. "Should I send the messenger up here?"

I looked around at the table. It was strewn with papers, some weighted down by a now-cold samovar. "No. I think . . . down on the second floor, the room with all the paintings? But not right away; let me get settled in there. And I think I want Quentin to meet me there first, too."

Yuri let out a soft inquiring whine.

"Yes, you come with me, too; you might notice something," I said to the dog, giving his ears a quick scratch. "Okay, let's go get ready to meet the bishop's envoy."

The infantry captain gave me a funny look before dashing down the stairs.

CHAPTER TWENTY-SEVEN

In Which I Confess

To my eye, the paintings that lined the room were remarkable—far more accurate and detailed to the human form and the scenery that surrounded them than what I had seen in the baron's study. Quentin had suggested that they likely had come up from the south, through the capital, but it could be that the previous bishop had brought the artist to Batavis to work for him as well. Wealthy noblemen were often patrons of the arts.

Other than the paintings, the room was arranged with seating around the edges and small tables, a sociable sitting room rather than a working office with a desk. I'd picked the most ornate chair to sit in; Quentin was seated to my right and Yuri on my left, the latter sitting on the woven carpet that covered most of the floor of the small room. I was unarmed; I felt Quentin's three pistols and officer's sword were more than sufficient.

When the bishop's envoy arrived, escorted by the infantry captain, I rose to my feet, bowed, and addressed him in Latin.

"Please take a seat." I gestured to a chair near the door and then followed the gesture by seating myself. "I am sorry for any misunderstandings that may have arisen in the course of my correspondence with His Excellency. I really hadn't planned on taking this keep at all; nobody actually hired me to, but in truth, I felt provoked by the actions of His Excellency's soldiers when they fired upon us unprovoked."

Quentin gave me an incredulous look, his eyes widening. This was exactly what he hadn't wanted me to say.

"I is good meet you," the man said in Latin. "I am good meet you," he corrected, sighing heavily. "Good you am . . . you are sorry." He shook his head, switching to the local Gothic dialect. "Do you speak Gothic? Latin conjugation is not my strongest skill."

"Yes," I said. I waited for him to speak, and my eyes drifted, distracted, to a painting of a partially clothed woman with a severed head on a plate.

After a moment, the envoy spoke. "It pleases me, and will likewise please His Excellency, that you have offered an apology for your unprovoked attack on the rightful bishop's property," he said. "While the man who hired you may have offered you riches, he is in no position to provide access to the bishopric's treasury, and the upper fortress is impregnable."

As he continued, I felt confused. Hadn't I told him that nobody had hired me and that the bishop's men had fired first? I exchanged a quick look with Quentin. Either he was reciting a memorized speech given to them by the bishop, or his understanding of Latin was very rudimentary. After a moment of reflection, during which I decided it was unlikely that he had feigned his difficulty in conversing in the language, I became aware of an expectant silence.

The envoy looked at me nervously, his hands clasped behind his back as he waited for my reply.

"What did you just offer me?" I asked. "Perhaps my Gothic is not so good, after all."

"Indulgentia plenaria," Quentin said, giving the proper Latin name to clarify. Seeing the puzzled look on my face, he explained further, switching to Magyar. "In the Roman church—perhaps the eastern church is different?—it is a sort of special grant. He is saying he will grant that you will not be punished in purgatory for your sins of transgression against the church by occupying the lower keep, provided you leave it."

It is sometimes accounted rude to converse in front of someone in a language they do not know, but I did not want the bishop's envoy to know that I was a Mikolai rather than a Marcus, and answering Quentin's question in Gothic would have taught that lesson to the envoy. "There is a similar practice in the eastern church; they call them permissive letters," I said. "He offered nothing else?"

"No," Quentin said. "I think his master must not have very much money to spare, but maybe this is just the opening offer."

While the envoy fumed quietly, I scratched Yuri's head, staring at a painting where a crowd of naked people huddled among flames, one being lifted up toward sunny clouds. If there was punishment accounting for sins in the hereafter, I had far worse things to worry about than taking a fort in an action that left only a handful of men dead. I could vividly picture a woman stating uncertainly that the rebels had stolen sheep from the village, her voice rising to turn the statement into a question moments before an enchanted sword swiped through her neck and sent her head rolling in my direction. The destruction of the village and the slaughter of nearly all of its inhabitants was something that still haunted my dreams at least once in every month.

Yuri whined, nuzzling my hand. I brought my attention back to the present, scratching under his muzzle. "I appreciate His Excellency's concern for the well-being of my soul," I said, my voice tightly controlled. "Quentin, please show the gentleman around. I wish His Excellency to know that we are taking good care of his property during the absence of his soldiers."

Quentin stood. "Yes, Lord Marcus Corvus," he said, granting me a title I had even less claim to than "Colonel."

After he and the envoy left, I stood, pacing in a small circle around the room as memories flashed back in front of me and I tried to account for each drop of blood that had stained my hands either literally or metaphorically. After a few circuits, Yuri decided it was a fun game and began trying to trip me up by running back and forth around my legs. I was angry for a moment, but it's hard to stay angry at a dog who just wants to play.

After I rubbed his belly, he told me I was a wonderful person and licked my face. Then there was a knock on the door, and I opened it.

"The other bishop has sent a message, sir," the infantry captain told me, holding up a sealed letter in her hand.

I took the letter and opened it, reading it carefully. The other would-be bishop—the one encamped outside of the upper fort with the army—didn't seem to believe I'd been hired by his rival. He was, however, prepared to offer me a considerable sum for possession of the lower fort, suggesting that the cover of dark night would suffice to conceal this activity from the guns of the upper fort. He was willing to forgive my crime as well as grant me a sum that, based on Felix's estimates of the value of the first day of tolls, amounted to roughly a week's income from river traffic.

I didn't feel confident that the letter was sincere. If he didn't trust me to tell him the truth (and we really hadn't—we'd said quite a lot of nothing while implying, suggesting, and insinuating many untruths), wouldn't he feel justified in deceiving me in return? While his force was small, they could be quite dangerous, particularly if we simply allowed them into the lower fort.

I wanted to discuss the offer with my officers, but the envoy was with several of them, so it had to wait. The Rimehammer cousins were giving him an impromptu tour through the storehouses, with Captain Felix spouting numbers like an accountant and Lieutenant Ragnar asking the envoy questions about the organization of the storehouses, purportedly with the purpose of ensuring that we put the correct goods in the correct places.

The envoy seemed generally unhappy, and Quentin gave me a welcoming look, so I approached. Perhaps it was a good time to try to resume negotiations.

"I hope my officers aren't boring you too much," I said. "Have you eaten? I believe I can arrange to feed you lunch. I was beginning to get a little peckish myself."

"That would be appreciated," the envoy said.

I waved a hand in the general direction of the envoy. "Come with me back up to the sitting room, then. My men will see to bringing up food and drink, and we can perhaps resume our conversation."

Quentin and Georg both gave me a quick military salute—crisply in the former case, and somewhat awkwardly in the latter case—and then dashed off in different directions. Georg was heading in the direction of the kitchen; Quentin was heading elsewhere, which suggested to me that he wasn't going to be of any help fetching food.

"Your men are quite quick to obey you, Lord Corvus," the envoy said. "I look forward to resuming our discussion. Perhaps you have now had time to consider the horrors of purgatory?"

"Perhaps," I said with a shrug, "but I think I would like to converse about earthly matters instead."

By the time we reached the room with the paintings again, Quentin was waiting for us with an aperitif of brandy, having fetched a bottle from somewhere (probably the storehouses). He poured each of us a generous serving, handing the envoy his glass first. While the envoy was taking his first sip, I turned the conversation to the paintings; they were very fine, and I was curious about who had painted them and what they portrayed.

The artist had come up from Tuscany, accompanied by one of his sisters, who had played the part of the model for Salome in the painting of

John the Baptist's beheading. That painting had been the first one purchased by the old bishop back when the old bishop had been a mere priest
(albeit one of high birth) before the old bishop had become the artist's
principal patron. The artist was gone now, although his niece Giselle was
in charge of the maidservants here in the lower fort.

Quentin had just poured the envoy his second glass of brandy when
a trio of maidservants arrived, one bearing a pitcher of wine and the others bearing laden trenchers. The maidservant with the pitcher set it on
one small table before moving two other small tables with the practiced
air of routine, the feet of the little tables landing almost exactly on barely
visible divots worn into the woven carpet.

Evidently, the previous master of the lower fort had enjoyed taking
meals with company in this room. The trenchers went onto the tables;
the maid with the pitcher poured wine for me, eyed the envoy's glass of
brandy briefly, then set down the pitcher and handed each of us a gilded
fork for use with the meal. I thanked the servants (earning myself a surprised look from both Quentin and the envoy); the three maidservants
blushed and curtsied almost as one before hastily departing.

We exchanged polite comments on the food before the envoy
worked his way around to making an improved offer. He told me that
his master was willing to let us keep the tolls we had collected during
our brief occupation of the lower fort, provided we did the would-be
bishop the additional favor of driving off the pretender encamped on
his doorstep. It was not something he was able to do himself, not without great risk, and the Batavis council had staked out a firmly neutral
position in the succession dispute. The indulgence, he added, was worth
considerably more.

After exchanging what I hoped were several meaningful glances with
Quentin, I told the envoy I would take his offer under advisement, not
quite rejecting it but not expressing any great enthusiasm either. I focused
most of my attention on appreciating the food, which was not as hard as
it was good.

This may have been a clever negotiating tactic in other circumstances,
but the envoy didn't offer anything more. As I saw him off on his way, I
thought of the letter in my pocket. It seemed, on the face of it, to be a far
better offer; but could I trust a man who wanted to sneak his forces into
the lower fort by cover of night? At the least, it seemed like a very optimistic strategy, one that relied on inattention.

The distance was not so great between the two forts (only a couple hundred yards), and even if the cloudy weather hid the moon, the clouds were not so thick as to totally block the light. I could imagine that if I held the upper fort, and the rival claimant to my bishopric was moving his forces into the lower fort, it would signal that I no longer had any reason to hold my fire. After all, the mercenary bandits holding the lower fort had chosen sides and would no longer be amenable to negotiations.

CHAPTER TWENTY-EIGHT

In Which I Take Sides

held up the letter that had arrived from the second would-be bishop (the one with the small army camped outside the upper fort) while we had been entertaining an envoy from the first would-be bishop (the one holding the upper fort). "The real question is, can I trust him at his word?"

Quentin swayed back in his seat. "Of course," he said. "He's a priest and from a high noble family. It would be an insult not to take him at his word."

I suppressed a derisive snort. My experiences with being under the command of nobles and priests had not given me great respect for either. The baron we had last worked for had wanted to dissolve our contract after someone (possibly the baron himself) had arranged for a noblewoman to be found in my bed after a night of drinking too much.

The last priest placed over me had been, if anything, worse. Major Alexei Pavlov, the chaplain who had been—at least nominally—my last immediate superior in the chain of command in the army of the Golden Empire. Supposedly, he had been an alchemist, but I had never seen any evidence of that, and the only devotion he exhibited was to alcoholism. He had managed to disappear entirely during a battle—presumably fleeing in cowardice—leaving me in command of a detached portion of General Spitignov's task force in the middle of winter in hostile Avaria.

"I can understand that he will take offense if we accuse him of lying," I said, "but I was asking what might happen if we did take him up on his offer."

Ragnar cleared his throat. "The man is suggesting subterfuge, and all but accused us of employing subterfuge likewise. We don't even know that he really is a priest, or that he really has a warrant from Rome to succeed to the bishopric."

Quentin shook his head stubbornly. "He has a force of steam knights and a small army," Quentin said. "And an arcane-powered mech. Those don't grow freely on trees. Nor is pretending kinship to a duke something a man can do lightly, at least here in the civilized parts of Europe. I don't know what it's like in the Union of Kalmar."

Ragnar bristled at the implication that Scandinavia wasn't a civilized part of Europe. He was about to voice some kind of angry objection, but I held up a hand and he held his tongue.

Quentin continued, ignoring or not noticing the silent exchange between Ragnar and me. "I don't doubt that he's come with the backing of Burgundy, and that means he can't possibly be pretending to have a warrant from Rome. The duke's position has been quite precarious from the start—just five years ago, Leon stripped his predecessor of half of his French possessions. Backing a brother's false claim to have a warrant from Rome would be devastating for the duke."

Felix rubbed his nose. The older Rimehammer cousin had a sour look on his face but was nodding reluctantly. "I'm convinced," he said. "Honor is currency between nobles and their vassals. If it came out that this would-be bishop lied to us to stab us in the back after we let him into the lower fort, it'd cost him dearly while gaining him . . . almost nothing, really, even if he thinks he can defeat us without too many losses. Betrayal for the sake of betrayal is the stuff of fairy tales. I say we take him at his word."

I looked around the room. "But . . . isn't that also true of the other one?"

Quentin hesitated. "Well, yes," he said.

"And don't they both claim that they have a superior right to be bishop?" I asked. "One of them has to be lying about that, at least."

Felix nodded; Quentin shook his head. Both opened their mouths to speak, talking over one another. After a moment, I waved Quentin to silence, letting the more senior officer go first. Felix thought that it was the kind of lie that one could get away with, meaning that it was no real harm to reputation. It was like the difference between a priest visiting a brothel or having a secret mistress, he added, a comparison that provoked a muffled feminine snort from behind a painting depicting thirteen men enjoying a meal together.

As Yuri and I stared at the painting, wondering who else might be listening to the conversation, Quentin explained that he thought both of them had good reasons to claim the title, making the dispute a matter of one of them having a flawed opinion about church law, or imperial law, or about how the two of them interacted with one another.

"Very well," I said, standing up. "If we can take both of them at their word, we send a message to the duke's brother accepting his offer. He has the better bid, so the lower fort is his for the taking. We have to leave it sooner or later, and tonight is none too soon for me."

There was a sound of muffled footsteps from the direction of the painting, which faded rapidly at a running pace. Whoever had been listening was gone. I wrote and sealed a quick note signaling my acceptance of the plan; Felix delegated the delivery of the message to Georg.

In anticipation of the need for rest, I took a nap that afternoon, waking up a little after sunset and then standing watch on the wall as darkness fell. It was a cloudy night, diffusing the moonlight to the point where shadows were blurry instead of being as sharp as they usually would be with a moon in the first quarter. The clouds stayed high in the sky, however, and no fog fell to truly obscure sight.

When the duke's brother and his soldiers made their move, there were still men vigilantly pacing back and forth along the walls of the upper fort; those men surely would be able to easily see the duke's brother's men as they left their campfires. The army traveled in single file, heading straight down the hill away from the upper fort before reaching the towpath beside the river and turning to march east along the river to the lower fort.

As if they weren't already obvious enough, every sixth man in the column carried a shuttered lantern with one shutter opened, creating a splotch of brighter light ahead of him along the towpath. The boilers of the eight-legged steam horses gurgled softly, throttled down to a minimum slow walking speed but clearly audible to my ears, a clear contrast to the crickets and the faint sound of music echoing across the water from the taverns of Batavis.

I watched the upper fort nervously. At any moment it could break out into a bustle of violent activity; if that happened I would have to run for shelter, as I wasn't wearing my armor. For all I knew, preparations were already quietly in motion from behind the concealment of the walls. From the upper fort to the lower fort, the range was short enough for arque-buses to have deadly effect (especially with the advantage of elevation), let alone mortars and cannons.

On the other hand, they might be waiting for orders from the pre-sumptive bishop himself, or they might simply not be paying attention. I shook my head. There was no point in speculating; I had orders to give. "Go tell the men at the western gate to start opening it already," I said. "I don't want the Burgundians waiting outside." Not, I thought to myself, when they could be waiting under artillery fire.

"Yes, sir," the soldier said, turning his face away from the distant camp-fires and pointing it at a spot about two feet to my left. He walked to the stairs carefully, running his hand along the top of the wall. He was so distracted that he nearly tripped on the first step, catching himself along the wall. It was good that I'd told the men on watch not to bring lanterns up to the top of the wall tonight; if he'd been carrying one, he surely would have dropped it, and that would have risked starting an accidental fire.

I watched the file of men and machines slowly approach, the steam knights near the head of the column and the lone mech bringing up the rear. The column stopped about ten yards from the gate, and the man at the head of the column took a deep breath, cupping his hands around his mouth just as the gate began to open. He stood there for a moment, a puzzled expression flashing across his shadowed face as he watched the portcullis rise.

"Hello the castle?" he asked in heavily accented Gothic.

I leaned out, both hands resting on the wall. "Well met," I called out, sparing a quick glance up the hill. I didn't see any signs of attack from the upper fort yet, but that could change at any moment. "Come on in," I added, hoping they would hurry up.

The man peered upward, his eyes scanning back and forth across the wall for a moment. Then he looked back to the column, shouting in an unfamiliar French dialect asking if they should go in.

A voice shouted back an affirmative, and the column moved forward, eight-legged steam horses in the lead. I drew back from the edge of the wall and hastened down the stairs to greet them inside the wall, watch-ing my step carefully so that I would not stumble like the soldier I had sent down before.

When I met him by lantern light, the would-be bishop seemed sur-prisingly young for his appointed office—perhaps in his thirties. His name was Raphael, and he spoke excellent Latin, though his Gothic was less than fluent. Later, I would learn that he also had a very good command of Greek and Hebrew and that—in spite of first impressions—he was usually very good at keeping his seat on a steam horse.

As it was, the first thing I said to him was a question about how many fingers I was holding up. This was because moments after he laid eyes on me in the courtyard, he fell off the steam horse with a sudden start, his eyes widening in shock even before he started to overbalance. Fortunately for me, Raphael's first response to my question was to shout "Stand down!" to his men in French, or there might have been real trouble.

I had every logical reason to trust the Burgundians, as Felix and Quentin had told me, but they had plenty of reasons to distrust a motley crew of foreign mercenaries who were wrongfully in possession of a bishop's toll castle. My men might have outnumbered them, but the Burgundian knights had fine mage-tempered armor. They also had a more experienced war mage with them—not Raphael himself, who required the use of a ritual circle and a calm environment to exercise anything other than his particular talent for reading auras, but the other priest in their party, a retired abbot who was Raphael's chief advisor.

The abbot was something of a specialist in the invocation of elemental power, accounted a master of four elements. His control of fire was deft enough to light arrows on fire in flight. He could summon what I thought of as fire-imps (he called them "cherubs of light"), small manifest spirits that, if unchecked, could wreak chaos on any force reliant on gunpowder. But it was his claimed mastery of earth and water that impressed Felix the most; the abbot said he could instantly drain water out of an earthen tunnel and then reinforce it against collapse . . . or cause it to collapse.

Much of war is siegecraft, and in a late-night, six-way conversation involving myself, Raphael, the abbot, Raphael's knight captain, and a very quiet Georg, the experienced Captain Rimehammer was happy to explain at length how many sieges had been decided by tunnel action and how. Perhaps the numbers were becoming fewer now, he speculated, with the rise of the great bombards and smaller cannons, highly effective against the older fortifications that protected most of Europe's castles and walled cities; perhaps more sieges would be decided by tunnel work in the near future, as star forts with great cannon-proof earthworks became common.

We settled payment, though Raphael said he was in no hurry for us to leave the lower fort. His aura-reading talent had settled his worries about my intentions. The payment he'd offered me amounted to the last of his coin on hand, and he had been nervous about trusting a man he was certain had misrepresented himself.

"You certainly don't have to rush out on a dark and moonless night like this one," Raphael said. "The river can be tricky enough in full daylight when you're trying to ferry heavy equipment across. I feel like I was lucky not to have anyone or anything slip off the edge of the towpath. We can talk more in the morning."

I nodded. "Georg, pass word to the men to stand down and tell them they can bed down," I said. "All but the most minimal of watches. They could still send a force down the causeway—I want men watching it at all times."

Georg's salute was passable this time as she scampered out of the room.

"Oh, to be a young man with that sort of energy at this time of night," groaned the knight captain, the solid iron-gray bar of his joined eyebrows briefly furrowing with envy beneath the wrinkled bald dome of his forehead.

Raphael tried and failed to hold back a short laugh as he glanced at the door that Georg had just left through. "Ah, well, never mind that," he said.

CHAPTER TWENTY-NINE

In Which I Champion a Causeway

To my surprise, negotiations resumed over breakfast the next morning. Things were a little chaotic because Raphael's men had locked up the highest-ranking servants in the lower fort; a precautionary measure, he said.

Raphael wanted to hire me for one more service—not, he clarified, my whole company, but me personally. He had an idea in mind that could avoid a lengthy and bitter siege.

"Trial by combat," Raphael said. "It's an old tradition, but . . . with you, it's a real option, if he takes the challenge."

"You have seventeen knights with you," I said. "Three of them officers." I glanced over at the knight captain, who continued silently spooning groats into his mouth. Getting no explanation from that quarter, I directed my skepticism back to the thick black substance in the small teacup in front of me, and then back full circle to Raphael.

"Father Waldemar Hellenbodus is a war mage," Raphael said. "A strong one. He fought at Varna. If he sent a champion, maybe Sir Guy could take him on, but if he decided to take the field himself, no ordinary knight would be able to stand against him in a trial by combat. You, though . . . I've seen your aura."

I rubbed my temples. I didn't want to admit that I didn't have any real training as a war mage, so I looked back down at the cup in front of me and its dark contents. A quartet of tiny cups had been brought out by one of the presumptive bishop's servants; Raphael, the abbot, and the knight captain had each drained their cups already. I sipped tentatively. It was bitter and sweet at the same time.

I set the cup back down. "Suppose I faced him and lost. What then?"

"Well," Raphael said, "at that point, I would be obliged to give up my claim to being the Bishop of Batavis. Which is why Old Sourpuss over there is glaring daggers at me."

I turned, taking in the abbot's frown. "And if I don't take your offer?"

"Then you go off on your way with my blessing, and I hold this fort until Father Waldemar or I figure out how to break the impasse," Raphael said. "Likely, we eventually fight a battle. Perhaps someone else intervenes to force one of us to back down—the emperor, maybe, or Rome." He shrugged. "I can't offer you coin in hand, but I promise I'll find a way to pay you."

How far was I willing to put my trust in this man? He seemed to be willing to trust me with his future as prince-bishop; my first instinct was to respond to trust with trust. The talent for reading auras might seem weak, but it allowed him to extend a sense of absolute faith effortlessly down from his relationship with God down to his relationship with ordinary mortals—and speaking as an ordinary mortal, that faith was seductive.

"I'll go get my armor ready," I said, standing up.

"Oh, no," Raphael said, shaking his head. "I need you to borrow the armor from one of my knights. You have to look like my champion. Sir Wolfgang's armor, I think? Nobody can know you're my champion."

The knight captain nodded. "He's the tallest we have," the knight captain said. "If it doesn't fit, we'll try to make adjustments."

"But . . ." I paused. "There are enchantments on my armor," I said.

The abbot nodded. "I have a protective vestment you could wear under Wolfgang's plate. It won't have the mass to anchor to like your armor does, but you could power it nonetheless. If you know the standard fourth protection of Saint Jerome?"

I stared at him blankly.

The abbot turned back to Raphael. "Are you sure . . ."

Raphael nodded. "God has placed this man in my path for a reason," he said.

My stomach twisted. I felt I didn't deserve the man's faith, and yet I couldn't bring myself to dispel his confidence in me.

The abbot laid out the orichalcum-threaded robe on the table. "Now, you must be very careful with your pronunciation," he said. "The incantation starts here, on the right shoulder. I will repeat it for you, stanza for stanza, and you will repeat it back to me. Clear pronunciation and rhythm is critical, as is the focused intent. Then we will draw up a salt circle for a binding. It will probably take two or three tries before it takes. These vestments were made for me thirty years ago, and I rarely lend them out."

Laying my finger on the right shoulder of the robe brought the orichalcum threading into focus. It was much like Hebrew lettering, I thought to myself. No, it was Hebrew lettering, of a sort. I muttered along under my breath as I traced my finger along the vestment.

The abbot kept talking. "Now, the first verse is 'Shir heharim . . .'" The abbot's voice stopped suddenly. Presumably, he'd turned and looked at me and realized I was staring at the garment instead of him. "Pay attention," he said with an irritated tone.

The robe flared with bright turquoise light as my finger finished tracing the line. "Sorry," I said. "I got distracted."

"I thought you said you didn't know the standard fourth protection of Saint Jerome." The abbot was irked.

"I don't," I said. "I'm paying attention now, though, I promise. Go on?"

The abbot gave me a hard look. "Joking around like that is inappropriate and disrespectful," he informed me. "You will suffer long in purgatory with an attitude like that."

I watched the abbot leave, still uncertain about what the standard fourth protection of Saint Jerome was. Was it really just the Hebrew poem sewn across the shoulders of the robe? I read back over the words, this time silently, trying to commit the bit of verse to memory. There was a tiny glimmer of light, even though I hadn't said a word aloud. And that, dear reader, is how I learned the fourth standard protection of Saint Jerome.

Seated atop an unfamiliar eight-legged machine, I held an equally unfamiliar lance in my right hand, upon which flew an azure- and gold-striped pennant, a flag I'd never seen before arriving in Batavis. I wore unfamiliar mage-tempered armor, the suit smaller and lighter than Ruthenian steam knight armor; only the horse beneath me was steam powered. Underneath the armor, I wore a badly fitted arming doublet, the abbot's enchanted vestment wrinkled up beneath it.

Behind me stood the abbot and Lieutenant Quentin Gavreau, the former wearing formal robes and the latter wearing his own mage-tempered cuirass. Beside me was Lieutenant Ragnar Rimehammer, the ancient war-hammer I'd given him at his side, his swordstaff at the ready, his face hidden behind his helmet. From the minute motion of the helmet, though, I knew he was watching the messenger.

For reasons unknown to me, Raphael had decided to send Giselle, the niece of the artist whose paintings adorned the sitting room—a woman he'd kept in a locked room until I'd finished putting on the unfamiliar armor. She was wearing a wine-colored silk gown; a long blonde braid ran down her back and just past her belt, swaying gently along with her hips as she walked up the causeway, a gently rolled scroll of paper in one hand.

A pair of guards watched from the upper fort. They had arquebuses close at hand, but they made no motion to ready them.

"Hello the castle!" Giselle called out once she was near, holding her empty hand to her mouth. "I come bearing a message from Raphael de Burgogne." She held up the paper, unfurling it. "He offers trial by combat, promising he will vacate his claim if his champion is defeated."

The guards acknowledged her message, one of them disappearing to speak with others. A little while later, the gate slowly opened, revealing a small cannon, about a dozen soldiers, and an older man in white and gold robes with a pointy hat and a staff with a curled end. By the miter and crosier, I inferred this was Bishop-presumptive Waldemar himself.

After exchanging greetings, pleasantries, a hug, and a short discussion of the health and well-being of both parties, Giselle handed Waldemar the paper; he read it twice, then spent a long moment looking at me. I waited patiently behind the line of salt laid down by the abbot, meeting his gaze as best as I could through the tiny slits of the helmet's visor.

Waldemar read the paper again, then leaned forward to whisper in Giselle's ear. "Who is his champion? The man with the pennant, on the steam horse." Father Waldemar pointed.

"I recognize the armor from last night, Father. I believe he is called Sir Wolfgang," Giselle whispered back, blithely failing to address the man as either "Bishop Waldemar" or "Your Excellency." She continued, "I believe he is a knight banneret. Devout, but not very bright. No magical talent to speak of."

"Perhaps Raphael is looking for a way out," replied the would-be bishop, ignoring the informality of the address. "He cannot simply walk away from his unwise claim. Who is that man standing as his second?"

"One of the mercenaries. His name is Ragnar," Giselle said. "I know it's him because of the hammer—he knows it's enchanted, he wouldn't possibly let someone else have it."

Waldemar nodded thoughtfully. "Raphael is a clever young man to arrange for a neutral witness for his defeat." He stepped back and then spoke loudly. "Go, and tell them I have accepted his challenge. When I win, he shall quit this land and go back to Burgundy."

"Yes, Your Excellency," Giselle said back loudly. She curtsied and walked back down the causeway, stopping just in front of the line of salt laid down by the abbot. "His Excellency accepts the challenge of the usurper," she said. "May I return to the upper fort?"

The abbot nodded. "You are no hostage here," he said.

She walked back up the causeway. I watched the blonde braid of her hair sway gently back and forth until it disappeared behind the waiting soldiers, assuming that Ragnar's vision was fixed in a like position. The gate stayed open after she passed, the soldiers waiting ready for any sudden treachery. I could not fault their readiness; out of sight behind me were a pair of Swedish walking guns, one to each side of the open gate.

Mentally, I rehearsed the incantation I'd learned from the abbot's robe, the cloth of the vestment tingling against my skin underneath the arming doublet. Sitting in the summer weather on top of an idling steam engine is not the most comfortable thing in the world, even if it is a cloudy afternoon. I waited, uncomfortably warm and nervous, still behind the abbot's line of salt.

Then Father Waldemar reappeared, wearing armor that looked to be halfway plated in orichalcum and on top of a horse. He was still holding a staff, but a different one; this one was battered, the tracery of black showing where the silver had tarnished inside the runes. A pointed helmet topped with a crucifix replaced his miter. Giselle also reappeared, looking out of an arrowslit next to the gate.

Slowly, the priest began to ride down the causeway. I opened up the throttle on my steam horse and shifted it into first gear. Moments later, it started forward slowly, the iron hooves trampling over the line of salt. The priest's head jerked back, and a moment later pulled his horse to a stop, looking at me. He turned his head back for a moment, then turned back to face me.

I kept my steam horse moving forward at a slow walk, uncertain if I was supposed to level my lance or not. Was he readying his first attack?

"May I know your name?" Father Waldemar asked, shouting to be heard clearly over the steam engine and a distance of some thirty yards. As an old man, he was likely hard of hearing.

I throttled my eight-legged machine to a stop. "I am called Marcus Corvus," I called out, matching his volume.

Under his breath, Father Waldemar cursed creatively for a dozen heartbeats in his native Gothic, then smoothly digressed into muttering in Latin. Rain started to fall. Another verse of dactylic hexameter and his silver staff dipped to touch the smooth and well-worn stones of the causeway. Ice sprang from the tip of his staff, sheeting down the slope of the causeway toward me.

Belatedly, I realized our duel had begun.

CHAPTER THIRTY

In Which I Slip and Sled

The ice was transparent, flush against the stone. Past the thin line marking the edge of the advancing ice, there was little difference to be seen between ice with more rain falling on it and the natural wetness of the stones behind Father Waldemar. His staff whirled and he continued chanting in Latin.

For now, the eight iron hooves of the steam horse were flush against the stone; they had firm traction. If I throttled the steam horse forward, would the hooves smash through the ice from the weight behind them, or would they slip? Considering my unfamiliarity with steam horses, I would rather dismount, I decided, muttering the protective charm under my breath. Turquoise light reflected off the inside of my armor.

I placed the lance in its holder, unlocked the kite shield from its slot in the side of the steam horse, and dismounted. On both ends of the causeway, I could hear people asking each other questions. Why had I chosen to dismount? Would Waldemar follow suit or ride me down? I paused, looking at the selection of hand weapons on the side of the steam horse as I clung one-handed to the saddle, ice slick under my feet.

Perhaps dismounting had been a bad idea, I thought to myself as I went through my choices. My bronze sword, being too distinctive, had been left behind. I had the choice of two straight swords, one longer than the other; then there were an axe, a warhammer, and a flanged mace. The axe looked most familiar of all the weapons—I had little confidence in my swordsmanship—but I felt confident it would not be of much use against the priest's armor. The warhammer, then; it had a spike on one end. I stuck it through a loop on my sword belt; then, realizing the sword belt had another such loop, stuck the axe on the other side.

Turquoise light flared inside my armor as a barely visible whip of force lashed through rain, deflecting raindrops on its way to strike me; the line of force bounced when it met me, whipping into the steam horse. The mechanical horse's boiler ruptured with a flash of golden light, venting steam. I cried out in surprise and then gusts of wind started to whip up around me.

I needed to fight or the priest would simply knock me down or send me flying off the causeway. My open hand twitched, fingers tying an invisible knot, a glowing line of force lashing out at the priest. The loop settled around his armor and then suddenly broke with a flare of golden light. He was protected. I retied the knot, looping it around his horse's neck, and the priest reached out to break it with his hand.

The horse, however, was unsettled, rearing out of control. Father Waldemar was an experienced horseman, but he was also an old man with one hand on his staff. In reaching forward to break my spell with his other hand, he had necessarily released the reins just as the horse was in the process of experiencing an unfamiliar and unusual sensation. The priest tumbled backward onto the causeway as the horse bucked and stepped forward on its hind legs; then the horse screamed as its front hooves landed and failed to find traction on the icy causeway.

My stomach lurched as the horse started sliding toward me, its hooves sliding over the wet ice. The truly impressive thing is that the creature hadn't fallen over yet, but that would surely change soon. I had to act quickly or be swept down the icy causeway all the way back to the lower fort. I put one foot in the stirrup of the steam horse, then the other on the saddle, and leaped forward over the sliding and screaming horse, maneuvering the kite shield in front of me in both hands. Turquoise light flooded the back of the shield as I pushed hard on the enchantment of the vestments, the song of the mountain—that is, the fourth protection of Saint Jerome—on my lips.

Living horse met steam horse with a crash and a scream behind me; it didn't sound good, but I was focused on my own landing. My reasoning was that a kite shield was not so different from a sled, though icy stone is considerably less soft than snowy ground. There was a blinding flash of light as I hit, and then the inside of my armor went dark as my momentum sent me sliding up the icy causeway. Steel scraped on stone as I slid past the edge of the ice.

Father Waldemar and I both stood up at nearly the same time, the dented kite shield at my feet and his silver staff in his hands. I was younger, and my sudden voyage through the air had been Intentional, but his fall had come first. For a moment, we looked at each other, and then I heard him chanting.

I dashed forward quickly, but not quickly enough, for it was a very quick spell; a thunderclap sounded as he slammed the butt of his staff on the ground, a sudden wave of concussive force knocking me off my feet and into the air as the causeway itself shuddered. I slammed against the chest-high wall guarding the edge of the elevated causeway, fumbling with the hammer at my belt as the priest started a new incantation, this one low and sonorous.

I had heard him clearly, and in desperation, chanted back at him, repeating his previous phrase back at him on my knees, slamming the hammer against stone in a diagonal strike that was neither straight down nor straight at the priest, the hammer bouncing out of my hand and away from me.

Father Waldemar's feet clipped the chest-high wall as he was flung into the air away from me, and he tumbled out of sight as he threw a small object with one hand. There was a distant wail of feminine despair and a fiery blast. Then nothing.

"How many of me do you see?" The voice sounded familiar, and there was a refreshingly cool draft brushing against my face.

I opened my eyes. It was a Swedish man. Lieutenant Rimehammer, I thought to myself, but what was his given name? Ragnhild? No, that was a woman's name. "You're Ragnar," I said, pieces falling back into place. I felt around with my hands. I was sitting against a wall, but what was this? "I have an axe," I said, announcing my discovery.

Ragnar frowned. "Can you stand up?"

"Hmm," I said, collecting my wits about me slowly. My first attempt failed. One leg of my armor was fused straight, the joint melted together, and that made things a bit awkward. Still, I could stand; I heard a cheer in the distance. I turned and saw the lower fort, a mix of mercenary soldiers and Burgundians clustered in the gateway behind a halfway disassembled steam horse.

Then I remembered everything and limped over to the opposite wall, peering down at Father Waldemar's body. There was another priest standing next to him, this one wearing normal vestments rather than armor; I saw one of Father Waldemar's arms twitch, bringing a hand up. I backed away from the wall. At that moment, I felt glad I hadn't killed the man, though I learned later that he did not survive his injuries.

"I won?" I asked.

"You definitely won," Ragnar said. "Let's head down."

I slipped on a patch of ice that Ragnar didn't notice, his feet treading firmly on it as if it were dry ground. Fortunately, Ragnar caught me by the arm; unfortunately, the sudden spike in pain revealed that my arm had been seriously injured, broken in two places during the fight. Later, after we removed the ruined leg of the armor, I discovered fresh pain; my leg was also injured seriously.

Walking on it gingerly, I could get used to the pain; but our surgeon was also a physician. After setting my arm, he inspected my leg closely. It was cracked, he told me, the bone not out of place but threatening to slip apart in two pieces if placed under strain. I should splint it, even if it seemed in place for now, he added, and use a cane to keep weight off it if I could.

Raphael went from being a claimant to the title of prince-bishop to the undisputed holder of the title; even depleted as it was, the treasury of the bishopric could and did provide coin for my services as champion. He strongly suggested I buy a sword. Batavis is famous for its enchanted swords, though swordsmiths elsewhere sometimes copy the signature wolf mark used by Batavis's thaumaturges.

I already had a sword; its bright bronze blade had sufficed for the tasks I had set it to. However, with the prince-bishop personally introducing me to one of Batavis's finest sword sellers and offering to cover the price as part of my earned pay, I ended up with a wolf-mark sword of my own. It was small and fancy-looking, with runed silver inlay down the blade and decorative gems set in the handle; it was suitable for wear at a dress party and quite possibly originally commissioned for a noble lad not yet grown to full size.

We stayed in Batavis for a little while, long enough for the swordsmiths to fulfill a special commission for wolf-marked swordstaves. The Batavis swordsmiths hadn't seen the likes of the Swedish weapon before, but a sword blade was a sword blade, was it not? That gave me an excuse to stick my curious nose into their shop—supposedly to provide guidance as a customer with exacting and unique demands, but in practice to satisfy my curiosity.

Johann volunteered to accompany me as my assistant, as he was quite interested in the enchantment process. This kept him out of mischief, unlike most of my other junior officers. Felix didn't tell me any of the details of the mischief the others got up to, although I know that Ragnar somehow managed to spend or lose every last coin he had on hand without the excuse of purchasing a new sword. We also lost and gained a few soldiers, something that seemed an inevitable part of operating a free company.

With a cane occupying one arm, the other bound in a sling, and the pain of my injuries distracting me, I felt remarkably useless. I could supervise what was in front of me; I could make a simple decision, if someone brought it to me; but I couldn't keep a train of thought moving for very long. The pain was too much unless I dulled it with brandy or poppy juice, which had their own dulling effects on my intellect.

The morning before we loaded ourselves onto a trio of smaller boats headed up the Oen, I had another dream involving being pursued by the hunting hound with the green eyes, the one I'd dreamed about before. Brandy and poppy juice before bed meant I woke with a fuzzy headache that obscured most of the details beyond the rust-colored fur of my pursuer, though I felt for some reason that the dream had been important.

We didn't quite fill the three boats by ourselves, and they took on other passengers traveling to (or at least toward) the capital. One was Giselle, the woman who had been in charge of the maidservants in the lower fort, her long blonde hair tucked out of sight under a close-fitting black mourning cap. She wore a matching black dress and carried a heavy bag; when she saw me she flinched. Ragnar later informed me that she was hoping to find work in an uncle's household.

These were not steamboats, so the trip was very quiet. I spent a considerable portion of it napping in the sun near the front of the boat. The wind was favorable on the first day; on the second day, it died down, and the boats were towed by oxen moving alongside the river. That evening, Fyodor, marking out the course on a map, suggested it would likely take several weeks if the wind had run out on us; the visibly pregnant young weather-witch sitting next to him took that poorly.

On the third day and thereafter, we experienced unusually brisk wind that, unusually, blew perfectly straight along the river during the daytime. It would stop in the evening, at which point we would anchor and a certain very tired-looking pregnant woman would go to sleep. The boatmen were at first appreciative and then grew increasingly unsettled. One boat captain approached me nervously and asked me not to summon up unnatural winds; I told him I had done nothing of the sort.

I'm not sure if he believed me or merely decided it was imprudent to dispute me; in either case, the boatmen were glad to see our backs when we reached the imperial capital of Oenipons.

INTERLUDE

A Letter from Vindobona

Dear Abraham,

I am well, and so is Sara. Thank you for your well-wishes and prayers. It is interesting news you gave us of Constantinople and the sultan's projects. Perhaps one day we will travel to visit, or to stay; with Sigismund II in his declining years, the future is uncertain, and there may be some disturbances here in the Empire. The Margrave of the East has decided to invest greatly in improving the fortifications of Vindobona, though whether he is concerned about Avaria rising, Avaria falling, or his fellow princes encroaching is not clear.

Our little village continues to grow thanks to the fact that the margrave considers building a rail bridge into Vindobona proper a lower priority than expanding those fortifications, and our permanent lodgers have by this time moved out into new homes. The spur line ends this side of the river well outside of the floodplain, and it brings bustling business in commerce. The rooms we have put to good use as an informal boarding house for travelers arriving by rail; it is a better class of traveler than those who arrive by foot, and we have seen all manner of persons pass through our halls.

Two weeks ago, we played host to the officers of a mercenary company, which did not have any business in the city itself but sought to travel upriver—there have been heavy rains to the west and their options were scarce. They paid well, but were such a motley assortment of foreigners that I fear the north must be coming apart in the emperor's old age; once relaxed on their own terms, the officers conversed among each other in at least three different languages, none of them Gothic.

The oldest one was a polite man with faded blond hair and a red beard running to gray, who spoke Gothic very fluidly but with a heavy accent; I thought he was the commander, until a taller man with dark hair and a very odd air about him arrived. They called him the Raven or Colonel Crow; he had with him a most odd-looking sword, a bird for a handle and the end bent in a forward-facing crescent. I do not mean it looked like a Turkish scimitar; it looked halfway like a sickle. And it was bronze!

I am not so sure he is a man if he carries a bronze sword instead of a steel one. Perhaps he is something allergic to cold iron, rather than just a man. The village was positively aswarm with crows for three days. He is supposed to be some sort of wizard, but some things that are not human may seem as such, and some wizards become something other than human when they dive deeply into the magic.

Between the birds and the more ordinary frictions and fears associated with the presence of soldiers in a small village, we were all pleased when they took a chance on an aging paddlewheel barge—that is the barge belonging to Captain Odelbrand that I mentioned in my last letter, the one who had a load of barley go to mold before he could make it upriver. They are supposed to be going all the way to the capital, though with Odelbrand's boat and the height of the river, it would probably take them two or three weeks to get to Batavis—they will have to burn coal the whole way, and that will mean stopping to load coal at least half a dozen places or giving up on steam power and getting a tow.

A week later, I had another unusual lodger, this one a woman traveling by herself who had purchased a passenger ticket. She had two artificial limbs and a rifle; she didn't say what business she had carrying a rifle about, but I assume she was a hunter. Her hair was bright red, the color of a raging fire. She didn't talk very much with me because she couldn't speak Gothic very well. She sent a letter downstream and took passage on a boat upstream.

We are all hoping that the margrave's fortification project is pure wasteful folly and war does not arrive in Vindobona—though we do not wish the sultan overrun by the French and their allies either, now that King Janos has married Princess Marie.

—Joachim

A Letter to Vindobona

Dear Fritz,

If my landlord has been pestering you about my whereabouts, tell him not to expect me back—I have departed Vindobona forever, and there is nothing for him to do but sell my things. The only thing left in my room of any value is the mage-lock I put upon the door, but I am sure he will enjoy the brief fantasy of recouping back rent.

If Margelein asks, tell her I am journeying with a powerful thaumaturge and will return to Vindobona a rich man. Yes, I know, I told you to lie and tell her I was traveling by invitation of a master thaumaturge who wished to take me on, but what I thought was a jumped-up land-knight with some kind of affinity for charming birds is no such thing.

Also, if my aunt asks, I have decided to flee sinful Vindobona to study diligently at the Batavis monastery, having become very pious. She can be disappointed later, but at least she won't try to visit me there. But yes, I have found a master thaumaturge to learn from, if I can convince him I'm a worthy student.

He fixed a steamboat's dying firebox, an antique with unreadable inscriptions, without so much as a preparatory circle, and no, before you ask, not a blood sacrifice either. You must stop listening to those dreadful lectures where Herr Doktor von Stetten dredges up every rumor he's heard of alternative practices from Lithuania, or Tripoli, or Mandaria, or wherever his latest purchase comes from.

Well, he did bloody his nose when he slipped, but that was after he let loose, and the firebox is like new now. The river is running fast and high and we're still steaming ahead! We'll likely make Batavis soon—we may be there before this letter reaches you, in fact, even if it is going down the easy direction of the river.

—J.v.Z.

CHAPTER THIRTY-ONE

In Which I Capitalize on Opportunities

Logistical arrangements took up the better part of our first week in the capital. This involved leasing a fallow field outside of town with a barn on it, and shortly thereafter raising a second barn, which the lessor expected to be able to use after our departure. I was neither the first nor the last man to bring a small army to camp outside of Oenipons, and the terms the landholder offered were both pragmatic and shrewd in small ways like that. In consideration of our misadventures in Dab, it seemed wise. It was also cheap, even for the whole season, especially considering the lower price of food.

For farmers, transporting goods to market can be an expensive prospect and inevitably involves some spoilage along the way. Everything becomes more expensive by the time it reaches the city, especially once it passes from the farmer to a carter to a grocer to a cook, though city folks also generally have more money to spend; and some things, like eggs and milk, don't transport particularly well at all. We were not working in town; at least, most of us were not—I will say a little bit more about that later— and were working from a reserve of money.

I hoped to soon augment that reserve substantially; the baron's letters of credit were meant to pay off his whole contract and then some. Felix was busy with managing the logistics of the company, and I was in no condition to socialize amicably, so the infantry captain was placed in charge of scouting out the capital to determine the lay of the land. As this primarily meant trying to make contact with wealthy nobles, she brought most of the gently born troops with her, including a disproportionate share of officers.

We might also find an employer, though once the letters of credit were redeemed we would be in no rush on that account. Since the previous winter, the Ravens—or Colonel Raven's battalion to anyone with the patience for a formal introduction—had seen multiple battles. The accumulation of injury, trauma, and untrained or lightly trained recruits meant that we were due a rest. I particularly believed that I was due a rest, and out of respect for my injuries, my junior officers contrived to give me one.

The men were put on a mostly voluntary rotation of liberty; they would be on their own for lodging and food in Oenipons, but they would also find it diverting. A few of the more enterprising ones would take up odd jobs in the city, some of them permanently as they thought better of being a mercenary soldier.

For me, sitting in a rocking chair on the porch of our newly raised "barn" and watching Yuri attempt to assist in the herding of sheep—something he was not well suited for—was all the excitement I wanted. The shepherds were tolerant of this as long as he didn't distract the real sheepdogs too much, and the sheepdogs were greatly impressed by Yuri's size and athleticism.

My pastoral vacation lasted for only a little while. As the titular Raven of the Raven's battalion, my appearance in Oenipons was part of the price required for us to exchange our letters of credit for real money. Somewhere, Felix found (or commissioned) a stylish mantle to conceal my slung and splinted arm and a walking stick topped with a stylized raven's head to serve as a cane.

Comfortable neither in limb nor in mind, I focused mainly on avoiding offense, cultivating a taciturn air. Evidently, stories of my role in the installation of Prince-Bishop Raphael of Batavis had spread, albeit in a somewhat chimerical form. Confronted with increasingly fictitious accounts and curious questions, I tried to maintain an image as taciturn and modest.

Yes, I had agreed to serve as the prince-bishop's champion, and I had somehow won. No, I did not have any opinion on the pretense of Waldemar; it was regrettable that a man who had been known as a great champion of the faith and a hero at Varna had fallen. As far as I knew, he had sincerely believed in his pretense to the throne of the bishopric. Yes, I had taken the lower fort quite quickly, as such things go, but matters had been slightly exaggerated, and it was not without loss. There had been unseasonable ice on the causeway later, but I didn't recall seeing any ice while taking the lower fort.

It seemed to be assumed that Raphael had summoned me to Batavis and that I had already been working for him when I took the lower fort. I did not correct this misapprehension. Then came a summons I could not have declined politely even if I had an appointment with a financier: an invitation to call upon a duchess known to be close to Princess Anna, one of the emperor's grandchildren.

This excited Quentin greatly. The princess, he informed me, was known to be a great beauty, and I might be able to lay eyes on her fabled figure at a gathering. In fact, such was her beauty that it proved King Janos was a remarkably level-headed ruler.

This chain of logic required further explanation. Princess Marie was not ugly, he reassured me, but Princess Anna's beauty was storied. It was said that her eyes were so brilliantly blue that only the new alchemically synthesized cerulean dye from France could match it; knowing how bright that blue was from a bolt of cloth that had been part of our payment from the Burgundians, I filed that fact away carefully. He also told me that her complexion was flawless, marked only by the delicate rouge of health in her cheeks; her chin a perfect heart shape; her nose pert, short, and straight; her bosom generous and her waist delicate.

And Janos had to be aware of that beauty. Emperor Sigismund II had sent King Janos not simply a miniature but several life-sized paintings of Princess Anna by southern masters of the art of portraiture. He'd also had the princess tutored in the Magyar language from an early age in an attempt to make the match.

And yet Janos had passed up a legendary beauty for a dowry of modern French muskets and soldiers trained in the way of Emperor Leon's new model army. And now Avaria would gain ships clad in Corsican brass, which never fouls, and would surely be able to fend off the depredations of the vile sultan who presumptuously styled himself as an emperor of Rome due to his possession of Constantinople, unlike Emperor Leon I, who had been acknowledged within Rome itself as an emperor in Rome.

As we were in public, I decided to cut the political digression short—not out of lingering loyalty for Emperor Koschei ruling from a city that he called a third Rome upon Tanais while calling himself the legitimate inheritor of the purple mantle on the basis of the affirmation of senators who had fled Constantinople before its fall, but in recognition of the fact that we were in the capital city from which Emperor Sigismund II ruled his empire.

The elderly man had been crowned by a pope and considered himself Emperor of Rome on a sacred basis, and Quentin was therefore quite close to expressing public heresy in expressing his views of Leon the Usurper. After suggesting that he not discuss politics, I asked Quentin about the proper forms of address and how I might recognize the princess if she happened to be visiting the duchess.

"Amelia told me that you're simply a marvelous dancer," the duchess said, a gloved hand patting my chest in a manner that seemed quite familiar considering the circumstances. Her voice was bubbly, fringed with liquid giggles lubricated by the white wine in her glass. "I simply must have you at my next ball."

"You flatter me unfairly, your grace," I said. I wasn't quite sure who Amelia was, but I did know that my leg hurt after the walk from the carriage. The stairs had been particularly troublesome. I lifted the mantle covering my slung arm delicately, then let it drop. "However, I fear I should warn you that dancing is wholly beyond me at the moment. I'm afraid I haven't fully recovered from the injuries I acquired during my engagement in Batavis."

The duchess offered her condolences and led me into a sitting room, where there were half a dozen people sitting and half a dozen more standing. Four of those who were sitting sprang to their feet, bowing or curtsying to the duchess; they sat down once she took her seat on a couch, patting the empty space next to her. This put me across a low table from the two people who had remained seated on the duchess's arrival. One was an older man—the duchess's husband—and the other was a young woman.

Unlike the other women in attendance, this young woman wore no powder or rouge, though a few neatly inked sigils lined the left side of her jaw. Her face did have a sort of rugged handsomeness to it, with a strong confident jaw and crooked nose; her eyes were a muddy brown. Pockmarks on her cheeks spoke of a childhood brush with illness, yet she had the calm confidence to remain seated while the duchess walked in, suggesting she was either familiar to the point of rudeness or of comparable stature.

The duchess turned to the young woman. "My dear cousin, I introduce to you Marcus Corvus, a mercenary captain who leads a free company," she said. "Hopefully he can break your losing streak," she added, picking up a deck of cards from the table.

"At your service, your grace," I said, nodding respectfully. It was likely that the cousin wasn't also a duchess, but Quentin had told me to err on the side of generosity when addressing someone whose title I didn't know.

She blinked and frowned. "I should hope so," she said, a chilly note entering her voice.

"My apologies, Marcus is from very far away," the duchess said, flipping through the cards one at a time to make sure they were all present and accounted for. Then she shuffled and dealt as the duke and I exchanged polite comments about the weather.

The three of acorns was the lowest face-up card, landing in front of the young woman. We picked up our hands. I had both the banneret and seven of acorns—the cudgel and the devil—and led the latter with confidence. The cudgel was a guaranteed trick I could save for later; the pope and high king were in the deck, and with the others having only one king and one captain for high cards between them, the hand was as good as won already.

Gloating early would be poor sportsmanship, so I schooled my expression as best as I could as we played out the hand. The young woman made the questionable call of dropping her beater three on the captain, with the king coming behind to recover the trick, but I pulled back the lead with the cudgel and led to the void to take the last trick.

We won more hands than not, and the young woman's scowl gradually softened. It was not difficult; the duke and duchess played without regard for what was in each of our hands—as if one could not tell which card was which after she'd taken the care to be fair by showing each one front and back to all of us—and that often cost them a trick or two, especially during hands where most of the beater suit was buried.

After the duchess tired of losing and put the cards away, I made my polite excuses and stood. The seat I vacated was immediately filled by a middle-aged landgrave, who stared most rudely at the young woman's pockmarked face for the better part of a minute before stammering out some kind of self-introduction combined with a series of breathless questions, folding himself in half in a seated bow. The young woman silently mouthed a rude phrase in Magyar under her breath; when no raven materialized to gouge out the man's eyes in response to her wish, she smiled brightly and offered polite, in-depth analysis on the likelihood that the

Avars would be at war with the sultan next year, based on the probable state of King Janos's treasury and the political influences brought by his new wife.

I circulated around the room, focused on committing names and titles to memory and trying to bring up a certain Silesian baron's foundry whenever the subject at hand veered onto the subjects of bells (once), artillery (three times), or what I had been doing before championing Prince-Bishop Raphael's claim to the bishopric of Batavis (four times). Someone with some kind of family ties to the baron, his wife, or the margrave would have the leverage to eventually get the full value of the letter of credit back out of the baron, regardless of the baron's willingness to pay.

The margrave's wife's second cousin was deep in conversation with me about his interest in Venetian commerce when the young pockmarked woman walked out of the room, favoring me with a brief measuring glance that turned into a look of surprise when I directed only a brief smile and polite nod in her direction before turning back to the man. He was the heir to a small but wealthy holding, and I suspected he was in charge of the treasure of his father, the burgrave; he certainly seemed to know quite a bit about matters of money.

CHAPTER THIRTY-TWO

In Which I Pursue a Purse

Discussing the duchess's party with Quentin in a café, I discovered that while the express function of balls is dancing, they are also excellent for conversation and befriending the nobility, even if one is unable to dance. He was quite disappointed that I'd turned down the duchess's implied invitation to her next ball, and moreover that I'd done so in such a way as to intimate that I was disinclined to accept any invitations to balls. In the future, he told me, I should try to avoid refusing invitations—it is easier to decline an invitation by note after accepting than it is to get one back after having mistakenly refused it.

Indeed, depending on the nature of the invitation, I might perhaps send someone else in my stead, perhaps a handsome and charming cuirassier, such as Quentin himself. With that in mind, I refrained from telling Quentin that I had expressly declined (by note) an invitation to a different ball, which had arrived by messenger earlier that morning before Quentin had risen, hosted by an unfamiliar margrave. After all, it was too late to undo that decision as well, and there was little point in disappointing Quentin further.

By way of aiding my understanding and his, Quentin drew several family trees as we discussed the duchess's various guests. The woman I had played cards with—well, "cousin" could mean nearly anything to a noble, as nobles needed to keep careful track of their relations, both for purposes of inheritance and for arranging marriages. The western church forbade third cousins from marrying without special dispensation, and a noble could not simply pretend not to know who all of his great-great-great grandparents were in the way an illiterate peasant might.

The fact that magical talents tended to run in patterns through family lines added extra interest in lineage for nobles. One of the few books that Quentin's mother had made sure he read cover to cover was a treatise on the natural patterns of inheritance of unnatural talent. Some talents seemed to run in a male line or a female one; some talents skipped generations regularly, while others seemed to leave a line forever once they died out.

While literate, I took his point without insult. As the youngest son of the family, my father was already old by the time I left home. I had never met my grandfather, and only three of my aging uncles were still alive the last I had heard; I doubted I knew all of my first cousins on my father's side, much less their children and grandchildren. It was hard enough keeping track of my close family with half a dozen older brothers; it was likely that by now I had at least one new niece or nephew I hadn't met.

At first, I thought Quentin was simply desperate to enjoy himself to the fullest. However, the longer I stayed in the capital with him and the more I learned from him, the more I realized that he was trying to fulfill his familial duty. As a noble stepson out of the line of inheritance, he lived on the edge of the noble class and risked falling out of it once his mother grew old enough. He would be a potential drain on his family's assets unless he proved himself.

He was not temperamentally suited to the priesthood, nor was he a mage. He could prove himself a great hero through service in war; if he'd done so well enough in Wallachia, it might have let him exercise his tenuous claim to a Wallachian title. An advantageous marriage would do just as well, however—or simply befriending the right high-ranking noble.

That is not to say that he didn't become distracted easily by a pretty face or gaming tables—he and Johann both. After Johann heard that I had won ten out of twelve hands with the duke and duchess, he wanted to take me to every gambling den in town. (Not that he played any better than they did.)

I did attend—though did not dance at—one ball, taking it as an opportunity to corner a man I'd met at the duchess's party. The margrave's wife's second cousin proved unwilling to cash out both letters of credit from his burgrave father's treasure. However, he did work out some kind of four-way deal involving an anonymous individual known to the duchess. While I wasn't clear on the terms between the three nobles, our side of the deal seemed as generous as I might have hoped for—nearly full face value on the first letter of credit and three-quarters of the value on the one with the delayed term. We would be able to winter peacefully in Oenipons, as I had hoped, giving us ample time to train, recover, learn, and weigh our options for our next course of action.

The cash traveled back to our temporary headquarters, accompanied by several curious nobles and their bodyguards. This included the young woman with the pockmarked face, who wore a deeply hooded cloak and stayed near the back, accompanied by a very vigilant man in full mage-tempered plate, who carried half a dozen orichalcum-inlaid triple-barreled pistols.

I was keenly aware that these nobles and others like them in Oenipons were potential next employers. As I greeted them with outward calmness, the infantry captain and several junior officers were rushing frantically behind the scenes to stage an exhibition drill as entertainment for our noble visitors. Ragnar made sure to put the men with our new enchanted wolf-mark swordstaves in the front rank, where the nobles would be like-liest to notice them.

I could sense that at least one of them was a full mage, though it was hard to tell which. Likely several were talented. The feeling was very diffuse, and I felt quite unsure. My lack of formal education in magic was taking a toll on my confidence; while I was sure that some purported wizards were fakes (such as Banneret Teushpa), I had no idea why or how I would sometimes feel certain someone was a mage before they used magic.

At the end of the demonstration, the nobles applauded politely, by all appearances duly impressed. By twos and threes, they went back to their carriages, but the woman with the pockmarked face lingered. When we were alone, or rather nearly alone but for her well-armed and well-armored protector, she stepped close.

"You announced yourself at my service earlier, when we first met," she said. "Did you mean that?"

I winced. "I—That is, ma'am, I could be," I said, glancing away from her soft muddy brown eyes. "It is a figure of speech, isn't it? We are not under contract, though, so I have no pressing reason to refuse you."

"Hm," she said. "You will stay here through winter."

"Yes, your grace," I said, interpreting her statement as a question about our plans and remembering my manners. I had never learned her precise standing within the Gothic nobility, and if I had been given her name at the duchess's party, I had forgotten it. Her lips curled up at my affirmation and then back down at the form of address, though only briefly.

"Hmm." She slipped off one of her gloves, then slipped a jeweled ring back on her bare hand before holding it out palm-down. "You may kiss my hand."

In the moment, I wished I had Quentin whispering in my ear. Was this some sort of impropriety, or was it a normal sort of noble thing? I glanced over at her guard, but the slits of his visor offered no clue. I reluctantly took her hand in mine and gave it a gentle peck on the ring, my lips barely contacting her skin. When I straightened back up and let go of her hand, the bodyguard still hadn't moved.

The woman bit her lip momentarily. "Hmmm." She looked me up and down. "You may be at my service later," she said as if granting me some great boon. "But, to be clear, take care that you do not leave this district before winter."

As I watched her bodyguard assist her into her carriage, I realized that her first statement about winter had not been a question at all, but a command. Who was she to offer me orders without having hired me? The carriage jolted into motion with a soft hum, proving that it was powered by an arcane flux engine. One powering each axle—no, each wheel—separately. An engineering extravagance and a thaumaturgical one.

Thinking about who could afford such an extravagance, everything suddenly fell into place. The horseless carriage powered by a cutting-edge arcane flux engine. Her discomfort at my addressing her like a duchess. The way that everyone treated her as important, even though the duchess had not addressed her with a title, only speaking of her as a cousin. The plain face, even—while I had not known many nobles, everyone always seemed to think that noble breeding brought beauty with it. She had to be the daughter (or niece or granddaughter) of one of the emperor's best mages.

Magical talent and noble status tended to correlate but did so imperfectly. While, on average, a duke would be more likely to have magical talent than a peasant (or even a lesser noble) the most powerful mages are rarely conveniently born to the very highest titles. They do, however, tend to gain substantial status and wealth, and often gain a well-born noble wife. The daughter of a powerful imperial thaumaturge might readily borrow the carriages he enchanted and maintained, and could easily have a duchess for a cousin through her mother's side.

Or father's side, if the thaumaturge were a woman, I thought to myself; but no, if the noble blood was on her father's side, then she would have a proper noble rank that would place her neatly in the noble hierarchy, and surely that would have been brought up during introductions. No; most likely, she had a noble mother and had gotten her looks and some measure of magical talent from her lower-born mage father.

It would not surprise me if her father was our mysterious benefactor, in fact; a powerful imperial mage would be able to collect on nearly any debt held by a noble, even one in an outlying march, and was likely compensated well in cash to make up for his lack of hereditary landholdings. Additionally, if her father was the ultimate source of the money delivered, she might feel entitled to give orders on that account, which explained a great many things.

I was distracted and deep in thought as I approached the converted barn, and so the voice took me by surprise.

"Your new woman is very beautiful," a bitter voice said in a feminine register. The words were in Slavonic, and they came from above.

Looking up to the open hayloft, I saw a rifle barrel resting in an artificial hand, both glinting in the setting sun. The red-orange gleam of the reflected sunlight nearly matched the color of Katya's hair.

CHAPTER THIRTY-THREE

In Which I Become Happy

I stared in shock and surprise. "Katya, it's so good to see you!" Then I finished processing her statement. "What? Who? I don't have a new woman," I said.

Katya frowned, her rifle barrel drooping an inch in a direction I found discomforting. "Do not lie to me just to spare my feelings," she said.

Since the woman I had just been talking to had pockmarked cheeks and a crooked nose, I wasn't sure who Katya was referring to. The only new woman in our company was Georg. "I've not taken up sleeping with new recruits," I said stiffly.

"No. The noble lady. You kissed her hand," Katya said. Her rifle barrel drooped several more inches down and sideways. She spoke more quietly. "You called me a murderess. I was a fool to think you wanted me back."

Technically, the one using that particular word had been Vitold, but as I had been more or less in agreement with Vitold at that moment, I didn't feel I had grounds to object, and so remained silent, my heart racing and my mind frozen.

She sighed, her voice taking an edge of complaint. "I understand. She is so much more beautiful and not a murderess. I left you alone and you found a better woman."

I shook my head. That Katya was deadly I could not contest. That she was ugly? That I could dispute. "You're much more beautiful than that woman," I said. "I can't believe you think that you're that ugly." I paused, considering that her lost limbs could be the source of her anxiety. "You may be missing a few pieces, but . . . your eyes, your hair, your lips, your chin, your cheeks, every inch of your face puts hers to shame."

"Lies!" Katya said. "I have not gone blind. I saw what she looked like. I saw you kiss her hand."

"You don't see very well, then," I said heatedly. "When did you last look in a good mirror? In my eyes, you're ten times as beautiful as her. And as far as the hand thing goes, I was just being polite to her because I think her father might hire us."

Katya stared at me. She blinked slowly, putting her rifle down to free her hands, which touched her face and then slid down to the reinforced metal plate that braced her artificial limb and enclosed her upper torso. "But . . . and she has . . ."

"Enough!" I shouted, losing patience with her bout of self-delusion. The fingers on my hand nimbly twisted out a knot; Katya yelped as a line of force looped around her good leg, pulling her out of the hayloft and into my waiting grasp. I hadn't accounted for the full force of a fall from the height of the hayloft or the fact that one of my arms was in a sling, though, and thus we fell in a heap with me on the bottom, Katya's hands gripping my shoulders.

"You're beautiful," I said weakly. "And I want you back."

Katya looked down at me, a bemused expression on her face. She said something—I'm not sure what though, as the pain from my arm flared when she took her weight off of it, and I passed out.

I learned several interesting but unprintable expressions in Venetian after our better surgeon and resident physician confirmed the story about how I had reinjured my arm. The bones were still in place; fortunately, Katya had impacted my arm with the softest portion of her body. Her mechanical leg, on the other hand, had cracked at least one rib, and an impact with the chest plate that braced her mechanical arm had left a large lump on my head. It would be best if I spent most of the next week or two resting as much as possible.

Having established that my injuries hadn't been the result of an attack by Katya and that they didn't need any more immediate attention from me, the surgeon enlisted my help in convincing Katya to let him check on her stumps. He'd been the one to amputate the ruined part of her leg in the first place, and after a fall like that, there could be complications, he informed me.

A very aloof Katya reluctantly accepted my suggestion. A few wipes with an alcohol-soaked rag and a few minutes of prodding later, he pronounced Katya fit, told me to send for him if anything got markedly worse with my condition, and excused himself from our presence to attend to a bottle of grappa. Quentin had picked up the bottle for the surgeon somewhere in Oenipons as a special treat; evidently, treating his commanding officer was a special occasion for the surgeon, especially when said officer knocked his head.

By the quiet muttering in Venetian I heard as he left the converted barn, he'd been worried more about my head injury than anything else, but I seemed lucid enough, and he didn't want to be in range when Katya and I started yelling at each other. I could have told him that I wasn't planning on yelling at Katya, but getting his attention at that point would have required yelling. Given how my rib cage felt, I didn't intend to do any more yelling at all if I could help it. Such a thing seemed likely to immediately pain my ribs and cause greater pains of several kinds in the aftermath.

I'd already yelled at Katya to try to shake her of the delusion that she was uglier than the imperial thaumaturge's daughter—and lost control in a manner that I had no inclination to repeat. Instead, I spoke to Katya quietly. I told her that I loved her, had missed her, and that she was beautiful; I filled her in on our travels and asked about where she had been and how her travels had gone.

In as detached and aloof a manner as I had yet seen from her, she answered my questions in a mechanical monotone as she recapped the various rumors (many of them wildly inaccurate) left in our wake in Dab, Vindobona, and Batavis. She'd traveled by rail to Vindobona and then up the river by horse—by several horses, logically, as she mentioned having "another change of mount" halfway up the Oen. I wasn't sure how much money she'd had with her when she started her journey and didn't press her on questions that popped into my mind.

Had she violated any laws against horse theft or game-poaching along the way? I did not want to know, and I also certainly did not want to sound as if I was accusing her of lacking a moral compass, even though I felt uncertain if she had one outside of her loyalty to the Golden Empire and her personal loyalty to me. My chief worry was that if I brought up the former, she would question the latter.

The fact that she had chosen to travel up the Istros instead of taking a swifter and easier trip downriver to the western edge of the Golden Empire was evidence that I was still important to her. True, she had been highly upset and unreasonable over a misunderstanding and showed a completely deranged perspective on feminine beauty, thinking herself exceptionally unattractive; but people are often quite unreasonable in the grips of jealousy.

In spite of her aloofness during our conversations, she readily assumed the role of caretaker in the absence of the surgeon, repeating as orders his suggestion that I rest as much as possible. She fetched pillows stuffed with straw and brought me meals—I drew the line at using a chamber pot during the day when I could simply walk to the latrines we had dug, though she insisted on my walking there under her supervision, her mechanical arm curled around my waist.

Though I worried that acting as my personal attendant during a period of enforced rest would cause her to lose the remainder of her lingering affection for me—surely if being strong and capable was attractive, being infirm was unattractive—the opposite pattern emerged. As she took care *of* me, she cared more *for* me. My insistence on the fact that she was blessed with greater beauty than the thaumaturge's daughter was met with weaker denials and eventually with fetching blushes. Her right hand lingered longer when she touched me with it. Three days into my enforced rest, she kissed me gently when she thought I had fallen asleep, and two days after that, she let me kiss her when both of us were clearly awake.

That evening, we became closely acquainted with each other's scars, old and new, opening up about the stories behind them. I learned that she'd gotten the odd star-shaped one when she'd sat on a board with a nail in it after falling through the roof of her father's carriage house; she learned that I'd had my leg toasted by Father Waldemar's powerful fire magic, leaving an odd pattern of burns correlating with the joints of the armor I'd been wearing.

While my arm still ached, I felt I was in paradise. Pleasant days stretched into luxurious weeks, the excuse of a fresh injury excusing me from social engagements in the capital for long enough that the invitations slowed to the slightest trickle. As my injuries healed, I grew restless, turning my attention to my company.

During the mornings, I supervised drills or worked on our mechs. My afternoons I devoted to sessions on brainstorming tactics, strategy, and logistics with whichever of my officers was in town, or picking Johann's brain to see what I could learn from him about magic. He seemed eager to expound on everything he knew, yet seemed disappointed at the end of each of our sessions.

Harvest time came, the farms bustling with hectic activity; I started to feel out of place. Yes, the farms were peaceful and familiar; yes, Katya had returned to me; but to be idle (or at least otherwise occupied) as farmers around me harvested fields underlined that I was not home on my family's farm. The strangers here were us, a free company of soldiers, preparing for our next mission—whatever that mission might be.

A sense of obligation began to settle in my stomach. Ignoring invitations became harder, not because there were many, but because I was keenly aware that we did not have a next mission yet. Even if we did not want a next mission until springtime, I could not afford to snub the nobility, and my excuse of sudden infirmity was wearing thin.

I needed to show my face again. I started writing letters back to those nobles whose invitations I had evaded earlier, saying very little directly but trying to make it clear I had not declined their invitations for lack of desire to rub elbows with them . . . even though I would rather have spent my time with Katya on the farm instead.

Naturally, the first reply I received was an invitation to a ball. The second was an anonymous love note, signed only "A," from a noblewoman interested in eloping with me. The second page of that letter presumably included instructions on how to secretly contact her without her relatives learning about it, but an angry Katya snatched it up, crumpled it into a small ball, and tossed it into the fire before I had read more than the first paragraph of the first page.

I felt her subsequent insistence that I decline the invitation to the ball unreasonable, but wisely decided not to push the point. Instead, I reassured her that she was the only woman for me, both verbally and nonverbally. She seemed to fully believe me when I whispered it again in her ear; and still showed no signs of her previous worries when I cleaned off the ink staining her face and tidied up the smudged papers on my desk.

Still, I could not decline every invitation, I told myself. The soldiers who had pledged their loyalty to me would be ill-served, and I could not in good conscience neglect their long-term welfare.

CHAPTER THIRTY-FOUR

In Which I Am Courted

I was reluctant to put Katya into the position of reprising the role of Leontina Odobescu. A fictitious Wallachian noblewoman could be the belle of the ball in the hinterland of the Gothic Empire near the Lithuanian border; however, even with Avaria in between, Oenipons was connected to Wallachia directly by river. The imperial capital also played host to nobles from across all of Europe; I'd met several Castilian nobles and seen, from a distance, an emissary from the sultan who ruled Constantinople.

The risk of discovery was too great. Other risks were also too great; I could recall all too clearly Katya setting a sharpshooter's perch on a rooftop after the ball in Dab. No, I would not be bringing "Leontina Odobescu" with me to any balls in Oenipons, even if—as I assured her—I would be delighted to dance away the evening with her nestled in my arms. And, as Quentin had informed me, the balls were valuable occasions for conversation and business, not simply for dancing, so I would have to attend them. It would be better if Katya stayed out on the farmland, keeping Yuri company and keeping a watchful eye over our mechs and men.

Besides, she would have to leave her beloved rifle behind—it was not a weapon the city guard would be pleased to see enter their city. However, the more reasons I marshaled against Katya accompanying me to the city, the more upset she became. Jealous suspicions flanked my phalanx of excuses, and they were not armored well enough to stand against tears fired out of angry eyes. By way of apology—and socially acceptable armament—I ended up giving her the sword I had gotten in Batavis, telling her that the gems in its hilt matched her eyes, that its length was a perfect match for her arm, and that it was no less precious than she was. I did not feel even one moment of regret as she unsheathed the sword, examining the blade; the smile that broke through her tears was worth all the treasure in the world.

Besides, it was a practical gift. I did not need it for the battlefield, and it seemed a waste as a mere fashion accessory. Katya had no magic and was no stranger to the use of a sword as a sidearm; it was not as if a sharpshooter burdened with a rifle had the hands free to carry a halberd. (Not unless the halberd was also a rifle; I suppose such is possible, given that I saw a man with something resembling a halberd-musket once, though it was short for a halberd and looked awkwardly heavy for use in either role.)

Katya, with her new sword and perhaps a concealed pistol or two, would accompany me in Oenipons as my hooded and cloaked bodyguard through the streets. She would accompany me anywhere that entrance did not require an invitation or some level of social standing. If I went to a ball and a woman seemed to be falling in love with me, I should make excuses to avoid dancing with her, perhaps feigning injury, and I should keep to the ballroom and with mixed company—and under no circumstances should I allow any noblewomen to entice me into a taking a private tour of an estate. Even, I told her, ones with appearances as plain as the woman whose hand I had kissed in front of her.

Katya stared at me for a while in silence after I said that; uncertain as to what feelings lay behind her emerald eyes, I stared back.

"You really mean that," she said. "You actually think that she is ugly."

"Next to you, she is plain in the face," I said. "Ugly seems an unkind thing to say. Not that I would insult her by telling her either to her face."

She shook her head slowly and sheathed the sword. "But you think I am beautiful. In spite of my shortcomings."

"Yes," I said. Having learned my lesson from when I had tried to convince Katya she did not need to be jealous of the baron's daughter in spite of said daughter's more generous physical attributes, I said nothing more about the shortcomings Katya may have been concerned about, nor did I produce estimated measurements to try to quantify Katya's concerns before dismissing them. Nor did I talk about the pockmarked woman's potential strengths as a partner or why men might appreciate her in spite of the plain nature of her face.

Instead, with the wisdom of gained experience, I wordlessly took hold of her hand and kissed it. When she gave me a bemused look, I pulled her hand back up, kissed her wrist, and continued onward until I'd finished kissing away any doubts that she had about my affection for her.

"Free-Captain Marcus Corvus of the Raven battalion," the servant bellowed.

It was my third ball of the season, and I walked forward into the room with a confidence I had not felt before. That confidence lasted eleven steps before a pair of hands seized my freshly healed arm with startling forcefulness. My arm twinged.

"Marcus! Finally! I've been trying for—" A feminine voice briefly paused as slender fingers ran from tricep to bicep. "It's wonderful to see you. You simply must honor me with a dance!" The woman was wearing a bright green gown trimmed and accented with cerulean; her hair was the color of well-aged cheese and tied in cerulean ribbons. After a moment, her familiar face registered.

"Of course, milady. I'd be delighted to dance with you," I said as I tried and failed to remember her name. It was the daughter of the Silesian baron who had employed us. What was she doing here?

A particularly feminine sort of softness pressed on both sides of my elbow as I was pushed in the general direction of the dance floor, the baron's daughter flashing a victorious grin at a knot of staring young women.

"What are you doing here in Oenipons?" I asked, trying to ignore the fact that in her excitement at seeing a familiar face, she had (surely unintentionally) pulled my arm improperly close to her own sternum.

She batted her eyelashes as she looked up at me. "I've convinced my father that it's time I found a husband," she said. "Unfortunately, he has to manage the factory closely right now, but my aunt had been wanting to make a trip to see the capital soon in any event, and I told him she could chaperone me, and . . ."

The excited bubbling of words out of her mouth continued as I glanced around, trying to look for an older woman who might curtail her ward's enthusiasm, perhaps a woman with hair somewhat faded from the color of aged cheese. Then the music paused, the current dance ending, and I took the moment as an appropriate one to extricate my arm from her front and place my other hand on her back.

We danced closely, enough so that the cerulean ribbons in her hair threatened to tickle my nose on several occasions. By the sharp scent of the ribbons, they had not been dyed for long; either the ribbons had come fresh off of a boat, or some enterprising dyer in Oenipons itself had gotten his hands on a measure of the alchemical solution.

Unlike at my two previous balls, I found myself pressed by dance partners; the jealous and curious eyes drawn when the baron's daughter dragged me to the dance floor had turned into admiring eyes once the music started. One woman, wearing an entirely cerulean dress, tried addressing me in bad Romanian and worse Magyar; apparently, it was being put about that I was some kind of dispossessed blueblood from Wallachia or possibly Avaria.

Between Katya's adoption of the identity of "Leontina Odobescu" in Dab and Quentin's tenuous claim to a Wallachian title, it didn't seem like a surprising invention, though I was surprised when I needed to deny being a secret envoy for a dead Wallachian prince.

When I had been an officer of the Golden Empire, I could clearly remember overhearing that Prince Vlad had been sent to the Undying Emperor by the sultan as part of the settlement of peace after the Golden Empire took Wallachia; I could also remember hearing that the ship he had been on, the *Ceres*, had arrived in Tanais as a drifting hulk, a dead helmsman lashed to the wheel and the rest of the crew swept overboard. In all probability, Prince Vlad lay somewhere on the bottom of the Cimmerian Sea; perhaps one of his cousins or siblings was stirring up trouble on the sly and blaming it on the drowned prince instead.

I was glad that I hadn't spent the last year fighting in Wallachia, but the young ladies I danced with told me very little about the latest news from the mouth of the Istros; those who were interested in such things going on in faraway lands tended to be interested in asking me questions about what things were like. Since I preferred that my background remained mysterious in case my *de facto* desertion from the army of the Golden Empire had been noticed by the imperial bureaucracy, I tried to cut those lines of questioning short with dips and other flourishes.

My arm was appropriated by the baron's daughter again after the dancing died down; I then finally met her aunt. This was an older dark-haired woman who apologized for not being able to speak the Magyar tongue, seemed to have no idea that I had worked for the baron, and was most curious about my thoughts on the state of relations between Avaria and Venice.

When I left the ball, I told Katya that I had encountered the baron's daughter. Katya did not seem happy about this event; however, upon our return to our lodgings, she was thoroughly affectionate even as she continued to frown. Twice she referred back to the left sleeve of my shirt, sniffing it as if to refresh her memory of the scent of the baron's daughter's perfume; but afterward she cleansed her palate thoroughly with me. I fell asleep holding her.

When I woke in the morning, I discovered that Quentin had accepted an invitation on my behalf. It was, he told me, one I could not possibly ignore; after he showed it to me, I found myself in agreement.

It was an invitation to attend the opening session of the emperor's winter court, as the escort for a landgravine whose name I did not recognize. This was not an invitation I could comfortably decline—nor was it an invitation I felt comfortable accepting without knowing more information. I pressed Quentin for details. Escorting a noblewoman to a session of an imperial court seemed likely to bear complications as well as benefits.

Quentin's advice on the subject was that I needed to accept, but that I should be cautious at court. The landgravine was an unmarried woman who held title in her own right from her father's early death; as such, she was highly eligible, and I should be wary of suitors jealous of my position as escort. Quentin himself sounded a little jealous of my invitation, for that matter; he had quite a bit of information about her already written up in his notes, including several good likenesses that he had drawn.

We sent Georg off with a quick affirmative reply for the landgravine and sat down to go through Quentin's notes. After going through the landgravine's family tree (all the way out to her third cousins, though her father's side of the chart was mercifully sparse), proper forms of address, the historical tax revenues of her estate for six of the previous eleven years, and some speculative plans Quentin had made for a possible modernization of her castle, I was eventually able to steer Quentin's advice to the subject of the protocol of the imperial court.

We practiced bows and forms of address—mercifully, I should expect my duties to consist entirely of standing around looking fierce and only speaking in the unlikely event that someone addressed me—and then Quentin did his best to fill me in on who else might be present at court from the top down. In addition to the exceptionally beautiful Princess Anna, Emperor Sigismund II had ten other grandchildren, several of whom might be in attendance—as well as two or three of his children.

The duke and duchess whom I had already met would almost certainly be in attendance.

Quentin also had numerous specific pieces of advice on the imperial couple: Sigismund II was old and tired easily, so the session would likely not be too long. The empress—his second wife—was a little younger but had aged poorly, going to fat and senility in a most unseemly way. I should expect her to sometimes mutter nonsense to the emperor, but to pay no attention to it; the emperor still had affection for her in spite of the ravages of age. The emperor himself was rumored to be half blind, which probably helped; but he was still quite sharp. Liars were often caught out in court, so I should keep answers short and vague but honest if the emperor asked me any questions.

The invitation did not specify whether the landgravine was simply going to court to be seen or if she had some kind of petition to present. It was possible that the landgravine had been intrigued personally by my showing on the dance floor. It was also possible that she wanted to be seen with a famous mercenary captain on her arm as a show of force. In the event that she was insulted by a noble with whom she had some kind of dispute, it would be wise to remember that I was not obligated to challenge an offensive noble to a duel on her behalf. Indeed, since I was not technically a noble myself, that could be seen as presumptuous.

That was a relief, though I hadn't imagined there would be any situation in which I felt the need to challenge anyone in Oenipons to a duel.

CHAPTER THIRTY-FIVE

In Which I Face Justice

Landgravine Wilhelmina von Gschwendtberg and escort," the footman announced in a bored voice, and we continued forward into the room, the landgravine's gloved hand tucked genteelly into the crook of my right arm. At my left hip was my sword, in an awkwardly wide leather sheath accommodating its unique bend.

The empress lounged on an oversized cushion, her slim form taking up a small fraction of the available space within the seat of her throne. There was a certain subtle firm roundness to her waist that spoke of the emperor's continued virility despite his advanced age. Her skin was smooth, her hair a lush shade of brown without a single strand of gray, and her ears came to gentle points. Perhaps Quentin had been misled on the subject of her appearance by one of his peers, a youthful joke played on an outsider who had not yet had the privilege of attending court.

In spite of her apparent youth, she took deliberate care to move slowly. She whispered frequently but very quietly, her whispers somehow failing to echo against the walls of the room; I could not make out everything she said, and neither could the emperor. Once in a while, he would tilt his head and she would clasp his hand and lean inward, repeating herself at a louder volume, easily comparable to that of a mouse who is mostly certain the cats are asleep.

"I said, the landgravine's escort is a mage," she muttered softly as the footman continued his steady patter of announcements. "The one from Batavis, probably. I haven't seen him before."

The emperor's chin dipped in the smallest of nods as he gazed in the general direction of the entryway, his clouded eyes unfocused. Power

swirled indistinctly, and I grew certain that the emperor himself was probably one of many other mages in the room.

"Pasha Mustafa, with escort, astrologer, and interpreter," the footman
announced behind me, and the landgravine paused, craning her neck back
to look.

I looked as well; the astrologer met my eyes as I took in his curious
hat and the pouches at his belt. His eyes widened, and he steered the sultan's emissary and attendants to the opposite side of the room while giving a nonsensical explanation involving the "fading of Jupiter"—Jupiter
was at that point waxing as a matter of astronomical reality, and with its
disk slowly growing fuller, there was clearly no reason to talk about the
"recent fading of Jupiter" as some kind of omen requiring Pasha Mustafa
to go to the right-hand side of the court instead of the left.

After a few polite conversations with other nobles, in which the health
and marital status of several dozen other nobles were discussed and half
a dozen contradictory explanations for Pasha Mustafa's presence in
Oenipons were aired, the landgravine took me aside to make sure I knew
how to behave in the imperial court. The landgravine cautioned me that
with the empress present, I should use plurals when addressing their majesties, as the emperor was unaccountably fond of her and had allowed her
considerable authority when she was younger, but that I should not expect
the empress to say anything.

"You mean she won't say anything directly to me, right?" I asked. "She
hasn't stopped talking for more than a dozen heartbeats since we stepped
in the room."

The landgravine's eyebrows twisted toward each other, and she looked
at me for a solid moment before letting out a little giggle. "You have a
strange sense of humor, Captain Crow," she said, then frowned, leaning
close to me and whispering. "But don't tell any more jokes about the
empress, or make any fun of her condition."

"Ah, that," I said, making a curving gesture in front of my belly to
show that I understood she was referring to pregnancy. An old man with
a pregnant young wife could be very sensitive about a large range of jokes.

The landgravine grabbed my hand forcefully, pushing it down to interrupt the gesture. "Right. Don't even mention it. So. Address him as 'their
majesties,' bow to both of them, and so on. The other thing—if you have
to say anything, make it short and simple. No exaggerated boasts about
everything you've done or flattery for the sake of flattery; he can smell

lies. One word answers are great. You've been doing a good job of keeping your lips buttoned so far."

I nodded, filing the information away. "Is it his talent, or a spell, or some kind of enchanted item?"

The landgravine shrugged. "I'm not sure," she said, "but he always knows when a petitioner is lying."

That seemed like a good talent for an emperor to have. Conversation quieted other than the empress's whispers as she told the emperor which directions he should point his head to appear as if he was looking at each of the two petitioners in his first case.

Most petitions were heard quickly; in most cases, the emperor gave an immediate disposition. Most were about issues that crossed borders within the Gothic Empire, particularly relating to river travel and rail travel, and most of the petitioners were merchants rather than nobles. Just when I thought I had figured out what sort of issue required imperial attention, though, a city councilman from Oenipons presented a petition involving local sumptuary laws as related to French dyes (cerulean in particular).

The Gothic Empire is old, grown up around feudal allegiances forged by Charles the Hammer and later his grandson Charles the Anvil—for the most part at sword point or lance tip. Sigismund II governed nothing and everything; whatever fell through the seams between the patches of his empire was his problem to deal with, personally or by delegation. It was, I would later realize, very different from Koschei's feuding ministries; at the time, of course, I thought of the ministries of the Golden Empire as one great faceless bureaucracy.

After a dozen petitions from low-born merchants, Pasha Mustafa looked annoyed. After another twenty, he began to sweat nervously. When the emperor's chancellor called his name, he bounced up on the toes of his feet, the motion sudden enough to set the pasha's belly into a brief wobble. He started forward, followed a moment later by his startled interpreter and one of his escorts, an attendant carrying an ornate scroll.

Pasha Mustafa presented his credentials, handed a small jeweled box to the emperor's chancellor, and offered a simple petition: He wished for a privy audience to discuss certain matters; after a quick whisper from the empress, the emperor beckoned the chancellor forward. The empress grabbed the box from the chancellor, who looked worried as the empress opened it.

"Perfumes and a miniature painting," whispered the empress. "I see. Grant him an audience with just the privy council in attendance, my love. We won't want this bandied about in front of the whole court. Anna may prove useful yet. She may not know Turkish, but she proved her tongue for languages with Magyar."

The emperor frowned at his wife, then turned his sightless gaze back on a point roughly three inches above Pasha Mustafa's head to tell the emissary he would grant a privy audience in four days' time. (In the emperor's defense, the sultan's emissary was a short man, and his translator had done most of the talking for him.)

After dismissing the emissary, the emperor took up the case of a dispute between a duke and a margrave; a river had shifted course during the last ten years, and the boundary between their lands was alleged by the margrave to have shifted along with it. As the margrave's representative droned on, the emperor and empress had a barely audible whispered conversation on another topic. I am not sure the margrave's representative noticed; he was engrossed in reading aloud from a set of prepared notes.

Princess Anna was not in attendance; evidently, she had been shirking her duties of late, preferring to avoid public appearances more and more after Leon the Usurper's daughter married the King of Avaria. Sigismund II would, the empress assured the emperor, have another princess to dote on soon enough, and Anna was old enough to want purpose in her life. She was certainly old enough to marry, and where else would she find a husband? Faraway Castile?

The emperor, for his part, seemed to have concerns that sending the princess east might be taken poorly among his coreligionists, a sign of desperation and loss of faith, and felt that the surrounding terms of any arrangement were of crucial importance. Inheritance was not such an orderly affair among the Turks; Avaria also had a border directly with the Gothic Empire. A princess was worth more than a vague promise of goodwill, especially when the arrangement could provoke controversy.

It was surprising they would have such a conversation publicly in court, especially while a high noble's complaint was being aired, but their whispers were soft and—oddly—didn't echo at all. I could imagine they were speaking quietly enough to believe they had privacy, and nobody was presumptuous enough to disabuse them of that notion.

At the end of the margrave's agent's scripted speech, the emperor said he would send a man to survey the river and thereafter would grant his judgement, dismissing both parties without providing an immediate settlement.

After that, the court descended into informal conversation and light snacks. The emperor chatted amiably with a trio of high nobles, the empress only occasionally whispering to let him know to turn his head a little more one way or another. A little while later, a discreet footman whispered in the landgravine's ear, instructing her to approach the throne.

"You're overdue to marry," the emperor said brusquely. "Your cousin sent me a written petition asking me for your title on those grounds."

The landgravine curtsied deeply to the emperor and empress. "Yes, your imperial majesty. Do your imperial majesties have a particular husband in mind?"

The empress smirked; the emperor gestured his hand dismissively. "Pick one soon," he said, brusquely. "I understand you have a selection of suitors. Is that one of them?" He pointed almost directly at me while pointing his face at the landgravine.

"He has not offered a proposal, your imperial majesty," the landgravine said, curtsying again.

The emperor turned his head slightly to the left, the empress telling him when to stop. "Will you? And who are you?"

"No, your imperial majesties," I said reflexively. "I am called Marcus Corvus, your imperial majesties." True, at least technically. I bowed twice, aiming one bow in the direction of each imperial majesty as all Quentin's lessons about court etiquette jumbled together in my panicked mind.

The landgravine looked piqued, though perhaps not severely offended.

"Not that there's anything wrong with Miss Landgravine von Gschwendtberg, your imperial majesties," I said hastily, trying to avoid offense. "She's very beautiful, as you can—um, I mean, as at least one of your imperial majesties can see."

"Are you calling me blind?" The emperor leaned forward, his face pointed in the direction of mine. The landgravine's hand slowly slipped out of the crook of my elbow as she took a cautious step sideways.

"Uh . . . yes, your majesty?" I said, bowing deeply. "My apologies if I am mistaken. I'm sure you had a very good eye for beauty when you could see things; your wife is very beautiful."

A sharp, surprised inhale sounded to my right as the landgravine flinched, her shoulders and ears coming together involuntarily. The inhale was quickly followed by more breaths as she continued breathing in and out very quickly.

The empress's expression was like a storm, her lips firmly pressed together and her eyes flashing. The emperor, however, cracked a smile. "Truth. Yes, she is."

He turned back to the spot where the landgravine had been standing. "Remember what I said."

With that, we were dismissed. I took the landgravine's hand, placing it in my elbow as I steered her away from their imperial majesties. Once she stopped hyperventilating, she asked me why I had lied about the empress being beautiful, which I took as a sign that she had breathed herself into a delirious state; rather than answering, I signaled a servant carrying a basket full of savory stuffed pastries and handed her one.

"Eat," I said. "It will calm your nerves. I hate to see a beautiful woman in distress, and it's my duty as your escort to protect you from distress, in any event, so please let me help." To be honest, I hated to see anyone in distress, but all things considered, I felt like offering her a compliment might make her feel better.

CHAPTER THIRTY-SIX

In Which I Am Not Hired

Even after escorting the landgravine back from the imperial court, I was unable to sit still. I was excited, concerned, curious, nervous—and perhaps several other feelings besides. Most of all, I was confused, and I felt I needed to talk through everything I had observed in the court, ranging from the city man's concerns over cerulean to the discussions of marriage to the dispute over the wandering river. I wanted insight that I was keenly aware I did not possess. I felt I was barely beginning to understand nobility; royalty was in another category altogether.

After emerging from an alleyway near the landgravine's lodgings to escort me back to our lodgings, Katya had no insights to share. Her father was a member of the landed gentry with a substantial estate, but as the younger child of his short-lived lower-born second wife, she'd grown up largely ignored in favor of his third wife's children and his first wife's grandchildren. In the contention over inheritances and advantageous marriages, she'd been a bored observer her entire life, climbing trees and buildings and practicing her marksmanship instead.

My talk would draw attention, she told me as we walked through the streets. I should watch carefully; there were many dangerous people in the imperial capital, and she lacked a rifle. The sword was very nice; she had tested it and it was very effective, but it would not protect me against someone else with a rifle, and I was not wearing my armor. Perhaps later I could shop for something I could wear in polite company that might protect against sharpshooters?

With her artificial limbs, sword, and the way her head kept swiveling cautiously to the rooftops, other pedestrians gave us a wide berth, though her presence did not deter either of the ravens following us. Perhaps they, too, anticipated mayhem; but if they did, they were disappointed when we arrived at our lodgings without incident.

Quentin and Georg were both present, and I sat the both of them down and brewed a pot of tea while I talked. And talked. And talked. By the time I served them tea, I found both of them had started taking notes; I continued. I told them about how the nobles were dressed; how the sultan's emissary's astrologer had behaved; the cases that went before Sigismund II that day; my refusal to consider marrying the landgravine (to Quentin's visible relief); and the lengthy discussion that emperor and empress had about Princess Anna's prospects of marrying and learning Turkish.

Once I had talked myself hoarse, I poured two more cups of tea, one for myself and one for Katya, discovering then that she had quietly slipped upstairs without my notice. I gulped the first cup of cold tea and sipped the second slowly, nodding at one question after another as Quentin and Georg reviewed the high points of my manic monologue. They had some doubts, however.

"Princess Anna to marry a Turk?" Quentin shook his head. "I can barely credit it. Sigismund led an army against the sultan's father thirty years ago. If one of my new friends here in town had said they'd overheard such a thing, I would have called him a liar."

"It didn't sound like they were certain about it," I said, "but the empress clearly wanted to. Out with the old princess, in with the new one."

Georg turned over a page. "Did she say which one of the emperor's children was expecting a new child?" Georg asked. "Or is one of his grandsons getting married? That would also be a new princess."

"I thought the empress herself was pregnant," I said. "She said there would be a new princess soon enough and patted her belly."

Georg's eyes rolled. "Colonel, she's at least fifty years old. She's just fat."

"Probably closer to sixty," Quentin interjected. "The elder of her two daughters is pushing forty. But never mind that; a new baby princess won't really make much difference. Did the emperor say which cousin was petitioning for the landgravine's title? Was it Albrecht?"

"No," I said. "That is, he didn't say."

"It was probably Albrecht, then," Quentin said, then sat back in his chair. "Beastly how Sigismund just tries to shove women into marriage. Emperor Leon would never do such a thing."

Georg took issue with that statement, and as the argument developed, I slipped upstairs to find Katya. The pressure of my feelings had eased; now that I had pulled the safety valve and released everything, I was completely out of steam. Seeing the window of our room open and no Katya in sight, I poked my head out of the window and invited her to come down from the roof.

"You told the landgravine you would not marry her," Katya said, peering around the corner of a chimney. "Would you marry me?"

"Yes." My response had been immediate, without even a moment's thought. For nearly a dozen heartbeats, both of us were silent as we considered my answer. I cleared my throat. "Now, will you come down?"

She slowly nodded. Wordlessly, I retreated from the window; shortly, Katya alighted on the floor, her metal leg thumping sharply. We did not exchange any more words, neither of us quite ready to speak more on the topic that Katya had broached.

There were no more invitations to the imperial court, although I attended a certain number of balls and masquerades. In a small village near Oenipons, the banns were posted announcing that a Ruthenian traveler named Mikolai would wed Katarina Borova of Khazaria. Having announced to Katya that I would marry her, I could see no cause for delay, nor did I want to lie to a priest. It might have been more convenient to get married in Oenipons, but I neither wished to lie to a priest, nor did I wish to reveal my real name and origin to the nobles of Oenipons; thus, a short trip into the Alpine hills was in order.

When I returned to tell Katya the happy news, however, she told me that I still needed to approach her father for permission to marry and that a wedding could not possibly take place without her father's presence and blessing. This conversation was loud enough to attract the attention of Fyodor and his weather-witch, however, and instead of being taken down, the banns were hastily edited to announce that Fyodor of Ruthenia would marry Nema of Nowhere, the latter name being a pseudonym for a woman who had peculiar concerns about her true name being misused by a priest but was sufficiently pregnant to belay any objections by said priest caused by her refusal to provide her actual name.

The wedding took place on midwinter's day, which was none too soon; Fyodor became a father shortly after the new year arrived. I was later told that the priest of the little village congratulated the lucky couple on having produced a child after what he described as a miracle of Saint Anne—a pregnancy lasting a mere fortnight after their wedding night. Though, he hastened to add, he was too humble to write to Rome to report the miracle on their behalf. Such miracles had occurred in his village before, and there was no need to involve the hierarchy in such matters.

For my part, I would rather have been stuck in a small, snowed-in village up in the mountains than endure twelve nights of festivities in the company of various nobles while Katya waited silently outside. That is not to say that the baron's daughter or the pockmarked thaumaturge's daughter or any of the others were poor company—even the sultan's emissary's astrologer was polite when we found ourselves forced into conversation on Sylvester's Eve, though the card-playing duchess told me later that it was impolite for me to converse with him in Turkish at the card table.

Winter was the season for rumors and dalliances. I soon learned from the baron's daughter that I was not the only one who had heard of the plans to marry the elusive Princess Anna off to a Turk. Later versions of the rumor that materialized during the twelve festival days grew more specific, referring either to the sultan himself or one of his male relatives or perhaps Pasha Mustafa or another high-ranking subordinate. Cognizant of my position as an outsider, I refrained from contributing to those rumors.

Instead, I focused on looking for work—and, on advice from Quentin, on mending fences with the landgravine. Purportedly, I wrote a series of sonnets reassuring her that I had said I would not marry her because I was beneath her notice, and that she was indeed a very lovely woman; these sonnets were both authored and delivered by Quentin. Quentin also penned a cryptically worded but vaguely threatening letter addressed to her cousin Albrecht, imploring him to give up his claim to the landgraviate, which I signed as "Colonel Marcus Corvus" with the mark of a crow. For the price of one very brightly polished silver penny, I convinced one of the ravens hanging around to go deliver the letter, saving me the cost of hiring a messenger.

Albrecht responded to the letter by hiring a free company and riding to Oenipons in the cold depths of winter—or rather, by riding halfway to Oenipons before slipping on the ice, cracking his skull, and having his body delivered to the city gates by a confused free company of mercenaries who wanted the landgravine to pay them what her cousin had promised for the trouble of making a winter journey to take on the Raven's battalion.

After that, the landgravine sent me a note that thanked me and warned me of the possibility that a disgruntled band of unpaid mercenaries might soon launch an attack on my encampment. A week later, I received a fresh invitation to a winter ball hosted by the duchess. At that ball, the pockmarked woman, the one I had figured was most likely the daughter of an imperial thaumaturge, approached me at a moment when both of us were otherwise alone, fan in hand.

"Is this your way of courting Wilhemina?" The pockmarked woman's question, offered in fluent Magyar, was the most direct question I'd been asked all night. Faced with surprised silence, she plowed on to clarify. "Love poems and *pro bono* killings?"

"I am not at all responsible for Albrecht von Gschwendtberg's death," I said in the same language. "All I did was send him a letter."

"His son alleges that your letter bewitched him," the pockmarked woman said. "Your letter or your familiar. You're a war mage. You could have written a spell into it."

"I didn't even write the letter!" I replied without thinking. "And the raven was practically a stranger to me. He's local to the area and had heard about me through the grapevine. That was the first time I said more than two words to him."

Above the fan that concealed most of her face, the pockmarked woman's eyebrows quirked. "If you didn't write the letter, who did?"

"My man Quentin wanted me to make up for her hurt feelings," I said. "He wrote the letter. The poems, too."

"I see," she said. "But you still haven't answered my question. Are you courting Wilhemina?"

"No," I said. "Absolutely not."

"I see," she said. "When the weather warms and the passes clear, you will travel south."

I raised an eyebrow. "Why?"

"Because I will be traveling south. You did say you were at my service, did you not?" A smile reached her eyes over her fan. "Besides, you are the duelist who killed the great Waldemar, the witch who cursed Albrecht von Gschwendtberg, and your mercenary company is larger than the emperor wishes any Rhaetian noble to hire into their house guard. You will have to travel elsewhere for work in any event."

"I said I could be at your service," I said, "but that still requires some payment, and if we are too large for a house guard, surely we are too large for a traveling escort."

"Hm." She nodded her head curtly, and turned away from me.

As I stared at her retreating backside, I believed that last vocalization, not quite even a word, to be the end of the matter. She had wanted an escort to see her over the mountain passes and perhaps further; all she really needed once the pass cleared was a rail ticket to travel from Oenipons as far south as Tridentum. The train through the pass would be protected well enough; if she was traveling even farther south, she could surely hire an appropriately sized escort in Tridentum.

CHAPTER THIRTY-SEVEN

In Which I Come to an Understanding

The streams were running high with snowmelt when I next gathered all of my officers in the same place at the same time. The first train through the pass had been sent on its way to Tridentum just two days before—as soon as a diviner had announced the way was clear enough. The train had returned the next day; the pass was clear enough for travel.

That event reminded me that we had not found an employer in the imperial capital of Oenipons. In light of the pockmarked woman's comments at the ball, I was pessimistic about finding employment anywhere within Rhaetia. It was time for us to consider our plans for departure. Our most plausible choices for directions of travel were northeast down the Oen, southwest up the Oen higher into the Alps, or directly south through the Rhaetian Pass.

Northeast back down the Oen would bring us back to Batavis and the friendly Prince-Bishop Raphael; it would also bring us to the great Istros, which ran from the western edge of the Gothic Empire into the Axine Sea, where it formed the border between Wallachia and Rumelia (and therefore the border between the Golden Empire and the Sultanate). The advantages of the northeastern route were numerous and apparent to officers ranging from Katya (who wished to return to Khazaria for me to meet her father) to Fyodor (who wanted to bring his new wife home to meet his mother) to Captain Rimehammer (who preferred to steer the company north toward his commercial contacts).

The disadvantages weighed privately in my mind. I did not want to be recognized as the suspected spy that I was not, nor as the deserter I was in truth. Torture and execution seemed likely if I returned to the

Golden Empire through Wallachia. Any effort to sneak around imperial authorities in Wallachia would likely bring us into contact with rebels and dissidents who had even greater reason to want me dead. The thought of returning to the site of the massacre that haunted my conscience was nearly unbearable.

As the sun set, I sat with Katya in the hayloft, open to the light breeze that smelled of the coming of spring. We ate and drank; by the time darkness fell, most of the other officers had finished dispersing to their quarters and tents. The soft echo of chatter, music, and laughter from the other side of the barn promised that the mood around the fire pits we'd dug was festive; only Yuri, a pair of disinterested sheepdogs, and even less attentive sheep were in sight. I must confess the heady combination of privacy and an unseasonably frisky breeze that was early for spring went right to our heads.

When a figure in a dark hooded cloak walked softly into view, I froze, startled. Katya, not seeing the figure, writhed and wriggled to make up for my sudden lack of motion, informing me that I should not stop. The stranger paused, turning to the left and right but not quite placing where the voice had come from; the deep hood prevented the person from seeing the open hayloft.

Concerned that Katya had hissed out her statement in Slavonic, but realizing that anything I said could be heard by the unseeing figure below, I clapped my hand over Katya's mouth to signal her silence and worked to satisfy her complaint nonverbally. The stranger walked closer to the barn and out of view and then rapped a fist on the back door of the barn, three sharp knocks that were clear but not especially loud. Then it was Katya's turn to tense with surprise.

A short time later, I hastily donned a pair of trousers, climbed down the ladder, grabbed my sword, and walked to the back door of the converted barn. Peering through the crack of the door, I could make out a jutting jaw with a line of runes and the tip of a crooked nose; it was the pockmarked woman, the one I had deduced was the daughter of an imperial thaumaturge, shifting side to side impatiently and raising her hand to knock more loudly. Not a threat, then; I set down the sword and opened the door.

Her eyes widened and she licked her lips involuntarily. Then she lowered her fist. "I thought perhaps I had found the wrong barn. We leave in the morning," she said. "I have payment." She held out a pouch and jingled it.

I blinked. It took me a moment to recall our previous conversation. I looked at the pouch. It did not look large enough to hold more than a few hundred coins at most. I was not sure how to politely tell a noblewoman that she was grossly unfamiliar with the kind of pay demanded by a substantial force of armed men. A pouch of coin that size might pay for rail transport for the company, but it could hardly cover the wages. "Um . . ."

She pushed the purse into my hands. It felt different than I expected somehow; when I opened it, I saw something surprising. In place of the mixture of silver coins of varying purity and size that normally would occupy a coin purse, there was nothing but the glitter of pure fine gold. I had never seen so much gold in one place, and every coin was a Rhaetian guilder that looked as if it was crisp from the imperial mint, uniform in size and thickness.

"You will be detaching some soldiers from your service," she added. "The landgravine will make her arrangements with them."

"Um . . ." I said again.

"Your honor is bound up with protecting her," the woman explained impatiently. "So release one of your officers and an appropriate number of men with him. The man who wrote the poems is an officer, is he not?"

I nodded.

"Good," she said, patting me on the shoulder. "Make him the officer, and the responsibility will slide onto his shoulders. Now, show me to my night's lodgings and pass word to your men."

"Um . . ." I said for a third time.

Her hand lingered on my bare shoulder. "Is there something wrong?" She squinted up at me, her hood falling back.

Behind me, I could hear the sound of metal clicking on metal from the hayloft as Katya finished clasping the metal chest plate that braced her mechanical arm. Remembering Katya's earlier bout of unreasonable jealousy over the pockmarked woman's appearance, I delicately removed her hand from my shoulder and stepped back to put some distance between us. "We haven't agreed to a contract, ma'am."

"Ma'am?" She frowned; then shook her head. "I don't need a contract. I have the payment you need, and you are therefore at my service by your word. Do you have something better to do? Or some other obligation you have taken on?"

"No," I said, "but . . . where is your bodyguard?"

She batted her eyelashes artfully. "I trust that you can protect me well enough, Marcus Corvus."

I frowned, possibilities percolating through my mind. Katya may have been an independent woman when she was the age of the pockmarked woman, but that was only because she had a distant relationship with her father. "I wouldn't want to steal you away from the capital under the nose of your father," I said, "especially if this is his money and not yours."

She inhaled sharply, biting her lip; then let out her breath, relief showing on her face. "The purse is my own. My father . . . He has been in Luxembourg all winter," she said. She paused, thinking for a moment to choose her next words very carefully. "He should expect that I will take a lengthy trip this spring. A courier was sent to tell him as much already."

From the careful way she chose her words and a tingling of my developing intuition for the social maneuvers of nobility, I felt that I was being told the truth but that there was something important she hadn't told me. After a few moments of careful consideration, I realized an important gap at the end of her statement. A courier had been sent . . . but she had not said anything about a reply. "Do you think your father will respond negatively to the courier's news? I know that not having received a reply yet isn't the same thing as having received permission."

A tight smile turned up the corners of her lips without reaching her eyes. "My father's response to the courier contained no objections," she said through a stiff rictus of exposed teeth.

I paused. I didn't have the full story, but if her trip was authorized by an imperial thaumaturge, perhaps the secrets she wasn't telling me were matters of imperial importance. "Very well," I said and showed her to my bedroom. The weather was warm enough that Katya and I could sleep in the hayloft. First, we needed to tell my other officers of our plan to start traveling first thing in the morning.

For a moment, I worried that Quentin would object to being left behind to protect the landgravine; then I considered the detailed file he'd written up on the landgravine, her holdings, and her family tree, including drawings he'd clearly put hours into. Thus, I was not surprised by his exuberant hugs and thankful praises when I found him and asked him if he would be willing to leave my service to offer protection to the landgravine. I told him he could ask for any volunteers that he liked to support him.

For her part, Katya was disappointed that we would go south through the Rhaetian Pass instead of north to the Istros, but I did my best to make it up to her later that night before we bedded down for several hours of sleep.

I woke before sunrise; there was already a short line of soldiers waiting patiently outside of the barn. At the front of the line were several of my officers with urgent questions regarding the source of the loud knocking that had awoken me from my slumber; trailing behind them were some men who had volunteered to go serve the landgravine with Quentin. In spite of the fact that Quentin already had my permission to take them on, each wished to make doubly sure that I told them individually and face-to-face that they were released from my service and free to fight under a different banner.

As the last waiting soldier slowly walked away, muttering to himself in Romanian under his breath, a dozen crows took off from the roof of the barn. They flew off in half as many different directions, dispersing. The soldier tripped as he looked up at the cawing birds, then froze white-faced on the ground for a full dozen heartbeats as he watched the crows fly off into the distance. When their cries began to fade, he scrambled to his feet. He did not resume walking slowly and muttering; instead, he skipped, singing as he went.

I am not sure why he was so happy; if I said he looked like he was on his way to his lover's house, I would be guilty of casting aspersions on the landgravine's virtue. Perhaps Quentin had a chance at wedding and bedding her, but he was nobly born and a cuirassier officer who had just been made the captain of his own independent squad of men. A roughrider from Transylvania who had perhaps a dozen words of Gothic at his command surely could not be expecting anything of the sort.

Having settled some matters of command, I carried out my morning ablutions and then woke our new employer. If we wished to buy space on the train, I informed her, our departure might need to be delayed. The second train of the morning had been canceled, the second engine sent on by itself with only a single car full of imperial knights to catch up to the first train—and none of the passengers who had expected to take the second train. Cargo was piled up high outside the station.

The pockmarked woman lazily yawned. "We were not going to take the train anyway," she said, then yawned again. "The early trains of the season are quite crowded and expensive. Besides, the train does not go all the way to our final destination anyway. Are we ready to depart yet?"

"Ah. Not quite, ma'am," I said. Recalling figures that Captain Rimehammer had brought up earlier, I frowned, performing a few quick mental calculations.

Accounting for the extra time and supplies, taking the train wasn't really a more expensive way to get from one point to another, not if you had to pay wages along the way for travel; the main difference was that marching was considerably slower and less pleasant. Especially with snowmelt-filled mud along the way. I could only hope that the old Roman road was well kept in spite of being mostly supplanted by the railroad.

CHAPTER THIRTY-EIGHT

In Which I Lie to an Officer

When we reached the road that paralleled the tracks of the railroad from Oenipons into the pass, imperial soldiers stopped us, their captain desiring some discussion with me and my officers while his men searched our wagons and carts. He told us that he had orders to give us; notwithstanding our lack of allegiance to Emperor Sigismund II, we were expected to obey his commands to the letter.

His first order was that we were to keep clear of the tracks as much as possible. They were built for trains, not wagons and carts, and they needed to stay clear for trains. We should not walk on them either. If we stood in the way of the trains, we would surely die, either as a result of being hit by said trains or by a firing squad charged with executing those guilty of interfering with imperial transit. If we damaged the tracks, the latter fate would also find us. Thus, we were to stay off the tracks.

As the Gothic captain discussed all the ways in which we were forbidden to interact with the tracks, his lieutenant silently mouthed along, eyes glazed with boredom. Then the lieutenant shut his mouth and came to attention, helping draw my attention to the fact that the captain had now changed subjects. I learned that Princess Anna was missing, perhaps kidnapped by inimical forces. If we had seen anything that might give a clue—any suspicious activity, riders in the night, or even just a truly, remarkably beautiful woman dressed in peasant clothes and out of place—we should speak of it.

At that moment, Banneret Teushpa suddenly remembered that he needed to tend to the engine of the self-propelled charcoal kiln, excusing himself. He had not previously shown mechanical interest, but I would hardly object to the self-proclaimed wizard applying his decidedly non-magical capabilities toward a more useful endeavor than the occasional sleight of hand tricks that he practiced to entertain his fellow soldiers. Especially not when the imperial captain required my full attention.

Not that I could help the Gothic captain solve the mystery of the missing princess; the only rider in the night that had passed our way was a homely woman, clearly not the elusive Princess Anna—not that I had seen Princess Anna personally, only a portrait of her. I paused. I had seen a life-sized portrait of her recently and had been told it was an exceptionally good likeness. Perhaps I could promise some assistance.

"I have not seen any sign of Princess Anna or of any possible kidnappers, but I do know what she looks like from her portrait, so I will take care to keep my eyes open," I said. "Her face is distinctive enough that I'm sure I could recognize it daubed with an inch of mud from a mile away, if she but turns to glance in my direction."

The imperial captain snorted. "I'm not one of your noble employers to be impressed with wild boasts," he said. "No man can recognize a face from a mile away."

I felt unreasonably insulted but swallowed my pride. "Of course not," I lied, wincing inwardly. Likely the officer was a shortsighted man who blithely assumed all other men were likewise shortsighted to the point of being half-blind. Someone else could correct his misapprehensions. "I was just excited. Still, if I see her, I will send word at once."

The officer waved me off; thus dismissed, I waited while the imperial soldiers finished checking each wagon and cart. Along the way, they asked questions of most of my men. They did not ask questions of either of our civilians, though; the weather-witch glowered too fiercely as she nursed her baby, and the pockmarked woman was completely beneath their notice as she sat next to Banneret Teushpa on the self-propelled charcoal kiln.

They looked right past the plain-looking woman as if she wasn't there—I have seen sometimes that men simply ignore homely women in such a way, pretending they do not exist, and I felt sad for her at that moment. Soon enough, the imperial soldiers finished their search, and we were on our way.

Though there was some mud, it was nothing compared to the deep morass I had experienced every spring in Ruthenia. Additionally, the Roman road was well kept, even if the train was far faster and more efficient. Sometimes trains break down; but also, the limited capacity of the trains made tickets too expensive for many travelers. The Rhaetian Pass was too much of a major route for trade and travel and too close to the imperial capital to be neglected.

It took a full week before Drusipons came into sight, a city nestled among the mountains. Even if it was a good road, as such go, we were moving heavy equipment through the mountains and had not spent much time marching recently; many of us were not in good condition for such exercise. We set camp outside of Drusipons, and I announced to the men that they could each take a day's leave in four separate shifts as we rested, repaired, and resupplied.

The city was abuzz; by imperial orders, the entire city had just been searched from house to house over the course of several days, the entire militia called up for this purpose. The first train to leave Oenipons the morning of the princess's disappearance stopped in Drusipons before the second train had caught up to it, and it had been thought the princess might have been hidden in the city somewhere.

One lurid rumor Vitold brought back from a bakery, along with a sack of morale-boosting pastries, suggested that Princess Anna, rather than being kidnapped, had thrown a jealous fit and taken a boat downriver to Avaria to challenge Princess Marie to a magical duel for the hand of King Janos. It was a ridiculous rumor—I had never heard of princesses dueling over a man's hand—but I could not dismiss it out of hand. She had been brought up to be Queen of Avaria, and the shattering of childhood dreams can drive people to very unreasonable actions.

The next morning, the pockmarked woman tried to convince me that as her new bodyguard, I should be fitted into the armor she had brought. It accounted for half of the luggage she had strapped onto the back of an anonymous-looking donkey and bore royal heraldry. It was of mage-tempered Corsican brass and close-fitting; unlike the mech-sized wizard armor I had built with parts from a steam suit, the legs and arms were true-fitted, meant to be the same length as the wearer's limbs, gauntlets over their actual hands, and boots over their actual feet. It would, she asserted, be suitable for escorting her into buildings, aboard ships, into very small boats, and over light-duty footbridges that would collapse under the weight of a mech.

For my part, I hadn't crossed any such flimsy footbridges over anything worse than a stream I could walk through, and had no need for small boats, and I told her as much. By contrast, while my existing armor was large, it was also very well protected, with over ten times the sheer mass of armor. In addition to the superior protection provided by my existing armor's thick steel plates, the flux engine powered the suit's lightning-fused actuators with far more strength than I personally had.

Nor did the suit's expensive construction do it any favors. Corsican brass was praised for its use as a metal for hull cladding, resistant to corrosion and fouling—it was not known for its strength and hardness, and it was extremely difficult to get in quantity unless you were a shipwright working for Emperor Leon's navy. In spite of its brilliant gold color and the cachet generated by its rarity, mage-tempered Corsican brass was consequently barely as strong as mundanely tempered steel. And that was without considering the additional protection I could gain by powering the protective magics of my wizard armor!

"First, this is also wizard armor," she told me, turning the breastplate upside down and showing me the orichalcum-inlaid runes on the back. "The strength of the protective enchantments is limited only by your own power. These are state of the art."

"I see," I said. The runes on the back of the breastplate looked familiar; I had similar runes inlaid inside my old armor.

She continued. "Even if you were to need the extra protection, you could not wear it where we are going. In Venice, the roads are canals, and much of the city consists of buildings placed directly on the water. They use very small boats to get around the city."

This was the first time the city of Venice had passed her lips as her intended destination. I raised a finger, wanting to interrupt with more questions about my present employer's plans.

She grabbed my arm and continued. "I have faith in the strength of your arms without any flux engine." She squeezed my bicep, a smile quirking her lips under her crooked nose. "But what is most important is that you must be presentable and present. Ideally, I would have brought a tabard or cape for you to wear over the armor, too, something fashionable, but I barely had room in my bags for clothes of my own."

I may, at that point, have mentioned that Prince-Bishop Raphael had provided us with a bolt of cerulean fabric as part of our payment, hoping that perhaps the prospect of hiring a tailor to make her a dress of the color that was the latest rage in fashion would distract her from her project of fitting me into more fashionable armor. This did not shift her focus in the slightest.

As for the fitting of the armor, the procedure was simple but slow. First, we would attempt to put the piece on and see in what ways it fit me ill. (Mostly, I was longer of limb.) Second, I would lie down on a flat surface, generally an empty cart, and touch the piece of armor. Third, she would hold one hand on the piece of armor and the other slowly kneading the corresponding part of my flesh that it was supposed to be better fitted to, reciting Latin poetry with me until I was bored enough to nod off momentarily. Then the woman would pinch me awake once the armor was done.

Katya and Johann both watched us very closely during this process, the former with a sour frown and the latter with a look of utter fascination.

When I asked Johann how massaging my leg helped reshape the metal of the leg armor, he said he didn't see how it could and then paused expectantly, quill in hand, as if he were the one who had asked a question of me.

Katya, that night, asked me the same question, albeit in a rather different tone. I gave her much the same answer at first before hastening to add that I would rather it had been Katya's hand rubbing my leg.

After three days of the fitting process, the pockmarked woman had a tailor fetched from the city to work on a cerulean cape and matching pennants to accent my newly fitted Corsican brass wizard armor, using up most of the cloth Prince-Bishop Raphael had given us. Then we set off down the road to Tridentum, again traveling parallel to the railroad.

INTERLUDE

From the diary of Quentin Gavreau

I may have damned myself by lying to a priest—is that a special sin, or is it like regular lying? At the least, it will be awkward when next I seek confession. Not that I think I can do so in this bishopric without causing trouble. I will write more tomorrow.

As we take ship up the Oen, I find myself once again putting pen to paper. There is much to celebrate—after all, we took a fort without a shot fired, and then settled a succession dispute by winning a duel. And by "we" I mean the colonel himself. For such a momentous event, it was over quickly—they stood a distance apart in the rain, talked to each other, and then for some reason the colonel dismounted.

The warrior-priest on the other side of the duel didn't either dismount or ride the colonel down, which I found confusing; then there was a flash of multicolored light and the priest's horse reared, throwing him. The horse slid down the causeway and then the colonel leaped into the air holding his shield, sliding unnaturally up the rain-slicked causeway until the priest blasted him with some kind of spell. The colonel slammed his hammer down, there was another flash of light, the priest flew right over the side of the causeway, and that was that. Less than a minute.

The priest's daughter Giselle is with us on the boat, which is what brings his death back to mind. Ragnar tried talking with her, but she's not in any mood to have words with him.

I have a new sword—an enchanted sword, bearing the famous Batavis wolf mark! If I should find myself out of all eight shots from my honeycomb pistol and my enchanted pair, perhaps I will use it. In related news, my purse has grown thin.

We have reached Oenipons! The less said about the trip itself, the better, I think. Since the colonel forced me into his service, I have become used to all sorts of rough magics unlike what I saw in the parlors of Paris, but . . . I will say only that I now regret taking the pistols. They are very lovely and bespelled besides, yet yours truly knows the value of a following wind. Sea power is the lifeblood of France from Cyprus to Loegria, and trade is still mostly carried by sail.

Today, I have no jealousy of Fyodor left in me, for I have seen a woman who must be the second-most beautiful woman in Oenipons (the incomparable but untouchable Princess Anna being the first). This woman has captured my heart with but a twinkle of her eyes, and Her name is Wilhemina von Gschwendtberg. I have since learned everything I could about Her, and She is above me, though not so far that I cannot dream. I am but a pretender to a distant title I may never claim, and She is a landgravine in Her own right . . . still, if She needs a champion, a hero—perhaps I can be that for Her.

The von Gschwendtberg maids dally often at the Flying Carpet—it is a coffee house that serves in the Turkish style. I have made myself a regular there, dropping hints and making friends; the hook is set, and their ears will soon be filled with tales of derring-do by the company bearing the banner of the raven—of mighty trolls, three-headed dragons, men who transform into bears. Once they have heard of my many feats at arms and my idle status as the company rests and rearms, I am sure that She will seek my services as a champion—for the landgraviate faces some matters of dispute most easily settled in a duel between men.

I have made a considerable study of her situation, and her cousin Albrecht, and I am certain I can take him either with pistol or lance. If it must be with sword, though, he has a keen reputation, and I am less confident in spite of my wolf-mark blade. I will be practicing my bladework accordingly. I have thinned my purse to the point of beggary by paying a membership fee for a local salle d'armes; they teach mainly the children of upwardly mobile merchants, but such a place is not beneath my dignity when I have barely used my old sword in the last year.

After all, I have been a soldier! The lance and my pistols are my principal weapons, the sword a last resort for when those have failed—and my artistry at war with pistol and lance have been impeccable.

Today there were three crows perched outside of the door of the salle d'armes. I felt the need to clarify that I did not intend to break my blood-signed contract placing me at the service of the Raven's battalion. The colonel allowed some to leave his service in Silesia—perhaps there is hope for me as well. My dreams still lie with Her—but She does not notice me, though now Her maids all know my name.

January 6th—it is Twelfth Night again. I have kept this diary for two years now, and it is rather less than half-filled. My sister will be very disappointed in me. I think she expected me to fill it before she saw me next. Though I do not know when that will be, so perhaps I will manage that task, after all.

Fyodor has married the witch, which disappointed me more than I can account for—since I thought my heart already broken and trampled by Wilhemina these last several weeks. She chose the colonel to be her champion and escort her to court, and worse, her maids say she proposed a marriage to him right in front of the emperor! But he said no, so she is too embarrassed to show her face in public again. I do not know if I should feel insulted on her behalf or relieved that the colonel prefers his own woman to her—and yes, it is the same, the fire-headed, one-armed sharpshooter who rides like a man, climbs like a monkey, and shoots like a demon. Not remotely a peer of the beautiful landgravine.

I will do but what I can; yet I fear God's plan for me involves the mountains of Wallachia and an oath to a prince I have never met, rather than being Wilhelmina's champion and consort. It was a pleasant dream, one in which I joined the ranks of true nobility without further trial and travail (beyond a few duels, at least). No, it is my fate to be bound to the Raven until I die or meet the son of the Dragon.

Today, I am a free man! I am now waiting with a hand-picked squad of men outside the landgravine's lodgings. Dreams can come true!

Two Short Letters

A Letter addressed to Yaroslava Ivanova, District of the Lower
Tanais, Rome-Upon-Tanais, Upper Quarter, Palace of the
Seventeenth Heir-son, Eastern Wing

Beautiful Cousin Yarka,

*I pain from the lack of reply from your grandfather. Please tell me you have
not gotten engaged in my absence—and pray speak well of me to him!
Supervising (or "assisting") General Spitignov is a very delicate assignment
that precludes my taking leave from deployment in Wallachia.*

*Indeed, by way of an example, it will be some time between the writing of this
letter and when I can place it in the hands of the imperial post—for I am writing
in northern Rumelia of all places. Ognyan was not convinced by pure reason
alone that reports of the missing prince south of the Istros must have been confused
with one of his brothers or cousins—Radu the Handsome is one of the sultan's
loyal officers—and could not be dissuaded from an empirical investigation.*

*I am confident that Ognyan is more puissant than any mage-prince the
sultan has chosen to exile to northern Rumelia to guard the border, and we have
a strong company of steam knights with us, but still, no matter is certain in
warfare! Comfort is scarce in Rumelia, and I fear that the general will yet trigger
open war between the Golden Empire, the vile Turks, and the barbaric Avars.*

Until we meet again, I am yours—

—Igor Vladimir Tsarevich

*P.S. Unable to prove General S. wrong—verifications that younger Vlad
present at monastery in Moldavia, Radu dispatched to Thessaly by Sultan
Alaeddin and would not in any case force Rumelians to renounce the sultan's
prophet, General S. insistent that greater magics used and that Danesti cousins not trained in such.*

*P.P.S. We are to go north and west and cross the Istros—reports that the
southern Sarmatian Mountains crossed in force. This letter will go north and
east and to the Istros with the steam knights and may arrive after my next
letter, luck depending.*

*P.P.P.S. Please tell your grandfather that I have been patient as a saint
in putting up with the delusions of General Spitignov—panicked delusion.*

There is no possibility one prince could go from place to place so quickly unless he had wings with which to fly. Clearly Ognyan has been gulled!

A Second Letter addressed to Yaroslava Ivanova, District of the Lower Tanais, Rome-Upon-Tanais, Upper Quarter, Palace of the Seventeenth Heir-son, Eastern Wing

Treasured Cousin Yarka,

We are now fixed in an encampment in the southern Sarmatians, in a fort we have raised next to the ruins of an older castle on the banks of the Ordessus River—the countryside is full of nuisance and uprising, the prince supposedly around every corner. His allies from Avaria, however, are not so omnipresent—the general caught them on their way through the mountain passes. Their leader, a woman, clearly thought herself a real war mage; she bore one of those oversized Gothic swords that have come into fashion in the west among "double soldiers," and wore wizard armor fit for a prince. Any mere boyar would be jealous to possess such!

Upon her capture, she swore she would not tell the general anything; and thus inadvertently preserved her life, as Ognyan Spitignov is determined to extract from her the essential secrets that I doubt she has. Her screams echo from the top of Mount Cetatea daily; she has, by this point, none of her toes remaining. I feel confident she has nothing to tell us; she was promised to the Dragon's son as a child, and is little more than a puppet of Avaria.

Fervently yours—
—Igor Vladimir Tsarevich

The following excerpt is taken from *Ragnar Rimhamar, Gentleman Adventurer,* with permission of the publisher.

"Ragnar," the princess said breathily. She involuntarily licked her lips as she leaned dangerously close, mesmerized. "I can see why Giselle sorrows from your absence," she said. "But I must keep my purity. As a princess, it is my only currency."

"Fear not," I said, nobly resisting temptation. The most beautiful woman in the world had come to me to beg my assistance; I would not be so churlish

as to stain her honor simply because (like so many women before her) she had fallen under the spell of my irresistible masculine charm. "I will keep you at arm's length."

The disappointed princess and I swiftly discussed the necessary arrangements. With my cousin being Mikolai's accountant, I knew what price would warrant the company's hire, and I knew also which among our officers might be indiscreet upon sighting the princess—Lieutenant Quentin Gavreau. The princess would find a ready excuse for why Mikolai needed to send him away.

Then her bodyguard returned, and our conversation had to come to a rude end as the man frog-marched me out of the establishment. Though it pained my dignity and likely harmed my reputation with the owner and regulars, I allowed the princess's bodyguard to do so rather than serving him a lesson on the foolishness of manhandling a great warrior. I knew when and where outside of the palace I needed to make my midnight stand; as much as the princess might have desired my continued company, our conversation was better kept short, lest any suspect.

Unfortunately, someone did suspect! The fiendish Turks either divined her plans by dark and vile magics or had a paid informant in that establishment— for later that night, as I walked through silent streets, I found myself ambushed by six turbaned men, each the size of a walrus, speaking with womanly voices—voices of boys who never had the chance to become men.

The leader drew his scimitar first, a great curved blade as wide as a dinner plate near the tip and as long as a full-grown codfish. "Halt, Ragnar Rimhamar! You shall not assist the princess! She belongs to Sultan Alaeddin now! Surrender now, and you shall keep your hands! Take one more step in the direction of the palace and I shall cut them from you, for you are a thief of women and such is the penalty for thieves!"

"Foul fiend!" I said. With one motion I drew my hammer with my right hand and my pistol with my left; before the eunuch had finished raising his sword high, I had placed a neat black hole between his eyes. For a moment, he stood still, eyes crossing to examine one another through the space where his nose had once been; I, however, was still in motion, my hammer swinging low. With a loud crack, my blow shattered the right knee of the second eunuch and left knee of the third.

I knew I had to be swift; with a shot having been fired, the guard would be searching the streets for the affray. Still, I was outnumbered; as the first three eunuchs hit the ground, their massive bodies causing the road itself to shiver like a shy virgin greeting her lover in a snowbank, I jumped back. Three elephantine scimitars, each large enough to behead an ox, rang out like bells as they struck the cobblestones where I had but a moment before been standing.

"I am no thief of women," I said. "Only of their hearts."

The enraged eunuchs engaged euphorically, grinning gleefully as I parried a hail of swift-swinging scimitars. They had me back on one foot defending myself; even with three of their number lying on the ground, my opponents outmassed me by nearly ten to one, as each was easily twice my size.

"We are the sultan's slaves, and so shall be the princess!" cried one of the eunuchs, his oddly high-pitched voice sounding like a little boy's. "She shall perform lewd and unnatural acts for his decadent delight!"

Frost began to glitter on their blades as I parried again and again, my defense against their greater reach and strength afforded through the mundane magic of superior skill; but my silver hammer grew impatient. My next parry shattered my opponent's sword, the blade brittle from the cold placed upon it; and as my opponents gasped, I struck at the limp sword of the next, shattering it as well. As my disarmed opponents fled through the night, the last of the six stood alone.

"Oh woe! I cannot defeat such an opponent on my own!" the last eunuch said, tears rolling down his face and onto his troll-sized body. "I have failed the sultan!" He then beheaded himself, death being less dishonorable than disarmament or disability.

I could hear the rapid clanking that announced the approach of the city guard and decided to depart. I raised my hammer high. The sympathy of a certain one of the old gods must have been with me, for a bolt of lightning came down from the heavens. The flash of light briefly blinded the guards, shutting their eyes for long enough that I could escape unseen. Perhaps I could have explained to the guards my mission, and perhaps they would have approved; surely no God-fearing Goth would approve of the sale of the princess into slavery!

However, in that moment I deemed discretion the better part of valor and rushed away in a swirl of snowflakes and soot, a winter storm rushing through a warm spring night. I was none too soon, for by the time I arrived at the back wall of the palace, the princess was already dangling from a knotted bedsheet some ten feet from the earth. Two heavy sacks already lay on the ground directly beneath her, tossed out of the window ahead of her trip; I moved them out of the way and positioned myself to catch her.

"Thank you, Ragnar," the princess said as she swooned in my arms. "I could not have held but a moment longer, and would have died without you there to catch me."

Unable to help herself, she stole a kiss from me before I set her on her feet. I carried the heavy sacks to the stables where I had left my horse, and then we rode through the night to the camp, with her wearing a hooded cloak to conceal her appearance. As we neared the camp, I warned her that it was better nobody knew of my heroic deeds on her behalf; she should pretend she slipped out on her own, or better yet, say nothing at all, and react to me as if I were a stranger. After all, I would not want my cousin or my colonel to think I had exceeded my authority by making arrangements with a soon-to-be-client behind their backs; nor did I wish to attract trouble from imperial authorities if she mistakenly gave me credit in too public a setting.

"You can never be a stranger to me, Ragnar," the princess said, wiping a tear from her eye. "But it is for the best that we pretend that we have never met."

CHAPTER THIRTY-NINE

In Which I Take a Fork

It had been easy enough to detour around Drusipons with the bulk of my wagons and supplies, as it lay nestled in a river confluence to one side of the old Roman road. Tridentum, by contrast, sprawled to both sides of the old Roman road, fresh buildings and bustling commercial activity displaying the wealth of the city. It was the southernmost tip of the rail line from the imperial capital and the main point of cargo transfer between the rail line and riverine transport on the Adige. The surrounding mountains also hosted rich veins of silver and the southernmost imperial mint, producing coin of good purity.

I am not sure which factor contributed more greatly to the city's wealth; but either way, I needed to march an army directly through the town in order to pass through.

While a small group of soldiers without heavy equipment might pass into a bustling city with little notice, Raven's battalion was not small and had substantial heavy equipment in the form of steam knights, mechs that looked like more steam knights, artillery, and the necessary logistical supplies to support both artillery and machinery. I had hoped that my new employer would ease the way using her connections as the daughter of an important imperial mage, but after helping me don my fashionable (if questionably useful) brass wizard armor she said she would stay behind.

She insisted that she needed to keep Banneret Teushpa company on the self-propelled charcoal kiln. Perhaps she was fond of being entertained by sleight-of-hand tricks; perhaps she was feeling shy about her appearance being remarked upon by strangers in a city where she wasn't known. After a brief and evasive discussion in which she made it clear that no explanation would be offered for her behavior, I gave up.

Nor was Quentin available to assist in negotiations; he had been left behind in Oenipons in the care of (or rather, to take care of) a certain highly eligible landgravine to whom he had addressed a variety of flattering poems and promises. The particularly clever part was that those poems and promises had been sent in my name with only my partially witting assent, a bit of cleverness that made me all the more certain that Quentin was an effective negotiator even as it irked me.

This far south, the Swedes were out of their linguistic element; the local Gothic dialect was the next best thing to incomprehensible for them, and the main trade language in the area was Venetian. I picked our chief surgeon, who spoke the local Venetian dialect with native fluency, and then Georg and Johann, hoping they could get by using Latin. Katya and Yuri also accompanied me. Four men, two women, and a dog, none with anything more offensive than a pistol or sword, seemed to be the limit of what the skeptical guards were willing to allow through the walls without special permission.

Since we needed to enter in order to obtain special permission, I left it at that. Nominally, Tridentum, along with the surrounding lands, were governed by a prince-bishop, much like Batavis; however, while the prince-bishop's cathedral loomed over the city, most day-to-day authority within the city rested within the hands of a mayor elected by a council of prominent citizens. I expected that I would probably need to speak with several different people in order to arrange passage.

Vitold slipped through unnoticed a few dozen paces behind me, walking close behind a cabbage cart, as if he was a good friend of the farmer.

It was at the train station that I met with local authorities. The train station was not the location I had in mind for meeting with the local authorities, so I should explain how that came to be before discussing the results of that meeting.

While we walked into town, a train arrived from Oenipons on its regular schedule. Among the passengers of that train were Pasha Mustafa and his entourage. The astrologer pointed me out with considerable excitement and consternation, and then the pasha went to a cluster of bored city guards.

"Seize that man in the golden armor," Pasha Mustafa told the guards. "He is guilty of *lèse-majesté*. It is he who is responsible for the scurrilous rumors which caused the princess to flee the capital!"

The city guards were at first reluctant to do the bidding of a man who was clearly a foreign dignitary, but after verifying the importance of the personage making the request of them and receiving a small jingling purse from one of said personage's attendants, they decided to approach me to make an arrest. Not wanting to provoke a violent incident, I handed my sword to Katya, telling her and Yuri to stand down while I presented myself to the uncertain guards. I proclaimed my innocence; the pasha said he had proof from his astrologer and that my sins were written in the stars.

"At least one of Landgravine Wilhemina von Gschwendtberg's maids knew of such a rumor not three days after the first winter court." The rotund and well-dressed pasha pointed up at me. "This man was none other than the landgravine's escort to the first winter court."

"Yes, I was," I said. "And their imperial majesties discussed the subject that very day, though I didn't hear them come to a final decision."

"They discussed the matter privately!" Pasha Mustafa's face grew red. "See? This man spied on the imperial privy council itself! I knew he was untrustworthy the moment my astrologer examined his aura!"

"I didn't say anything to the landgravine or her maid about it!" I said hotly. Only Quentin and Georg, I almost said, and then stopped myself. Quentin, who wrote numerous letters in my name to the landgravine, and who carried most of them there himself. Could I have truly been the one to start the rumor?

The emperor and empress *had* been whispering quietly, and the regular attendees of the court were clearly used to tuning out what they heard whispered—if they even heard it clearly at all. I had barely heard it, after all, and my mother had always told me I had keen ears. Perhaps that had not been idle flattery. With a sinking sensation, I began to suspect that I truly *was* guilty. And if I was guilty, did that mean that the astrologer— the man who had spouted complete nonsense about Jupiter—really could perform magical divination by watching the stars and planets?

It troubled me to think that my conversation with Quentin and Georg could have shifted a star or planet in the sky. True, the stars were innumerable, but they were clearly greatly distant, bright pinpricks occluded by the closer round discs of the planets—which, like the moon, had a brighter and darker part. The heavens moved like clockwork. Were my actions then predestined? Had a star in the sky caused me to tell Quentin that Princess Anna might be sent to marry Sultan Alaeddin?

While I considered these philosophical matters and reflected on what I had seen in the last several clear starry nights, the city guardsmen must have continued walking with my armored arms held in theirs, because I suddenly realized that they were locking the door to an iron-barred cage set on an elevated platform by the town square. There was an unfortunate individual already locked in a set of stocks; evidently, though, I merited more special treatment.

I was still wearing my wizard armor, and the bars were merely cold iron; I could perhaps pry them out of place, if it came to that. For now, though, I would claim innocence and wait patiently. I had not spied on any privy council, and my private report of the emperor and empress's comments on the possibility of Princess Anna's marriage did not seem like it qualified as an act of *lèse-majesté*. I had not been speaking disrespectfully, simply honestly presenting what I had heard. I waited, watched, and listened.

Barges came and left; so did another train. As the sun set, one last barge arrived, pulled upstream by a small boat. It carried a marble pedestal with some kind of statue wrapped in cloth, the crew of boatmen accompanied by a nervous-looking young man wearing an apron and carrying a sack full of tools. An artist, I surmised, as he tried to get the boatmen to unload the statue, invoking the name of the town's mayor; but it was late and the young artist did not have any extra money to offer to the boatmen. The barge was left anchored close to the town square.

Night fell, the weather growing chill, and I grew hungry. Hours passed, and the town grew quiet. Then a figure approached my cell. Vitold. Metal clinked in his hands.

"Shh," he whispered as I stood up. "I'm getting you out of here. Hang on."

"But if I leave, how will I prove my innocence?" I whispered back.

"Think, Mikolai," he whispered back. "We're at the edge of the Gothic Empire. It doesn't matter what they have you in here for; we leave town and they won't be able to do anything. Now shut up and let me focus."

I sighed. Perhaps Vitold was right, I thought to myself as a thick fog began to roll across the town square. Wait—shouldn't the fog hug the river? It was sweeping in from the town to the river. The door to my cell popped open, and I hesitated. "What's with the fog?" I asked.

Vitold looked over his shoulder. "I told them to wait until we got back," he said, an edge of complaint to his voice. "I guess they got impatient. What was this all about, anyway?"

I could hear the creak of wheels and the tread of boots inside the fog. A baby wailed, and the fog momentarily swirled in place before resuming its advance. "The pasha thinks I'm responsible for Princess Anna's disappearance," I said, shaking my head. "I hope that notion doesn't spread."

"Oh. Yeah, we don't want that getting put about," Vitold said. "How did he figure it out?"

"I'm not sure," I said. "His astrologer somehow divined the source of a rumor. Supposedly."

Vitold's face twisted in confusion. "How could he figure out where Princess Anna was from a rumor?"

"I don't think he knows where Princess Anna is," I said. After all, I didn't know where Princess Anna was. I did, however, know where my army was—in the middle of a city they didn't have permission to enter— and I also knew where a mostly empty barge was. At my insistence, we offloaded the statue, which turned out to be a statue of a man holding a trident with a gilded head carved delicately out of marble.

I was amazed that the delicate marble trident did not break. No wonder the artist had been nervous; one nasty bump on the river and his statue would have been ruined. It was only later, as we were drifting downstream, that I found the other trident lying under a pile of canvas—a real one, also with a gilded head, likely the model for the marble version. While I didn't know the artist's intentions in bringing a second trident, I guessed that he had also been worried about the marble trident breaking in transit.

CHAPTER FORTY

In Which I Encounter a Gentleman in Verona

Using the self-propelled charcoal kiln as an impromptu cooking stove, Vitold prepared me a quick meal of thick, fluffy pancakes. Katya insisted on serving them to me, which demonstrated her practiced familiarity with her mechanical hand. (She even straightened the dinner fork afterward.) When I suggested that I was perfectly well and wanted to check to see who was steering the barge and talk about our plans with our client, Katya refused to leave my lap, wrapping the blanket more tightly around us.

"You need to rest," Katya said, loosening my belt to a point where standing up would become cause for embarrassment. "You are now full of pancakes and warm. Sleep."

Reluctantly, I allowed myself to be pushed back down in the cart by the warm weight of Katya. It was less comfortable than usual since she had not taken off her arm; the metal chest plate that served to brace her mechanical arm was hard.

The river was flowing well with snowmelt, and Tridentum had passed well out of sight. The trident, however, remained with us. I had slept in well past sunrise, as well as the change of shifts between the night crew who had stayed awake and those who had slept. As other officers had matters well in hand at the changing of the shifts, there was little for me to do but worry.

The gilded and painted trident was a reminder of the city we'd left behind; hopefully, the artist had seen his statue installed without breaking the carved trident, which was the most delicate part of his work.

Also, I hoped I had not become a wanted fugitive across the Gothic Empire; I knew that within the Golden Empire, notices sometimes circulated from the capital regarding fugitive persons who had offended the pride of the Undying Emperor. An accusation of *lèse-majesté* was a serious matter.

Under my fretful handling (and perhaps two or three throws at a practice target after I decided I liked the balance of it), the gold leaf began to wear off the points of the trident, showing verdigris beneath. Recalling what I had read about bronze, verdigris, copper, and gold in the alchemical text, I had an idea, which I then discussed with Vitold. For my part, I set a fishing line while Vitold disconnected the charcoal kiln's engine and went to work.

Two hours later, the kiln was functioning as a high-temperature furnace fueled by some of our precious coal, Vitold had a pot of a muddy-looking brown paste prepared, and I had caught seven bream. Six I laid off to the side; it had taken me that long to find one large enough for what I wanted to do. The fish was sliced almost (but not wholly) in half, the brown paste evenly applied to both sides as Johann watched with growing curiosity, and then I sandwiched the head of the trident inside the fish. Vitold, armed with needle and thread, stitched the fish shut around the head of the trident while I held the haft.

I wore a thick pair of double-layered leather gloves, mechanic's coveralls, and the protective mask of my old trade, a translucent layer of hard resin blurring my vision. We had rarely worn the masks past training; they protected one's face from high-pressure steam venting unexpectedly, but they distorted vision horribly, and the rigid things sat uncomfortably on the face of anyone with a normally sized nose. Vitold opened the door to the kiln, and I shoved the trident deep within, praying that alchemy really did work as mundanely as the book seemed to describe.

Heat, then steam, then steam and smoke poured out of the kiln door, but I held the trident firmly. The haft warmed in my grip, paint peeling off of it. The air smelled of burned fish; I still waited until my hands were uncomfortably warm, then pulled the trident's head out of the kiln. The fish had become an unrecognizable lump of black charcoal; Vitold helped knock it loose with the flat side of a three-quarter-inch wrench.

"Orichalcum!" Johann seemed to suddenly find alchemy considerably more interesting now that he was faced with its product. "You've turned it into solid orichalcum!"

"Well done, Vitold," I said, holding up the trident to the sky. If I understood the alchemical process correctly, the trident had only a very thin layer of orichalcum on its head.

"You will mage-temper it next?" Johann asked, leaning forward.

I paused, bringing the trident horizontal. "How would I do that?" I paused.

Nervously but eagerly, Johann stepped forward, a small knife appearing in his hand, then hesitated. "You are sure you wish me to . . ."

I nodded.

Johann swallowed, then slashed his left arm and squeezed, chanting in bookish Latin as his blood dripped hissing onto the trident's head. He stepped back.

"Is that all?" I asked.

"Well, it's blood-seasoned but not quenched. Then it would go back in for the time that the smith thinks is right," he said. When I didn't say anything, he hastily spoke again, with a questioning air. "If it's not burned all away, it will remain connected to me? Then the process is repeated, sometimes?" He looked at me, swallowing nervously. When I stuck the head of the trident back into the kiln, he breathed out a sigh of relief.

When I pulled it out again, I slipped off one glove, then pricked my fingers on the sharp tines, repeating his incantation under my breath. Then I turned back to the kiln again to put the trident's head back in a third time, but I had not put my glove back on. When my bare hand touched the haft, I realized how hot it was to the touch and dropped the trident with a shout of pain. There was a hiss as it landed on the damp deck of the barge.

After Katya had bandaged my burned hand, Johann asked about the inscription on the haft of the trident, spelled out in a tracery of fine orichalcum wire sunk a fingernail's width deep.

"It is just how some of the orichalcum melted and ran along the shaft as I handled it," I said, then paused. "In truth, it does look like the writing of the old people of Cimmeria," I said, recalling the scratches on an old copper pot long gone to green. "Yes, it is Hleode. Their writing does not quite use an alphabet; each symbol is an icon for a word." After I'd complained to the little old grandmother about learning the dead language of Latin with its five declensions, only spoken by scholars and mostly badly, she'd insisted I learn the tongue called Hleode and its nine declensions; then made me promise that if she died before me, I would burn her hut, for that was the Hleode tradition—a hut was built when a new generation of a family entered the world and burned when the last of that generation died.

"But what does it say?" Johann leaned forward curiously.

I rotated the trident in my hand, considering several possible directions in which the words might have been meant to be read. "Spear triple-instrument man serves, will man follow, direction heart pulls," I said in Hleode, skipping over one or two symbols I couldn't recognize. Perhaps I would remember them later. I shook my head, switching to Latin, a language more polished by civilization. "The trident serves the man, following his will and his heart."

"Oh," Johann said. "It looks like rather more than that."

"Hleode writing was abandoned for good reason," I said. "Each word is a picture broken down to straight lines so that it can be cut into wood with a knife. It takes a long while to write anything, and there is little chance of writing small neat letters legibly."

We reached Verona in the evening. Some tense negotiations resulted in permission for a few of us to come ashore to purchase provisions before going on down the river; while the city authorities could stop us from passing through by raising a chain anchored on either side by the city wall, they felt the wiser course of action was encouraging us to continue along in haste.

With only a handful of us allowed the liberty of the city for a few brief hours, our employer—the pockmarked woman whom I presumed to be the daughter of an imperial thaumaturge—insisted that she be among that limited number. I, naturally, had to go with her as her bodyguard, wearing my new armor and—by her insistence—also the cerulean cloak, though I should keep a respectable ten paces behind her once we had cleared the docks. She would signal if she needed more direct assistance.

Verona was alive into the evening, and the pockmarked woman flitted from taverna to taverna, drinking only a few sparing sips and saying only a few sparing words; she was there to prod and to listen, asking about the state of the Venetian Republic's trading fleet and its spring convoys; of diplomacy between the Sultanate and the Republic; the sea-weather; and what wars might be in stock for the campaign season on the fertile fragmented soil of the peninsula that had been almost entirely Roman for roughly a thousand years.

War is, after all, mostly a warm-weather affair; most warm seasons in my lifetime had seen armies on the march in the Roman peninsula, home of the condottieri. There were outstanding disputes between Milan and Venice, though armies had not yet started marching about. Perhaps once I had delivered my employer to Venice, the Raven's battalion would find employment locally.

She kept her hood up, for the most part, but still drew attention; one gentleman followed her out of a taverna with the slightly unsteady gait of a man who lacks sobriety.

"I love you!" he shouted at the pockmarked woman.

She turned, startled; his subsequent explanation that she was the most beautiful woman he had ever seen seemed cruel, considering her decidedly imperfect features. When she did not respond to the provocation, he doubled down on his sarcastic teasing by announcing that she was fit to marry him—and he was a scion of a great noble house!

Above the street, a young girl, perhaps thirteen, choked off a sob as she slammed her window shut, cursing the man for his fickle cruelty—presumably empathizing with the pockmarked woman. (It just goes to show that not all pretty young girls are cruel to ugly women; some sympathize with them.) His persistence suggesting a threat, I approached from behind, gripping him by the elbow.

"Unhand me," he cried out, turning to face me.

I released his elbow while thinking of what to say; I settled on a diplomatic statement. "It is not seemly for a nobleman to chase a woman through the street," I said, echoing something that Quentin had told me by way of an explanation of his own behavior and his failure to speak with the landgravine directly before she had invited me to escort her to the imperial court.

"True," the man said, adjusting his puffed sleeve, "but that doesn't give you the right to lay a hand on me! I ought to demand satisfaction."

I looked down at him silently for a moment as I tried to understand what he meant. A curious pair of ravens fluttered over to investigate, one perching on each of my shoulders while I pondered and then gave up. "What sort of satisfaction do you feel entitled to?" I asked.

"Ah," the man said. "Nothing, really, I'll just be heading back into the tavern. Mercutio must be wondering why I ran off."

A smile quirked on the pockmarked woman's face after the man had gone; she went up on her tiptoes to deposit a kiss on my cheek by way of thanks, which made me glad that Katya had not come and then immediately worried that perhaps Katya had come. After I had finished looking for rifle barrels on the surrounding rooftops, I found I was more than ten steps behind the pockmarked woman.

CHAPTER FORTY-ONE

In Which I Ride the River to the Sea

We made our way out of Verona without killing anyone or misplacing any personnel, though after I had ushered the pockmarked woman onto the barge and cast off, I discovered we had picked up several stowaways. Given that their presence was not particularly well concealed, perhaps I should simply refer to them as non-paying passengers. However, even that description may perhaps be misleading.

It was a party of three, a gentleman named Proteus, his servant, and his servant's dog, the latter named "Granso" for reasons that escaped me. (Editor's note: "Granso" is the Venetian word for "crab.") They had been in the process of negotiating (by which I mean demanding) passage to Milan when I had interrupted matters by asking if all supplies had been loaded. Receiving an affirmative reply, I had not waited to order us to cast off. While sneaking aboard a barge full of potentially violent mercenaries to demand unpaid favors may seem an act of dubious wisdom, the fact that Milan lay to the west and our direction of travel was to the east of Verona should remove any doubts with regard to the subject of the wisdom of the gentleman and his servant. As for the third member of their party, I will say simply that Yuri was glad for the presence of a canine playmate and was more tolerant of fleas than I would have been.

When morning arrived, Proteus asked me impatiently how much longer it would be until we reached Milan. During the resulting conversation, he asked for a refund of the price of his passage. As he had offered no payment in the first place, I was happy to oblige his demand, putting him and his servant ashore in the countryside without a penny paid. His servant's dog, Granso, showed little interest in following them, preferring

Yuri's company; I had to give Proteus's distraught servant several pieces of venison jerky in order to entice Granso into departing with his humans.

I considered this a poor sign and was glad to be rid of such an ill-favored duo. Even General Ognyan Spitignov could command the loyalty of his own dogs, in spite of his halitosis and his tenuous grip on reality. (Granted, dogs are fond of many scents that humans are not, including fresh manure and old carrion; both of those scents being reminiscent of his breath, perhaps dogs enjoyed his company because of his breath rather than in spite of it.)

The great Pados River sprawls into a swamp at its end, and that swamp spreads north all the way to the Adige's mouth and the vast tidal lagoon that protects the city of Venice proper against invasion. We moored the barge on a piece of land that seemed solid and then spent several hours waving at passing fishing boats before a fisherman felt bold enough to approach; I pressed a sum of silver into his hands, telling him we would be ready customers for fish for a few days and that a small number of us would want passage to Venice during a high tide in the near future.

My first choice for a companion was our surgeon; as his native tongue was Venetian, I thought him likely familiar with Venice. It turned out that while the surgeon was indeed familiar with Venice, he was unwilling to show his face. Banneret Teushpa volunteered to assist with this problem, claiming he could render the surgeon unrecognizable even to the surgeon's own mother. I felt uneasy about this claim but thought that perhaps the man who pretended to be an illusionist might have a talent for the art of disguise as well.

The Cimmerian rider drew a few quick light lines with the ochre stick, muttering under his breath. Then he made a heavy stroke across each eyebrow, put the ochre away, and gestured grandly. Off to my left, Ragnar muttered approvingly.

The surgeon held his breath nervously, patting his face. Other than his eyebrows having turned the color of rust, he looked much the same.

"You won't feel any difference that way, but look," the Cimmerian said, pulling a small silver signaling mirror out of his pocket and handing it to the surgeon.

The surgeon stared into the mirror, inspecting his slightly altered eyebrows. I suppose the man was too polite to complain about the inadequacy of the disguise, for he slowly nodded, handing the mirror back to the junior officer. "Are you sure it will hold?" he asked, nervously. "There are wizards in Venice."

Banneret Teushpa grinned confidently. "A skilled illusionist may be able to dispel it if they know it's an illusion, but the whole point is that they won't know it is an illusion at all. I especially like using ugly faces like that."

The surgeon rubbed at his chin. "Warts can be a bit repulsive," he said. "I'd rather be just unmemorable."

"Fine," the well-born Cimmerian said, rubbing out one line and drawing in two more, muttering under his breath. "A little less ugly, but there you have it. That satisfy your vanity, *dottore?*"

"I suppose it does," the surgeon said, eyeing himself again in the mirror. "Now I look old, but at least nobody will think I'm poxed or hexed, and that sort of thing matters here. You will come with me?"

With some trepidation, I added the self-proclaimed illusionist to the list. Without Quentin, I felt I needed Georg at my side to help navigate the treacherous waters of etiquette. Additionally, Quentin's presence as a dashing handsome military officer had proven to be effective at drawing and holding the attention of nobles when it was desirable. Fyodor was preoccupied with helping to care for an infant, Felix looked too old and grizzled (especially considering his peg leg), and that logically left Ragnar.

I did not trust Katya in social situations, but I did trust Felix to competently manage the main bulk of Raven's battalion; thus, I decided to bring the infantry captain along as the second-in-command of our expedition to Venice proper. The bulk of our company, waiting in the swamp, would be short on officers as a consequence.

We glided into the city on quiet oars over dark waters. As we approached closely, the surgeon started to give the fisherman detailed directions, guiding us to a grand-looking house that had seen better days. A coded knock on the water door and an introduction of himself as a "friend of Maestro Zilioli" later and he was allowed inside, accompanied by one Swedish lieutenant, one Cimmerian banneret, and the pockmarked woman, who all pronounced themselves also friends of Maestro Zilioli.

As I did not pronounce myself such, I and the others were given directions to more humble lodgings that cost coin. I wasn't quite sure who

Maestro Zilioli was until later when Georg told me it was the surgeon; I didn't recall ever hearing his name, and his signature on his contract had been completely illegible.

In the morning, Banneret Teushpa, wearing Venetian clothing, came by to give me his report: Our employer had secured an invitation to a masquerade, where she would be able to make contact with Venice's upper crust and negotiate arrangements. Exactly what kind of arrangements she sought to make were unclear to the Cimmerian, who told me that I was expected to escort her on the trip to the masquerade in fully polished armor, with my new trident being the perfect prop for me to dress as a masked Neptune.

The Cimmerian hastened to tell me that he would be happy to improve upon my costume, handing me a plain leather mask covered in scribbled writing.

"This is what our employer wants me to wear?" I asked. It looked plain; if I polished my new armor, it would look like I was making a mockery out of the idea of wearing a costume, a heavily armed bodyguard who had offered the thinnest pretense of being part of a masquerade.

"I believe it will suffice," the Cimmerian said evasively. "You should hire a gondolier to take yourself to the house we are staying at—she will expect you at least fifteen minutes before sunset. Wear a heavy dark cloak over your cerulean one on the way over, so as not to attract attention."

I put the infantry captain in charge of the men while Georg polished my armor, cleaned my cerulean cloak, and informed me of everything she knew about Venetian etiquette. This was not much, and most of it sounded like it came third or fourth hand through rumors, but it was better than nothing. She tried to convince me that the Venetians elect a principal leader through a complicated series of elections involving the drawing of lots and several rounds of voting; it sounded like propaganda made up in the Gothic Empire to make fun of the Venetians' government, and I told her as much.

I assumed the reality was probably something like the Roman Republic, which the Venetians clearly admired. In the meantime, the captain let her men explore the city by twos and threes, letting them have liberty but giving them strict instructions to keep an eye out for each other. By the time I was ready to set out, all of the men had by turns gone to the center city and taken a trip down a lane named the Street of Comedy, finding a bridge near there with friendly locals posted to greet strangers.

Each pair or trio returned from that particular tour in good humor, so I concluded Venice had good street theater; it was a pity I was stuck inside polishing armor. Georg helped me hail a gondola, and we rode in style as anonymous master and neatly dressed servant. When we arrived, there was another gondola waiting.

Ragnar opened the water door at my knock; he was wearing a rather more elaborate mask that included a great curly red beard. The woman next to him was a stranger with long blonde hair who held a strange mask, a featureless black oval with no straps. It did not look to be held on by glue either; rudely, she didn't introduce herself before engulfing herself in a heavy, concealing cloak, though I would later learn her name was Bianca.

The pockmarked woman was wearing a more elaborate getup; I think it was meant to evoke Venus, a more sincerely divine counterpart to my mockingly simple military "Neptune" costume. Her mask looked to have been modeled after the face of Princess Anna with added gilding and feathers, though her muddy brown eyes peering through the eyeholes gave lie to the illusion of similarity to the princess.

For reasons related to the balance of weight, Georg went to the other gondolier with Ragnar and Bianca, who only slipped her dark mask off into her sleeve after her face was thoroughly covered with a hood. She gave both gondoliers directions in fluid Venetian and in halting Gothic asked Ragnar to sit down; then we were off to the masquerade, taking a circuitous route that circled past some buildings three times. Our heavy, anonymous cloaks attracted some glances but no bullets or arrows. We were far from the only suspicious figures passing through the canals of the city of masks; Venice seemed to take notice of neither a Gothic thaumaturge's daughter nor a Ruthenian mercenary.

At the party, Bianca was far from the only woman with a simple dark mask, mouthless and strapless—not even the only one with long blonde hair, which seemed to be more common in Venice than it had been in Tridentum or Drusipons. The dark mask was one of the more popular styles of mask among women, in spite of the fact that it did not allow for verbal conversation; it was kept in place by biting onto a button on the back of the mask, as I learned by watching other women take breaks from wearing theirs.

There was also a mouthless mask worn by many of the men, but that mask was held on by normal straps or hooks and had a chamber in front of the wearer's mask so that they could be easily heard—and could easily slip a wine glass underneath. As far as I know, Bianca didn't sip a single drop of wine during the entire party, though many Venetians asked her questions about us that she answered with a gesture, a bow, or a shrug.

Our entrance had caused a stir; we were clearly foreigners. I barely qualified as masked, Ragnar's red beard-wig was a unique spectacle, and both of us were armed with deadly "props"—myself with a trident, and Ragnar with his hammer. Ironically, in spite of his mask being a far better depiction of its subject, he was less well recognized than I was; few Venetians were familiar with Norse myths, but they swam in Roman ones.

One particularly drunk Venetian mage asked me shyly if I really was Neptune; most of the other mages that I sensed avoided speaking with me, sensible of the fact that my brilliant trident had genuinely sharp points on it. The pockmarked woman dragged one man after another to meet me, most ranging from middle-aged to old; at least a third of them gave me the feeling that they were magically talented in some way.

She would then go dance with them, relying on music and motion to mask her words—not that I quite understood what she was saying. She did not speak very directly most of the time that I listened, and I was distracted by Bianca's attempts to tease and confuse Ragnar by trading accessories and outerwear with other black-masked blonde women behind his back. When he did successfully pick her out anyway, the hint of a smile crinkled her eyes behind the mask. I was not surprised when the two of them disappeared from the ballroom, separated by a dozen heartbeats of time and a knowing glance.

The night was late by the time we returned to the house; the pockmarked woman thanked me with a peck on the cheek, telling me that she would send word with news when she had it and hinting indirectly that perhaps the Venetians would want to hire Raven's battalion.

CHAPTER FORTY-TWO

In Which I Meet a Dolphin

I never received a message from the pockmarked woman; I waited for two days, and then the course of events turned in an unexpected direction one evening when I was out at a taverna with the infantry captain and a squad of our soldiers. After the barmaid's third delivery of wine pitchers to our table, a strange woman squeezed her way between two soldiers to sit down with us. I thought at first that she might be a messenger and then wondered if she might be a prostitute; groups of soldiers in drinking establishments seem to inevitably attract practitioners of the world's oldest professions.

The woman opened her cloak and leaned forward. Through a combination of curiosity, admiration, and jealousy, her daring decolletage drew the eyes of nearly everyone around her. The good-luck stone around my neck grew cold as the delicate tracery of her necklace glimmered briefly, its amber beads casting a yellow light. She spoke softly with a musical voice that cut through the noise of the taverna, but I had trouble attending to her words as my attention was drawn elsewhere.

What drew my attention was a sharp yank on my arm as Georg suddenly stood and bolted for the door of the taverna, her eyes wide in panic. I turned away from the spectacle of glimmering amber beads resting atop a generous expanse of feminine flesh, then shook my head. The infantry captain and her men could handle themselves while I dealt with whatever concern Georg had.

I caught up to her on the walkway next to the canal.

"Enchantress," she blurted out. "That woman was casting a charm."

I frowned, closing my eyes and extending my other senses. "She doesn't feel like a mage," I said. "The old man in the corner, two people upstairs, and to a much lesser degree the barkeeper, yes," I added. "But she doesn't feel any more like a wizard than you do."

Georg frowned. "Right. You would have the aura sense. You can pick up strong or active mages, especially ones that can invoke lots of power, but wizards with more subtle types of magic or people with lesser talents just don't have the same sort of power radiating from them. Master wizards can mask themselves, too; but in her case, I really doubt she's powerful enough to really register on her own. She was using a focus," Georg said, by way of explanation.

Her hand briefly and unconsciously touched her own necklace before rising to pinch the air in front of her chin, as if she was stroking an invisible beard, and then she continued. "People who have just the smallest bit of magical talent don't have the kind of power you need to cast spells, but if they've had the training, they can trigger and shape a spell from a focus that's been enchanted by someone more powerful. And that necklace of hers—those thirteen amber beads, the septagram with the golden point leading to her throat—that's a spell focus."

"Really? Hm," I said, then looked down at her. She seemed to know quite a lot about this subject. The most logical explanation was that she had been trained, which meant that either she or the baron's daughter was a focus wizard. "Can you use a spell focus?"

Georg looked at me for a long moment. "Yes," she said, her voice guarded. "I thought you knew that from the start," she added, "since you recognized me right away. All I can really do on my own is feel certain types of magic—I can feel them on my skin. It's like . . . dry wool in wintertime, just before it sparks on you? Like how Fyodor can read the winds just by looking up into the sky."

"Fyodor can read the wind?" I asked. "Really?"

"Yes," Georg said. "He's a little embarrassed that it's all he can do, his grandfather was a mage capable of actual spellcasting. I understand why he might not have opened up to you about it." She paused, gathering her courage. She raised her hand up, her palm hovering a few inches away from my arm. "You are scary," she said very quietly.

"Huh," I said. We talked for a while longer by the canal, as I was curious about how she had received her training.

Georg had been trained along with her mistress, who had inherited the talents of both of her grandmothers. The baron's daughter had a real talent for both enchantment and illusion. Not strong enough to cast a spell with a few words and a gesture, but with a few hours to spare and a clean surface to draw out a chalk circle, it was a different matter. For the baron's daughter, working around the limitations of her limited power meant learning how to make spell foci (which required more power than Georg had) and learning how to use them (which required almost no power at all).

After my curiosity had been satisfied, we returned to the taverna, but there was no sign of the woman with the daring decolletage, my infantry captain, or her men. The enchantress had absconded with an entire squad of soldiers while I had been trying to figure out what was going on. Where had they gone? I went upstairs, pushing past the objections of the bouncer with a shove that left a dent in the wall. They were not gambling; nor were they in the businesslike bedrooms that lined the next floor up from the gaming rooms.

A chilly wind swept through the taverna as I stormed back down the stairs. An older man, who may have been the proprietor, shrieked at me at length while I did so, something about having called the city guard to either jail me or shoot me and toss me into the canal.

"Where did my men go?" I asked, and the man ran up the stairs, a growing wet stain on the inside of one leg of his hose.

Most of the customers of the taverna were making themselves scarce, but a few, more bold than others, told me that the siren had led them out the back entrance. Some further questions revealed that "siren" was local slang for women who worked as recruiters for ship crews, and that my soldiers were most likely in the process of being press-ganged. With the Venetian navy drawing heavily on the Venetian citizenry in their continued conflict with the sultan, merchant ships and foreign traders alike were desperate for sailors and oarsmen to keep them running.

I found this irksome. The building shuddered briefly as I walked out of the mostly vacant taverna, and lines of ice glittered as they formed a hexagonal webwork of lines across the canal. I beckoned to a gondolier, and he paddled quickly in the other direction, past a half-dozen city guardsmen with chattering teeth, breaking through the small lines of ice forming on the surface of the water.

The guardsmen had clearly not dressed warmly enough for the unseasonable cold winds suddenly blowing, I noted to myself. Likely, I needed to prove I was ready to pay above the ordinary rate. Rummaging through my pocket, I found a silver florin and held it out, the bright metal gleaming; the next gondolier passing by hesitated, then paddled forward. I gave the man a brief explanation of my predicament and asked where I was likely to find and recover my men.

The coin vanished a quick moment after hitting his palm, and the gondolier briefly glanced in the direction of the city guardsmen. The city guardsmen responded by looking away, and then the gondolier told me he had an idea of where I might look. He would be happy to take me there, and to the other ports of the city as well—if I had more coin where the florin had come from.

His first guess about which direction my men might have gone was wrong; the florins I spent after the first were silver flashes of futility. Perhaps my men were silently aboard a ship; perhaps they were on a ship that had already left; perhaps they were in one of the grand houses that lined the canals. The enchantress had gotten herself and my men out of sight, and there was no trail to follow on the waters of Venice.

As the night began to give way to early pre-dawn gray, the gondolier's exhaustion began to war with his greed. Georg's exhaustion had already won victory over her; she was lying down in the boat wrapped up in her jacket.

"We have nearly circled the city," the gondolier told me. "You will have to find another gondola if you want to keep looking."

I looked out at the dark ships and sighed. "I am afraid I may as well stop looking," I told him. "My men have vanished," I said heavily, trailing my fingers through the water.

A bulbous head poked above the water of the canal. The creature had smooth gray skin and a long nose; I had never seen the like before. In a surprisingly high-pitched voice, it asked me what my problem was, revealing an even row of white conical teeth. The gondolier didn't seem to be put ill at ease by its presence.

I told it that some of my friends had been lured away, probably to a ship, but I didn't know which. Could it help me? I would be back later, I told it.

The creature giggled and submerged. I turned to the gondolier, who had a worried expression on his face, and told him he ought to pole for home.

After a brief morning nap, I woke, crunched down a handful of roasted coffee beans, and then rushed off to track down the harbormaster or the

Venetian equivalent thereof. After questioning several nervous passersby, I found a well-dressed man familiar with the business of the harbor.

"The convoy just left for Negroponte," he told me. "If your friends were hired as oarsmen, they're half a day's journey out already."

I made several suggestions for remedying this problem as I lifted the man by his shirt. The fabric was well made and did not tear, and the man remained surprisingly calm as I shook a finger in his elevated face.

"The Serene Republic is at war with the sultan," he told me. "Nothing to be done about it. The Venetian navy needs every galley it can get its hands on, and what the navy doesn't hold left this morning for Negroponte. You're out of luck—there just aren't ships to be had, let alone a fast galley, and certainly not one whose master is willing to deal with a Lithuanian. A fishing boat just won't get you there."

"I'm not Lithuanian," I said, by way of clarification.

"Some distant barbarian foreigner," he clarified. "Lithuanian, Danish, Mongol, doesn't really matter. You're not Venetian or Dalmatian or Greek—you're not from anywhere near here. Now, would you put me down?"

I returned the man to his feet reluctantly and looked out across the water.

CHAPTER FORTY-THREE

In Which I Do Not Talk to Mermaids

After a long day of investigation, I was tired, hungry, and felt the need for a pitcher or two of wine and dinner without company. The best I could do in crowded Venice was to find a taverna where nobody knew who I was, seeking solace in the company of strangers by sitting at a small table meant for two. The other seat was occupied by my gauntlets, with my helmet sitting above it, perched on the tines of my trident.

"He talks to mermaids," the man sitting two tables down said, revealing the fact that I had failed to find a taverna where nobody knew who I was. "I heard it from Marco."

Concealing my disappointment in my lack of anonymity, I ignored him and signaled for the waitress, communicating to her with a gesture and a coin that I desired another pitcher of wine to accompany my dinner. The man may have had a sense of who I was, but I consoled myself with the fact that he knew me only through inaccurate rumors; talking to mermaids, indeed!

I had only talked to dolphins, who were a little more bold about visiting the closer parts of the lagoon and occasionally even swam in the Grand Canal. My second conversation with the dolphin had been more fruitful, but I had neither seen nor talked to the mermaids. The dolphin had a few things to say about mermaids, a mix of compliments and insults. Due to the prurient nature of much of the dolphin's commentary, I shall not repeat it in writing—dolphins may be creatures of the sea, but they have a very earthy nature and a surprising interest in humanoid anatomy.

Mermaids largely stay clear of Venice. It's too busy, too noisy; the water is much too dirty, and there are too many women around—mermaids,

I have since learned, tend to be insecure about their appearance, since their land-bound rivals generally have legs. They also look rather different from dolphins when they surface, although perhaps with very bad vision blurred by exhaustion, one might only see a dark shape breaking the surface of the water.

However, in defense of the man's misapprehensions, I had indirectly communicated with mermaids. After I had spoken with the first dolphin, he had talked to his friends, and one of his friends had talked to a mermaid, who had then discussed my situation with other mermaids. One of those mermaids knew of a ship that the Venetians weren't using that I could have; it was on the bottom of the ocean. It was a ship that had drowned its master, its keel made from the tree of a liachiad with neither care nor permission, and the god of the sea had refused to let it rot.

At least, that is what the dolphins said that the mermaids told them. I'm not sure how much credence to put in the specifics of the story; dolphins are clever enough and greedy enough to lie, unlike most dogs and a few delightfully innocent humans.

However, I am confident that dolphins, lacking hands and fingers, are incapable of tying ropes; after draining the second pitcher and departing the taverna, I saw that a whole pod of them were pulling knotted ropes as they pulled the liachiad-keeled ship into the lagoon with the high tide, a dark shape mostly below the water, only the forecastle peering above the water. When those dolphins credited the mermaids with tying ropes to the ship, I believed them on that point.

"I didn't think you would bring me that ship tonight," I said to a familiar dolphin swimming ahead of the rest, pulling my visor up. My belly felt heavy from what had been an overindulgent dinner involving several extra helpings of a grain mush that the locals called polenta, lightly seasoned with mushrooms, and my feet were unsteady from the third pitcher of wine.

The dolphin laughed; I knelt at the edge of the boardwalk and we chatted amiably for a while until a second dolphin swam up to hand me a knotted rope and chide the first dolphin for his laziness. As the dolphins swam away, I eyed the mostly submerged ship dubiously; while I appreciated that the dolphins had brought me a ship, it was in no condition to catch up with a convoy of great galleys.

"What are you doing?" A well-dressed man stood behind me; behind him were about a dozen confident-looking city guards.

"Getting a ship," I said, holding up the rope. Taking in the position of the arquebuses in the hands of the rearmost quartet of guards, I let the rope drop, hastily lowering my visor. Three bullets rattled off my breastplate as the quartet of guards revealed that they lacked the confidence they displayed; the fourth shot missed, dropping where the dolphins could see it.

I tapped the butt of the trident on the boardwalk. "Hair-trigger guns you have here," I told the well-dressed man through my visor, my voice echoing through the narrow slits. "No harm done. Except to my men, taken by one of the sirens your lot tolerates."

"You can come quietly, or you can come shouting, but you will come with us," the well-dressed man said.

I paused, considering the last time I had permitted myself to be arrested. It had been a chilly, hunger-filled, and embarrassing night in the cage in the town square. "No," I said. Ice rimed the boardwalk as the warm Venetian spring air was replaced with a chilly wind. "I need a ship," I said. I reached down, tugging the rope with one hand experimentally. The ship, thoroughly waterlogged, didn't budge; it had settled into the mud with only some of the forecastle visible above the water.

"That ship lacks a mast and sail," the well-dressed man said, raising empty hands and adopting a conciliatory tone. "I'll offer you a deal—come with us, answer a few questions, and I'll cheerfully pay your passage wherever you like, on one of my own galleys."

"If you fetch a mast and sail, I'll make my own way with this ship," a deep voice said, sounding like my father.

The man stepped back to confer with the guards; too late, I realized that the voice must have been my own. There was nobody else standing near me. Was that a promise I could fulfill? How could I possibly be confident that the ship could sail? I looked down at the ship, grounded in the mud, waterlogged, and encrusted with barnacles—a ship that should have rotted away to nothing centuries ago. I stared out at the water, distracted, and did not notice the pair of bold guards rushing forward until they shoved me off the pier.

My thoughts turned away from the mysterious voice and my ownership thereof (which had significant implications for later thought) and toward the problem of my sudden downward trajectory. The dolphins giggled unhelpfully, thinking it very amusing that I was being pushed into the water. I flailed my limbs in panic and hit the surface of the water with a great splash.

Down I went into the dark water, sinking under the weight of my armor. Water rushed in through my visor, and I pulled it open to see better. My orichalcum-plated trident had landed point-first in the muck, and I walked along the muddy bottom toward the precious weapon, intending to pull it out before climbing back out of the water. When I gripped the trident with both hands and pulled, though, there began a great rumbling noise, and the curious dolphins scattered away as my visor slowly fell back down into place.

I pulled harder, able only to see the muddy ground through the narrow slits of the visor, and the rumbling continued. My lungs began to burn from the effort of holding my breath, and my vision began to dim around the edges just before becoming obscured entirely as air rapidly began to bubble up into my visor. I breathed deeply, new strength coming into my arms, and yanked. The trident popped free of the muck, and I looked around. A confused fish flopped next to me on the muddy ground, which was strewn with all manner of trash and detritus. I was no longer underwater, though water was still draining from the ship. The hull of the ship creaked as it leaked at the seams, water spraying in all directions as the aged wood bowed outward from pressure applied in a direction the planks had not been built to resist.

To either side of the ship, water lapped at the sides of the muddy spit of land I was now standing on. Behind me, I could hear shouting and the ringing of bells, which I ignored as I considered the ship. If it truly had been preserved from rotting, perhaps something could be made of it; but water was sunk deep into the very timbers. The bronze ram looked like a solid hunk of verdigris lying in the mud. Experimentally, I scraped at the corroded ram with my trident; perhaps some kind of alchemical treatment could restore the ship, I thought to myself.

I pulled off one of my gauntlets, hooking it on my belt, running my hand along waterlogged and barnacled wood as I walked around the right-hand side of the ship. My overindulged stomach twinged as I reached the rear, my hand touching the keel that the dolphins claimed the mermaids told them had been cut from the tree of a liachiad. It felt solid, and for a long minute, I held my hand there, closing my eyes. I could almost imagine trying to talk with a tree spirit.

After a bit, I opened my eyes, walking around the left-hand side of the ship. This side, I noted, seemed free of barnacles, and in much better condition. I shaded my eyes from the bright noon sun, rapping my knuckles against hard dry wood. It felt a little waxy. I made my way to the front of the ship, my empty stomach growling; I was quite hungry, I realized. Clearly, the polenta hadn't been filling, I thought to myself as I took in the bright white painted eyes of the ship. It really did look like a face, with the brilliant bronze ram gleaming in the sunlight.

The tide was lower, and I realized that the mud was no longer sucking at my boots; it had dried somewhat. I looked over at the boardwalk, but I didn't see the well-dressed man anywhere; indeed, the boardwalk itself was partly missing on either side of the muddy hill I stood upon, and the taverna behind the boardwalk tilted at an angle that made the building itself look as if it were drunk. Next to the leaning taverna, there was a long pole that looked to have been fashioned from an entire tree trunk, and piled next to it was a heap of canvas.

"He is awake," said a familiar voice in Slavonic. "I told you he would wake up again."

Focusing my eyes, I could see Katya—and, standing next to Katya, Captain Felix Rimehammer, my second in command. Both of whom, if I remembered correctly, should have been waiting on the coastline south of the lagoon with the rest of my company. I turned my gaze back to the ship, looking for clues on the right-hand side of the ship. Its surface also felt waxy and was—quite suddenly, from my perspective—also free of barnacles. My stomach growled again, complaining of its emptiness, and I felt remarkably thirsty.

I turned my gaze back to the boardwalk; Katya was approaching at speed.

"Seven days and seven nights," Katya said quietly as she opened my visor. "You made me worry."

A collection of giggles sounded behind me as she went up on her tiptoes, pulling me down for a kiss. Mostly high-pitched raucous dolphin giggles; but there was also one dulcet contralto chuckle, throaty and far closer to human-sounding. Just not quite.

CHAPTER FORTY-FOUR

In Which I Receive a Donation from a Generous City

I have trouble crediting that an entire week passed in the blink of an eye with my hand on the ancient larch keel that had once been a liachiad's tree; I know that tales have a way of growing. However, from the depth of my hunger and thirst afterward, I reasoned that it had been much longer than the trance I had fallen into when I picked up my sword after my battle with the Magyar war mage. The time was also long enough to effect a change in attitude of the authorities of the city of Venice, which had been hostile before I touched the ship. In truth, I must say I found Venice to be a generous city in the end.

In addition to the sail and mast that my voice had demanded, the city of Venice—as the leading manufacturer of galleys—also kindly donated oars and a second smaller mast and sail; they had realized, as I had not, that my sunken galley had been originally built to accommodate two sails. I did not have the three hundred oarsmen the ship needed for its three banks of oars, and the city of Venice was rather tight on skilled oarsmen at the moment, but they were willing to donate the required one hundred eighty oars, plus spares. (Editor's note: The astute reader may note that three hundred does not divide evenly by one hundred eighty. Fortunately, Mikolai enclosed several helpful diagrams, so I may explain that the ship had three levels of oars on each side, with the lowest (shortest) oars handled by a single man and the upper two handled by two men each.)

It was up to me and my men to install the masts and sails; while the Venetians accounted themselves skilled shipbuilders, most of their expert carpenters and shipwrights were superstitious, unwilling to approach the new spit of land closely for fear it might cause an earthquake. Their superstition derived from an odd coincidence that, if one is familiar with natural philosophy, may be well explained. It is known via consultation with elemental spirits of the deeper earth that earthquakes are the result of small slips of great masses of rock stuck together by friction, and these slips are not precise, leading to aftershocks as the great masses make smaller and smaller shifts until they once more settle into place.

Evidently, not long after the sudden earthquake that lifted the ship out of the water (and caused some damage elsewhere), the Venetian gentleman who had originally attempted my arrest was reinforced with a pair of mages and another dozen regular guards. As the first of them set foot on the newly arisen muddy spit, a perfectly ordinary aftershock hit and knocked most of them off their feet; as even the mages were a bit superstitious about earthquakes, they promptly fled the scene.

As a result, the men of Venice were, as a whole, quite reluctant to come closer than a hundred paces from my newly salvaged vessel and the muddy spit of new land it was beached upon. Close to half of my battalion was housed nearby, though, brought back on fishing boats. Once the heated emotions of our confrontation had died down, the city's authorities must have been swayed by the fact that I had been wronged. They not only invited my soldiers to join me but performed an extensive investigation, reporting that the siren who had stolen a squad of my soldiers was a notorious Turkish agent working for the Sultanate, one with a long history of stealing good Venetian men to slave away on boats, secretly owned by the sultan and his omnipresent agents.

Upon reviewing their report, I asked why she did not look or sound Turkish; they told me she was born of a Wallachian woman who had converted to Turkish ways, citing as evidence the fact that she had spoken some in a dialect that sounded much like the dialect of Dalmatian pirates. While I decided not to argue the point further, I privately remained skeptical of the quality of their investigation. The Romanian tongue spoken by Wallachians is much more closely related to Venetian than to Dalmatian, the latter being more similar to Slavonic.

With assistance from the acolyte (who was familiar with tree magic) and Johann (who was passingly familiar with enchanted boats), we were able to graft the new masts cleanly onto the stumps of the old one and hang the sails, both the small one and the little one. At the insistence of Ragnar, I handed a princely sum of coin to a heavily cloaked Bianca in a boat laden with our sails. Ragnar claimed that the Venetians had special secret processes that they performed on sails for the ships of their navy; we had received untreated sails, but Bianca could fix that for us.

I was skeptical; but the sails returned marked with the design of a black raven and felt subtly different to the touch. They had been alchemically or magically treated, perhaps both. Once we had hung the sails, the few of our number with sailing experience speaking to the other, I announced we would leave with the next high tide, calling for all my soldiers to come aboard by then. I spent several hours negotiating with dolphins for help getting us off the muddy spit; they seemed to dislike the idea of showing up to a particular spot at a particular time to work, and I had to promise to dump two barrels of pickled fish overboard in order to get them interested.

Pickled fish do not often swim in the sea, but they have a distinctive and interesting taste that one dolphin particularly liked and the others were curious about. As high tide approached, a strong wind blew in from the sea. Gainfully employed adult Venetians mostly went about their business after only a few amused glances; drunks, prostitutes, and children proved a more attentive audience. The crowd that gathered to watch us leave was small and motley.

Once I felt reasonably confident we had everyone aboard, and the acolyte had finished feeding her infant, I gave the signal to the dolphins to pull and asked the acolyte if she would kindly assist. Many of the watching Venetians lost their hats to the lagoon that day, as the swift reversal of the direction of the wind came as a surprise to them. In one case, the hat revealed a gloriously long stream of blonde hair, which blew wildly in front of a black, mouthless mask—Bianca had come to see us off.

Moments later, there was a giant slurping sound as the ship, pulled by dolphins below and pushed by wind above, tore loose from the muddy spit. The dolphins let go of the ropes and scattered as the ship shot forward. That is when I discovered that it is difficult to steer a ship with its rudder facing forward and a ram trailing behind it; this makes sense given it is the reverse of the usual arrangement.

I watched as Bianca shrank into the distance. At one point, she pulled out Ragnar's favorite silk handkerchief, slipping it under her mask to wipe away a tear; then she pulled her hood over her hair and slunk away. Perhaps she would let the woman with the pockmarked face know that we had left; preoccupied with first my missing men and later the ship, I had not seen the plainer woman since the night of the party. The woman I presumed to be the daughter of an imperial thaumaturge had told me Venice was her destination, but on a certain level I missed her company and wished she had come along with us.

It wasn't simply that she had more formal training in magic than I did and I desperately wanted to learn more; she had been pleasant company in spite of her lack of beauty, making up for a lack of physical attributes with a very comprehensive education. She spoke half a dozen languages flawlessly; she was well versed in natural philosophy; and she even had a sort of confident poise about her that is usually reserved for women attractive enough to presume they will usually be the center of attention.

Of course, there was the annoying factor that she seemed to believe herself entitled to order anyone about at any time, but as Venice rapidly receded from sight, I felt like I missed having the direction she gave us. We had entered Venice on a mission; now we were lost. When Katya had been jealous of the pockmarked woman at first glance, I thought she had been unreasonable; but now that I missed her company, I felt Katya must have had some deep intuitive insight into the woman's intellect and force of personality.

On being questioned, Katya insisted otherwise, though she did not seem to be pleased that the pockmarked woman's personality had begun to grow on me. She took me belowdecks for two tongue-lashings, one metaphorical and the other literal, adding up to something of a mixed message.

It took us longer than I would like to admit before we managed to get the ship turned around, sailing southeast to where half of my company waited, along with our heavy equipment and livestock. We then spent three days in the swamp planning.

That is to say, Captain Felix Rimehammer saw about purchasing foodstuffs via the fishermen while trying not to think about the fact that we could find employment in neither the Gothic Empire nor the Venetian Republic. Lieutenant Ragnar Rimehammer moped belowdecks packing and repacking inventory, as sullen and distracted as some boys ten years younger than his true age; and if anyone mentioned Venice's unusually numerous bounty of blonde women or the masks Venetians liked to wear, his mood soured further. Lieutenant Fyodor Kransky's new wife's goodwill was too valuable for me to consider trying to pry him away from her side when the two of them had an infant demanding attention.

Lieutenant Vitold Szpak and the other mechanics spent three days taking apart machinery ill-suited to shipboard use and experimenting with the use of gears, ropes, oars, and chains while trying not to think about how a mercenary company might avoid running out of cash with which to continue purchasing fish by the barrel. The casualties of this exercise included the self-propelled charcoal kiln. Katya, as the only other officer with any kind of seniority, excused herself to the crow's nest after giving me two orders. First, I should for the time being avoid speaking with any beautiful women, or women I thought were plain-looking with intriguing personalities. Second, I should go back to speaking with Georg and Maestro Zilioli and figure out which direction I needed to sail to go home.

I did not ask Katya whether she meant to insult Georg's appearance or personality; the former lady's maid was comely enough, if one ignored her ill-fitting men's clothes, and generally a skilled conversationalist, though she had been a little less cheerful since our departure from Oenipons. I did, however, take her second request to heart. I had asked to marry Katya; she had told me that I needed to seek her father's permission. Her father lived in the Izh District, in the eastern part of the Golden Empire.

The Mikolai Stepanovich who had enlisted as a mechanic of the Imperial Army was a very different-looking man. The last two years had shaped me; I had finished my growth, filled out, and learned a great deal about magic and the world. If I returned home, it would be as a different man. Only my old armor could mark me as the alleged steam knight that General Ognyan Spitignov thought I was; but I had new armor made from Corsican brass.

With that, I made two decisions. First, I would head east, back in the direction of the Golden Empire. Perhaps I would have to fight along the way; perhaps not. During my journey I would stop in Negroponte and Constantinople; perhaps my missing men had been taken to one of those ports by the siren's call, the former if they had been taken aboard a Venetian convoy, and the latter if the Venetians' claims about the siren proved correct in spite of their implausibility. Second, I would disassemble my old armor, removing any temptation to wear it and with that, any possibility of being identified as a current or former steam knight of the Golden Empire. The arcane engine at the heart of it—the flux engine—I would repurpose. With Johann's help, perhaps I could help keep Vitold from setting the ship on fire in his attempt to construct a working rowing engine.

CHAPTER FORTY-FIVE

In Which I Meet a Mermaid

After a long night working with Johann on the flux engine—he had insisted that the elemental gate was far too small to supply enough flux to move an entire ship, and rebuilding it had taken all night—I woke to a strangely uneven rocking motion, the ship turning momentarily to one side for half a second before lurching back on course. Between the waves and the odd torquing motion, I found reason to rapidly rush to the railing, donating some share of the previous night's dinner to the fishes of the sea.

Rebuilding the arcane engine and enlarging its gate appreciably had given me a better understanding both of how it specifically worked and also of thaumaturgy in general. Arcane flux engines are more complex because they utilize a pair of elemental gates rather than a singular gate; flux, unlike heat, has two polarities. Johann was eager to answer all the questions he could and seemed to be learning new things along with me; evidently, he hadn't been encouraged to experiment as a student in Vindobona. Teaching me thaumaturgy inspired him to experiment, up until the point where he was tired enough to drop his athame across the exposed lead of the open flux engine.

The lightning sparks generated by the unmediated animosity between the two flux gates—and rapid heating of the athame under the passage of arcane-generated flux in combat between them—nearly set the ship on fire, and that tempered Johann's desire for further experimentation that night. We closed up the rebuilt arcane engine, leaving it charged with fighting vigor.

Evidently, after Johann and I had called it a night, Vitold had felt comfortable enough with flux-related mechanics to connect the engine to the actuators with flux cables, and the actuators to the gears. This was a surprise to me, as flux engines are extremely rare within the Golden Empire and were not covered in our training as mechanics within the Imperial Army.

After stopping the arcane engine, I told Vitold he needed to synchronize the drive chains better, or perhaps better yet use a single central wheel on both ends with the one by the engine driven by all the actuators instead of two separate sets of actuators driving two separate sets of gears.

Vitold's response was to tell me he couldn't send a single main drive chain directly through the mast. I gave him authorization to disassemble anything he needed for parts to get a proper rigid linkage on the wheels we'd turned into main gears.

Until he did, we would be dead in the water. The acolyte was asleep and the wind was once again trying to blow us back to Venice, so sailing didn't seem to be an option. Some of the men who had been on sea-going ships before seemed to think there was some trick that let one sail into the wind. I assumed that it had to be some variety of tightly controlled wind magic, kept secret by sailing masters; our weather-witch's magic was less subtle, though dependent on her mood, attention, and wakefulness, all of which were depleted by an infant of several months.

Having failed to find Katya anywhere on deck or below, I looked up, knowing by that point that she tended to gravitate to the heights for better vantage whenever she could. Unsurprisingly, I spotted a few strands of red hair blowing in the wind over the crow's nest. I waved up at her; she waved back at me merrily but made no move to come down. As captain of the cavalry, she was in charge of reconnaissance, and she'd decided that meant she was in charge of the heights of the ship.

I had tea, eggs, and toast by way of a late breakfast. The tea was cold, the toast nearly stale, and the eggs fresh. (The fresh eggs were courtesy of the hens we'd brought—rank having its privileges, Captain Rimehammer had ordered the cook to save some for me.) Thus nourished and preferring to stay out of the way of the retrofitting of machinery, I took a perch near the aft end of the ship, sitting next to a very morose-looking Lieutenant Ragnar Rimehammer.

"What's wrong?" I asked.

He sighed heavily.

"Is it about that blonde woman?" I elbowed him in the ribs.

"Her name is Bianca," Ragnar told me. "It means white. She was born with white hair."

"Maybe you'll see her again," I said.

He fished a copper coin out of his pocket and pitched into the waves with a splash. Motion swirled beneath the waves as the Swedish lieutenant stared blankly.

"Well, she does have lovely blonde hair as an adult," I said. "Not so far from her natal white. Makes the name easy to remember."

"Too easy," Ragnar said. "I think I love her."

A splash sounded, and out of the corner of my eye, I saw a wet mass of brunette hair duck below the waves. "Well, you could go back to Venice," I suggested, "sooner or later. Maybe after things calm down."

Several flashes of yellow light flickered under the water. Ragnar shook his head. "After that spectacle? All of Venice felt that earthquake. And Bianca, she can't just leave. Not with her family in the state it's been in."

A blonde head emerged from the water and then the upper half of a woman's torso, very partially concealed by wet strands of hair.

"Hello, men," said the blonde mermaid, waving with a copper coin held between two of her fingers. She bobbed in the water, demonstrating a certain level of buoyancy that pulled my eyes to the waterline like a flux-charged magnet.

Ragnar looked up, then shook his head. "I'm seeing things," he said, standing up and turning around. "I should go try to catch some sleep while the boat isn't rocking too much."

"Hey!" The mermaid waved with both hands, bobbing vigorously.

My eyes tracked the bouncing for a moment, then turned upward to meet the mermaid's eyes. "I'm afraid he's a bit out of sorts," I said, apologetically. "He usually doesn't ignore women like that."

The mermaid sank down into the water, down to the level of her lips, blowing bubbles. "That's kind of you, but I'm not a woman," she said. Her head disappeared in a quick somersault, a flash of scales and fins showing for a moment before her blonde head perked back above the water, followed by the uppermost six inches of her chest.

"Yes, I see. You don't have legs," I said.

She frowned. "Yes," she said sullenly. "And legs are the best part. They're very tasty."

"You mean they look nice?" I asked. I had heard of attractive women being referred to in culinary terms before.

"Yes," she said quickly. "I meant they look very nice." She pouted.

"Don't feel sad," I said. "You look nice, too. Besides, it's okay if you don't have legs. My woman is missing one, and she's still beautiful to me."

"Really?" The mermaid perked up, wiggling and jiggling upward until her belly button showed.

"Really," I said.

"Would you like to come for a swim?" she asked.

I demurred; we spoke for a while. I had many questions about boats and sailors and the sea, and so did she; she'd seen our ship when it was below the surface, and there were many things about ships that she didn't understand.

Then Katya called down that she saw sails. A few moments later, the mermaid's eyes suddenly widened and she dove forward under the water, swimming under the ship and out of view. I stood, looking up to the crow's nest, where Katya had set down her spyglass and shouldered her rifle, which was braced, ready, and pointed in a direction not very far from me.

I waved up at her and she put the rifle down, setting it back in a piece of canvas fastened to the inside of the crow's nest.

My climb up to the crow's nest took longer than I had expected. While I had climbed trees before, they do not wobble with the waves, and the motion of a mast with the rolling waves can be amplified by the leverage of its height.

I wanted to discuss the sails that Katya had sighted; Katya wanted to discuss the mermaid. As Katya felt much more strongly about the subject of the mermaid and I had no information about the sails she had sighted, we talked about the mermaid, and I reassured Katya both verbally on the subject of my fidelity and nonverbally on the subject of the sufficiency of her physical endowments. (From prior experience, I knew explicit verbal reassurances on the subject of Katya's visible insecurities would imply that I had taken notice of the mermaid's generous proportions.)

After this reassurance process was complete, Katya talked to me about the sails she had sighted while I put her prosthetic arm back on, securing the metal chest plate that provided the necessary bracing for the mechanical limb.

There had been three ships, with pointy triangular sails that looked unlike the large square sails that our ship had; and they were sailing with the wind, coming closer quite quickly though not quite directly at us, lined up single file front to back. She took her spyglass back out, looking for a minute until she found them; following the direction she pointed the spyglass in with my own gaze, I saw a trio of ships heading directly toward us, spaced in a wide triangular formation with the point at the back.

"They weren't headed exactly in our direction before," she said before I could comment on the inaccuracies in her previous description. "Only partly moving in our direction. And they were lined up in a straight file front-to-back before, too, not abreast like they are now. They have changed direction and formation."

While I could think of innocuous reasons why ships might shift direction, I found this development cause for some concern. Even in a rural farming village in the hinterland of the Golden Empire, I had heard of pirates; during the war with the Sultanate over Wallachia, news sheets regularly brought us stories about innocent, peaceful merchants and fishermen of the Golden Empire captured and enslaved by the cruel pirates funded and supported by the Sultanate.

This then justified special tax levies in support of further development of railroad lines and the construction of the Golden Empire's first pair of purpose-built warships. Designed to match the state of the art in French naval technology while optimizing maneuverability and stability, they were built on a novel circular hull, able to move in any direction at command by the use of any two out of their six firebox-powered paddlewheel engines. The use of six separate arcane engines (paired with six supplementary coal-burning furnaces for higher speed maneuvers) would ensure the continued operability of the vessels even after taking substantial damage, as in principle they could continue to operate effectively with any pair of opposed paddlewheels.

These warships remained under construction for roughly three years and "in sea trials" in the Cimmerian Sea for the remainder of the war while the sultan's piratical navy continued to dominate the entire Axine Sea outside of the Cimmerian Strait. No pirate would have ever voluntarily approached them, as their profile was so distinctive as to be entirely unique—the most visible part of their superstructure was their central elevated artillery battery, the smokestacks for the supplementary coal furnaces having been built sideways in order to try to maintain clear lines of sight.

However, my ship simply had a pair of square sails. While its bronze ram attested to some military purpose in its construction, it was not visible above the waterline. Pirates—or well-armed merchants more generously supplied with space in their cargo holds than with moral scruples—could easily mistake us for an easy target.

In fact, since at the moment we were dead in the water, our sails furled and Vitold's rowing engine currently under construction, we likely qualified as an easy target, as we were completely stationary—anchored with our nose pointed against the wind. I had already learned firsthand that it was difficult to control the direction of a ship moving backward.

The following two excerpts are taken from
Ragnar Rimhamar, Gentleman Adventurer

Though I thought the previous six defeats at my hands had dulled their appetite and thinned their numbers, the agents of Sultan Alaeddin found us once more while we camped outside of Tridentum, arriving at a moment that was both indelicate and inconvenient.

We had shared the road with a merchant caravan; the factor in charge of the caravan was a Venetian and had brought his daughter with him, a lovely brunette named Jessica whom he hoped to marry off soon.

As the factor had no sons, he had decided to give his daughter a hands-on education about finance and trade, so as to ensure that his future son-in-law would be likewise educated and able to take over running his business when he grew too old for the rigors of the road and had to retire from the business. According to his varied complaints, this sad event would take place sometime within the next ten years; five years; and by the time we reached Tridentum, ought to have occurred some two years in the past.

Not trusting the local officials and criminals of Tridentum any further than he could launch them from a catapult, the factor camped his merchant caravan next to our encampment and headed into town to negotiate matters related to pricing, passage, and the exchange of goods without risking theft. After seeing him and the colonel off on their way into the walled town, I returned to the privacy of my tent to polish my armor—you must understand that as an officer, naturally, I had a private tent.

No sooner had I unpacked my traveling chest and sat upon the blanket laid on top of my cot than the flap to my tent twitched, and there stood Jessica. Several dark curls had worked their way loose from her braids, framing her face as she gazed into my eyes, biting her lip in a vain attempt to restrain her passion for but a moment. Her elbows nearly met as she pulled her arms behind her back, the motion thrusting her chest toward my eyes as her fingers danced to untie her dress and stays.

"We must be quick," she said. "My father will be away for but three or four hours, and I am painfully hollow inside for the lack of you. I must have you for every minute, no, every second that I can before he knows of my absence."

"But . . ." I said, attempting in vain to restrain her lust. This was a respectable daughter of an honest factor! "Surely it is unwise for you to bed before you wed," I said.

By way of response, she let the dress fall to the ground, revealing her full glory. "Take me," she said, breathless. "Take me, or I will die of a broken heart."

What else could I do but take her offered gift in order to save her life? And so, I did . . .

"Hold," Jessica whispered in my ear. "I hear footsteps. It may be my father's guard captain."

With catlike quickness, I leapt to my feet, tossing a blanket over the dark-haired beauty's naked form where she lay. As there was no time to waste, I took hold of my pants and jumped into both pantlegs at once to save time.

A finger tugged at the tent flap. "Ragnar?" asked a female voice, a moment before the flap was pulled away to reveal the princess, her golden hair shining in the sun. Within a perfect heart-shaped face, two cerulean pools bracketed a pert little nose. She was breathing heavily, her ample bosom straining at the confines of her dress over a waist that still seemed impossibly small.

"Princess," I said, bowing respectfully. "What brings you to my tent?"

"Georg and Johann came back from town without the colonel, and all the men are distracted," she said. "When I realized that for just this moment nobody was watching over me, and that you were all alone in your tent . . . I am sorry, I succumbed to the temptation to see you." Her soft hand moved forward as if pulled by an invisible force, caressing the muscles of my chest.

Keenly aware that the second most beautiful woman in the encampment was only a few feet away, I shook my head. "We must not, Princess," I said with an ashen taste in my mouth. "It is unwise in the extreme. You said so yourself. In your position, any doubt of your purity could be your ruin."

The princess shuddered, her finger tracing up my chest, then neck, then chin, lingering on the point. "One kiss," she said. "One kiss is all I ask."

When the most beautiful woman in the world places her finger upon your chin and begs, could you hold strong?

"But only one kiss. And then you must go," I said, unable to look away from the twin cerulean pools welling with unshed tears.

As her tongue prodded at the seal of my lips, I heard booted footsteps approaching with haste. Perhaps the factor's guard captain; perhaps a fellow officer who would have harsh words to say about my corrupting our honored employer. "Quick!" I said. "You must hide!"

And so I crammed the most beautiful woman in the world into my traveling chest (with her panicked cooperation) and latched it shut.

This third visitor proved to be Georg.

Georg, as I have said before, was on the slight and short side for a soldier, but very well-kempt with a neat goatee that he waxed regularly. While one might have considered him a pitiful weakling in a prior age where might of arm was more essential to martial success, he was educated and disciplined enough that I thought of him as an officer in training, who had learned to shoot a gun and keep the pointed end of a sword in the direction of an enemy coming to grips with him.

He was also quite handsome, perhaps second only to myself; but his inferior height and musculature unfortunately brought with it a lack of confidence when it came to women. Whenever a woman flirted with him, he was consumed with wooden awkwardness, apparently unable to believe any woman would truly find such a puny specimen attractive.

Lieutenant Quentin Gavreau had taken on training him as a sort of personal project; unfortunately, with the departure of Quentin to serve as the knight champion and guard captain of Landgravine Wilhelmina von Gschwendtberg, Georg had been sad and sullen in spite of my efforts to take him under my wing and build up his confidence. Even now, he seemed slightly ill at ease with my shirtless state, staring down at my chest with what I could only assume was naked envy.

"Georg? What is it?" I asked.

"My apologies, I did not mean to wake you if you were sleeping," Georg said, averting his eyes. "I have news from Tridentum. The colonel has been arrested."

Conscious of the small man's jealous discomfort and how it would undermine his confidence further the longer he compared my physique to his, I tossed on my shirt. "Is he very upset about the attempt to arrest him?"

"I don't know," Georg said. "He just let them do it. They're holding him prisoner. But we don't know what he plans by it. Pasha Mustafa told them to do it."

I sighed. "Help me put my armor on," I said, recognizing the name of one of the sultan's officials. "We will have to fight the sultan's agents at any moment. I have defeated them seven times already, but I would prefer to be prepared."

No sooner did we finish donning my armor than the side of my tent was sliced open in a flash of scimitars. This was no overweight, muscle-bound eunuch; this was one of the infamous fanatical hashishim, those who are known as assassins. The man was clad in black silk, a scimitar greased with vile poison gripped in each hand, an unearthly look in his eyes. The blades rang harmlessly against my armor as I blocked with my arms, hissing noises following spatters of vile venom against Swedish steel.

"Have at you," I said, slamming a gauntleted hand against the silk-masked face.

There was a sickening crunch as the assassin's jaw proved itself inferior to my fist, and the man fell, taking my tent down with him. One of the tent lines caught on the corner of the blanket that hid Jessica from view, revealing for a moment a shapely foot.

"The princess!" gasped the assassin through broken teeth, pointing with one of his blades.

Fearing a deadly assault on the person of a beautiful woman, I bore down on the assassin, hammering gauntlet after gauntlet down into his face until he stopped moving, either unconscious or dead.

"Oh, no, the princess!" Georg shouted. "They're stealing her away!"

I turned to look; two shapely legs sticking out of a bundled blanket kicked, struggling helplessly in the arms of a second assassin. Could I catch up? I lunged for a pistol, and another scimitar chopped down to destroy the gun before I could load it. A third and then a fourth black-clad assassin appeared from somewhere unseen to batter me with blows. My armor held—but against fanatics whose treated blades ate away slowly at steel, how long would it continue to do so?

"Georg! Stop the kidnapper!" I dropped to the ground and rolled to where my hammer lay as the short man ran after the second assassin, finding courage in my words as he called for assistance. Deeming him harmless and myself to be the true threat, three more assassins revealed themselves by striking at me.

I could not say that the princess was safe inside of my luggage without revealing her true location to the assassins; nor could I leave her side. Silently, I apologized to the poor kidnapped Jessica as I fought back against the assassins in earnest, one against five, my hammer cracking limbs and crushing skulls. One, two, a third; and then I felt a burning sensation against my arm. The poison had finally penetrated my armor. It was sheer agony.

I fell to my knees, shouting out something halfway between a prayer and a curse; when the hammer fell from my hand, ice crackled outward from the point of impact, freezing the feet of the two remaining assassins fast to the ground.

Still driven to kill, they cut at their own legs, trying to break free; and then gunshots sounded, and they were still. Though their detestable poison had brought me low, I was in the middle of a camp full of allies, and those allies had arquebuses to bring to a swordfight. Yet again, I had foiled the agents of the Turks—and that for the final time. We would deliver the princess to her secret allies in Venice without any more interference from the agents of Sultan Alaeddin; of those allies in Venice I can say little, for that is a secret that must be kept.

I will say only that we left Venice aboard a quinquereme—which, I think, was the first of its kind to sail the Aegean Sea in a thousand years.

CHAPTER FORTY-SIX

In Which I Fly Through the Air
with the Greatest of Ease

My presence in the crow's nest had allowed me to personally discern that the ships had altered course and formation in an alarming manner, albeit only after taking our principal watchwoman out of service for an extended period of distraction. After testing the fastenings of my clothing for durability, I shouted down a warning before making a hasty descent down to the deck.

Alighting on my feet, I doffed the gloves I had worn on the way down (they were now ruinously abraded and uncomfortably warm) and hastily explained the news to a startled Captain Felix Rimehammer before heading to the forecastle to don my armor. Georg followed in my wake, having transformed herself from Felix's personal assistant to my *de facto* squire around the time we arrived in Venice—her principal squirely duty being to assist me in and out of my new Corsican brass wizard armor and ensure it sparkled afterward with the aid of a polishing cloth.

It was only after I had stripped down to my smallclothes that I considered the possibility Katya might object to having a woman involved in dressing and undressing me, but it was too late at that point. Even with Georg's assistance, getting my armor on took too much time; and on my return from the forecastle, I found that Captain Felix Rimehammer was deep in discussion on the problem of our lack of maneuverability.

Lieutenant Fyodor Kransky was of the opinion that unfurling the sails and waking his wife would be unlikely to allow us to evade the incoming vessels, which could now be seen clearly by him from the deck. They were manned by sailors with more experience and had arrays of sails that looked both larger and more complicated; we and they would face very similar amounts of wind whichever direction the wind was pointed.

Lieutenant Vitold Szpak had a lengthy report to make on the status of the rowing-engine, the gist of which was that it wasn't quite ready yet, and he wasn't sure how long it would take, other than the fact that it wouldn't get any closer to ready while he was standing around discussing matters.

I made several decisions in short order with immediate effect. We would unfurl our sails right away and weigh anchor. The wind blowing us backward would earn back some of the time I had lost to my negligence.

Fyodor would wake his weather-witch wife and then prepare artillery. The steam knights were to warm up their boilers and then carry cannon. Vitold would work on getting the rowing-engine ready, along with anyone that the elder Rimehammer cousin thought could be spared. Banneret Teushpa, being well-educated but otherwise nearly useless as far as I was concerned, would be entrusted with the tiller at the rear of the ship, which I told him was a fine honor and a sign of great trust. He would be in charge of making any decisions about maneuvering if neither I nor Captain Rimehammer could send him directives.

I would perch in the forecastle, ready to speak with or signal to the approaching ships. If we were fortunate, they were merely interested in trading goods and gossip at sea. Briefly, I worried that our defensive posture might provoke a hostile response; and then I put the possibility out of mind. A convoy of merchants choosing to approach us directly could not mistake us for aggressors when we were adrift.

My cerulean cloak flapped behind me, and I gripped the orichalcum-plated trident in my left hand, watching the ships come closer. If the eyes painted to either side of our ship's ram made a face, I was perched on the crest of the ship's hairline, where I could see; the vantage from the main deck was too low and blocked by the foresail we had unfurled. We wobbled as we drifted slowly backward. From where I stood, I could not see Katya in the crow's nest, the backward foresail blowing between us.

The blonde mermaid's head popped up out of the water. She swam after us for a few minutes before deciding to hold onto the ship's ram. "Why are you sailing backward?" she asked, arching her back artfully as she brought the whole of her torso above the water to look up at me.

"We're not very experienced at sailing," I told her. "We don't know the magic for sailing into the wind."

She giggled musically. "Where's your friend?"

Assuming she was referring to Ragnar, I shrugged. "Busy trying to get the oars working." Ragnar's moodiness had led his cousin Felix to order him to go assist Vitold instead of helping organize soldiers on deck.

"So you do have rowers after all?" She smiled winningly, licking her lips. "My sisters said there weren't enough men on the ship to row it."

"No, that's true," I said. "We've put together a rowing-engine. Much more humane than having men stuck below working the oars." My mind briefly flitted back to my missing men and their likely fate as galley slaves.

Her face fell. She opened her mouth to ask another question, but I held up a finger in warning and she fell silent. I could hear the men on the approaching ships talking in the Dalmatian dialect, their accents a little strange to my ear but their words easy enough to understand. They spoke of plunder and of easy targets, puzzled but encouraged that our crew very obviously lacked sailing experience. They spoke of signaling each other, and surrounding us; the ships on either side let out more sail, building speed as they raced to surround us and block off possible escape routes.

They were also loading their bombards; each of the three pirate galleys was armed with a single great gun fixed forward, larger than anything in our arsenal.

"I do not mean to be rude," I said, "but from what I hear, I think the ships who approach have ill intentions for us, and I am afraid I must try to speak with them."

She huffed, causing a distracting bouncing motion through the violence of the sudden contraction of her rib cage. "Surely you cannot hear each other over the wind and waves yet," she said. "Sound is so muddy and unclear above the water."

I shook my head. "I can hear their voices clear as bells on a winter night," I said. "More clearly than I can hear your sisters whispering below; the surface of the water reflects most of the sound back down into the deep. They think blonde hair looks poorly on you."

The mermaid frowned sternly, her arms crossing in front of her chest. "You're lying! They said it was very cute!" She looked me in the eyes, and her face fell as she took in my mirthless expression.

"They're wrong about that," I added with haste, trying to reassure her. "Don't listen to them; your hair looks lovely. But I must try to dissuade the other men from attacking us." I looked up, the ship growing nearer. I would need to shout to be heard clearly. Straightening my posture, I took a deep breath and then shouted as loud as I could in the Dalmatian dialect.

"Hello the ship! We are the Raven's battalion. If you attack us, it will be at your peril!"

A splash sounded as the mermaid dove beneath the water, her hands clasped over her ears. The men on the approaching ship—now barely a few thousand yards away—rudely ignored my shout, though I thought I had spoken loudly enough to be heard at such a distance. Sound carries well over water, after all; I could hear their voices, and I doubted any of their shouts were a tenth as loud as mine. They should be able to hear me easily.

In the absence of a reply, I sent Georg back to tell everyone to prepare for imminent hostile action. She returned with Johann in tow; he had many questions to ask. Some of those questions were simple; some were more complex; and one made me stop and think:

"Are you going to cast a shield now, like you did in Batavis?"

This seemed like a good idea; on my perch on the forecastle, I was an exposed target, and the pirates could very well have sharpshooters. I closed my eyes, concentrating on the protective magic in my armor, pushing outward. I opened my eyes; a soft turquoise glow lit the edges of the wood beneath my fingers. Closing my eyes, I tried to feel the shape of the magic. Did the protection extend to the whole of the forecastle?

Overhead, I heard the distinctive crack of Katya's rifle, followed by a splash down low that made me worry for a moment, wondering if Katya had shot the friendly mermaid; then there was a great booming noise, and I felt a great shock, a sudden wave of exhaustion taking hold as a deep yet short splash sounded, something small but heavy entering the water with great speed. Katya's rifle fired again, and I opened my eyes. The center galley was driving through a bank of smoke, slewing sideways with its tiller (and therefore rudder) pushed to one side under the weight of a dead helmsman. As I watched, there was a third report from Katya's rifle, and the mainsail lurched as a rope snapped. In the crow's nest, a man pulled out a black and red flag attached to a rope, waving it in the wind as he looked toward the galley to our right.

On both sides, the two flanking galleys were turning under oar power, bringing their bombards to bear. I closed my eyes tightly, the Hebrew incantation from the abbot's vestments tripping over my tongue as I sought to reinforce the shield, which I now knew protected not only myself but the ship as well. Both fired within a few seconds of each other; I staggered as the first shot was deflected into the water, and then fell as the second shot bounced away from the other side of the hull, deep splashes sounding one after another.

The turquoise light flickered out as I got up on my hands and knees, and then I was rocked by the nearer and louder sound of my men returning fire. Our guns were smaller but more numerous, Swedish walking guns and steam knights' cannons with a few other light field pieces and a pair of mortars. All of that fire was focused on the ship to our left, Fyodor having determined that it was better to try to put a single enemy out of action than to disperse our fire. The lighter chatter of arquebuses followed in both directions, and a second more ragged volley sounded from my steam knights as I regained my feet, pushing at the deck with the butt of my trident.

The ship to our left was smoking, showing that somewhere a fire was burning its way through sails and rope; its deck was awash in blood, and its oars were in disarray. The ship to our right stroked steadily forward on its single bank of oars, its crew unable to see the carnage on the opposite side of our taller ship. As they neared, I realized our ship's greater height was an advantage in any boarding action.

"Now!" Banneret Teushpa's shout from the aft of the ship surprised me. I had left him in charge of the helm of a ship whose sails were slowly pushing it in the wrong direction, a ship dead in the water waiting for either a weather-witch to provide a friendly wind or for Vitold to finish hooking up his rowing-engine. My expectation was that this would occupy him harmlessly without insulting his dignity.

As I fell flat on my back, I realized three things. First, as I looked up into the sky, I could see that our sails were furled. This implied that, second, Vitold must have finished hooking up the rowing-engine. As I rotated through the air, I quickly inferred from the scene below me that the pirate ship, which had been nearly directly in front of us earlier had lost a third helmsman while its crew tried to correct their course from its earlier slew, which had then brought them quite close to the bronze ram on the front of our ship.

Gripping my trident firmly, I noted that the impact between the two ships had considerably slowed the forward course of our ship, with the two halves of the pirate galley entangled in our oars. My own trajectory, however, had not slowed, and the water was rapidly approaching.

CHAPTER FORTY-SEVEN

In Which I Rise to the Occasion

I hit the water with arms and legs spread wide, the better to slow my fall by creating a large splash. Weighed down with over a hundred *grivnas* of Corsican brass, however, I still sank below the surface rapidly. Screams and gunshots were muffled; underwater, the louder sounds were the creaks and groans of wooden structures coming apart, the thrashing splashes of men in the water, the squeals of dolphins, and the beautiful songs of the mermaids. Sound is indeed richer underwater, and I spent several stunned seconds appreciating that fact before I started trying to swim upward.

Fortunately, dolphins are very helpful creatures, fond of humans in general, and I had little difficulty convincing one that I ought to be conveyed back to the surface. The more difficult part was holding on; seawater is slippery, and dolphins are both smooth and shaped quite unlike a horse, donkey, or mule, which accounted for the entirety of my previous riding experience.

On our third attempt at an ascent, my head finally broke the surface of the water not far from a small, leaky boat filled with pirates. As I filled my aching lungs and the spots faded from my vision, the pirates briefly discussed my presence and decided to paddle away with blistering swiftness. Most of the aft-half of the pirate's galley was still floating, though poorly; of the front, there was no sign other than a spreading field of flotsam and desperate men.

The galley slaves had the worst of it, being chained to their benches. As the dolphin brought me to the ragged floating wreck, I told him I would appreciate it if his friends tried to keep the chained men from drowning. I had not yet seen any familiar faces, but the fact that some of my own men had been stolen away put the fact that the slaves were not voluntary participants in piracy at the front of my mind.

I said nothing about the pirates themselves, a fact that would cause me shame later as the dolphins spent considerable effort bringing several dozen thoroughly drowned galley slaves back to the surface and very little on the pirates in the water. Dolphins are, in general, optimistic creatures, particularly on the subject of how long a human might be motionless while simply trying to conserve its air; perhaps if their attention had been focused on the unchained men, more men might have lived.

The only galley slaves that survived from the pirate galley we had rammed were some of those in the still-floating aft-part of the wreck. Unfortunately, even though I struck the chains off them as quickly as I could, my bronze sword cutting through the cheap iron like a sharp knife through overcooked beets, I could not save all of them either. If the children's fairy tales that Felix later told me were true, perhaps a few of those who slid into the ocean were rescued by mermaids and chose to stay with them below the waves. It is sometimes said that a mermaid's kiss is a fine comfort to a drowning man.

Unfortunately, I cannot accord those tales the status of confirmed truth. Children's stories are often made up to entertain them, and the mermaids I spoke with were not forthcoming on the subject of their private lives. All I know is that they displayed some undisguised interest in human men, some degree of insecurity in their appearance, and odd feelings about the unfair fact that human women generally came supplied with two lovely legs instead of a tail. That particular reserve might be peculiar to the mermaids that roam between the Aegean and Axine Seas; Felix, upon being challenged, claimed the mermaids of the distant north were more forthcoming.

The rate at which the wreck of the rammed galley sank slowed as I proceeded on my mission of rescue and salvage. Wood generally floats, men and wood together tend to be roughly buoyant, and anything much denser had already slid off into the ocean. By the time I had finished severing every chain I could find, the cannons and arquebuses had fallen silent. One pirate galley had fled, and the third was a blood-soaked hulk riddled with grapeshot.

The battle completed, we rescued as many men as we could from the wreckage, whether pirates, galley slaves, or other captives. This included many of the slaves on the intact hulk, as the decking had afforded them some protection against the grapeshot fired by the steam knights' cannons.

In theory, that bullet-riddled hulk might have been repaired and set back into motion in spite of the damage from our artillery, provided one was willing to spend the effort on cleaning the dead and the debris off, mending the sails, and manning it with oarsmen. In consideration of our limited manpower, we limited ourselves to simple rescue and salvage operations before firing the hulk with the dead aboard.

While setting the ship on fire was not strictly necessary, it made me feel better. It seemed cleaner somehow. I also thought it was a more respectful way to give the dead pirates a funeral than leaving the bodies to slowly rot on a floating hulk. It burned almost to the waterline, sinking lower and lower under the weight of its bombard.

The bombard may have been valuable, but it was far too heavy to try to transfer from the hulk to our quinquereme. We did retrieve cargo that included silver, amber, spices, salted fish, olive oil, wine, grappa, and a very nice chess set carved in an exotic style out of ivory and ebony. There were also three or four captives who had not been put to work in the galley, including a nobleman who claimed his safety was worth a good ransom, two women, and a very pretty boy dressed in a feminine manner whom the women insisted was not a pirate in spite of his lack of chains.

The captain of the surviving pirate galley must have decided that discretion was the better part of valor; that ship was nowhere to be seen by the time we finished cleaning up after the battle, having sailed away at its best speed.

With a wakeful weather-witch, the wind moved us along at such a clip that the blonde mermaid asked me if I would drop a line off the aft end of the ship for her to cling to. She was tired; we were moving quite quickly; and she wished to follow us. If we gave her a tow, then she could relax and later call her sisters to let them know where to follow. Cognizant of the role the mermaids played in bringing me the ship in the first place and increasingly aware of the fact that a man in metal armor with the water of the sea beneath him is well-served by having friendly aquatic creatures nearby, I granted her request without reservation.

The lot of a galley slave is not a pleasant one. Men chained for long periods are likely to develop sores, to fall ill from the bad air, and a whiff of grapeshot tends to be accompanied by wounds that can easily be infected in the filth of the rowing benches. Even men not struck directly by grapeshot or round balls or the shrapnel of an explosive shell may be blasted with splinters or have part of the deck fall in upon them.

In the next two days, eleven former galley slaves and three former pirates died from their wounds, infections, or as a violent consequence of attempting mischief of some kind. We tossed their bodies overboard with as much ceremony as we could afford, funeral services being conducted by a former slave who claimed to have been a monk.

He was at least fluent in Latin, although I am not sure the proper Latin service in the western style includes commending the soul of the deceased to the Archangel Lucifer, bringer of light, and imploring said fallen angel to torment the damned soul of said deceased without mercy. This particular prayer was only included in four out of fourteen cases, adding to my sense that it was a very irregular addition to the liturgy.

With favorable winds whenever the weather-witch was awake and more experienced sailing hands ready to help transform partially favorable winds into forward motion, we made quite swift progress even before repairing and replacing enough oars to bring the rowing-engine back into action. We did not encounter any more pirates as we sailed on, or at least, none that came close. We did see a French cruiser in the distance near Crete. The spinning paddlewheels, the gleam of Corsican brass, and the markedly larger size of the vessel made identification easy.

The journey was pleasant, and I spent half my time in the crow's nest. It is ironic that the most private place on the ship was also the place with the best view. I explicitly discouraged Katya from shooting the blonde mermaid, telling her that it was difficult for a man in metal armor to remain afloat without assistance from aquatic animals. I did not mention that in my case, it had been a helpful dolphin; I felt sure that the friendly mermaid would have been similarly willing to assist had she been closer.

The blonde mermaid continued to inquire after Ragnar's well-being; I was happy to inform her that he seemed to have shaken off most of his saddened mood. In rare private moments, he wrote poetry on scraps of paper; at sunset, he would go to the edge of the railing, peering in the direction he imagined Venice to be, whisper the poem under his breath, and then cast it into the sea.

The mermaid collected several of these poems, committing them to memory before the seawater blurred the ink into illegibility. She recited one for me; it was a sonnet about a masked woman with golden hair who guarded a ruby-red treasure. When the mermaid asked if the poem was about her, I paused for a moment. Recalling how Katya had reacted when I compared her assets to those of the baron's daughter, I decided it was probably kinder not to launch into a comparison of Bianca's attributes and how those attributes more closely matched the description in the poem.

Instead, I asked her if she guarded a ruby-red treasure beneath the waves, which helped move the conversation in a different direction without hurting the mermaid's feelings.

We stopped twice at small islands to take on fresh water and let off whoever wished to be let off; at the first stop this meant the two women, the boy, and half of the surviving former galley slaves; at the second stop, two of the former pirates, both men who spoke fluent Greek. The nobleman, after several days of telling me a ransom would be paid for his release, proved uninterested in being let off at a small fishing village; he said he would rather accompany us to Negroponte, where we would surely be able to collect a reward for our troubles.

So, I agreed to take him to Negroponte, thinking it would be no trouble at all.

CHAPTER FORTY-EIGHT

In Which I Am Called Roman

On the last day of our voyage from Venice to Negroponte, Fyodor's wife woke halfway between dawn and midnight to feed their complaining baby and expressed her dissatisfaction with the roll of the ship in the waves, the perpetual presence of salt spray, and the quality of the food available to her aboard the ship. In our cook's defense, he did provide her with two of our limited supply of fresh eggs from the chickens we had aboard as part of her breakfast.

Shortly thereafter, a strong and steady wind from the south propelled us with rapidly increasing speed until sails strained, masts creaked, and ropes flexed tautly, threatening to snap under the tension. By mid-morning, the blonde mermaid found she needed to either stay entirely beneath the water or entirely above with her tail skimming the water, splashing up a thin V-shaped wave behind her; if she was half in and half out of the water, the force of tension between water and air was too much. The novel experience of skimming along entirely outside of the water was something she found exhilarating at first, but she told me it grew uncomfortable if she did it for more than a few minutes at a time.

We arrived at the port city of Karystos on the southern tip of the island called Negroponte around midday. It was clear and sunny despite the intensity of the wind. Even with the wind rapidly dying down as we approached shore, Banneret Teushpa ordered the sails raised and the rowing-engine readied for braking action, which is to say oars digging into the water to slow our approach. (The Cimmerian had retained his appointment as principal helmsman; I could hardly do otherwise given the total success of his ramming maneuver.)

I should explain that the port of Karystos is sheltered in a semicircular bay that faces south. With a powerful and steady wind from the south, the local fishing boats (nearly all sail-powered) were unable to leave, and Venetian galley captains (conservative about risk) were concerned that even if they could row into the strong wind, its strength and constancy seemed an unnatural harbinger of ill weather.

In addition to the presence of a convoy of galleys scheduled to return to Venice and the local fishermen, a motley assortment of fishing boats and independent merchant vessels traveling either east or west had blown into the harbor, choosing to dock at Karystos rather than risk being blown further off course or having their sails torn off their masts. Thus, the docks at Karystos were quite crowded when we arrived. In fact, we had not crossed the whole bay by the time a small boat rowed out to greet us, a well-dressed young man standing in the prow while weathered seamen rowed steadily.

"There is no room, the wind has pinned all the ships!" the young man shouted in Venetian through cupped hands. "We are all crowded, as not even the fishermen are out! You must beach your vessel to the east of town or turn about under oar and seek a different harbor!"

I frowned, moistening one finger and holding it up in the air. The strong wind from the south had tapered to a mere gentle breeze. I cupped my hands in front of my mouth and shouted back down. "I believe the wind has shifted!" I shouted back. "It will probably blow back the other way soon enough! We can wait a little while, surely someone will want to leave port."

Natural philosophy dictates that for every perturbation of the natural order by magic, there is an opposed and equal, if less ordered, perturbation imposed in the absence of magic. With the weather-witch having called wind from the south, that would have placed a greater pressure of wind across the island of Negroponte, and the natural relaxation of that order would tend to result in an opposite flow of wind. (Or, as I later learned, circular flows of wind. The natural order of wind is one involving cycles, which I did not understand well at the time.)

The young man, who had clearly been given a message verbatim without considering that conditions might change as his boat was rowed out to greet the incoming vessel, rubbed his fingers inside his ears with a pained expression. "It's been blowing from the south all day long," he said, speaking in a normal tone rather than shouting. "What kind of dullard am I speaking with? And what manner of ship is this? Who paints eyes upon the sides of ships?"

As the other men in the boat denied familiarity with the style of my ship, I adjusted my cerulean cape and twirled my trident before tapping its butt on the deck. "A dullard with valuable cargo and no interest in damaging my ship's hull on unseen rocks in unfamiliar waters," I said, no longer shouting as loud as possible but still speaking in the sort of carrying tone officers must use on the battlefield. "Are you the harbormaster?"

"I came from the harbormaster," the young man shouted. "But his instructions were clear!"

"Conditions have changed," I told him, waving my hand in the air as Banneret Teushpa ordered the oars put into the water. Our forward momentum shortly came to a halt, the wave from the oars' braking action sending the rowboat bobbing wildly up and then back down. "Besides, my ship is smaller than a single Venetian great galley. Surely you can make room for just one more ship."

I wasn't actually sure of the comparison, as size can be tricky to measure by appearance alone without resorting to mathematical calculation. Our ship was taller with three separate oar decks above the waterline crowned with a full deck on top of that, with the forecastle rising even higher. Most of the Venetian galleys looked to be the same length as our ship, and most of the ones that were the same length looked to be wider, but all of them had only one oar deck.

After the harbormaster's messenger climbed back into his boat, we waited for a while. When a gentle breeze came in from the north, a flurry of activity on the docks followed.

It was still early afternoon when I exercised the privilege of rank to put myself at liberty and left the Rimehammer cousins in charge of the ship. Katya followed closely; Yuri changed his mind after considering the climb down the rope ladder required to exit the ship. I had not yet set foot on dry land when a bandy-legged and half-blind old man greeted me with effusive and unexpected affection.

"Such wonderfully rhythmic rowing! It is so good to see a Roman ship," the old man said in Greek as he rushed forward to hug me. His accent was unfamiliar to me. As he hugged me, he whispered in my ear. "Your oarsmen are very good. Guard them. We Romans, we must stick together. The Latins are worse than the Franks were, nearly as bad as the Turks—they will steal your men away with coin or siren spell."

I cleared my throat, pushing the man out to arm's length as I checked that my belt pouch remained tied shut and attached to my belt. In my best schoolbook Greek, I thanked the old man for his concern politely, wished him well, and found myself immediately invited to dinner. I attempted to demur, but as I did not wish to be rude and he was willing to follow me both to and from the harbormaster's office, I found myself obliged to accept.

Katya followed silently at a distance.

"He speaks like a proper Roman," the bandy-legged old man said pointedly to a weathered old woman, speaking past a bandy-legged younger man who was the actual target of his comment as he waved his hand pie in the air. "Good, polished, old-fashioned Greek like they spoke at the court of Alexios the First, if I am not mistaken."

"Dad, who is this stranger?" The younger man was not easily distracted.

I opened my mouth to answer, but the old man was faster. As interrupting him would be rude, I shut my mouth without a word while he provided an explanation.

"This is Markos the Crow," the old man said. "Captain of the dromond with the triple oar deck, and bane of the Latins." By now, I knew that 'Latin' to the old man meant 'Venetian,' while when he said 'Roman,' he was referring to Greek-speaking people like himself.

The younger man frowned. "You're from the funny-looking galley? The one that called up the storm to punish the harbormaster?"

"We didn't call up any storms," I said, ignorance leading me astray. "But I am the captain of the triple-decked galley that came in today."

Later, I would learn from the weather-witch that the truth was slightly more complicated. An equal and opposite perturbation returning the natural order of an unnatural clear south wind could (and in that case did) involve the rapid movement of a tempest from east to west, such as the one that raked the mouth of the bay just as the Venetian convoy was leaving. While she hadn't intended to call up that particular storm, its arrival was an indirect consequence of her actions.

The old man cleared his throat loudly. "And when the rest of your fleet of triple-deck dromonds arrives, the Latins will pack up and leave Euboea without a fight. They can't go to war with a new Roman Navy, not squeezed as they are between the French and the Turks."

I shook my head. "I'm not Roman," I said, holding up a hand. Before I could tell him that my ship was alone, he continued, overruling my attempt at interruption.

"Not by blood, no, but Rome has always had its adopted auxiliaries. And you, you're a Varangian," he said confidently. "For generations, you Varangians served as the most trusted guards of the Roman Emperor in Constantinople. Your people may have come from somewhere up the Slavutich originally, but you of the Varangian Guard are true Romans at heart now."

For a moment, there was only the sound of the old woman smacking her lips as she chewed on her own hand pie. My intention to speak was halted by confusion; I had been thrown off my mental course by the old man's reference to the Slavutich River. Did he know that I came from the Golden Empire? Or did he think merely that my ancestors came from there? Then I heard distant shouting in Swedish. Ragnar sounded both unhappy and drunk . . . and should have still been aboard the ship according to the orders I had left behind.

"Thank you for the meal," I said as I stood, bowing to the old woman first and then to the old man. "However, I believe matters have arisen that require my urgent attention."

The old woman must have been pleased by my politeness, for she slipped a hand pie in my coat pocket as I squeezed past her, ducking low to go through a door that was only a handspan taller than the old man himself. Jogging down the street with one hand on my belt to keep my sword from bouncing too much, I could see across the harbor to where the crowd from a dockside taverna had spilled out into the open. Several men were standing around outside with lanterns, one of them still wet from the sea and the other two looking like they could be his brothers.

By lantern light, I could clearly see three other fishermen. The first held tightly onto a twitching tail tied with rope and wrapped in a net; the second held a wheelbarrow supporting the weight of their catch; and the third held the rope around her wrists. The mermaid's golden hair gleamed in the lantern light as she whimpered around the knot of fabric stuffed in her mouth.

CHAPTER FORTY-NINE

In Which I Do Not Deliver a Passenger

In the doorway of the taverna, on the other side of the gathered crowd, Ragnar wore a sour look, a short middle-aged man tugging pleadingly on his arm as he spoke in what was either an unfamiliar Gothic dialect or a very badly accented version of a familiar one. "No, we really have caught a, how you say, *syoyu* . . ."

"*Sjöjungfru*," Ragnar said, snarling. "And they don't exist outside of my cousin's fairy tales. He makes up a new story about how he lost his leg every six months."

"What's the rich Frank saying? Is he going to buy the siren now? She has to be worth a lot of money." On the other side of the middle-aged man and speaking in fluid Greek was a man with an identical nose, slightly younger, slightly taller, with his shirt still damp with seawater.

"He still doesn't believe me," the middle-aged man said. "Look, it's just our bad luck that the Latin convoy is gone, but maybe the baron will buy the siren in the morning."

"At the price he picks," the younger man said, "and in scrip I can't spend off of the island. The Frank has gold coin; the harbormaster's assistant's brother said so." Shouldering the older man aside to grab Ragnar's arm, he pulled.

The drunken Swede, caught off guard, staggered forward several steps through the crowd of people. Sensing trouble, I broke into a brisk jog. Behind and to my left, a roofing tile slipped to the cobblestones below, shattering just as Ragnar removed his arm from the grip of the fisherman in a quick movement that left the local on the ground checking himself for a broken tailbone.

He took in the three fishermen holding the mermaid, then turned to the fisherman on the ground, slipping from deliberate and easily understood Gothic into an angry burst of his native tongue. "You think you can con me out of my hard-earned *örtugar* by tying up some big-titted whore with a severed dolphin tail and calling her a mermaid?"

While exceptionally loud, these words were too fast, too fluid, and too foreign for the middle-aged man to translate directly; although Ragnar's stance and clenched fists made his mood clear. The crowd began to spread in a half-ring, the universal human reaction of a crowd to an impending fight. The middle-aged man backed up, prudently holding up empty hands in a calming gesture; the fisherman holding the lantern, however, was less sanguine about Ragnar putting one of his comrades on the ground. He put his lantern down on the ground and switched his gaff to his right hand as he walked forward.

The mermaid whimpered through her gag. I jogged faster.

Ragnar slipped his hammer out of his belt in response to the escalation. I could only watch as the fisherman with the gaff swung the pole two-handed at Ragnar's head; fortunately, Ragnar was an experienced soldier, and the fisherman was not accustomed to trying to gaff humans. He parried, and when the hook on the end of the gaff caught against the hammer's head, yanked hard, sending the pole clattering to the ground.

A second later, a pinging noise announced the impact of the broken metal hook against a cobblestone. "Don't you dare," growled Ragnar, swaying visibly on his feet. He took an unsteady step forward, a quick dexterous motion of his right hand bringing the top of the hammer to the ground to catch his balance, muttering a startled oath under his breath.

The first cracking noise was the sound of a cobblestone breaking under the impact of the head of the inverted hammer; after that, there were many smaller cracking noises as the puddled seawater around the wheelbarrow froze solid. Ice ran across the cobblestones and up the net that wrapped the mermaid. The man holding the wheelbarrow jumped back, trying to snatch away his hands as ice ran up the handles. The wheelbarrow tipped over, the frozen net shattering as the mermaid and wheelbarrow more or less switched positions, landing with a loud thud followed by a muffled whimper.

Ragnar was still looking down at the cobblestones, working on finding his balance again. When one of the other fishermen stepped forward holding a knife, a quick motion of his elbows and rapid blur of frosted steel left his hammer upright in a two-handed grip. "Piss off," Ragnar said, enunciating in his best slowly spoken Venetian as his eyes focused on the fisherman, a growing layer of frost on his hammer catching the torchlight.

I don't know how many words of Venetian either Ragnar or the knife-wielding fisherman understood, but that phrase appeared to be one they had in common. A fresh damp stain melted through the frost on the fisherman's pants before he made a hasty exit from the scene, followed more slowly by the other fishermen. The one rubbing a possibly cracked tail-bone was moving the slowest and was bold enough to shout something about Ragnar paying one way or another before jogging out of view behind a row of houses.

"All of you, piss off," Ragnar said more loudly, swinging one leg around in order to turn to face the half-circle of onlookers. "Back to your drinking."

Slowly, reluctantly, the crowd began to disperse. Ragnar looked down at his now-crossed legs, making the unfortunate decision to try to move his other leg to get both of his feet pointed in something resembling the same direction. That was when he lost what was left of his sense of balance; I broke into a run, but wasn't quite fast enough to catch him as he went down on his hands and knees and then rolled to a sitting position.

"Lieutenant Rimehammer," I said gruffly after I had arrived and caught my breath. "What are you doing here?"

He snored gently in reply, his chin resting on the butt of his hammer, one leg sprawled in either direction, the scent of grappa filling the air.

After a few failed attempts to wake him and deciding I didn't trust any of the locals looking on, I reached the conclusion that I didn't want to leave either him or the mermaid here. So, I tossed the wheelbarrow aside, pulled the gag out of the mermaid's mouth, and slung the mermaid over my right shoulder with her tail as the heavier part to my rear; then picked up Ragnar and slung him over my left shoulder with his legs forward to try to balance the load.

In the absence of any fresh threats, most of the original crowd of onlookers had returned to looking on, along with a shadowy figure perched on the roof of the taverna whose rifle barrel glinted in the moonlight. Trusting that my back was well guarded, I walked back to the ship, boards creaking dangerously underfoot until I could slip the heavier part of my burden into the water. Along the way, I answered her questions with a series of assurances that Ragnar was mostly fine; he was not injured, but had drunk too much grappa.

After satisfying her apparent desire for more details about Ragnar's health by discussing the distillation process involved with the production of grappa at a level of detail that would have bored most non-mechanics, I carefully climbed up the rope ladder back into the ship, deposited a snoring Ragnar Rimehammer on the deck with an open question in my mind of whether or not he ought to still be called "Lieutenant," and then set about waking the elder Rimehammer cousin.

We were midway through a digression about stories Captain Felix Rimehammer had heard told about mermaids when Katya climbed aboard, telling me she thought it advisable that we depart promptly, as the offended fishermen were in the process of demonstrating that they were connected by friendship or familial ties to a large fraction of the population of the town. From what she described, I concluded that the fishermen believed Ragnar and I owed them a substantial sum on account of mermaid theft, emotional distress, and reputational damage.

With that in mind, we woke Vitold and began to warm up the rowing-engine as we made a quick head count. We were short three former galley slaves, but those three had been from Negroponte, so I had not expected them to return. More surprisingly, we still had the liberated nobleman aboard.

"I thought you wanted to be brought to Negroponte," I said, gesturing at the harbor and taking note of the fact that there seemed to be an increased number of men with lanterns moving about in the streets. "If that's your destination, here's where you get off. We're leaving."

"No, this is Karystos," he said. "Negroponte the city, not just anywhere on the island. This is the territory of the southern triarch. I need to get to the city."

I stood stock still for a moment, trying to picture the relevant charts in my head. "That is on the wrong side of the island from where we want to go. I could give you money to pay your passage on the next boat headed that way."

He shook his head vigorously. "You promised you would take me to Negroponte, and I promised I would reward you. I can't do that here. Promises are sacred!" He jutted his chin out defiantly, his arms crossed.

"Couldn't the baron of Karystos advance that reward on your behalf?" I asked. "Or one of the local merchant factors?"

At the mention of the baron, the noble swallowed, his face paling. "No," he said. "Just take me to the city of Negroponte. Like you promised."

I sighed. He was right; I had promised. "Very well. It will not take us that far out of the way, I suppose." I gave a signal to Banneret Teushpa; he gave a signal to Vitold; and with a lurch, the rowing-engine jerked the ship forward. After the first several strokes, we reached a steady speed, silently sliding out of the harbor.

Felix was at first slightly annoyed at the detour; but then realized that stopping at Negroponte would give us another opportunity to sell off the cargo we had not had the time to sell at Karystos and perhaps take on profitable cargo, something which had been in short supply at Karystos, given the fresh departure of a Venetian convoy.

While we were moving at a good galley clip, it was not so fast that the mermaid was pressed hard to keep up with us. She was very pleased with her rescue—both that it had happened and that it had been effected by Ragnar, thereby proving that he loved her enough to face down five angry fishermen with gaffs and knives and flaming lanterns alone. Her exuberance showed in the way that she leaped back and forth over the ram at our prow, for brief moments coming entirely out of the water; and while underwater, she sang loudly enough that I could feel the faint vibration coming up through the keel.

Once a school of her sisters arrived, she calmed down, telling them an abridged version of the story of her capture and release. As they talked amongst themselves underwater, she perched on the ram, sliding up the nose of the ship with her chest thrust out, and quietly asked if I might teach her the lovely language Ragnar had spoken when he was angry. She only knew Venetian, Greek, and Dalmatian; but that language, whatever it was, it was Ragnar's heart's tongue, and she needed to know it.

CHAPTER FIFTY

In Which I Bid Farewell to Negroponte

Could I ask a small favor?" The rescued nobleman had his hands nervously clasped behind his back.

"You may ask," I said. Whether or not I would grant the favor was another question.

"I was wondering if perhaps you might announce my arrival as loudly as you can," the nobleman said. "When we sail up to the Castle of Negroponte."

"Really?" I frowned. "Like a majordomo announcing a guest?"

"Just so, only louder." The nobleman nodded. "Being that we are arriving in a ship of a style that they will not have seen before, it may save some difficulty."

"But . . . there's no way that the Venetians at the castle know anything about me," I said. "I'm as much of a stranger to them as the ship. The convoy that left Venice while I was there hadn't yet called at Karystos." At least, according to the harbormaster.

The nobleman shook his head. "From what your officers say, I am sure that a description of you has gone by pigeon post from Venice to Pula, Corfu, and Negroponte. There is only a little news that can be sent by pigeon, but you were . . ." He trailed off, searching for a suitable word.

"Pigeon post?" I asked, puzzled.

"Yes, pigeons make very good messengers," the nobleman told me. "Though, you have to take them away from their homes, so they must be carried one way slowly before they fly back."

My mind raced, thinking back to the pet pigeon that Ehrhart had lost just outside of the border of the Gothic Empire, the one with a scrap of paper tied to its leg that was nattering on about going home. Had Ehrhart loosed the pigeon to send a message? I shook my head, focusing back on the present.

Given how many larger birds preyed on pigeons, I felt skeptical of the reliability of pigeon post and said as much, then continued to the real question. "You think that if I announce you, they will be quicker to give us permission to drop you off and pass through the strait? Why?"

"Er. Well, you're an impressive fellow," the nobleman said quickly. "Just wear your golden armor, that lovely cerulean cape, and have your orichalcum trident in hand, and they will surely know that you're a respectable gentlemage of means. Even if they haven't had word of you by pigeon post."

"It's Corsican brass," I said by way of a correction. "Fine. I'll announce you." I paused, trying to remember his name and title. "Baron Logos?"

He shook his head. "I gave that as a false name to the pirates. My real name is Constantine. I will write out the style of my introduction for you."

And so it was that I sailed to the gates of the Castle of Negroponte. When I saw cannons begin to shift in our direction, I commanded the oars put in the water to brake, walked to the highest point of the prow, holding my trident in one hand and unfurling a scroll of paper in the other. I took a deep breath before beginning my speech.

"Hail the castle! I speak as Marcus Corvus," I began, my eyes scanning the page. "You may have heard of me. Pause for one minute." I stared at the paper, realizing that 'pause for a minute' had been an instruction intended for me to follow, rather than part of the message. Reading ahead, I found several more instructions nestled into the introductory statement that the nobleman had penned. I shook my head, deciding to ignore them.

"I come to return from durance vile the noble Constantine, thirteenth of that name. He was held by those who enslaved many of his people, chaining them to oars until death. He has promised me a reward for returning him to his proper position of status and authority upon the island known by the Latins as Negroponte," I said, pausing to interject my own words. "He hasn't been specific at all about that reward except to say that it will be well worth any trouble. It certainly should not involve any cannonballs."

I glared for a moment up at the ramparts, where several bombards were still pointed in the direction of my ship. A watchman who had been holding a spyglass was now standing and waiting impatiently as a well-dressed man made use of it, pointing it in my direction. I looked back down at the paper, finding the place where I had left off, and then I heard the distinctive sound of Katya's rifle break the monotonous rhythm of wind and wave. Looking up, I saw a man with a mallet in hand fall down next to one of the bombards, a red stain blooming around the shoulder of his mallet arm.

"He was going to strike the phoenix stone of the bombard," Katya called down, justifying herself preemptively.

I took a deep breath, finding within myself the strength to shout more loudly. As I did so, for a few dozen yards in front of the boat, a triangular shape formed where the surface appeared calmer. "This is your last warning. Move to fire again and I will make you regret it."

The mallet-man at one of the other bombards dropped his mallet, stepping away from his bombard with both hands raised. The well-dressed man with the spyglass was now talking with several officers; I waited for them to finish before resuming the introduction. "You will call upon the retainers of Constantine within the city of Chalkis. They will take position within the Castle of Negroponte and within the harbor to greet us. Thus speaks Marcus Corvus, mercenary and renowned war mage."

I skipped over the line that called me "blessed of Poseidon" and "breaker of armies," as I felt no confidence that the former was correct, and the latter seemed a bit boastful. However, the last sentence seemed perfectly friendly, just a bit of well-wishing. "May the walls of the Castle of Negroponte stand tall forever, and may it be not today that a great earthquake casts the whole city of Chalkis into the sea, taking with it faithful and faithless alike in screaming horror. May the people of Chalkis see today only sunlight, and not the dark clouds of wings of carrion feeders hungering for flesh." I paused, spontaneously deciding to add a benediction that seemed of greater interest to normal persons. "And may your fishing nets never come up empty for weeks on end, leaving hunger in your bellies."

Having wished both the castle and the surrounding city good fortune in a friendly, if mostly oddly specific, manner, I rolled up the scroll of paper, handing it to Georg. Then I made a respectful salute with my trident, hoping that the soldiers and other important persons scurrying around on top of the wall would believe that I really was just delivering a lost nobleman to them. I steeled myself and kept one eye on the bombards as the rowing-engine engaged, prepared to try to shield the ship from harm if they decided to fire; but there turned out to be no need.

We did have to wait a little while in the harbor before Constantine's escort arrived to take us to the castle.

I had been impressed by how well-dressed the soldiers on top of the ramparts of the castle had been, but at the harbor we were greeted by a ragged formation of soldiers wearing their armor over more humble clothing. Their armor was generally poorly fitted, several were clearly inexperienced with handling arquebuses safely, and a third were barefoot. They were accompanied by half a dozen very well-dressed Venetian gentlemen with empty baldrics.

Constantine greeted the soldiers in Greek and the Venetians in their own tongue. Katya and I spent a pleasant evening in a soft land-based bed, Felix sold off much of our cargo and replaced it with other cargo he thought was valuable, and the next morning saw Constantine's reward delivered to our ship. This generously included a small chest packed with several *grivnas* of golden ducats, a jeweled and enchanted dagger, and half a dozen personal servants. I was also offered a trained giraffe, which had apparently belonged to a Venetian noble whose estate had been recently dissolved, but demurred; I could not see how to safely keep it aboard our boat in rough seas.

In the end, the only major complication that weighed on my mind about our arrival to the Castle of Negroponte was the unfortunate bombardier who took a bullet to the shoulder; Constantine promised that the man would be seen to. We set out in a well-rested and well-fed state, absurdly well compensated for the simple task of returning a kidnapped noble to his home island. It has not been my experience in general that nobles are generous without reason, but there are exceptions to every rule.

I had no experience with having personal servants, unless Georg counted in her role as my *de facto* squire. Knowing that Georg had been a lady's maidservant and that Katya had grown up in a wealthy family, I delegated the task of figuring out what to do with them to those two while I focused on teaching the mermaid how better to speak to Ragnar in his native tongue.

In the excitement over our sudden departure from Karystos, I had put aside the question of whether or not Ragnar should remain a lieutenant;

in the end, I decided to leave the matter of disciplining Ragnar to his cousin Felix, who decided to run him ragged in drills on the deck. I did, however, decide to promote Georg to the rank of banneret and Teushpa to the rank of lieutenant. After all, Teushpa had been a banneret for a long while, and even if his pretense at being an illusionist was unconvincing, Ragnar's misadventure brought it to my attention that I had never had to discipline the Cimmerian for misbehavior in spite of the fact that he'd been part of my company from the very beginning, which made him unique among my junior officers.

Once we rounded our way out of the northern gulf between Negroponte and the mainland, we were in the northern Aegean, in waters controlled mostly by the Sultanate. While the Venetians relied heavily on galleys, the fleet of the Sultanate included a number of steamers—not as large or as quick as the French ones, but as mobile and maneuverable as any galley with greater persistence and heavier artillery. As we entered the open waters of the northern Aegean Sea, I could not help but remember all the news-sheets I had read as a child about the helpless state of the fleet of the Golden Empire against a more advanced naval power—and of the rapacious nature of the Axine Sea pirates funded by the Sultanate.

Still, if I wanted to return home to the Golden Empire, the fastest route lay through the heart of the Sultanate—across the northern Aegean Sea, through the Hellespont, and across the Axine Sea. If I wanted to reach Katya's father, I would then take the ship through the Cimmerian Strait, across the Cimmerian Sea, and up the Kama River. It was a route traveled regularly by merchant ships, and the sea trade passing through the Hellespont was highly important to the Sultanate.

True, our galley looked a little bit different from a modern galley, but would that be any reason to block our passage?

INTERLUDE

A Letter Addressed to Yaroslava Ivanova, District of the Lower
Tanais, Rome-upon-Tanais, Upper Quarter, Palace of the
Seventeenth Heir-son, Eastern Wing

Esteemed Cousin Yarka,

If you wish ever for us to unite, bid from your grandfather the favor of speaking on my behalf, for circumstances have conspired to generate a failure that may be placed on my shoulders.

Did I not say the prince would not be able to be everywhere and everywhen that he was credited with unless he had wings to fly? Did I not say he was the greatest new mage of our generation? Please let that be known!

Our fort built upon the banks of the Ordessus is no more; I returned to it in daylight not a week after the fateful battle. Every hundred paces from the ruins of the old Wallachian castle down to the Istros, there is a spear thrust into the dirt, crowned with the remains of an unfortunate arquebusier of the Golden Empire.

I write now from Tyras as a loyal Colonel of the Imperial Army; unfortunately, duty (and certain unwarranted accusations of cowardice related to my continued survival by officers eager to lay blame anywhere but on one of the Emperor's old favorites) requires that I seek to bolster the defenses of Tyras. We must have artillery, mounted to fire at elevation—such as on the latest warships.

Yours to the very end, should it come to such.
—Igor Vladimir Tsarevich

CHAPTER FIFTY-ONE

In Which I Put Dreams to Rest

I sat bolt upright. I was breathing heavily, my heart racing, my body damp with sweat. With the blanket falling to my lap, the night breeze felt cold against my bare chest. Katya shifted, squirming to pull the blanket back over herself and blinking up at me sleepily.

The moon was full and high in the sky, so I knew that it was still night. The slow but broad rocking motion informed me that I was in the crow's nest; I could remember having joined Katya after dinner. Perhaps it was irresponsible of us to sleep in the crow's nest when it could have been used for a night watch, but we had determined that the crow's nest had two particularly desirable properties: First, it had privacy, which was in short supply after Constantine had given me half a dozen personal servants as a reward for his rescue and return to Negroponte. Second, it did not smell of livestock and sailors, which is to say soldiers, many of whom had not bathed in some time.

What dream had set me bolt upright? I focused, trying to remember. There had been a cave? Or perhaps an old ruined castle on a mountain. Or both? Leathery membranous wings crossing over the full moon. Eyes glinting in the darkness. A ruby, so dark as to be royal purple—like a gem-prince of the lesser amethysts. General Ognyan Spitignov and his sword—that I had seen in countless nightmares about a massacred village.

But no, there was something more; the Butcher of Belz's familiar face had lacked eyebrows and eyelashes, every last hair singed away by heat; and his grin was a stiff rictus rather than an expression of a maniac's emotions. And his sword—I remembered his sword sunk halfway into the earth, a crucifix. And the intense gaze I saw reflected in the blade; it had not belonged to General Ognyan Spitignov. The general's boots had dangled in the air behind the sword, on either side of a wooden pole.

As I sat there hyperventilating, Katya slipped her hand over my chest, driving the images away.

"The old nightmare again?" Her fingers were warm against my chilled chest.

"Yes . . . No, it was different." I paused. A fleeting imagined scent like roast pork faded, the last lingering trace of the dream. "I think in this one, he was dead."

"Hm," Katya said. "Was I in this dream?"

"No," I said.

"Am I with you now?" Katya asked. Finger by finger, her hand crawled up my chest and around the back of my neck.

"Yes," I said, my hands slipping over soft skin as I pulled her into my lap.

"So the nightmare is over. It will not come back." She kissed me with a sense of firm authority, denying me the opportunity to argue the point as she clung to me hungrily. It was not long before all thoughts of my dreams were pushed out of my mind by Katya; and then I fell asleep with her lying on top of me. The nightmare did not return.

Morning found me well rested and giving a sunrise language lesson to the mermaid following us. It would have been better if one of the Swedes was giving her lessons instead of me, but I didn't feel like testing Ragnar's disbelief in the existence of mermaids yet again, Felix was preoccupied with logistical matters, and none of the other Swedes could get by adequately in Venetian (much less Greek or Dalmatian).

I heard a footstep behind me and then a crash. The mermaid giggled, slipping below the water; I found one of my new personal servants kneeling with a tray in her hands. Two damp pieces of toast and one tea-doused egg remained on the tray; a third piece of toast marked the original point of impact for the teapot. A teacup was lodged in her dress. As she addressed profuse polite apologies to my boots, I took in the shade and length of her hair (light brown, with a braid that reached down to her waist) and tried to recall her name.

"Zaneta," I said as I gently took hold of the tray. "It's okay if you're a little clumsy."

"I'm not clumsy," she said to my feet. I could still see only the top of her head as she continued. "I just need more practice carrying things on trays. And on a moving ship."

Holding the tray by one edge, I made a sandwich from the tea-soaked toast, putting the egg between the two slices, and then set the tray down on the deck. After taking a quick bite (I was, after all, hungry) I reached out my free hand. "Here. Stand up," I said.

Her silky smooth hands, free of any callouses, gripped mine as she pulled herself up. Her face was streaked with tears. In the ensuing conversation, she insisted she had little practice with carrying trays; my ensuing questions revealed that she had some practice with painting, embroidery, playing cards, and supposedly some forms of magical entertainment.

Armed with knowledge from Georg about focus wizards, I asked if she was missing some necessary focus in order to succeed in her endeavor of recreating delightful music; she responded by flinging an angry slap in the direction of my face and accusing me of tormenting her with lies to further debase and humiliate her. As I stood there in surprise with my cheek stinging, she sank back down to her knees, rubbing the palm of her hand with a pained expression. Then she broke down crying again, begging me to punish only her for her insolence and not her family, which had already been punished sufficiently by their loss of triarchic status.

Now that I understood that she came from a noble family fallen upon hard times, I thought I understood her anxiety. I meant to reassure her by telling her that if she had second thoughts about entering my service, I would be happy to let her off at the next port to pursue an alternate career or take passage home; however, I only got as far as telling her that she could disembark in Constantinople before her eyes opened wide in fear. She bowed low and started wailing again, clutching my feet and begging me to give her a second chance before dragging her to the dreaded markets of the Turks.

Never before had I met anyone with such a terror of going shopping in a foreign city that the mere mention of bringing her to a city (not even of any intention to take her shopping there) was enough to raise such objections. That said, the seeming paradox of emotion she presented by alternating between attachment and anger was concerning, and I suspected that Katya would become concerned if Zaneta spent a great deal of time kneeling in front of me. I bade her stand and calm herself and then dismissed her from my presence, sending her to Georg.

We had very good fishing all the way to the Hellespont, a fact that was no more natural than the wind that blew us directly there. Being on friendly terms with mermaids and dolphins helped; the blonde mermaid in particular was excited to experience the novelty of fire-based cuisine and often took the lead in herding fish into our nets. The dolphins were more mercenary in inclination, interested mostly in cooperating on the basis of the fact that with a net on one side of their hunting formation, they could ensure that an entire school of fish was eaten all at once rather than most of them escaping.

While she was interested in the greater variety in taste, the mermaid's motivations in helping herd a diverse range of fish into our nets were not strictly culinary. One of Ragnar's poems mentioned an edible fish known as a *torsk*, and she was eager to try to impress Ragnar by getting his favorite fish to him. (Editor's note: Torsk refers to codfish.)

As I have no familiarity with *torsk*, I was unable to describe them in detail to the mermaid, which made this quest difficult. With each new species of fish she herded into our nets came inevitable disappointment, as one or another Swede on deck answered my question in the negative. While it is difficult to prove that there are no *torsk* anywhere in the waters of the Aegean, I soon came to believe they are strictly a fish of the north.

Within the Hellespont, however, the wind was no longer at our command; and, further, we did not wish to stop to fish. It is a narrow strait, a busy one, and due to the unusual nature of our vessel, we were assessed a passage toll that gave me pause. The logic the sultan's men employed was that since our ship had three times as many decks of oars as a regular galley, we should pay three times the usual tariff.

Even given that logic, the toll seemed high, and I convened a quick advisory council belowdecks, including Captain Rimehammer and those members of my crew who were familiar with the area—mainly Greeks and Venetians. Unfortunately, the single Venetian whose judgement I trusted best (Maestro Zilioli) deferred along with the rest of the Venetians once one of my new personal servants, Zaneta, told me that I should respond to their insulting attempt to extort me by razing Troy to the ground.

If I were an intemperate and uneducated man, I might have followed that advice; however, from my studies, I knew that the mighty fortress city of Troy overlooking the strait is no mundane fortress. Its reconstruction involved some of the most advanced magics of the Augustinian era, the foundation laid into warding patterns designed by no less than Virgil, one of the greatest Roman archmages.

Even if I were inclined to halt our voyage to lay siege to Troy with a single battalion of soldiers, I was not experienced in tunnel-magic to undermine walls (as was the case with the Burgundian abbot we had met in Batavis). Additionally, Troy's walls were well warded against magical attack, and those wards had been reinforced repeatedly over the centuries after Virgil's great project was complete. Indeed, those wards were why we did not have a favorable wind—the wards that extended into the rock cliffs effectively shielded the whole of the Hellespont from weather magic.

At that point in the discussion, Zaneta had another emotional outburst (something about lies, extortion, and fraud) and was swiftly removed from the proceedings by an alarmed-looking Maestro Zilioli whispering fiercely in her ear.

Further discussion with the Greek seamen we'd taken aboard established that the proposed tariff was more than triple the actual usual tariff for most merchants, and that the tolls charged were ordinarily related to the value of goods carried. That council complete, I returned to the forecastle, hailing the firebox-powered steamship that had blocked our path.

While not as large or as impressive as a French cruiser—it rode quite low in the water, and its hull was sheathed in lead rather than Corsican brass—the Turkish warship had two sidewheels, bombards both fore and aft on elevated firing platforms, and smaller guns lining its sides. If forced to fight, perhaps I could shield us from their guns, and perhaps our return fire would give us the edge; but then we would be shelled from the looming fortress of Troy. Picking a fight instead of paying a toll seemed unreasonable.

Instead, I discussed the matter with them reasonably, asking for a more reasonable tariff, discussing some of the particulars of our cargo, listing the rates I had been told were normal for merchant ships passing through, and so on. Clearly there was no fixed rate, and while there were no alternate routes to take a ship through to the other side of the strait, perhaps we were not so interested in passing through the strait today after all.

Once several merchant ships had queued up behind us, waiting for their own exchange with the Turkish warship, the fee lowered slightly; then I paid, sailing through without assaulting the walls of Troy.

CHAPTER FIFTY-TWO

In Which I Leave a Debt Unpaid

In the broadsheets that reached the village during the conquest of Wallachia, the sea guarded by Troy on one end and Constantinople on the other was often called the Sultan's Lake. It has other names as well. Traveling across it gave a strong impression of the strength of the sultan's navy, and we were treated to a close look at several more steamships by naval captains curious about our ship.

I kept a running count of ships; while the lighter escorting galliots with their conventional oars were more numerous, the greater weight of the steamships probably made them the more important part of the strength of the sultan's great fleet, which had terrified the ship's captains of the Golden Empire in the Axine Sea and now greatly worried the Republic of Venice in the Aegean Sea.

For my part, I wondered if the sultan's lead-sheathed sidewheelers stayed in the Sultan's Lake most of the time because the sultan was worried about losing them. There had been no word of the French having designs north of the islands of Crete, Rhodes, and Cyprus, but French cruisers were taller, longer, faster, and clad in Corsican brass. Though I had not seen the one near Crete close enough to gauge its armament, I suspected they were better armed as well.

While several of the sultan's sidewheeler captains were curious enough to draw near for a better look at our unusual ship, only one captain was curious enough to stop us to get a closer look.

Between our quinquereme's unusually high freeboard and the sidewheelers' unusually low freeboard, the sultan's most curious naval captain was treated to a difficult climb before coming aboard. The man was surprisingly young for a captain, with dark hair, bright eyes, and a beard that nearly matched the shade of Katya's hair; on viewing Vitold's rowing-engine, he agreed that we clearly did not have spare galley slaves for him to purchase for his galliot escorts.

He made an offer to purchase certain other members of my crew, including Vitold (on account of my crediting him the design of the rowing-engine we had built together with Johann), Katya (on account of her hair), Zaneta (on account of her "aristocratic beauty and poise," which I guessed was a polite method of referring to the fact that she had a comely figure), and two other of the personal servants assigned to my comfort by Constantine (on the grounds that surely I wouldn't miss "one or two hearty wenches").

I assured him that I did not have any slaves at all for sale, being that I ran a free company of soldiers rather than a slave-trading enterprise. After the red-bearded captain climbed back down the rope ladder to his side-wheeler, having been satisfied with my handing him the modest "gift" of a small waxed wooden chest I had found in the hold, filled with red threads of some kind that smelled like hay. (An irritated Felix Rimehammer later informed me that he thought the chest was of greater market value than Zaneta, which seemed a rather cruel assessment.)

After the curious captain's departure, I was thanked individually by several of the former galley slaves among our crew, as well as Zaneta. Zaneta's thanks were profuse enough to leave no doubt that her generous endowment was no illusion produced by padded cloth, and for me to discover that her red lips were that color due to scented lip-paint. Katya took exception to the latter, and I told Georg to keep Zaneta busy belowdecks out of sight of the crow's nest.

That night, I slept in the crow's nest again; Katya considered the climb well outside of Zaneta's capabilities.

In the morning, we reached Constantinople, and I declared my intention for us to stay in port for the day. I placed Captain Felix Rimehammer in charge of a security detail for the ship along with our mechs, our religious order of steam knights, and whomever else wished to stay. This included Vitold (who was concerned about the naval captain's interest in our rowing-engine), Fyodor (whose wife had assigned him baby-related duties while she napped), Zaneta (who, as I mentioned earlier, seemed irrationally afraid of going shopping in Constantinople), and nearly included Ragnar, who was inclined to continue moping and writing poetry.

I took him by the shoulders, looked him very firmly in the eye, and told him with every bit of controlled energy I could muster that he should put Bianca out of his mind for the day, go have the best time that he could, and then return to the ship by sundown.

"Yes, sir," Ragnar told me, blinking confusedly.

"So you're ready to get over Bianca?" I asked.

"Who?" He gave me his best befuddled look.

I smiled at his joking antics and waved him off down the gangplank after Lieutenant Teushpa. Then I gave Katya a little bow. "After you," I told her. I had decided to visit the city myself. It was true that I had not found myself in good favor with the sultan's emissary to the Gothic Empire, and this should perhaps have inspired me to greater caution during my visit to Constantinople; however, while Pasha Mustafa's astrologer blamed me for the sudden flight of Princess Anna from Oenipons, I did not expect to encounter the pasha or anyone else who knew me.

Even if he had planned to return directly to Constantinople to swiftly report his failure to obtain the legendary beauty as a wife for Sultan Alaeddin, which I doubted on account of all the stories I had heard about sultans chopping off heads of pashas who displeased them, Pasha Mustafa had perhaps a week's head start on us due to our delays in Venice. We had made excellent time traveling by sea; in spite of Constantine's claim that Venetians had circulated my description via messenger pigeons, I doubted very much that I featured in what little news traveled at the speed of wind.

Besides, I do not think it is possible for a man possessed of both an interest in history and the freedom of setting his own schedule to simply sail past Constantinople without taking port for at least one day. In my defense, I also felt it would be suspicious if I attempted to sail straight through the Strait of Constantinople without stopping to sell and buy at least some cargo.

Although, I find I must clarify what I mean by "cargo." In spite of Katya's pointed suggestions on that topic, expressed both before our departure and then later when we passed the women's slave market near the harbor, I did not count Zaneta as cargo to be sold. We did, however, stop at the men's slave market, as by that point I had remembered the Venetians' claim that the siren who had stolen my men was Turkish.

Though I doubted that the woman with the enchanted (and quite literally enchanting) necklace was Turkish, the Venetians, Dalmatians, and Turks all participated in a wide-ranging slave trade that spanned many kingdoms, with Constantinople being the final point of sale to a long-term owner for many slaves. This trade was only occasionally interrupted by wars between the Sultanate, the Republic, and Avaria, and even then not completely; the loyalties of trader captains are often most strongly attached to coin rather than country.

At the men's slave markets, Katya tugged on my hand, stopping me to point out a face that she found familiar, penned up with a bunch of other men under an awning.

"That man is Wallachian," she told me in an energetic whisper. "I met him in Wallachia."

I paused. "I don't think I have seen him before," I said.

Katya shook her head. "He was the rebel who told me where to find you. I asked him where the handsome Ruthenian prisoner was kept. He must have thought you were handsome. That was before I decided you were handsome. I thought he was telling me where Ilya was."

Curious, I took two steps toward the pen.

"If you take the whole lot, I can give you a special rate—three thousand *akcheh* a head!" The slave seller smiled brightly, his gaze taking in my armor as he addressed me in badly-accented Greek. "They are trained fighting men!"

I hesitated, unsure of what to say in reply, and the man repeated himself in Venetian before continuing.

"You do not need so many? Perhaps only a pair of guards? I will give you any two you want for seven thousand *akcheh*," the slave seller said, then shook his head. "Of course, I understand if you do not have *akcheh*. I would also accept one hundred Venetian ducats!"

"Where are they from?" I asked.

"They are Latins," the slave seller said. "They speak Venetian poorly, but they understand it well enough. For you, I see you have a beautiful concubine, an exotic Circassian with flame-colored hair; surely you have need of guards for your women's quarters. They are not yet gelded, but I will have it done for you for no extra charge. One hundred golden ducats for two trained, gelded fighting men as household guards!"

"How could I possibly trust slave fighting men?" I asked, crossing my arms. "Wouldn't they want to kill me in the night and take their freedom?"

"They are very far from home. They were captured by Ruthenians in the fighting in northern Rumelia, the northern vilayet that the Deathless

Emperor stole." The slave seller turned his head to spit, which I learned to be a regular custom among the loyal citizens of Constantinople when mentioning Emperor Koschei I in an outdoor setting. "They only have reason to hate Ruthenians, and they have no home to return to—between the Dragon's son and the Empire, half their country has been put to flame. For only one hundred—no, only ninety—Venetian ducats, you will give them new purpose."

"May I speak with them?" I asked.

"Of course, of course. You will want to make your choice of the best two." The slave seller smiled broadly, rubbing his hands together.

The slave seller looked a little more nervous when I addressed the man in Romanian rather than Venetian.

"What is your name?" I asked.

"Oh!" The man seemed startled by my choice of language. "Vesel, milord. Have you come to ransom us?"

"Vesel." I paused, trying to commit the name to memory. "Thank you, Vesel." I felt a strange sense of obligation to the man. His unwitting betrayal of his comrades had led directly to my rescue, and indirectly to my close connection with Katya.

Vesel and I spoke for a little while. The conversation was uncomfortable for both of us; I wanted to know what had taken place in Wallachia since my departure, and Vesel wanted to impress me with his valuable and marketable skills. Vesel didn't really want to discuss how he had been captured, as it reflected poorly on him; and I didn't really want to hear the professional assessment of the owner and manager of a whorehouse applied to Katya.

"You could still get a good price for her here, simply on account of her coloration; red hair, fair skin, and blue eyes are not so easily obtained here, and so her deformities and small breasts do not impede her value as much as they ordinarily would," Vesel told me at one point. "Indeed, you could probably trade her in kind for a swarthy and dark-haired woman with a truly spectacular figure, or a good figure and intact virginity."

Vesel clearly did not recognize the woman he had talked to a few years ago one fateful day before several of his close comrades had died. To be fair, Katya looked somewhat different: her face had been hardened by years of fighting and killing and she had two fewer limbs.

I did learn that he believed Prince Vlad to be alive and that the sultan's men did as well. Somehow, the Wallachian prince had survived whatever disaster had befallen everyone else aboard the ill-fated *Ceres*, washing ashore somewhere along the Tauridan coastline. From there, he voyaged west alone, traveling more swiftly than the news of his presence and unleashing devastating magic. Along the way, he left behind an intermittent trail of destruction across the sultan's prized northern holdings, Ruthenia's Axine Sea coastline, and both sides of the delta of the Istros, which briefly restarted the war between the Sultanate and Golden Empire.

That flare-up died after several exchanges of emissaries between the courts of Alaeddin and Koschei, though the fighting did not, with the rebellion spreading east into Moldova and south into northern Rumelia. After being sold across the border into the Sultanate by an enterprising officer of the Golden Empire who considered the logistics of sales revenue a greater benefit than anything else that could be done with prisoners of war, the local Rumelian slave factor put them directly on a boat south from Rumelia to Constantinople, reselling the captives immediately to a ship's captain for a profit that Vesel considered shockingly modest.

Vesel speculated that the slave factor had feared that one of them might know a secret way of sending a magical summons to Prince Vlad and that the Dragon's son would appear from the sky to fire another loyal village full of the sultan's taxpayers.

As Vesel and I continued our conversation, the slave seller grew impatient and skeptical of my intentions as a customer. Upon being presented with an individual price for Vesel and pointed questions regarding the subject of imminent purchase, I found that I did not consider my nagging sense of accidental indebtedness to be worth paying fifty ducats to free a man whose most productive form of employment in Constantinople would be either in assisting with the buying and selling of slave women or in operating a bordello. Especially not after his unkind words about Katya.

I sincerely bade Vesel the best of luck, telling him I would pray that he found a kind master. Then we went back downhill to visit the women's slave market. While I had not found any of my missing men in the men's slave market, there had been one woman officer numbered among my missing soldiers. There was a chance, however slim, that I might find a familiar face there in need of rescue.

CHAPTER FIFTY-THREE

In Which I Do Not Buy a Concubine

The women's market differed from the men's market in several ways, one of which was the more visible presence of both mechs and eunuchs. In spite of everything I had read about the traditional use of eunuchs as harem guards, I was caught off guard by the apparent fact that the sultan's preferred purveyors of certified virgins were in many cases eunuchs with mech guards. I cannot say I was certain in every case whether a seller was an intact man, a eunuch, or a woman, but at least a third of them seemed to belong unambiguously to the second category. Perhaps Vesel's future in Constantinople would involve such a transformation, even if he was granted the opportunity to pursue his natural talents.

As I searched the women's market, I found no familiar faces there, though Katya seemed surprisingly interested in browsing the wares of the market, making inquiries about pricing and skills that I often had to translate (though some of the slave-sellers spoke Slavonic).

After she lingered in getting a firm price on a Serbian virgin with generous physical endowments and no discernible useful skills, I took Katya aside to ask if she was looking to purchase a concubine and to assure her that I felt I had no need of any such. She agreed with me, and then dragged me to the next slave seller. Within ten minutes, she was inspecting the teeth of a Circassian dancer.

At the end of nearly two increasingly uncomfortable hours in the women's market, Katya told me that she thought Zaneta could sell for upward of two hundred ducats, perhaps as much as three or four hundred ducats if the seller could be convinced of her alleged talents in illusion magic;

and that we could probably get another three or four hundred ducats sell-ing the other five servants Constantine had pressed on us.

"It is not as if they are very useful," Katya said. "Constantine said they were a gift, and a useless gift is best sold. Especially since Zaneta will prob-ably soon become less valuable if she is not watched carefully." Katya gave me a guarded look.

"I don't . . ." I paused, realizing first, that Zaneta was a virgin; and second, that Katya was concerned that I would alter that status. "Katya, you're the one that I want. To me, you are far more precious than Zaneta. But for the third time, I am not going to sell her into slavery simply because you feel jealous."

Katya crossed her arms over her chest angrily, her artificial arm clunk-ing against the supporting breastplate underneath her shirt. "I do not feel jealous," she growled angrily. "It is the smart course of action. You are smart. So, you should do that."

I glared at her; she glared at me. With the silence between us, my ear caught the whispers passed between two Circassian women in the tent behind us, near the edge of the market, whispering in quiet tones only just audible above the rumbling boilers of the pair of mechs stationed by the front of the tent.

"He promised he would see us free even if he had to break us out of the sultan's palace," one of them was saying fiercely. "And take us to Kalmar! That's where the Varangians came from in the first place; I read all about it in the stories."

"Put aside all that nonsense about Varangian oaths! I wish you'd never begged the captain for that romance. You've read it half a dozen times now, and it's given you all sorts of stupid ideas." The second Circassian woman sighed loudly.

The first one must have shaken her head or made some kind of other negatory gesture, but did not speak.

"Besides, even if he would, and it wasn't a grandiose statement, I don't want to be broken out of the sultan's palace!" The other woman seemed irked. "I thought I would be sold to some fat loathsome merchant and put to work washing dishes for his wife if I didn't convince that foreigner to buy me. The sultan himself? I'm sure we will be very well treated, and Sultan Alaeddin is by all accounts a vigorously healthy man, at least. And his agent asked for both of us! A matched set, blonde and brunette."

It was at that point that Katya turned away from me, walking briskly out of the women's market. I followed, leaving the conversation behind.

Bereft of further conversation with my companion, Katya and I explored the city mutely for the rest of the day. She watched warily as I wondered at the sights of a city that I had read about in history books as well as heard about in the news. This had been the second capital of the Roman Empire and now was the home of the Turkish sultan who styled himself as the Emperor of Rome.

In keeping with the former and surprising given the latter, significant parts of the city were in ruin and disrepair, including the Hippodrome, the great entertainment center of the Romans of the East; others had been renewed and repurposed, in keeping with the differences between the religion and customs of the conquerors and conquered. I found every part of the city worthy of great curiosity, to Katya's impatient annoyance.

I myself was subject to some curiosity; Corsican brass is an unusual material for armor and the cerulean of my cloak was a rarer sight in Constantinople than it had been in the Gothic Empire or Venice, both of which trade more extensively with France. However, while I attracted many stares, few people were willing to approach me for casual conversation; at least, until after I stopped to converse with a bookseller and examine his wares. I had sampled my way halfway through a slender, freshly printed volume of Persian poetry when a voice interrupted me.

"Good day to you, stranger. I am called Mahmud. Who are you, and what brings you to this city?" The greeting was offered in French.

Thus confronted, I lowered the book, making a short, polite bow. "I am Colonel Marcus Corvus," I said in Turkish, sensing that some formality was called for on account of the fact that the man who had greeted me was quite well dressed and had two bodyguards near my own height (and somewhat greater in bulk). His attention seemed dangerously similar to the attention of local law enforcement. "I am just passing through the city, pausing to take a break from a long journey with many miles yet to go. Pleased to meet you, Mahmud. Have I transgressed against local customs?"

"No, no. I was simply curious. You look very French. Do you read Persian?" The man seemed hopeful.

"Of course," I said, "but I am not French," I added, switching from Turkish to Persian. "I have really only read a little bit of Persian literature, though, in the largest part just Omar Khayyam." Then I tried to name the few other Persian authors I could remember reading, or the titles of their works if I could not remember the author; I recall that Mahmud corrected me on the pronunciation of one name I had not remembered correctly.

"And, as a cosmopolitan reader, an educated man, what did you think of the poems you were just reading?" He leaned forward, unconsciously licking his lips.

"I am no expert in poetry, but I thought it pleasing," I said. "This Adni writes very lyrically. I can imagine singing those verses."

"Excellent," Mahmud said, a smile on his face. "The book is yours, then," he said, shifting to Turkish and making a quick cryptic gesture to the bookseller. "You will take coffee and baklava with me as we converse further."

The bookseller loudly refused my attempt to pay him, though when I tried handing him the coins a second time, they vanished in his palm while he continued his protests, glancing quickly over at Mahmud. While Mahmud's attitude seemed imperious to the point of rudeness, I was keenly aware that I did not actually know Turkish customs or manners especially well; and if I considered his statement as an invitation to join a wealthy local for coffee and baklava (whatever that was), it seemed an invitation I should be delighted to accept.

The coffee was served in tiny cups, exceptionally strong and sweet with a thin layer of foam on top. It was accompanied by crisp layered pastry filled with pistachios and walnuts, drizzled with almonds and a mixture of rosewater, citron juice, and honey, in which had been steeped something that I recognized only by virtue of having smelled a box full of little red threads earlier, when I had bribed the naval captain, a spice that Mahmud informed me was called saffron.

I had read the name before, but reading a word in a book does not tell you what a thing is. I told him that I found the coffee and the baklava delightful, for it was; and then we spoke of poetry, mathematics, natural philosophy, and other such subjects for a little while. In time, as the sunlight dimmed, I turned my questions to the city and the happenings therein; after all, it was my first visit, and I was greatly curious. Both of us were, by that point, quite animated, and after the eighth or ninth refill of our tiny cups, Mahmud confided in me that the city was in a bit of excitement.

An enchanted rope had just arrived in the city that morning, a gift sent all the way from an eastern prince. Its bearers had stopped to see the great Aya Sofya mosque and participate in prayer there; while so distracted, a bold thief had somehow made off with their basket containing the magic rope. Unfortunately, this necessitated closing the port to departures, news which I took with equanimity. After all, I was having a delightful time in the city, other than the fact that Katya was refusing to talk with me. (Which, I will confess, had slipped my mind.)

From his having brought up the Aya Sofya, the topic of conversation in our quiet lantern-lit garden then turned to architecture for another two cups of coffee and three platters of sweet snacks, until such time as we were interrupted by one of Mahmud's bodyguards. The large man brought unfortunate news; he did not wish to interrupt his master, but the messenger had insisted.

Mahmud excused himself while I took advantage of the privacy to kiss Katya's hand, tell her that I was sorry, and then feed her a piece of sticky baklava from my own fingers.

"And Mustafa is certain of this?" Mahmud's voice had a questioning note.

"Yes, my lord. His astrologer is never wrong. The thief is acting on the orders of the very same devil who stole the princess."

"How does the thief appear?" Mahmud frowned. "You must give the description to the guard at once."

"My lord, the astrologer's art does not work so precisely. The astrologer could describe the thief's master only because he had seen him in person. Find the master, and the thief will surely come to you. The devil is an uncommonly tall man with dark hair. He speaks fine classical Turkish as if he is from the old Seljuk court. His aura is strong and turquoise."

I froze in shock, leaving my thumb and index finger in Katya's lips partway through feeding her another piece of baklava. My magic always looked turquoise to me; I was tall; and my hair was dark.

CHAPTER FIFTY-FOUR

In Which I Walk Very Briskly

For a moment, I stood there in shock. Katya chewed and swallowed the piece of baklava and then playfully sucked on my fingers, not realizing the reason for my sudden inattention. Understandable, as she did not understand Turkish, and thus had not understood the quiet conversation being carried out in the anteroom of the coffeehouse that enclosed the private gardens we were sitting in.

"Katya," I said, very quietly in Slavonic. "We need to get out of here quickly and quietly."

She paused, pulling her head back from my hand, but not letting go. "Now?"

I nodded, pointing at the back wall as I took to my feet. Katya reached the back wall first, but waited for me, giving me a boost to help me reach the top of the wall and clamber over before following herself. As she did so, I heard bells ringing, distant shouting, and the rumble of steam engines being brought up to full—all sounds of alarm and concern. For half a heartbeat I thought I had caused the ruckus by leaping over the wall; then I realized that it was not in any way possible, as Mahmud had not yet returned to the garden to find me absent, and in any event the sounds of alarm were coming from the palace.

We had landed in an empty alleyway. After a short panicked jog, Katya told me that running would attract more attention, so we walked very briskly, as if we had considerable purpose but no fear of being detained. We did run very briefly twice, once to get out of the way of steam carts carrying soldiers, and the second time to get out of the way of a steam cart carrying a pair of mechs. Because we were going downhill, we found ourselves at the harbor considerably more quickly than I had expected.

As I climbed aboard the ship, I heard the rapid footsteps of a man running at a full sprint; turning, I saw Lieutenant Teushpa running by a group of marching soldiers. Since they did not stop him, I came to the conclusion that perhaps the soldiers were not concerned with some individual criminal or fugitive like the rope thief that Mahmud had mentioned, but rather an attack of some kind, perhaps a rebellion or some kind of intrigue. Nevertheless, having been wrongfully accused by Pasha Mustafa's astrologer of arranging the theft of a magic rope, I felt I needed to set out as quickly as possible.

I told Katya as much and then asked her to get a full count of who, other than Lieutenant Teushpa, was still missing; she gave me an odd look, but I didn't feel like explaining my reasoning. Instead, I waited for Lieutenant Teushpa to clamber up the rope ladder, giving him a hand and asking him much the same question.

He held up a hand, panting as he caught his breath, and then Katya came back, telling me that we were missing a total of four persons, including two lieutenants, an arquebusier, and a sailor.

"Felix said he told everyone to be back by sunset," Katya said. "It's not like Lieutenant Teushpa to be late."

Lieutenant Teushpa ignored the insult. As he finished catching his breath, he made a few dramatic gestures. Katya stepped back.

"Correction, one lieutenant is not back yet," Katya said.

"Ragnar," the Cimmerian said. "I know. I'd like to wait for him, but we can't, we really can't. Warm up the rowing-engine and make ready to cast off as quickly as we can. He's the one they're looking for. I'm sorry, I caught up to him in the sultan's harem briefly, but we got separated again."

For a moment, I felt offended that, having been recently promoted to lieutenant, my Cimmerian cavalry officer now felt he was ready to give me orders; then his last sentence clicked into place. I looked at his haggard face and at the mechs lining the harbor. Some bore cannons; others long, thin, menacing tubes attached to barrels, not structurally sound enough to be guns. Between the astrologer's continued persecution of me and my junior officers having thoroughly offended local sensibilities, I could not avoid agreeing with the insubordinate lieutenant.

"We're leaving, with or without Ragnar," I said. "Vitold, make ready the rowing-engine. Teushpa, you have the helm. Kransky, try not to make it obvious, but make ready to return fire If we find ourselves in a firefight. Felix, I want us untied from the dock without it seeming obvious."

Teushpa paused. "Someone else should take the helm, sir. I have an idea about how to get us untied without making it obvious."

I gave him a look. "Very well. I'll take the helm." We could talk about insubordination later; in the heat of the moment, though, I decided to trust that he had a good idea and walked back to the helm. Katya was speaking with the other sharpshooters, pointing at the tops; in a few minutes, she would be scurrying up to the crow's nest, and I would be alone.

Then I heard a splash, a wave of dark brown hair emerging from the water. "What is going on?" It was one of the mermaids; I told her that we found ourselves needing to depart swiftly, and that Ragnar, unfortunately, might not make it.

The mermaid smiled toothily, then ducked down below the water, repeating the news I had given, with the addition of a few choice words about how a certain mermaid could get rid of the stupid-looking blonde color on her hair. The blonde mermaid poked her head out of the water at the same time that we set into motion; sadly, I still did not see Ragnar anywhere. Katya had a better vantage point and a spyglass and made no signal.

"Ragnar is in trouble?" The blonde mermaid bobbed in the water as she swam after us.

"Yes," I called down. "He has gotten himself into trouble, unfortunately, and we need to leave. He's somewhere in the city."

One of the mechs fired its cannon, the ball splashing some ten yards behind the mermaid, who squeaked with alarm. I wasn't sure if the miss was the result of bad aim or intended as a warning shot, but a sidewheeler was turning in our direction, picking up speed to try to head us off.

"You can't abandon Ragnar!" The blonde mermaid sounded upset. "If he's in trouble, you have to save him."

My heart sank in my chest as I beckoned Felix over to the helm. I needed to try to shield the ship with my magic. "Sometimes, you can't save everyone," I said. "I'm sorry, but I don't think we can save him. We'll be lucky if we survive."

Felix jogged over.

"I don't know what got into my cousin," Felix said. "He's been moping and writing poetry . . . I thought the worst case would be that he got drunk and someone needed to carry him back to the ship again. Did he really break into the sultan's harem?"

"You know as much as I do at this point," I said. "I'm sorry, I really am. Maybe he'll escape the city by foot." I braced my hands on the railing, getting ready to try to shield the ship; the mechs began to fire cannons one at a time, and turquoise light flared under my hands, but I felt nothing. Then I saw the splashes of the shot, landing deeper in the water, and thought to look up.

There, up in the sky—a carpet with a hole punched in its middle, an intrepid Swedish lieutenant clinging to the fringes as it flew over the ship from front to back. As it passed over the crow's nest, it flipped sideways, beginning to spiral out of control, and a large basket fell off, dropping down and landing with a firm thud on our deck.

"Ragnar!" I shouted, watching helplessly as the carpet spiraled away, losing altitude rapidly as it flew south into the open sea, plunging downward. "That's Ragnar," I shouted down at the distraught mermaid swimming in our wake as the carpet hit the water. There was a great splash, and when the water cleared, Ragnar and the carpet were gone; the blonde mermaid leaped all the way out of the water, reversing her course.

Then I felt a great shock pass through my body, up from the railing, as turquoise light flared. "Faster!" I shouted down. "Can we go any faster?"

There was a rumble as Fyodor's team and the steam knights returned fire, some shooting at the mechs on the dock and some shooting at the sidewheeler slowly gaining on us. In the distance, I could see four more sidewheelers moving into motion. I heard a screaming baby and a shouting woman, and the steady breeze I had felt from our passage began to still. "Sails! We will have wind soon enough!"

There was a shot from the sidewheeler behind us, and I fell to my knees, suddenly tired, my hands slipping from the railing. I shook my head, staggering forward as the wind picked up, and the sidewheeler began to fall behind. Several minutes passed, and the sidewheeler's stern bombard fired again; I gripped the railing, thin wisps of turquoise light wrapping my fingers before flickering out. The shell splashed down fifty yards short, producing a great splash that momentarily obscured my view of the warship.

I sighed. I could not stop any more shots from the bombard. Was there anything else I could do? I wobbled my way forward, finding the basket sliding around on deck in the rough seas. The top of the basket had blown off in the wind somewhere; inside the basket was a coiled rope. I had a vague idea that perhaps the rope would be useful to the sailors, and in any event the basket sliding around on deck was a hazard, so I grabbed it, securing it between my knees as I began to pull the rope out, coiling it.

As I did so, I found that the rope had a curious amount of resistance to being pulled, as if a great weight was attached to the end; then two pale limbs emerged from the basket, clinging to the rope along with a blonde Circassian woman, who stepped unsteadily onto the deck with a surprised and delighted expression, reducing the amount that I had to lift by her own weight. A brunette Circassian was next, with a sour look on her face; when she greeted her blonde countrywoman, I recognized their voices from the slave market.

Third was a close-lipped auburn-haired woman, whose eyes promised thunder and turned away from mine; fourth was a woman with black hair and an expression that lay somewhere between amused and bemused. And that was the end of the rope; I peered into the bottom of the basket curiously for a long moment before one of the women addressed me.

"I am the youngest sister of Sultan Alaeddin," the auburn-haired woman said, by way of an introduction, bright moonlight gleaming off her richly colored hair for a moment before the gathering clouds blocked the moon. "If you know what is good for you, you will turn the ship about at once."

I opened my mouth, pausing for a moment as I considered how to frame my rebuttal to this argument; then there was a very loud crunch as the next bombard shot smashed into the side of the ship at an angle.

CHAPTER FIFTY-FIVE

In Which I Disobey Orders

I turned away, ignoring the auburn-haired woman and her presumptuous advice. True, she indubitably had an interest in continued survival, which was at risk from the bombards of the sultan's fleet; however, I did not think she fully appreciated the risks posed to most of the rest of us in the event of a surrender.

"Shut down the rowing-engine!" I shouted as the ship slewed sideways, suddenly bereft of perhaps a third of the oars on one side. "Oars up and all to the wind!"

The night sky darkened further as the weather-witch worked her magic, and the hull groaned as Felix grappled with the helm. The weather-witch stumbled, and Fyodor rushed to her side, holding his wife to help stabilize her.

The strait guarded by Constantinople is a narrow one, and has several sharp turns in it. "Turn the wind with us!"

The weather-witch nodded, grimacing.

Another bombard shell whistled by, clipping the railing of the ship; a man, screaming, slid overboard and into the rising waves. A soft hand grabbed mine, and a feminine voice shouted over the howling wind. Beneath my armor, my good-luck stone turned ice cold against my chest.

"You *will* turn this ship around at once!" The auburn-haired woman was nothing if not determined, tugging at my hand with both of hers, hints of red light flickering across her body.

"You will shut up and get out of the way," I shouted back, grabbing back. Diaphanous layers of silk tore as I picked her up and tossed her bodily down a hatch. A soft thump and a loud shriek announced her landing, and I made my way forward to better see the way ahead. Possessed of a measure of common sense and lacking the commanding attitude of the auburn-haired woman, the other three basket-women followed of their own accord, the black-haired woman in the lead and the Circassians following to get out of the way. The brunette Circassian paused to give me the very briefest of angry looks before following the blonde Circassian down the ladder.

After a moment's thought, I tossed the basket after them. I did not know how it worked, but it was clearly magical, and I didn't want it to fall overboard. Rain had begun to fall, reducing visibility and control; the weather-witch had no choice but to focus all her attention on commanding the direction of the wind, and we were stuck with the weather that came along with it. I could see the fresh wreckage of a less-fortunate ship to my right, likely a great galley. Reflexively, Felix veered the ship away from it, coming closer to the left side of the strait.

A bombard fired, more distantly, the splash barely audible over the howling wind and rain. We had opened the range to the lead ships, either through speed or sheer recklessness. Though it was easy enough to see the path through the strait by the diffuse moonlight that pierced the storm clouds, the rain made things tricky, and I could not see through rock. Ahead, I saw approaching cliffs and what looked like an end to the water. I knew that the strait connected the Sultan's Lake to the Axine Sea; so there must be an opening on one side or another, but which? I stared at the waves.

The current was flowing away from the cliffs to the left. "Hard left!" I called out. The weather-witch, by now lashed to the mainmast for stability, swallowed nervously, making circular gestures with her staff. The sails jolted from the sudden change of wind, and then the hull creaked and groaned as water came into view to the left. The sudden shift of direction sent some men sliding, at least one screaming as he toppled over the railing. By the subtle rattling, he landed on the shipped oars; I hoped he would make it back into the ship.

Behind us, the sudden change of the direction of the wind at the sharpest corner of the strait left a spiral in our wake, the wind roaring louder and louder, oddly similar to the sound of a train. Water began to spiral upward, tracing a rope-like path into the dark clouds—a waterspout. As we straightened back out from our turn, the view of the waterspout was blocked, and I looked back ahead of us. A while later,

Katya shouted, announcing she'd seen a sidewheeler, but it was delayed by the waterspout; ahead, cliffs drew nearer, another point at which the strait appeared a dead end.

With the chop of the waves, it was harder to see the current—but there it was. "Prepare for hard right!" I said, looking back at the men. My command was echoed back along the ship. "Hard right! Very hard right!"

The weather-witch's pointed metal staff whipped around like a baton; the ship groaned; and there, behind us, was a growing roaring noise as another waterspout grew. The weather-witch panted heavily, slumping forward; Fyodor grabbed her staff as it fell; and the wind continued to push us forward.

"Wind wild from here!" I shouted. "Felix, we need a little to the left, and it's open sea."

Behind us, the waterspout roared, following more slowly. "As much as the sails will take!" I shouted to the sailors. "Let's not be turned about by the waterspout!"

Daylight found us in the middle of the Axine Sea and uncertain of our precise position within that large body of water. We could say only that we were somewhere in its interior; the shoreline had disappeared some hours earlier and we had been riding winds of uncertain direction and speed against currents of uncertain direction and speed. At dawn, I left instructions for us to head north, and then headed belowdecks to check on the state of the rowing-engine. There, I found that both Vitold and the auburn-haired woman had been tied up. The former was snoring lightly, his head on top of a crate; the latter was gagged and glaring furiously.

"Why is my officer tied up?" I said in a mild tone, looking around at the assortment of soldiers, former galley slaves, mechanics, and personal servants who had chosen to shelter belowdecks and out of the way. The other basket-women edged nervously away.

"She was trying to get him to turn the rowing-engine back on and turn us back to Constantinople," Zaneta said. Dark circles ringed her tired eyes. She knelt down in front of me, bending her neck and lowering her gaze to the deck. "He was going to obey her. If you must, punish me; this mutiny against your officer is my fault."

I looked down at Zaneta's soft hands, the rough ropes snugly binding Vitold and the auburn-haired woman, and then at the guilty-looking mechanics and sailors standing around in stances that vaguely resembled military attention. Men with calloused hands, greatly experienced with ropes, knots, and in at least some cases grappling in close quarters. I had difficulty believing that Zaneta had acted alone against the auburn-haired woman and Vitold. He was short for a man, true; but he was a man accustomed to handling heavy equipment, and Zaneta was a physically delicate woman who struggled with anything heavier than a fully loaded breakfast tray.

I spoke, trying to reassure her. "Look, I don't think that—"

"Please, Master Corvus. You may do whatever you want to me. I only did what I thought was best." Zaneta shuffled forward on her knees.

I tried again. "It's not—"

"Anything at all," she said, bowing down to grasp my boots. "It was my insolence and my insolence alone to act against Lieutenant Szpak. You may punish me any way you wish. I was afraid of returning to Constantinople. Please forgive me. I will do anything you wish. Anything. No matter how degrading or humiliating or painful."

I paused, waiting to see if she was done talking. "It's fine," I said, looking awkwardly down at the beautiful woman clutching my knees. "You did the right thing. If the rowing-engine had come back on while we were in the strait, we would probably have all drowned in the wreck."

In the corner, the Circassians, already pale of flesh, surprised me by paling further.

Zaneta bowed down again, her head bobbing up and down over my boots. "Thank you, Master Corvus, for your understanding."

Uncomfortably, I disentangled myself from Zaneta's grasp and went to check on Vitold, waking him up.

"He should be over the compulsion," Zaneta said. Now standing, she slipped her arms around one of my elbows. "It's the enchantress you need to be careful of."

"I see," I said, untying Vitold.

Vitold denied all knowledge of having been enchanted. He'd been diligently working on detaching the stubs of the broken oars from the engine, and then someone must have knocked him over the head, for the next thing he knew he was tied up and lying in a puddle of bilgewater. Zaneta and I were both satisfied that he seemed back to his normal self, so I walked over to the auburn-haired woman.

"Hello," I said.

She glared fiercely, her eyes showing no signs of recognition. To be fair to her, she'd only seen me briefly the previous night.

"We met last night," I said. "I pulled you out of a basket, but you were being difficult, so I tossed you down here."

Her eyes flickered up and down as she reexamined me; then she closed her right eye for one moment, a flicker of ruddy light glinting in her blue iris. Then both her eyes widened, and she flinched away from me, saying something that, due to her gagged state, amounted to little more than a muffled wordless set of high-pitched squeals. Given the thoroughness with which she had been bound, her attempt to move away from me had an effect as limited as her attempts at speech—that is, the only movement she accomplished was rolling herself over onto her back.

I sent one of the sailors to fetch Georg since I knew that the petite blonde girl had enough familiarity with enchantment to identify the siren in Venice; then took counsel with her and Zaneta, huddled together in a quiet space belowdecks.

"What, exactly, am I supposed to do with an enchantress who can take control of at least some of my officers? Is there a way we could protect them?" I asked.

Zaneta nodded; Georg shook her head, giving Zaneta a sneering look and stroking the air beneath her chin. "Theoretically, yes; pragmatically, no. Enchanting that many protective amulets would be extremely difficult, especially without a ready supply of blank orichalcum."

Zaneta stamped her foot in frustration, folding her arms beneath her bosom in a way that highlighted the size of her feminine assets. "Do you have any magic-suppressing shackles?"

I paused. "I don't think so," I said. "Is there such a thing?"

Zaneta looked at me in disbelief, as if astonished by my ignorance; Georg nodded. My mind drifted back to my time imprisoned by the rebels, and I paused, thinking of another question. "If you try to use magic while wearing such things, will it make your arms feel heavy?"

Zaneta nodded vigorously. "Some of them tighten instead, but that's not very safe, you can lose a hand or foot that way. The modern method is to have the magic drain empower a weakness spell; that way, the more the prisoner strains magically, the weaker they become physically."

"I see," I said, and I did; but we still didn't have any. "What other choices do I have?"

Zaneta shook her head. "You could have her gagged and guarded constantly, but it would be a little bit of a risk. The safest thing would be to throw her overboard." She looked at Georg, as if expecting that she would protest; instead, Georg nodded vigorously.

"Well, you're not very chivalrous," Zaneta mouthed darkly in Venetian while holding her breath. Georg politely pretended not to notice.

"Is anyone susceptible? Could I put the two of you on guard?" I frowned.

"Um. Maybe?" Zaneta said. "She's more powerful than I am. I might have trouble countering her if she went for me when I was distracted. It'd take a more powerful mage with a strong will to reliably resist her even when his attention is elsewhere. I bet Lieutenant Teushpa could."

"Hm," I said, suddenly inclined to disregard Zaneta's judgement; if she thought Teushpa was a powerful mage, she was in no position to judge. I paused, thinking back on why I had dumped the auburn-haired woman belowdecks in the first place. "She was shouting at me to turn the ship back earlier. Why didn't she just enchant me?"

"I expect she tried, for what good it did her!" Zaneta let out a delicate but derisive snort, reaching out to feel my hair and my scalp beneath. My good-luck stone felt cool under my shirt. "She would have failed completely. You've proven very resistant to enchantment. I don't know why."

Georg looked over at Zaneta. Her eyes narrowed. "You witch, you've been trying to enspell the colonel this whole time! And not just now; don't try to tell me that was just a first test."

Zaneta suddenly pulled back her hands, eyes widening in panic. "I, uh . . ."

I shook my head. "Let's not get side-tracked," I said. "Focus on the sultan's younger sister. Zaneta's been with us for a while without causing any serious problems. Zaneta, have you tried enchanting Lieutenant Teushpa?"

Zaneta shook her head, then opened her mouth.

Georg beat her to the punch, blurting out a question. "The sultan's youngest sister?"

I nodded. "Any other ideas?"

When the two of them mutely shook their heads in reply, I walked over to the auburn-haired woman where she lay on the floor. I checked and adjusted the ropes, untying and resecuring her arms behind her back—the coarse hemp ropes had begun to chafe her delicate skin—then rolled her over, hoisting her with my left hand, using the convenient handle I'd created. "You and the other servants will have to clear out of the captain's cabin," I said. "I'll be sleeping there tonight. I mean today."

I rubbed my forehead tiredly with my free hand, then walked up the ladder back onto the deck and to the aft of the ship, ignoring the quiet whimpering I heard from the burden in my left hand. I looked south, to our wake; then sighed, setting down my burden and sticking my legs through the gaps in the aft railing.

After a moment, a brunette head popped above the water.

CHAPTER FIFTY-SIX

In Which I Bind a Redhead

Finally! You traveled very quickly," the brunette mermaid told me. "I wouldn't have been able to find you if the dolphins weren't so noisy."

I shrugged, then stood, leaning against the railing. "Sorry," I said. "We were in a hurry. The men of Constantinople were angry at us."

The mermaid pulled her head back in a gesture of surprise. "Oh? Must have been something bad in the Bosporus waters last night; my own sister turned on me." She shook her head, then swam higher in the water. "She bit me!"

As the mermaid jiggled the affected portion of her anatomy, I found that my eyes were drawn away from her face and down, to where a ring of circular dark marks defaced a particularly feminine part of a display of mermaid anatomy. "I see."

She nodded vigorously. "Yes! All I wanted was a few bites of—" She clapped a hand over her mouth, then finished with an entirely different sentence: "—really unkind to bite your own sister. We left her behind."

I sighed heavily. "We also had to leave someone behind. Ragnar. Also through fault of his own, sadly."

"Did he bite you?" The mermaid rubbed her bite mark distractingly.

I forced my eyes back up to the mermaid's face. "No, no. He caused the trouble with the men of Constantinople, though, and I think it's his fault that I now have to deal with this woman." By way of illustration, I reached down and grabbed the rope handle of the bound auburn-haired woman, lifting her into the air with my right hand; she squeaked through her gag in an alarmed manner.

"Oh? Is she dangerous?" The mermaid frowned. "Sorry, my sisters and I rarely have much experience with females of your species. I've heard they're a little more buoyant."

"Well, most of the time people account women less dangerous, but this particular one is a bit of a menace. I've been told I'll either need to keep her under close watch or toss her overboard."

The mermaid licked her lips. "She looks quite tender."

"High-born. She's the sister of the ruler of Constantinople," I said. "Doubtless reared on the finest delicacies, and likely never had to labor a day in her life."

The mermaid licked her lips again, then lowered herself back fully into the water to swim closer to the ship. The auburn-haired woman made a series of repeated rhythmic squeaks, trying to speak through her gag as she squirmed involuntarily with a strongly emotive affect. I wondered what she was trying to tell me; then I wondered if Zaneta was right about my resistance to enchantment and decided to take the risk.

"I will remove your gag for a moment to talk, but if you attempt to enchant me, I shall toss you overboard straightaway," I told her, flexing my arm to bring us face-to-face. "Is that clear?"

She nodded with wide eyes. I pivoted my wrist to turn her around by the handle, and with my free hand, I delicately untied the knot at the back of her head. A quick twist of the wrist later, I was able to pull the knot of fabric out of her mouth. She then proceeded to emit a steady stream of terrified Turkish, begging me not to throw her overboard and talking about how it would be a terrible waste if I were to let a beautiful woman be torn apart and devoured by sea monsters. Not that there were any vicious woman-eating sea monsters present as far as I could tell, but the Turks would not be unique in having unfounded superstitions about what dwells in the open sea.

I will grant that there are many books documenting the existence of leviathans and krakens and great serpents of the deep. However, as any dolphin will readily tell you after extended conversation on the subject, the largest beasts of the ocean are concerned primarily with one another, and only occasionally mistake ships for other large beasts; humans are largely irrelevant to their concerns, being at best a small and exotic snack with dubious fibrous coatings (i.e., clothing) that are likely to cause indigestion.

Not that I said as much at that point; instead, after she began to repeat herself, I tucked the index finger of my free hand under her chin and pushed gently up, my way of indicating that I wished to change the subject.

"We're not turning around and going back to Constantinople," I said, figuring I should start with basic facts. Then I let my finger fall.

The auburn-haired woman introduced herself in greater detail (her name was Gulben), described her close and dear relationship with her older brother (Sultan Alaeddin), and promised great riches would be given to me if I would but return her to the sultan unmolested and uneaten. I had trouble trusting this and touched my finger gently to her chin again; she paused mid-sentence, closed her mouth, and swallowed.

"Sorry, but I have urgent business to the north." This seemed kinder to say than telling her that I did not expect to live to spend any such ransom payment if I put myself back in the territory of the Sultanate. "I could hand you off to a third party, but I don't think many third parties would be willing to advance me even half of a sultan's ransom without having heard from Constantinople."

I sighed, staring into Gulben's dark eyes. "And, since you're an enchantress, just your voice is enough to set you free from any chains I might put you in. You've already tried to take over my ship once, and that marks you as quite a nuisance to keep around. I'm afraid I don't really have many options here." I really didn't want to keep her gagged for however long it took us to sail across the Axine Sea and reach land.

Gulben looked past me and into the sea. I risked a quick glance away from her to see what had drawn her attention; I could now see three heads bobbing along in the water in our wake, each one attached to flowing brunette hair. I looked back at Gulben, and she met my gaze, swallowing nervously. "I . . . I could sign a blood oath," Gulben said.

I looked confused; she looked surprised at my confusion. Then she described what we would need to do that. A freshly plucked quill, a bowl of purest silver, a little alcohol and gum arabic for mixing the blood into ink, and a clean blade.

"And you are willing to sign such a blood oath?" I frowned. A magical oath seemed like a lot of fuss to avoid being gagged and bound for most of a week. The latter scenario was uncomfortable, but it did not seem entirely unbearable. "You understand, I am not forcing you to do so; there are other alternatives."

She looked past my shoulder. "I . . . do not know how to enchant creatures of the sea," she said meekly.

I shrugged off her non sequitur, stuffed the gag back in her mouth, and called over one of the sailors, giving him a set of instructions to pass on to Felix. After he repeated them back to me (and I corrected his mistakes), he went off to fetch Felix, and I waited.

Katya arrived before Felix, her trusty rifle slung over her shoulder. She looked at me, looked down at the bound auburn-haired woman propped against the railing in a sitting position, and then looked back up at me. "You did not come up to bed," she said, jerking her head up toward the crow's nest. Then she stood up on her toes, grabbed my shirt, and kissed me thoroughly. When I came up for air, she pointed down at the bound auburn-haired woman lying at my feet. "Who is this, and how did she get aboard the ship?"

"Ah. This is Gulben. She's an enchantress who tried to turn the ship around." I paused, trying to think of how to explain exactly what had happened. "Ragnar dropped her off. Georg said . . . Well, either I personally need to guard her nearly constantly, I can toss her overboard, or she'll likely have a chance to try to turn the ship around again. She suggested she could take a magical oath instead."

Katya looked down at the trio of brunette mermaids trailing the ship. "So, she swears an oath to behave well or you throw her into the sea?"

I shook my head. "I'm not heartless. How long could it take to cross the Axine Sea? A few days? A week, maybe? I can put up with having her around me continuously for a little while. I could chain her up in the back of the captain's cabin at night while I sleep."

Gulben's body relaxed as she let out a muffled sigh. While the corners of her mouth could not move, I could see a smile enter her eyes.

Katya looked up at me, then down at Gulben, balancing on her mechanical leg while prodding experimentally at Gulben, first with a toe prodding at the auburn-haired woman's side, and then running her fingers through one of the dark red locks of Gulben's hair before tucking a bright red strand of her own hair behind her ear. Katya turned back to me, giving me a quick but thorough kiss and grabbing at me possessively for a brief moment in a way that I did not think was appropriate in sight of other humans. "You are a very sweet man," she said. "Ragnar chose poorly when he decided to rescue her."

Gulben emitted an angry-sounding series of grunts through her gag, losing enough of her composure to try to express some passionately held opinion related to Ragnar and her relocation from the imperial harem.

Katya ignored the noise, caressing my face affectionately. "I would be sad if you had to lose sleep guarding her." She pulled her hand away from my face, drew her jeweled wolf-mark sword, and began the process of cleaning and polishing it. Gulben swallowed, shifting in place. It was at this point that Captain Felix Rimehammer showed up, with Lieutenant Teushpa and Georg in tow. (I had asked Felix to round up all the magical expertise he could, except not to bother the weather-witch, who was in dire need of sleep. I assumed that number would include Zaneta and exclude Teushpa; I didn't realize Felix still believed Lieutenant Teushpa could perform anything more arcane than sleight-of-hand tricks for casual entertainment.)

A tray held a quill from one of the shipboard fowl, a familiar-looking silver bowl with a little bit of clear liquid in it, and a brightly cleaned and polished knife. Felix held a curled scroll of paper out to me. "With a little help from Georg and the lieutenant on what would and would not work, I believe I have come up with appropriate terms for Gulben to sign."

I nodded. "Good," I said.

"Don't you want to read it?" Felix asked.

"Do I need to sign it?" I asked. When Felix shook his head, I nodded. "Then I'm not the one who needs to read it to make any decisions, now, am I? I trust you, Captain Rimehammer. I'm trained neither in law nor wizardry; I doubt there's anything I could do to improve what you've come up with."

"She will need to read and understand to sign," Lieutenant Teushpa said. Fearlessly, he undid the enchantress's gag and then untied her hands, the latter being a rather more complicated process. I tensed, ready to grab hold of her and fling her away into the sea at the slightest sign she was trying to use her subtle yet powerful magic to beguile a magicless man who merely pretended to have real talents in the area of illusion.

But there was no sudden motion, no glimmer of red light. Instead, Gulben just rubbed her wrists one at a time before taking hold of the offered scroll. For a minute, she sat in silence, reading. She frowned, then looked over at Katya, who was still polishing her sword. She swallowed, then glanced briefly over her shoulder at the mermaids swimming in the ship's wake. She unrolled a little more of the contract, rolled up the section she had read, and then unrolled more of the contract. As she read, her lips narrowed, and by the time she'd unrolled the last section of the contract, there was only a thin, short, pursed line in the middle of her face.

She looked up at me. "I must sign this?"

I shrugged. "There are other options," I said. "I could just tie you back up. It's uncomfortable, but it's just a few days of discomfort. And if you really can't bear staying on this ship and being abandoned far from home, you can disembark. I know we're pretty far from land, but if you ask nicely, I expect that one of the dolphins would be willing to take you to the coast. Maybe even to part of the coast controlled by the Sultanate. It shouldn't be more than a day's swim." I'd read plenty of stories in which dolphins had rescued fishermen and brought them to shore, at least.

Gulben's eyes flickered briefly over to Katya, and then she turned her head to look back out at the mermaids for a long moment. Then she turned her head back to the scroll of paper in her hand and sighed. "I will sign," she said, in a very soft voice. Her eyes glistened. "I will need the knife now," she said, holding out her hand.

Katya turned, stepping between me and Gulben. Gulben gasped. Katya stepped back; a thin red line had appeared on Gulben's cheek. "That should do," Katya said. She flicked her blade again over the railing, a couple of drops of blood flying out into the sea. One of the mermaids lifted her head out of the water and shook her hair loose, then dove back all the way under the water.

And so, Gulben signed the contract. Teushpa claimed he was certain that the oath had taken hold; I asked Georg her opinion, and she nodded while Teushpa glared at me with a level of annoyance that nearly verged on insolence. After waiting for the signature to dry, Felix attached one end to a wooden rod and rolled the whole thing up, five and a half feet of paper bound up tightly for archival.

I thanked Felix, gave him my condolences on his cousin Ragnar having been left behind in the waters of the strait, and did my best to reassure him by telling him that Ragnar had the friendship of a mermaid who'd gone to help him. Perhaps she had simply lost her way, I added, and might show up shortly with Ragnar in tow; though privately, I suspected that after getting into a fight with her sister mermaid, she had gone a different way.

Gulben's face went through a remarkable series of contortions as she controlled her expression, keeping her now ungagged mouth sealed of her own accord, but I could hear her heartbeat race as I discussed Ragnar. At the end of my attempts at reassurance, Felix only shook his head sadly and limped away, his peg leg thumping more heavily than usual against the wooden deck.

CHAPTER FIFTY-SEVEN

In Which I Investigate a Fire

The weather-witch needed to rest for a substantial length of time; due to the compounded indirect effects of her considerable efforts at navigating the strait at high speed by wind alone, the weather was quite irregular for a while afterward. I have seen clouds, and I have seen fog; but we found ourselves with clouds not quite low enough for ordinary fog and not quite meeting the ground, yet engulfing half our mainsail. The tops and the crow's nest were out of sight.

As my sailors had greater confidence in my eyesight than their own, I was stationed in the forecastle to watch for reefs and rocks, or the sudden appearance of land; then I saw something that was neither of those things. It was bobbing up and down, clearly adrift rather than a piece of fixed land. Its sides seemed perfectly straight, though, and most of it was low enough in the water that it was difficult to see over the choppy waves.

After a moment, I realized it was round. A round floating platform, like nothing I had seen, wider than any ship, slowly rotating in place as it drifted closer to us among the waves of the Axine Sea. As I stood in the forecastle staring at it, I suddenly realized that the flower-like burnt protrusions around the edge were the remains of paddlewheels. There were six of them; then I realized what I was looking at.

"It's a battleship of the Golden Empire," I said in Greek, turning to the sailor next to me.

The sailor stared at me in disbelief, then looked back into the dim space of open air beneath the deep foggy clouds. "You see a ship?"

"Well, it *was* a ship," I said. "It was built as a steamer from the hull up, no sails or oars at all."

"Oh . . . it's so big," the sailor said, as he caught sight of it, his jaw hanging open in surprise, "and round. Which way is the prow?"

"I think it's actually smaller than a French cruiser, but I'm not sure. The width of the thing makes for a stable firing platform, theoretically." I frowned. Judging the size and distance of it was difficult, particularly with the unusual shape, but it did seem a lot larger than it had a minute ago. My eyes widened, and I turned, shouting back. "Brake! Brake! Reverse oars to brake, now!"

The oars strained with a splashing noise; then there was a loud *crunch* and I stumbled forward. For the second time in my career as a ship's captain, we had rammed a ship with me standing in the forecastle; this time, with the oars deployed to slow the ship rather than to speed its passage, I was not launched into the air in an uncontrolled tumble. I found I greatly preferred keeping my feet during the process.

"Stow the oars. I'm going to inspect the damage." Having avoided being involuntarily thrown out of my ship, I jumped out of the ship of my own accord, dropping heavily into a crouch as I did so. The impact was still hard enough that I instantly regretted my impulsive decision, pain shooting up my legs.

The damage to our ship was minimal. It had been designed for ramming, and the thick timbers that were meant to protect the sides of the battleship were, while thick and robust, not very firmly attached in place to one another. I may theorize that perhaps they had been fixed into place with iron or steel nails; or, alternately, that the fastening materials and supporting structure, whatever they had been, had been weakened by the fires that had gutted the ship.

For the ship was gutted; there was no question of that. The central battery was missing almost all of its guns, with the elevated castle that served as the central battery's rotating fire platform having been smashed apart. It looked for all the world as if it had been struck over and over again by a great mech wielding three giant mech-scale axes strapped together, their heads lined up so as to leave parallel lines whenever they struck. I was not sure whether this damage happened before or after the ship was raked with fire.

The ship's log spoke simply of having been sent to Aegyssus, there to help secure the mouth of the Istros against an increasingly energetic rebellion led by the presumptively alive Prince Vlad, serving double duty as both a floating battery and transport. (The latter because the railroad had been sabotaged in some particularly severe fashion.) The only survivors left aboard were a pair of soldiers who had been thrown into the brig for one or another mischief; after two days adrift with little water or food, they were barely coherent.

The ship had clearly been attacked with fire and battered by boarding mechs with heavy blades, but they claimed they had been in open sea with no alarm of any ship having been sighted when, out of nowhere, the ship was set ablaze. One said he was an expert gunner and would surely have been brought out of the brig and back on deck if an enemy ship had been sighted, and the other insisted he'd seen a monster through a porthole. While sea monsters are real, neither leviathans nor krakens nor sea serpents are known to have much tolerance for fire; the notion of a sea monster using fire to attack a ship may be therefore dismissed as an absurdity and the fevered imaginings of a man who was drunk enough even by the standards of the navy of the Golden Empire to merit being tossed in the brig to put him out of the way until he sobered up.

No; a fired ship is usually set alight by courtesy of an enemy ship, the result of the application of heated shot, a war mage, or the notorious fire projectors manufactured in Constantinople. This last possibility focused my suspicions southward. Perhaps a squadron of the sultan's navy had happened upon one of the Golden Empire's most valuable naval assets in the middle of the Axine Sea in the night. In spite of the nominal cooperation that the two powers were engaged in with respect to the rebellion that had spread from Wallachia into northern Rumelia, the officer in charge had been unable to resist the strategically compelling temptation to eliminate a significant portion of a rival naval force.

The only difficulty with this theory was the lack of any sign of impacts of cannon fire from the heavy bombards that were the staple armament of the sultan's ships, whether galley or sidewheeler.

Perhaps the enemy ships had closed to boarding range without giving signs of their intentions by overtly loading their guns, but how? Some clever deception? Magical fog? Both survivors insisted there had been no dense fog the night of the attack, but they did claim to have heard a sound like the flapping of great wings; in reality, obviously the flapping of sails, meaning that the Empire's greatest steamship had been defeated by the galleys that formed the second tier of Sultan Alaeddin's great navy, galleys moving under wind power no less.

After establishing that the attack took place at night and was carried out by galleys moving under sail power, I concluded that the real cause of the ship's defeat had been the negligent failure to ensure that night watchmen were assigned in sufficient number or even stayed awake, in spite of the giant samovars and the ample stores of tea that we found aboard. As someone who was or at least had briefly been an officer of the Golden Empire, I felt a sense of deep shame and embarrassment on behalf of my countrymen. They had taken a modern warship into battle against galleys that could have been built a thousand years ago, most likely galliots less than a tenth the size of their own vessel, and lost totally and completely.

I certainly found it more plausible that the sultan's navy was still preying upon that of the Golden Empire than the notion that Prince Vlad by himself had somehow wreaked such destruction while having only scattered mountain folk at his disposal and no warships. Perhaps the rebels had some river barges at their disposal, courtesy of captured traffic on the Istros, but those would hardly be seaworthy, much less able to ambush a steamship making a straight-line course that took it far away from land.

After we had salvaged what we could from the wreck of the ill-fated *Holmgard*, which included a surprising amount of intact copper piping and an intact cast-iron boiler, I met with my officers for dinner and an extended discussion. For some combination of reasons related to upper-class etiquette that I found confusing, or perhaps the size of the decorated dinner table we had salvaged from the small dining room attached to the *Holmgard*'s captain's quarters, this dinner included not only my officers, but Zaneta and the four women who had been either rescued by Ragnar (according to the delighted blonde Circassian), stolen by Ragnar (according to the less-delighted brunette Circassian), or kidnapped by Ragnar (according to Gulben, the suddenly meek auburn-haired younger sister of Sultan Alaeddin).

Other than the fact that Katya was an officer herself and seated between myself and Felix, there was a woman seated between every two officers, meaning that the seating alternated between men and women with the exception of a misplaced Georg at the foot of the table. Gulben was seated at my left hand, and reacted poorly to my theory that Sultan Alaeddin was responsible for the destruction of the *Holmgard*.

"Our captains would never disobey orders to risk restarting the war!" Her dark eyes locked onto mine defiantly for one heartbeat. Then she clutched at her stomach and looked down, shaking her head. "Unless you say so, Master Corvus."

"My saying it doesn't make it so," I replied drily, glancing over at Vitold, seated on her other side.

Vitold nodded. "He's been wrong before. But everybody knows that the Sultanate lets all the pirates in the world roost in Taurida," he said. "Most of his galley captains are little more than ravagers and freebooters. They eat babies and impale dogs on spikes! I remember seeing the illustrations on the news-sheets. Some of them even had horns and tails, the devils! You can't tell me the sultan's devil-pirates are disciplined enough to keep the peace!"

Gulben glared at Vitold, then looked down. "I hear and obey, Lieutenant Szpak," she spat out through gritted teeth in thickly accented Slavonic of a Rumelian variety. "I shall not tell you that the sultan's captains are devout and treat the slaves they take as lawful plunder of war humanely. I shall not tell you that the Golden Empire tolerates pirates and freebooters of its own. I shall not tell you that none of the ship's captains of the Sultanate have horns and tails and that the only devil made flesh is the Undying Emperor squatting in Tanais. I shall not tell you that you are an idiot who will believe any lie printed on a page!"

"Enough," I said.

Gulben's teeth clicked as she shut her mouth, humming at me in annoyance.

"The important question is this: Should we be worried that what befell the *Holmgard* will befall us?" I looked around the table, then repeated myself in Gothic after remembering that not all of them understood Slavonic. "Whether that was a squadron of Sultan Alaeddin's navy, pirates, some absurd Wallachian fleet conjured out of nothing by the rebel prince, or whatever those two men thought—"

"A fire-breathing kraken with a giant axe in each tentacle, perhaps?" Johann grinned, and there was laughter all around the table.

"That sounds like something my cousin Ragnar would come up with," Felix said, smiling briefly.

The blonde Circassian looked hopefully at Felix, not understanding Gothic; our surgeon, conversant in Gothic as well as Turkish, whispered a quick translation, and her face fell, disappointed.

Once the conversation had been steered back on track, we discussed the logs of the *Holmgard* and the survivors' testimonies, and decided that the ship must have drifted northeast from where it had been attacked; as we ourselves intended to sail further northeast to pass through the Cimmerian Strait, we would be moving away from the attacking ships which, in any case, would doubtless have come away from the engagement with looted money and captured slaves, the latter of which would be more profitably disposed in the south, in Rumelia, Trebizond, or Constantinople.

And once we crossed through the Cimmerian Strait, there would be no worry about pirates; true, the navy of the Golden Empire was no great force, but it could and did police the Cimmerian Sea.

CHAPTER FIFTY-EIGHT

In Which I Arrive at an End

We reached the Cimmerian Strait on a mostly natural favorable wind. It was a night with very thick clouds but only a little bit of rain and a light cooperative natural wind blowing almost exactly in the direction we wished to go. As we sailed between the fortress cities of Pantikapaion (belonging to the Sultanate) and Hermonassa (belonging to the Golden Empire), I saw that the latter's many cannons were fully manned in spite of the late hour, though the former had only a light watch of a few men, curiously enough.

Fortunately, in spite of our decision to pass through the strait at an hour at which persons would normally be asleep, none of the soldiers atop either fort's walls deemed our passage suspicious enough to sound an alarm or begin firing cannons. Either that, or all officers with the authority to make a decision had gone to bed and the soldiers stuck on watch didn't want to risk waking them. After all, even if there was a light rain, the thick clouds diffused the moonlight nicely and evenly, and there was no obscuring fog; if I could see the individual gun crews huddled closely around the cannons of Hermonassa, surely they could see my triple-decked galley with its sails billowing.

Once we were safely through the strait, I went back to sleep, waking with the dawn over the peaceful waters of the Cimmerian Sea. Though I was wary of the fact that there might be another circular battleship somewhere, we only saw scattered small fishing vessels as we sailed across the Cimmerian Sea. The fishing vessels kept their distance—understandable given that they had probably never seen any ship quite like our quinquereme. This left us with little to do but finish repairs, sail, and tell stories to one another.

I had not planned on whiling away the hours telling stories, but Fyodor had once been to the capital of the Golden Empire (our destination), and I begged him to recount the story of his visit; and that began a long round of storytelling by one person after another, with a large and gathering audience who made excuses involving mending clothing or polishing armor or some other quiet sedentary chore. (In Georg's case, the excuse was that she was polishing my armor.) The blonde Circassian particularly wanted to hear stories about Ragnar, and no less than seven of the Swedish soldiers obliged (with our surgeon acting as translator), though I suspect half of the stories about Ragnar were pure fiction.

As we drew within sight of the city called Rome upon the Tanais River— colloquially known as Tanais, as the city and river had been before the Undying Emperor received the fleeing senators who proclaimed him Emperor of Rome—I marveled at the architecture. The upper city with its palaces occupied a low hill on the south side of the southernmost mouth of the Tanais River; the lower city sprawled all the way up to the sea coast.

The upper city of Rome-upon-Tanais is a veritable city of palaces. Most of the Undying Emperor's wives had given him at least one son; each favored son of an emperor deserved his own palace, and the Undying Emperor's favor was fickle and changeable over the generations. Some had fallen into disrepair; others had been expanded upon by the more prosperous grandsons and great-grandsons of the Undying Emperor; below them huddled the homes and shops of ordinary citizens, along with warehouses and factories, and between those the ample wharves of a port that Fyodor had told me was often as busy as Constantinople. And yet, along the wharves, there were not very many ships, and only two or three were close to the size of our own quinquereme.

Then a red haze flickered into view, mostly obscuring the lower city. The red haze stretched fifty yards into the sky, taller than our mast.

"Out oars and slow to a stop," I called out, uncertain if it would be safe to steer the ship into the glowing red haze.

After we had stopped, I discussed the red haze with several local seagulls, who told me that in spite of its translucency, it was an impenetrable barrier of considerable solidity that was raised irregularly but not infrequently and that I had better fly all the way over it if I wanted to get to the city where all the lovely garbage piles were. The seagulls waxed rhapsodic about the quality and quantity of the garbage of Rome-upon-Tanais for some time before I made my excuses to cut the conversation short; at that point, they followed their own advice and flew high over the barrier.

Then the oddest thing happened: A brass boat with a glass top bobbed to the top of the water in front of us. The glass top opened, revealing a pair of men in military garb—one an enlisted soldier, and the other a junior officer of some kind, the naval equivalent of a banneret, whatever that may be called. (Editor's note: This is probably an ensign.)

They shouted up at us with demands to be let aboard; I shouted an affirmative answer back down at them in a more or less friendly fashion; then we lowered a rope ladder and the officer climbed up for more polite conversation at an ordinary volume. The enlisted soldier remained in the boat. After a few perfunctory polite greetings, he pulled a silver mirror from his jacket pocket and held it up to me. I stared at my image in confusion for only a moment before it was replaced by another face, that of a rotund man of considerably greater rank. He introduced himself as the Underminister of Harbor Security and wished to know the origin of our ship.

"I am Mikolai," I said, tapping my freshly polished Corsican brass armor with my hand and adjusting my brilliant cerulean cloak. Behind me, I heard a swirl of surprised whispers from those among the company who had only known me as Marcus. "I'm Ruthenian, a citizen of the Golden Empire. And this is my ship and my company." I tapped the butt of my trident on the deck and gestured at the gathered crowd of curious people.

The man holding the mirror slowly turned the mirror back and forth, muttering a quick description of what he could see. As far as he was concerned, we were clearly pirates, a motley crew of well-armed foreigners, our ship brimming with loot ready for sale, ranging from high-quality furniture to slaves. I felt a sense of relief that he did not recognize the dining table of the *Holmgard* as such; trying to prove my innocence in the ship's destruction could have been difficult.

"You seem to have quite a few soldiers on board. Foreign warships are not permitted to dock here," the man in the mirror informed me. "Unless you perhaps are one of our privateers, bearing a letter of marque?"

I demurred, saying I had no such document, having acquired the ship in Venice; and then he offered to sell me a letter of marque.

"Naturally, given the irregular circumstances, I must ask for some personal consideration," the man in the mirror said. "And, of course, with your cargo predating the letter, the tariffs will be quite steep, but if I make the letter out with a retroactive date, I can classify it as prize material and tariff it at a lower rate." He paused, counting under his breath. "Show me around again?" The junior officer slowly turned around in a circle. "Three hundred Venetian ducats or thirty thousand Turkish *akcheh*, and I'll put it a year back and make you a separated veteran of the naval service. No, I'll be reasonable and give you a discount. Half that plus the lovely red-headed slave."

Katya bristled. I put my arm around her. "Katya is one of my officers and *not* a slave for sale," I informed the man in the mirror bluntly.

"No, no, I wasn't talking about the cripple with the mechanical arm," the man in the mirror said blithely, waving his hand. "Goodness, no. She's one of your bloodthirsty pirates; I can see that readily enough. I meant the girl in Turkish silks." He then offered some further commentary on Gulben's appearance as contrasted to Katya's.

Katya's lips pressed into a thin line. I patted her on the back, keenly aware of how she must feel and appreciative that she didn't express those feelings aloud.

Gulben sputtered. "Giving me to some two-bit functionary of the Golden Empire as a bribe would be outrageous!" Her eyes widened and her hand clapped against her stomach, and she continued woodenly as she looked down, staring at her feet. "If you order me to serve that man, I will obey, Colonel Corvus."

I looked at Gulben and frowned. "Really?"

"Yes," Gulben said. She pulled her head up, speaking in an expressionless monotone. "I will wastefully humiliate and degrade myself in such a manner if you so command, for the paltry and insulting sum of a hundred fifty solid gold ducats."

The man in the mirror sputtered incoherently, surprised at Gulben's opinion of her own value.

"Gulben, I appreciate your willingness to volunteer for such a duty, but I do not think it is necessary," I said. "The underminister is making unreasonable demands. A whole *grivna* of gold is a ludicrous bribe for a docking fee, and he asked for more than two. No, he has seen we have a fortune aboard, and he wishes to rob us of it to dishonestly line his own pockets."

The man in the mirror expressed confidence in his negotiating position, temporizing for a bit and then asking for two *grivnas* of gold plus either Gulben or both of the Circassians. "There is nothing you can do here without my say-so," he added. "I control the barrier, and you cannot sell your goods for a fraction of their value anywhere else along the whole Cimmerian coast. Indeed, with a ship that size and no letter of marque, you cannot even attempt to pass through the strait without having it seized and pressed into service in the west. I hold every card in the deck, and you must accept what I choose to deal to you."

My annoyance grew. I glared. Gulben shivered. Vitold cursed under his breath, jamming his fingers under his armpits. Katya flexed her mechanical hand, a thin layer of ice falling off. Frost rimed the edges of the mirror and crept across its face. The two Circassian girls huddled together, teeth chattering. In the distance, there was the sound of cawing, a distant murder of crows having been stirred into action by some disturbance. Quite suddenly, every seagull within a hundred yards found that they wished to be somewhere else.

"Underminister," I said, addressing the blurry face in the frosted mirror, "I believe you are responsible for the security of the city against attack, and therefore will be held directly responsible for any damages to any buildings in the city from cannonfire."

"I have an impenetrable magical barrier between us," the eyeball said. "No cannon can pierce it!"

I looked at the red haze extending some fifty yards up from the sea, considering the angle required to clear it. Then I looked at the upper city, mentally calculating a crude parabola. Then I looked at Fyodor. "I think a demonstration is in order. Perhaps an air burst? I don't wish to cause the underminister any serious trouble yet, you understand."

"I have to use some sort of aiming point," Fyodor said cautiously. "And if we range low or the fuse runs long, I might just hit it."

Staring at the upper city through the red haze, I glanced from tower to tower, ignoring the alternating threats and confused questions being emitted by the mirror; then my eyes settled on one particular target. I could feel my good-luck stone warm against my chest. From what I could see through the translucent red blur of the barrier and the diamond-shaped panes of the windows spaced around the top level of the tower, the top room of the tower had not been used for some time; there was a thick layer of dust over everything, from the bookshelves to the glass case that enclosed a crudely stuffed hare with a bulging fat body. If someone had told me that the hare was the result of a crude effort at taxidermy by a twelve-year-old boy, proud of his first successful hunt, I would have believed them.

"That tower there, the third one from the left—I think it is long-unused. A good demonstration target," I said, gesturing expressively until I felt sure that Fyodor had confirmed his target. At a quiet order from Felix, a pair of burly Swedish soldiers bracketed the junior officer.

Fyodor selected a small and neatly decorated bronze cannon. Baron Asman von Vasco had been a poor employer in many ways, but his Silesian craftsmen were excellent with bronze, whether they were casting bells or cannon. Fyodor wanted to use our most accurate piece; that particular souvenir of our employment in the Gothic Empire was the gun he trusted the most. He measured and loaded powder, sighting along the barrel carefully and checking its angle of elevation as the ship rolled back and forth gently in the waves. After touching a slow match to the fuse, Fyodor carefully slid the shell into the cannon with a deft motion that pulled his fingers and face away from its muzzle before the shell butted against the wadding.

He paused for a moment, pushing the cannon just a little to the left as he waited for the motion of the waves for half a heartbeat. I was reminded of what Georg had told me: Fyodor could read the wind. The little adjustment likely meant that the wind had shifted a bit. What did he see when he looked into the sky? I wondered for a moment what the wind looked like for someone with the ability to see it directly. Then Fyodor struck the phoenix stone set into the butt of the cannon with his mallet, and I stopped thinking about his small magical talent.

My ears rang, and my nostrils filled with the distinctive scent of gunpowder as the shell arced through the air. Hopefully, it would explode high in the air close to the tower, a visible display of both our ability to fight back but harmless; if it did not, the damage would be limited to a long-abandoned tower.

Fyodor's aim was true to the tower, striking it directly. The shell smashed through the window I had noticed, smashing through a set of shelves and the glass case. As the shell ricocheted off the back stone wall and into the floor, lighter debris flew up into the air—the pages from a book and the detached dusty head of the crudely stuffed hare.

A moment later, the window disappeared in smoke and flame as the fuse finished burning deeper into the shell, reaching the store of powder within. An instant later, a varied assortment of debris came into view as it fell beneath the billowing smoke—scorched pages of paper, bits of ancient fur, an intact Persian rug, a silver mirror, half a dozen candles, the pieces of a hollow, carved, wooden duck decoy, and a jeweled egg that had somehow miraculously survived the blast. Perhaps it had been inside a smaller container of some kind.

Most of the debris rained down onto the top of a wall fifty feet below, the egg shattering as it hit the stone. Its attention initially drawn by the noise of the blast and then redirected by the falling debris, a curious raven flew overhead, looking for anything shiny or edible; picking over the broken remnants of the egg, the raven found a particularly bright and shiny silver needle, which it took up in its beak; however, while attractively shiny, the needle was brittle, and it snapped in two under the pressure of the raven's beak.

For a moment, I felt as though everything in the world stopped, freezing in place as the two halves of the needle fell to either side of the raven's beak; then the sensation passed. Then I heard a slow dull roar building as first dozens, then hundreds, then thousands of voices raised across the city. Less than two minutes after Fyodor fired, bells began to ring across the city; and within five minutes, every single bell tower in the city was ringing all at once. City guards ran this way and that; so did brightly dressed citizens and brightly but more impractically dressed nobles, long-toed shoes causing some of them to trip as they hastily ran from building to building.

The junior officer holding the mirror turned his head to look at the city, the pair of burly Swedish soldiers standing on either side of him. He turned the mirror to himself, wiping frost off with his shirt. "Sir, I can confirm that they have fired over the barrier." There was silence from the mirror. "Sir, are you there?"

I could hear the muffled and distant sound of shouting through the mirror, multiple voices that sounded as if they were quite far away.

"But he's the Undying Emperor! He doesn't die!" Between the lowered volume and the panicked pitch, I could barely recognize the underminister's voice.

"The House of the Seventeenth Heir-son requires your support, man, snap out of it," said a gruff angry voice. "With the Minister of Harbor Security under arrest, you are the only ones who can order the harbor cannons trained upon the Ministry of Internal Affairs."

The junior officer shook the mirror, ignoring the distant conversation. "Hello? Where did you go? Sir, what's going on? Sir?" By the second "sir," he had escalated from normal speech to shouting.

The red haze began to slowly fade. I looked at the city and the chaos therein. By wild coincidence, the explosion of Fyodor's carefully fused shell had happened only moments before Emperor Koschei of the Golden Empire, in full view of his assembled ministers, had suddenly stood bolt upright, let out a terrible gasp, and then dropped dead, collapsing suddenly.

The Undying Emperor was dead.

About the Author

Tomas J. McIntee is the author of the Accidental War Mage series, originally released on Royal Road. He is a lifelong lover of science fiction, fantasy, and alternate history. When not preoccupied with dancing, data science, medical research, recreational reading, long walks with his dogs, or voting systems, he quietly writes fiction of his own. McIntee's work is inspired by his interests and an eclectic education comprised of diverse degrees in mathematics, physics, philosophy, and the social sciences. He lives in Chapel Hill, North Carolina.

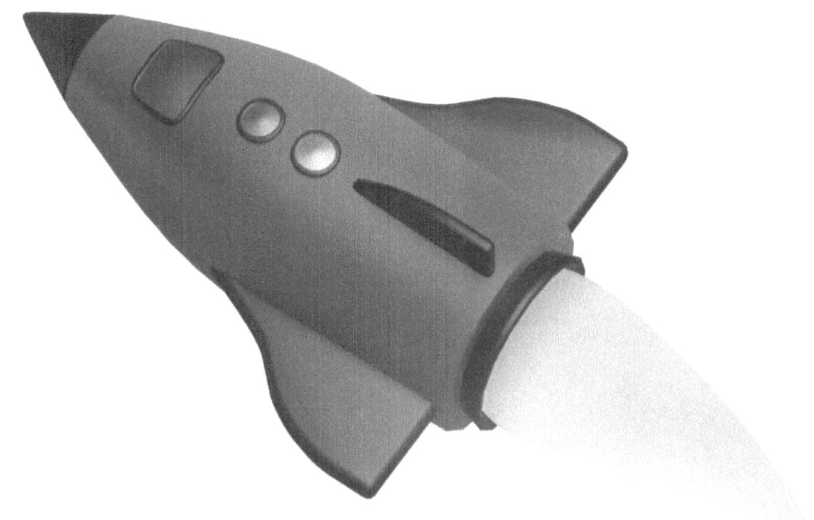

STELLAR
CONTENT AWAITS
follow us on our socials

podiumentertainment.com

@podiumentertainment

/podiumentertainment

@podium_ent

@podiumentertainment